HEART
OF A
FOREST

SYLVIA LOCKARD

For anyone who has ever not quite fit in a category the world put you in. Who felt like you had to hide pieces of yourself. Don't stop until you find someone who accepts all your facets.
Be you—all of you.

PLAYLIST

I Like Me Better ~ Lauv

Natural ~ Imagine Dragons

The Pines ~ Roses & Revolutions

Dusk Til Dawn ~ Madilyn Bailey

Beautiful Creature ~ MIAA

Young Love & Old Money ~ Elizabeth Gerardi

Storm ~ Ruelle

Someone to You ~ Roses & Revolutions

You Put a Spell on Me ~ Austin Giorgio

Power Over Me ~ Dermot Kennedy

Dandelions ~ Ruth B.

Walk Through the Fire ~ Zayde Wolfe, Ruelle

Game of Survival ~ Ruelle

like that ~ Bea Miller

Who's Afraid of Little Old Me? ~ Taylor Swift

CHAPTER 1

Ravenna Heldt eyed the blades on the blacksmith's table as they glinted in the afternoon sun. It wasn't proper for her to stare at the weapons, but they were fine craftsmanship, and she couldn't help but stop to admire them while she waited for the blacksmith's apprentice to finish with his customer. Though the kingdom of Ecanta was not high on criminal activity, a weapon was always a good accessory.

Even for a princess.

Raven fingered her dagger's hilt, hidden within the pocket sown into her skirt, unease and security roiling with that touch. A black rose seal rested on the hilt's end, the Loren royal insignia. A dangerous blade to carry—stolen and damning—but it reminded her of the dangers she faced… and had survived.

A cool summer breeze coated in cedar floated through the simple marketplace, teasing black locks from her red headband. Even in the warmest months, a chill clung to the air with the mountains so close to the town. Ravenna smoothed the long, brown sleeves of her dress and glanced out at her villagers readying their stalls. Ilasia, the capital of Ecanta, had a modest but vital marketplace in its center, which bustled daily. Vendors displayed items from their booths, selling ripe—though sparse—fruits, cloths, and even weapons.

The walls surrounding the marketplace couldn't block out the forest encompassing the city, the treetops stretching far higher than the walls could try. Stone stacked upon stone reached higher than any villager's head but not beyond a building's roof edge. Villagers roamed within, visiting the booths on either side of the rectangular trade section, filled to the brim with stalls and a few merchant homes. The scent of fresh baked bread mingled in the air with the forest's ever-present aroma, and the floral merchant's wares farther down the market. The remaining merchant homes rested beyond the walls in the next section over.

Ravenna returned her attention to the stall before her when the customer thanked Flint, the blacksmith's apprentice, and left. Behind the heavy wooden table, Flint arranged the knives and swords, careful of their edges. Leather bracers lined his strong but wiry forearms, a dark brown tunic and belt loosely cinching around his waist. Thin, as always, she wondered how he could work at the weapon forge.

Flint smiled crookedly. "Good morning, Your Highness."

Raven returned the smile and greeting. "Have you eaten breakfast yet?"

He cleared his throat and straightened the blades. Dark blond hair fell in front of his face, but she saw the flicker of discomfort.

No, he'd probably given whatever food he'd managed to buy to his younger siblings. Like usual. Sadness rippled through Raven. *This* was why she visited his stall first each morning. She touched Flint's restless hand gently and offered an apple.

With a grateful tilt to his lips, Flint thanked her. He leaned down to place it in his satchel at his feet. Deftly, Raven reached her hand forward across the wooden stall and slipped three coppers into his pocket. They landed silently.

Food was one thing her villagers willingly accepted—coin was not—but they it needed all the same. Over the years, she'd learned how to reverse pickpocket to give them more.

Saying goodbye to Flint, Raven nodded to her guard two steps away and turned to rejoin the group of two others. At least two always accompanied her beyond the castle walls, not including Ruben, her Head Guard and beloved friend. Though far from oldest guard, at twenty-six years, he had climbed in rank quickly with his skill and dedication. He was never more than a touch away. She strolled through the market with

8

him, the others paces away but scrutinizing villagers who neared. Over the years, she'd learned the villagers felt more open to interaction with only Ruben at her side.

The slight clanking of their uniforms followed her everywhere and was as much a comfort and staple to her life as the men themselves. The Royal Guard's armor was layered with both leather underneath and metal plating outside. The soft insignia of Ecanta—three trees with a mountain stretching tall behind—was stamped on their chests with the royal differentiation of a bronze shield encompassing the insignia and a crown resting atop. The shield signified the capital guard, the crown for the Royal Guard, and the bronze solidified them to her specifically. The red trunks and green leaves of the trees were stark against the brown and white-capped mountains.

With each stall her basket—and coin purse—grew lighter. Sometimes she bought items from one vendor and gave it to another, but always at the end of her trip, the basket and purse would be empty. Today, she bought a loaf from the baker, a red-faced man standing at his stall like always. He never missed a morning despite probably getting up at dawn to bake the mounds of fresh loaves on his table.

At the far end of the market, her guards fanned out, leaving only Raven and Ruben. A noticeboard faced the market's center, standing between two merchant houses, wide and filled with papers. Like the past two days, Raven found only small disputes between vendors and offers to trade goods. A clump of papers hung clustered in the middle, one over another. She lifted the edges and revealed a wanted poster.

Crimson covered the page, dominating what little representation of a face was shown under a dark crimson hood. A dash of a hard jawline, the angle of a neck. No one could ever recall the face of the vigilante, though no one knew why. A small smile tugged at her lips.

Red Hood.
Criminal and assassin. Any information on this thief and murderer must be reported immediately to the guards or Queen Vanera.
500 coppers reward.

Though the guards posted a fresh page each week, the image always became obscured by... *important* notices.

Lost marbles, please return.
One chipped cup, 5 coppers or best offer.

Her smile flickered again.

"What a nuisance," Ruben spat, his gaze held on the vague sketch.

"Do you really think so?" Raven asked lightly, looking up to him. His trimmed dirty blond hair shone in the morning light.

Ruben straightened, glancing down at her. "Absolutely. He assaults random people. And we cannot protect everyone."

"You cannot?"

He faltered at her teasing question, then caught her smile. Ruben sighed, with only a *slight* tone of annoyance, knowing she loved messing with him. "Regretfully, we cannot predict his targets since he picks nobles *and* villagers. And we don't know whether he's hired."

Raven nodded, letting the pages fall back into place over the wanted poster. "Such a shame."

"Yes," said a voice behind Raven, one familiar in a horrible—impossible—way that hitched her breath into her throat. "Such a shame that murder isn't punished justly in this kingdom."

Ruben stiffened beside Raven, but she lifted her chin and turned.

A young man stood feet away, and everything about him from his sneer and too-straight posture to his lapels and clean shoes proclaimed him a royal. The overly jeweled crown glinting in the afternoon sunlight only solidified it. For Raven, it wasn't the black rose on his lapel but his dark red hair, turning copper in the sunlight and matching his eyes, that proclaimed him a Loren prince.

Her breath hitched in her throat.

Why was a Loren here again?

Loren rested on the farthest edges of west Aloria. It was hundreds of miles away, and almost twice the size of her kingdom. Why would anyone take a trek that far to this corner of the continent? Especially after the last time a Loren royal had visited.

That damned voice—different yet similar to his brother. The accent, lilting at the ends of his words, froze her in place. No—she was stronger than this. Ravenna clenched her fist behind her skirts and took a stilted breath. "Well…" She paused, mind blank. What had they been saying?

Ruben spoke up, saving her like always. "My guards are working hard to catch the criminal." He dipped his head—barely a dip—but kept his hand on his sword. "Good morning, Prince Grayson."

Grayson cast a quick glance over Ruben, then laid his glare on Raven. "*Princess* Ravenna."

She smoothed her dress, a simple brown fabric she wore into the market specifically. Even with flowers embroidered on the hem and the ends of the sleeves, it wasn't the lavish lavenders and teals of her court dresses. Raven forced her chin higher, but her heart pounded in her temples, in her ears. She plastered her smile in place but blinked hard. Red, she only saw red behind her eyes. Raven forced them open.

Ruben shifted, his elbow lightly grazing hers, and that steeled her back into herself. She straightened. "Grayson, good morning. What brings you to Ilasia?"

Grayson raised a brow, a cockiness to the gesture. "The betrothal."

Cold rushed through her veins. Did he mean—

"It's not as if the first went well for either of our kingdoms, but…" Grayson smiled, the expression harsh and sharp. "Maybe this one won't end in fatalities."

This one? No, Mother couldn't have—could she? Throat constricted, Raven managed to say, "Yes. Let's hope."

"*I* hope to learn more about this Red Hood." Grayson flicked a finger at the partly obscured wanted poster. His copper eyes met hers steadily. "Good day." The prince nodded once and departed with a sneer. That sneer did her in.

She backed away from the notice board, away from the booths, feet stumbling a step. Distantly, she heard Ruben instruct the other guards to stand where they were. She knew he was protecting her from view. Protecting her like always. Breaths coming faster, she grasped blindly sideways for a house and slung herself into the alley.

Grayson's voice, his sneer, his angry, copper eyes—it all matched his older brother. Though *that* prince hadn't been alive, let alone in Ilasia, for a long time.

Panic swirled through Raven, the frantic emotion foreign after so many years. She tried to take deep breaths, finding only shallow waves of air.

Landon.

11

Blood, hot and horribly red, dripping down her arms and into her sleeves, drowning her dress.

Metal and leather squeezed into her palm, slippery with—

"Ravenna."

She blinked, focusing on Ruben before her, on *now*. The slight dusting of freckles on his nose and cheeks, the face she'd learned since she was a child, the softness around his hazel eyes. *Deep breaths.* She thrust her fingers into her dark hair, clenching them against her scalp. Her eyes widened on her best friend, whose face warred between caring and guilt. "*What* is he doing here?"

Ruben's thick brows dropped, entire face softening. His voice turned somber, "The Queen invited him. But I didn't know," he rushed out, irritation entering his voice. "I didn't know he'd crossed the border, let alone into the capital. It appears information is not passing as fast as travelers between cities."

Grayson had walked into and *through* Ecanta, all the way to her damned home without Ruben knowing? Anger flared bright within her, breaking through her panic, then crashed under her worry. "He—I—" Raven released a trembling hand from her hair. Black strands flew rampant, the ruby hair band hanging uselessly at her neck now. "Ruben —I can't…"

He laid his hand on hers, and she intertwined her fingers with his gloved pair. She managed a steady breath, holding onto Ruben's solid grip.

I can't let it get out, was what she couldn't say but he didn't need to hear to know.

After all, he was the only other person to share the secret. It'd been hard enough to keep composure when the Loren king and young Grayson had arrived, the body of their prince presented in a casket in the throne room. To stand beside her mother and Ruben as Queen Vanera expressed condolences and explained the accident that had befallen Prince Landon Loren. A wild boar in the mountains that had attacked and stabbed him, its body offered to King Loren.

The story Ruben had crafted to protect her. The boar he'd located and killed.

Vividly, she recalled the grief on young Grayson's face, the lack of anything on the king's.

Raven looked over Ruben's shoulder toward where the noticeboard stood.

But *why* was Grayson here?

The word 'betrothal' bounced around her mind, but… would Mother really invite a *Loren* here again for a betrothal without even telling her? They'd talked about a betrothal, but not an agreement yet. Then again, Mother didn't know the full history of the last… visit. Frustration and a twinge of hurt bubbled inside her chest.

Gripping Ruben's fingers tightly Raven pulled him farther from the view of others and forced her shaky voice to whisper, "Ruben, what if he starts asking questions?"

"We don't know that he'll—"

"Or if he—"

"Raven." His nickname for her broke her panic. "We'll get through this. I'll have guards follow him and make sure Grayson doesn't do anything." He removed his hand from her grasp slowly, with one last squeeze. "And you're more skilled with a blade this time. You can handle yourself."

A cold shiver shot down her spine, plummeting her heart into her stomach. She could do *worse* this time. She whispered, voice still shaking, "I don't want another time, Ruben."

Ruben rested his hand on his sword. "I'll do my best to make sure there won't be, Raven. But I've also done my best to ensure *you* can do the same."

She took a deep breath, because he was right as always.

Raven grasped the necklace that fell just to her heart. Glass pieces molded together with gold stitches, making a beautiful, perfect heart. She rubbed her thumb over the raised gold branches, the contrast with the smooth glass a comfort. Her own heart slowed, and her breathing smoothed. Her father had always told her she had a pure heart, a heart of gold. He'd fashioned the necklace for her, and she'd never removed it. Some days, like today, it was a reminder that she was good.

With a nod from her Head Guard, Raven straightened her dress, her spine, and her smile, then stepped out from beside the house. The composed princess yet again. Not the girl with fear in her veins and a dark secret in her heart.

She eased through the crowd that parted in her wake, a casual movement of the people, more a kind gesture than signaling her their ruler. Ruben gestured to the other guards to stay—to watch Grayson—then followed behind. Her steps quickened with each stride. She needed to talk to the *queen*. Try to stay calm, casual.

But with Grayson's copper eyes filled with almost as much hatred as his brother's, her heart was thrown six years back to when she was thirteen and naive and thought she'd found a friend. Someone to trust. Someone who liked her. Someone to save Ecanta from poverty.

But she'd been wrong.

He'd almost destroyed it.

And her.

LOX PUSHED OFF FROM THE WALL HE'D BEEN LEANING ON BEHIND TWO houses, gaze curiously latched on the raven-haired young woman across the market. He'd first been drawn to her beauty, those full lips catching his attention even from a distance—and probably larger coin purse given that she was obviously some noble's daughter. That dress's stitching, the poise to her steps, the amount of items she bought—there was no doubt. He always knew how to sift out the wealthy.

One of this thief's rules: only steal from the rich. Not even the slightly more fortunate, the slightly less poor. Poor was still poor, and he would not empty sparse pockets.

This city seemed full of sparse pockets.

The young woman sauntered across the marketplace, her steps much more hurried and concise than before. A tall guard followed in her wake, and others glanced up as she passed. Yes, a noble indeed.

She was beautiful and rich, but what worried him was her expression when that redheaded royal had approached her. She'd practically wilted. The bright smile that had captured his interest had been torn away by fear. Royalty had a tendency to do that to those they deemed lesser.

Lox eyed the alley she and that guard had whispered in, then headed to the noticeboard. The pair seemed more like comrades than protector and employer. He hadn't been near enough to overhear, but panic had been evident in her face if not the manner and too-quiet words. Something was wrong, and Lox always gravitated toward *wrong*.

It was how his band had grown from just him and Daran—his best friend—to seven men, all scarred and damned in their own ways. Some even cursed.

Lox skirted around the few villagers at this end of the market and turned to the noticeboard so he could read the papers pinned to the board and watch the young woman. He turned a sharp eye on the redheaded young man. What had that royal done to her?

He'd almost walked up to her—and not to pickpocket, no, she was off limits now—but that guard stayed close on her heels. And Lox's band had just entered the city, he didn't want to draw the guards' attention yet. But... Lox watched her cross the marketplace, sliding through the crowd easily. Panic still warred in her gaze, despite her smile, a deep-rooted fear that tugged at Lox to ease. He hated seeing people in fear because of another.

She exited through the creaky gate, that one guard in tow, and Lox shifted his attention to the notices. One referenced the daily court times of the queen for villager inquiries and disputes. A few requested assistance with the apple orchards this kingdom was known for and the additional crop harvesting. Loxley noted those papers were faded and recalled hearing the export from Ecanta was less this past year. He couldn't remember the last time he'd had an apple, actually.

Interestingly, most of the papers were layered in the center. He pushed the pages up with a single finger, and his eyes narrowed on a very vague sketch. How was anyone supposed to identify someone with *this* picture?

Red Hood. Thief—sounded right up his alley. Murderer—well, not all were bad. Scar had killed more than his fair share of criminals, and he was the jokester of the band. He didn't think there was a single one of his men who hadn't killed at least once. Maybe little Jon. But that boy had secrets that even Lox refused to push.

He retracted his finger, papers concealing the wanted poster again. A criminal seemingly protected by the villagers? *That* was also intriguing. Lox would definitely have to check out this Red Hood.

A chilled air swept his dark hair in front of his eyes, and he swiped it back, the goosebumps already flickering over his olive skin. He eyed the fabric vendor as he crossed to the other wall behind a house and out of the villagers' views—this kingdom might force him to purchase a longed-sleeved tunic finally. Maybe this was why he'd never brought the band to this corner kingdom.

They'd been traveling Aloria for years and hadn't considered this northeastern section. The sunny seaside Ocara, the warm greenery of Fovet, and the vast cities of Loren had been his shifting home for nearly ten years.

Lox gazed up at the forested canopy just beyond the wall to his right, breathing in the cool cedar-tinted breeze. Though, he had to say, he loved the atmosphere here. He hadn't been this surrounded by trees in far too long.

Maybe this kingdom would have something new, maybe even something for Beast's curse. The constant request from Beast to *stop looking* floated into Loxley's mind. But, bloody hell, he just couldn't listen.

Lox chose to walk behind the merchant houses instead of through the crowd in the market, not quite wanting the townsfolk's awareness yet. Once in the small alley, Lox spotted his man, Ramsey, farther down the wall. They always separated and observed a new town so they wouldn't be associated together so easily.

His comrade glanced over from observing the crowd when Lox approached. Ramsey's grin sharpened, the expression tugging his scar tight across his pale face. The line, from temple to corner of his mouth, flexed. "Boss." His gaze turned to the gate. "I thought you had a new target, but it seems you found yourself a girl—"

"That man there," Lox interrupted, jutting his chin toward the royal standing at the baker's booth. He met Ramsey's gaze steadily, voice hard as the blade he wanted to level with the redhead's throat. "Watch him."

CHAPTER 2

Black wooden doors parted for Raven as her guards held them open, revealing the massive throne room. She nodded to the guards. Ruben beside her, she entered with slightly stiff steps echoing in the mostly empty expanse. On the cobblestone path up the hill to the castle, a guard had stopped her and Ruben. Apparently, she'd been summoned by the queen. How convenient.

Why her mother always called her here to talk, she would never know. A simple heart-to-heart in the dining room could suffice. But no.

Marble floors stretched wide to the tall windows lining the left and right walls. A banner of the Ecanta seal hug on all four walls, with a silver crown ringing the symbol. It had changed from gold to silver when Raven was far too young. The first time in Ecanta history she could recall —a queen ruling a kingdom alone. Directly ahead, a raised dais held the three royal thrones, two guards standing on either side.

Raven kept her irritation and breathing in check as she neared the platform of thrones, determined not to lose her composure.

She stopped slightly off-center to face the throne on the left. Holding her gaze, Ruben bowed, and she forced herself to not throw him an annoyed look. He smiled, understanding and a little bit of laughter in the expression. He knew the way Raven and her mother's conversations could go. He turned to stand to the right of the dais.

Queen Vanera sat upon her silver throne, an opalescent path lead from the doors to the steps at her feet. Dark blonde hair styled into a bun rested at her neck. The encircling braid accented the perfectly perched silver crown. Her long-sleeved and high-necked blue dress covered most of her pale skin, lending more of her perfectly poised appearance. Green and silver embroidery lined the sleeves, neckline, and hem, matching Ecanta's colors. Beside her rested an elaborate, empty gold throne in the center of the raised platform, and a few feet to the right of that followed a smaller bronze one.

Vanera stared heatedly at the floor, lips pursed. Her gaze lifted and sharpened on her daughter, a small smile cresting before fading.

It always felt like this between them. Hollow and fleeting. It drew most of the anger out of Raven now. It hurt to see her mother still grieving after all this time. The emptiness that seemed to consume the widow queen.

After curtsying, Ravenna ascended the steps to her bronze chair, always trying not to stare at the empty seat between them.

She halted. In the seat of her throne shined a matching delicate bronze crown.

This again.

"Ravenna," her mother started, turning in the throne to stare at her with a tight smile. "Even in your simplest of attire, you must wear your crown."

"Yes, Mother," Raven said, bowing her head.

A small sigh preceded the rustling of the queen's dress as she stood. Vanera stepped across the dais, caressing Ravenna's dark hair, such a contrast to her own blonde strands. "I respect your reasons for not wearing it in town. But you *are* the ruler, the decider, the protector of your people. And this crown," she gestured to it lying in the throne's seat, "symbolizes that. It shows your pride in them. Wear it for that if no other reason."

The princess nodded and opened her mouth to speak—

"Ravenna!" came an excited voice from behind.

Raven turned to the windows on the left wall. A woman in an indigo dress strode over, beaming. Gold bangles jingled with her movements, and Raven wondered how she hadn't noticed her until now. The Rova's light purple eyes unsettled most people, but Ravenna had gotten used to it over countless years. The fortune teller raised her hands gleefully, dark curls bouncing as she glided toward Raven.

No wonder her mother was in a horrid mood.

"Mira," Raven replied, hugging her. It had been almost two months, and Mira's warmth radiated into her like the sun. She'd missed the woman's joyfulness. "I didn't know you were coming to Ilasia."

Mira's multitude of gold bracelets sang as she gripped Raven's shoulders. Mira tilted her head back, letting her lavender gaze travel over the princess. "I couldn't wait. Besides, I had some things I needed to check in on."

"Outlaw clienteles, no doubt," Vanera mumbled, distaste layering her tone.

"Only outlaws want to know their fortunes, to see what luck—if any —is on their side," Mira said, winking at Ravenna.

Queen Vanera scoffed, sitting at her thrown again.

Mira ignored the queen. "Look at you—I can remember when you were just a little sprout." Brushing her long black ringlets to the side, she circled Ravenna, looking her over fully.

Fortune tellers were rare, even rarer since true magic had been almost extinguished from Aloria, but the Rova tribes were still strong in the far, far northwest on the edges of Loren and all the roads they traveled between cities, earning coin for their tricks and trade. Only the Rova could access magic anymore, and even then, it was a brief touch, a glimpse into one's future, to see the touch of magic on one's life or an item. But no creating, no altering, just seeing and sensing magic. And Mira was as elusive and mysterious as magic itself.

Mira was the second Rova she'd ever met, Ruben's wife, Esme, being the only other. But Esme had stopped practicing her culture's talents long ago. Raven couldn't help but notice the stark differences in Mira's brazen Rova appearance and Esme's always pinned back curls. And Esme's milder demeanor. Culture wasn't strictly one representation, she assumed.

Did that mean Raven would be a different queen than her mother?

Raven lifted the crown from her throne and donned it. The weight kept her hair in place better than any ribbon. She caught Ruben's warning gaze from her left and turned back to her friend. "Mira, are you visiting for anything special? The betrothal?" Raven almost spit the word.

Vanera's light brows rose, a rare expression. Nothing startled the Queen.

"Grayson Loren was in the market." Ravenna met her stare. "How long have you been planning this?"

They had talked about *needing* a betrothal, about possible trade deals, but nothing further. For Grayson Loren to arrive meant there had been more planning, she'd just not been part of it. That shouldn't sting, but it did. Their distance always stung.

Could she really blame her mother entirely, if she was the one who chose not to stay during the trials and court discussions?

The soft *clink* of armor shifting came from her left, and she resisted the urge to look at Ruben again. She knew he found her challenging her mother dangerous yet amusing territory. She was still irritated that he hadn't told her the portion he'd known.

Mira gasped, eyes widening, and looked between the queen and princess. "Your mother hasn't—*Really?*"

"*Mira.*" Vanera waved for Raven to sit and waited until she did—though her sigh was barely repressed. "We are hosting a ball this weekend."

"Mother—"

Vanera held up a slim finger. "I know, it's short notice for you, but... considering the last time we had visitors." The queen pursed her lips. "I didn't want to upset you. We need gold. The crops are dwindling even more this year."

"And spending money on a gathering for entertainment will remedy that?" Raven asked, trying—and failing—to hold back her tone. One week's notice? That's what she got?

Vanera set her with a stare, grey-blue eyes as sharp as Raven's hidden blade, then sighed. "Yes, Ravenna. Because they will come for a competition. And we need their support."

"A competition?" How long had her mother been planning this? Raven's heart thudded. "And what prize can a starving kingdom offer, Mother?"

Vanera's brow creased.

"You, darling," Mira said, striding onto the steps between them, before the empty King's throne. "They will have a chance to court you."

A betrothal *search*. The breath eased out of her lungs. That meant she wasn't solidified to Grayson Loren. There could be someone else. But who else?

She'd always expected this, to be courted and married to a prince, the highest bidder so to speak—or literally. The other three kingdoms all had princes, making a marriage with her the only option for combining any kingdom's power. Even with a starving kingdom, less and less crops and import over the years, Ecanta was still second largest territory and had the strongest lumber in Aloria. Once her nineteenth birthday had come five months prior, she knew the time to be a true princess neared. Yet the suddenness of this arrangement surprised her.

Raven straightened her shoulders. *Princesses don't get to choose their fates.* And she was fine with that.

The last time had been… an attempt, although a disastrous one. She made her voice steady. "Who else are we inviting, Mother?"

"Who cares," Mira chimed in, throwing her hands in the air, bracelets chiming.

"Mira," Vanera snapped, then took a breath. "I invited the two neighboring kingdoms, as well as some… not so near."

Fovet and Ocara were the only remotely *neighboring* kingdoms, and they were still days' travel from the edges of Ecanta. The scattered remains of Valara's deserts crested the northern center of the continent, separating Ecanta from all other territories beyond Ocara, which bordered and controlled most of the sea trade. The only other way out of Ecanta was the rocky Gilan Pass on the northwest, but that went into the desert, a route no one took since Valara fell near two decades past and all trade routes were lost and forgotten. Fovet spanned the distance between Ocara and the northwestern Loren, which stretched the entire west coast and then some of Aloria. Unless there were some newly discovered islands she didn't know about, that meant Ocara and Fovet would bring their eldest to vie for her hand.

She blinked, startled. How had Grayson gotten here faster than anyone else if he was the farthest? Panic started to rise again, and she forced it down. A glance at Ruben, his solid form always near, steeled her composure.

And Ocara—could she even consider that option after Papa? She couldn't even think about that kingdom without also remembering the night the guards had informed her King Eldric wouldn't return from his trip. The night she'd lay alone unable to sleep while hearing her mother's cries down the hall. The drowning was an accident, but she still feared the ocean and the kingdom.

"They are expected to arrive the day after tomorrow," Vanera stated, interrupting Raven's thoughts, "though it appears the Loren prince came early." Sadness tinted her brows, and she dipped her head. "I regret the way you learned of this, given it is your future on the line. And… the last time…"

"I'll do my best to make them feel welcome," Raven said with more determination than she felt. Anything to stop her mentioning before. She nodded toward the queen.

Her mother evaluated Raven's face, eyes lingering on the crown. "You'll have to get used to wearing a queen's crown once you've married. A queen must never take off her crown."

"I understand, Mother."

The fortune teller took the princess's hand and laid it palm up. Though not able to wield magic like the Vala or Javir from the fallen kingdom of Valara, Mira could see its presence. How it touched lives of the fortunate—or unfortunate, if that touch was a curse. "You'll find a handsome one. But even if you don't, the power's where it's at." Mira winked a purple eye and grinned at the queen.

"Yes, a *strong* kingdom," Vanera corrected, "is good."

Covering a chuckle, Raven stood. "I'll go pick out my dress."

Vanera reached for her daughter's hand and squeezed once.

Mira moved beside Raven. "Maybe you'll be lucky like your mother here and find true love." With a strange tilt to her lips, she added, "Our lucky princess."

Raven glanced at her mother. Mentioning father never boded well with the Widow Queen.

Hurt crossed Vanera's face, pinching her features. Like regret and sorrow all tied into one. A sorrow so deep it cracked her beautiful appearance for a moment. Then, it smoothed like a solid glass pane of perfection.

Seeing those rare glimpses of her mother's pain always tightened her throat. Raven swallowed it down. If the queen chose to push the grief deep within her, Raven would do the same.

She nodded to Ruben, who would remain in the throne room to discuss the guard with the queen.

Leaving the room, Raven gladly shifted her thoughts to the women behind her. Those two women had a complicated acquaintanceship. The fortune teller had been a regular visitor of the queen and princess for all of Raven's life. Yet Mira's appearances, whether scheduled or spontaneous, always seemed to dampen Vanera's already somber moods. Raven wasn't sure what about Mira caused that, maybe the Rova's excitement made the queen focus on her own sadness? She'd never understand her mother, it seemed.

At her bedchamber door, she dismissed her guards. Sighing, she paced the length of her room. Raven met her reflection's gaze in the mirror. The bronze crown looked absurd with her marketplace dress. She furrowed her brows. But her mother was right—the crown symbolized her pride and care of Ecanta. It would show them she protected them.

Better than a red hood could… right?

Raven sighed, wishing the crown's weight felt less crushing and more comforting like it used to. Wishing that she felt as regal as her mother appeared in her silver crown. Regal… yet lonely.

Ever since Raven's father had died… well, it had been a hard time on them both. Unlike most royal marriages, Vanera and King Eldric's had been one of true love. And true heartbreak at the end.

That was the only thing she knew about love. She couldn't recall the happiness on Vanera's face, only the joy she could recall of her father.

Not all royal marriages involved love. She doubted hers would. But princesses didn't get to love.

Love—happiness… and pain and grief.

Did she really want that?

CHAPTER 3

O n the eleventh strike of the clock, dressed in burgundy tunic and trousers, Raven laced up her boots and grabbed her black satchel. It held all the tools she'd learned to lean on over the years in this role—her lockpick, an extra knife, wrapped and bundled herbs, and a roll of elixirs, though she had been wary of the elixirs for a long while.

She told herself the elixirs Mira had gifted long ago were clever combinations of herbs, not actual potions from the merfolk. This was a hard tale to fall for, considering she wasn't sure what herbs might melt a flower like one elixir had done, and the shimmer the elixirs left once poured... that made her wonder sometimes. It helped that she'd never seen a mermaid or knew anyone who had. But that wasn't hard to say, seeing as her kingdom was high in the mountains, far from the oceanside and ports of Ocara where it was said mermaids frequented.

She checked the sword strapped to her left thigh, and the black rose dagger at her hip. All in place and sheathed. Stealth and shadows were her work of trade at night. Slipping out of her room was easy, since Ruben slept eventually, and the other guards patrolled when he wasn't on duty, but tiptoeing to the east end of the castle unseen would test even the best thief's stealth.

She entered the mostly empty storage room and struck a match. By the light of a lantern she kept there, Raven rolled up the corner of a rug to reveal a trap door. Grasping the cold metal ring, she tugged it open and lowered down her satchel. After settling inside, she closed the door, encasing herself in the darkness. The musk of earth filled her nose, comforting her as it did each time she used this passageway. Her next breath was slow and full. A small smile lifted her lips. Every weight from being the perfect princess lifted and faded away.

Raven pulled a garment from her satchel. She donned her crimson cloak, clasping it around her neck, and tugged the enchanted hood over her face. Warmth radiated over her eyes and skin from the fabric and its magic.

The princess remained in the castle, and the Red Hood exited into the village.

Leaves rustled above, eerie in the darkness. Raven crept along the tree line following the walled road down to the marketplace from the castle. Periodic gates around the market allowed entrance for the merchants living upon the hills on either side. She chose a gate she'd oiled last week, easing it open without a single creak.

The marketplace rested in the middle of Ilasia, with mostly merchants' houses surrounding it and others spread outward. Upon the highest hill, the castle overlooked the entire town, only a few nobles' houses around it, and Ruben's. He had quarters within the castle, but he and his wife, Esme, lived outside.

Scaling a tree, Raven stepped onto the roof of a merchant stall. The marketplace was too open when the crowds had retired to bed, too vacant for her to traverse as the Red Hood. Feet silent as leaves touching the ground, Raven crept along the tops of the buildings until she reached the farthest stall. Then, she leapt down, ducking into the shadows and holding her breath to listen for the telltale sound of armor.

Silence gave her the cover to walk to the noticeboard. Her gloved fingers lifted her wanted poster as well as the fake notices pinned over it. One small note, written in crimson ink, rested below. She unpinned it, clutching it in her fist, and made her way through the shadows to the closest gate.

She paused, unfolding the note to read the proposed request. One word lay scrawled in uneven and shaky red letters on the page: **Barren.**

Raven dug a match from her satchel and burned the paper. Anger threatened to shake her fingers.

Quickly darting back to the shadows, Raven breathed evenly, trying to erase the child's scratched letters from her mind. She'd already picked the weaponsmith Barren as her target, even investigated her suspicions, but to see this... it clenched her heart. A shuddering breath escaped her. She'd seen those misshapen letters before, on a child's drawing in Flint's house when she'd brought the children breakfast last week. They knew. And they'd asked the Red Hood for Barren's punishment.

With a betrothal on the horizon, tonight could be the last night for the Red Hood. She'd savor it. Those children deserved it.

Hood pulled tight, Raven turned the lock of Barren's door with her lock picks, the hinges quiet in the still night. Four months ago, she'd crept through the shadows of his living room and pulled him from his small bed to beat him close to death. Four months ago, she'd told him he had one more chance or she'd return. He apparently thought himself sneakier than her.

Idiot.

Her hide boots moved soundlessly across the wood floor, shadows sticking to her like they were her own. Targets like these were both the hardest and the easiest. Two years ago, when she'd first donned her red cloak, Raven had vowed to give everyone a second chance, no matter their deed. A promise to herself that grated on her conscience when they didn't live up to that chance.

The first repeat offender had been a nobleman who'd worked his servant too hard, a child he hadn't fed enough but gave lashings in excess. Poor girl had died by his whip. Raven had debated an entire day over what to do. Every second she'd taken had been one he'd abused another child. And Raven had whipped him that night. A month later, a boy—barely over fourteen and this time hidden better—had disappeared from his house. The next night, Raven had revisited him, the face of those two children in her mind, setting her resolve.

One more chance, that's all she gave with crimes this heinous. One chance to change, to correct their ways, and they got to live.

She'd gotten another chance—Ruben had ensured that—so they received one, too.

A cruel bastard, a beater, a murderer, a rapist, and now a child molester. This would be the fourth man to die at the hands of the Red Hood. The fifth man Ravenna had killed.

Barren's bedroom door lay ajar. Raven removed her elixirs and held the blue in her left hand. She readied her favorite dagger with the other and slipped inside. He lay asleep on the bed, loud snoring grating her ears, mouth hanging open.

Raven unstopped the vial and slipped two drops of the elixir into his parted lips. Indigo shimmered over his mouth, across the weathered skin of his face, as the elixir immobilized his limbs. She poised her knife to his throat, blade longways, and covered his mouth hard with her gloved hand. Black eyes opened frantically, settling on her hood with an eerie calm.

Soft heat tingled across her face—eyes, nose, lips, laying on her cheekbones—magic settling and seeping in to mar her features from his view. It spread to her throat, where she knew it masked her voice.

"Hello, Barren," she whispered, twisted voice like ice against his ear.

He swallowed, throat bobbing in the darkness. Raven removed her hand, keeping it ready in case he yelled.

"No… please… don't." He whimpered, body shaking against the bed frame, unable to move more than that shudder.

"We were here before, Barren." Raven squeezed the handle of her blade so she wouldn't press it further into his neck. "And I told you exactly what would happen if you touched another child again. Was I not clear?"

Barren nodded, sweat pouring down his neck.

"So, you understood the consequences."

Another shaky nod.

"Yet you touched," she spat, "you *used*, Flint—a boy who went to you for help."

"P-please—"

"No!" Raven roared, moving in close, gripping his shirt tight in her fist. "Now tell me, how do you want to die?"

His watery eyes roamed from her hooded face to the window. He shook his head roughly, lank strands falling across his forehead. "Don't be cruel."

"I'm not cruel. I'm just." She clenched her fist so hard she thought her gloves might rip. With one swift move her knife dug into the wood beside his head, a thud ringing through the house. Raven's voice deepened to a lowness she didn't think possible, sharper than her blade and colder than the heart they thought she had. "How do you want to die?"

They got to choose. Another thing she despised about the big trials in court—no matter the crime, they hanged.

The bastard looked into her hooded eyes, not managing to find a focal point with the enchantment, and all hope leaked from him. This was it. And he had to choose or she would. His lips trembled with his whispered decision.

He picked quick. Though, part of her wished he hadn't. But Raven wasn't a monster.

Just her heart was.

Flint and his younger siblings' tired faces in her mind, those shaky red letters bright against the paper, Raven plunged her knife into his neck, slicing across with precision to end this for them both.

Icy water washed away the blood on Raven's gloves and knife, the stream quietly trickling through the trees beyond the walled market district. She sat beneath a tree, checking the shadows for life, and leaned heavily against its strong trunk. The deep red of her cloak blended against the tree bark, the fabric an almost perfect match. Raven paused to stare at the crimson forest around her. Some spots were burgundy, some a brilliant bright ruby. Here, it was intermingled. She took a deep breath of cedar coated air and sheathed her blade.

Taking a life, even a horrible one like Barren's, grated on her soul.

She had to admit, she was angrier than usual with this kill. Part of that was because Flint was so nice and undeserving of that treatment. The other part, the darker part, knew it was anger from Grayson this morning. The way he'd instantly made her feel small and scared. The way she'd reverted back into a wounded little girl. But here, in the forest and cloaked in darkness and enchantment... she was the danger. She was death and shadows. *She* was to be feared.

Barren had been the main weaponsmith in the village besides Win at the castle, and she'd seen too often someone walk from trial after paying gold, their station ranking higher than their crime. In trials, if actually convicted, death came sure and swift. She just removed the trial, but that was okay… right? Because, as the princess, her declaration meant justice. It was just a secret declaration.

And she talked to them first, warned them. She *tried*. Sometimes they didn't.

Raven liked to think her people could be redeemed if given the chance.

She had donned this hood to do better for her kingdom. To right the wrongs left unseen. Did killing a criminal make her better… or worse?

Could she even be redeemed?

Or would her heart be darkened forever?

She leaned her head back, noting the small strands of moonlight breaching the verdant canopy above, and sighed. When she'd ventured into the forest behind the merchants' houses for the stream, she'd seen Grayson Loren headed into the southern region. What was he doing out this late? Visiting his twenty occupants at the inn? The damned campaign he'd brought with him to parade his wealth and power. She knew traveling royalty needed an adviser and guards, but *twenty* people? Part of her itched to find him and listen in at his camp or the inn, wherever he was staying. When the other princes arrived, he'd be given bedchambers at the castle.

She couldn't follow Grayson; it was too risky to stay out as the Red Hood tonight. Barren would be found by the morning, sooner if anyone visited him.

Regretfully, Raven returned to the shadows of the forest and wound back to her hidden passage on the east side of the castle. The weight of another life spilled by her hands bore down on her, easing the guilt of her very first kill. But not enough. Her actions could never quite erase that guilt.

That cruel bastard would be on her conscience forever.

RAVENNA SEARCHED THE SHADOWS OF THE FOREST FOR HER GUARD, WORRIED *they'd gone too far behind. Mother had said it would be good to spend time with* the prince, to build a friendship before the betrothal, but she didn't think Landon wanted friendship. Didn't think he even knew the word. She shouldn't have let him send the guards on an errand. Shouldn't have let him pull her deeper into the unfamiliar area of the forest. Verdan was not a city she knew, all these forests a stranger to her.

His easy smile had lured her in to a sense of comfort, a sense that he might be kind enough to like her. His words, however, showed a different side of him.

"I'll have a second castle here," Landon Loren pointed to the mountainside peeking through the canopy above. "Far from the filth of that village."

Anger spiked within her alongside a twinge of embarrassment. Over the few days he'd been here, Ravenna had found Landon was skilled at making people feel embarrassed for something they shouldn't. She straightened her crown, slightly too big for her head, even at thirteen years old.

"I like the village," she said, touching a crimson tree trunk to keep her balance. She loved the deeper color they took on farther from the castle. "And that would require taking down a lot of the forest here."

"Yes, it would." Landon spread his arms. "So much lumber to export! This kingdom needs more trade, more coin coming in. I'll increase the lumber output by building more."

Unease settled in Ravenna's stomach. The trees were beautiful, and she'd heard stories that the fae originated somewhere deep in the forest. Where would the faeries live then?

"Ecanta is smaller, but I can make it better than Loren," he continued. "This kingdom will bow to me like Loren does to my father. I won't be a disgrace like my brother. Hideous, I'm glad father—"

Raven stepped forward, lost in his ranting. "But the forest—"

"No 'buts.'" Landon spun, pointing a finger in her face, making her flinch. "Tsk tsk. I'll have to toughen you up, little princess."

Ravenna pressed her lips together, wanting to speak but not to anger him. Mother had said to be nice, and what she wanted to say was decidedly not.

Landon laughed. "Those stupid guards—I can't believe they just left when I asked for something." He picked a leaf from a low-hanging branch and crushed it in his hand. "I hate guards. They follow, and they watch and tell you what you can't do." Sunlight shined through, turning his copper hair to an almost fiery auburn. He smiled, sauntering toward her. "I do like how you follow me, though." Landon brushed the back of his finger down her cheek.

Ravenna jerked her head back, revolted at his touch, and pushed his hand away. "No, don't—"

He stepped close, face inches from hers. Those copper eyes turned to fire. "You don't get to say 'no'—you'll be my queen. And you'll be whatever little queen I want you to be."

Stars above, he really was horrible. She shook her head. "You will never be king here."

She'd tell mother what he said. There had to be someone else. Anyone else.

Landon leaned back, assessing her from crown to hem. He smiled. Metal sang against the sheath as he slowly brandished his blade. "You shouldn't have done that."

Ravenna ran. Footfalls and curses followed behind in pursuit. All she could think was to run, to find her guards, to find Ruben. They hadn't gone too far from where Landon had sent them off. He could still be close—

Her foot caught on a protruding tree root, and she crashed to the dirt, screaming. Her crown clattered distantly. Leaves slid under her hands as she tried to stand, pain stinging in her palms and knees—but something hit her head.

Darkness.

Numbness.

Pain radiated from her chest. Her eyes shot open, a scream vibrating her throat. Ravenna looked down to find blood on her ripped bodice, a knife carving into the skin below her collarbone. One clean line ran straight down, and the blade was turning to the side for another cut.

She struggled, but Landon kneeled over her. Ravenna twisted her shoulders, managing to knock away his blade. White hot pain seared as the knifepoint slashed jaggedly in a horizontal line. The knife fell.

"You little—" Landon cursed, falling backward.

Ravenna crawled to her knees, then had one foot under her, the other, rose higher —come on, just a little farther—come on—a sharp knock on her back sent her back to the forest floor with a cry of defeat. She brought her elbow back to smash into Landon, she didn't care where. He grunted, and she clawed her way forward.

Nails scraped her back, ripping through the layers of her dress collar, another set tearing the flesh of her arm. Tears brimmed and fell as she crashed down again. Landon twisted her and lifted her by the neck, making her face him. His fist clenched around her throat, not only stealing her air but squeezing her skin and neck. Black spots clouded her vision, rough bark dug against her back. His knees weighed down her legs.

"You'll pay for that, little princess," Landon Loren spat. He leaned to the side, admiring his handiwork. "Not a bad L, even with your interruption."

Ravenna grasped for his hand, trying to pull it away. Dull red eyes glared in inch from hers, pure hatred flaring within. She'd never look at copper the same again.

Panic flooded through her veins. Her fingers reached around her for something, anything, to lessen his grip. Dirt, only dirt, why was there noth—wood. Solid wood covered in something soft. Her eyes bulged, and she seized the branch. Raven tried to lift her arm high to bash his head but couldn't angle her hand higher than his stomach. Blinking hard, she channeled her strength and thrust upward.

Her world dissolved into blood.

The object didn't hit him, didn't push him off. It went through, buried deep into him. Soft flesh, a squish of muscle, and then a hard stop as her hand met his abdomen. Whatever was in her hand hit bone deep within, the harsh scrape reverberating in her palm.

Copper eyes, a dull match to the blood, widened along with her own.

Landon slowly looked down. His hand unclenched, freeing her throat. Air— glorious air—rushed into her lungs on a ragged breath. His hand remained around her neck despite his shock, though loose enough for her to see—oh gods.

His dagger protruded from his stomach, Raven's hand still gripping the handle. A second passed, then hot liquid trailed down her hand. Her fingers shook, releasing the blade.

On a gasp, she coughed and tried to move. Her hand slipped on the ground, now slick with… with…

Landon moaned and sank backward, still staring at his blade.

Trembling fingers grasped the handle, not yet worn to his grip, and pulled it out. More blood gushed from the wound, and he whimpered.

Raven pulled herself to the side, crawling backward but not looking away.

Red, too much red, stained her dress, already sticking to her hands and arms and face.

Landon Loren looked up, hatred gone from his eyes and only a cold, blank fear remaining. He tilted and fell to the ground.

Crashing of leaves underfoot and jangling armor sounded from her right. Raven couldn't move. She stared at Landon's body, feeling the blood coating her, tears streaming down her face. Blood still flowed from the gaping wound on his abdomen.

The footsteps stopped. "Ravenna..."

She turned. "Rue—" Tears overtook her voice, she couldn't finish his name.

Ruben had only been with her personal guard for a year, but she'd seen him in the castle for longer. Since Papa. Her guard, her friend. Here. But too late.

He stared, blue gaze assessed her bloody figure, torn dress, ending with the knife next to Landon's body. Ruben nodded, sheathing his sword.

"He—I didn't mean—I couldn't..." Ravenna gestured to the blood on her chest and the knife.

Ruben knelt, taking her small hands in his. He wiped away the blood on her collarbone with his sleeve. A pause. Rage darkened his face.

She glanced down at the bloody gouge of an "L" carved into her pale skin. The red and jagged surface a harsh contrast.

He straightened her heart necklace, placing it over the cuts.

"They're going to be mad," she said, thinking of the Loren king and her mother.

"You'll be okay," Ruben assured her. He held her gaze, lifting her chin to see his sincerity. "I'll take care of it."

She nodded but stared down at her bloody fingers. Her hands numbed, hot from liquid while she grew cold inside. Frozen and hollow.

Was this what a heart felt like when it darkened?

CHAPTER 4

Raven awoke shaking, trembling from inside out, but that wasn't what shook her body. She opened her eyes to find Ruben leaning over her bed, his hard hands gripping her shoulders gently but forcefully. She blinked, and the nightmare faded—only a nightmare, but one rooted in something all too real.

"Raven," Ruben whispered.

He was here. Like before and always, he was here.

She tried to say something but tasted salt—tears. Slowly, she reached up to wipe them away, but her fingers couldn't still. A sigh, or maybe a whimper, left her lips, and she crumpled against her best friend.

Ruben held her tight, using a gloved hand to erase her tears.

She could still feel the hot blood on her hands and arms and... everything. Coating her. But she felt so cold. Iciness spiraling inside.

Or was that just the guilt?

At the doorway stood two worried maids, who had probably called for the guard standing next to them. And as usual, they'd found Ruben.

It had been years since he'd comforted her from nightmares, but they fell into the roles easily.

The women and guards shared sympathetic glances and backed out of the doorway. Normally, the princess shouldn't be allowed alone in her bedchamber, let alone on her bed, with a man, but Ruben was the sole exception. He'd been the only one to help her in worse times than these. Back when no one had known how to look the grieving child in the eye.

Ruben's hand smoothed down her hair, and her gasps eased into breaths. Eventually, she moved back, and he caught her eye.

She nodded, and he released her, moving to stand beside her bed. He kept his gaze trained on her face, then the walls.

"Are we going down to breakfast now?" His eyes shot to hers, holding the real question.

Raven left her bed, clad in her night dress, for the closet and grabbed her tunic and pants. "No."

Ruben smiled and turned for the door. "I'll grab the swords."

Swords clashed in the crisp morning air, the sharp *shing* of metal rang throughout the courtyard. Dawn had just broke, the sun's rays barely cresting the treetops surrounding the castle.

The abandoned cobblestone courtyard had been overgrown with weeds and grass until Ruben had ordered some recruits to clear enough room to spar six years previous. Its hidden pathway still covered with bushes allowed the Head Guard and princess to practice their swordplay in private. A royal learning swordsmanship was not *proper*, especially a princess. However, Ruben had insisted she wear and *learn* a weapon since she was thirteen. Since the first Loren prince's visit.

Panting, Raven heaved her sword against Ruben's. His strength always outmastered hers, but he'd taught her ways to outwit stronger opponents. Raven whipped her heel behind Ruben's, knocking him off balance. He caught his footing—but not before she leveled the tip of her blade at his chest.

Ruben grinned, looking at his princess like a sword wasn't an inch from killing him. "Nice move."

"I'd say the same," Raven said, lowering her blade to her side, "but I won."

Her Head Guard laughed, a deep hearty sound, and sheathed his sword at his waist. His movements were silent, the metal plates of his armor rested on the stone near the entry. Only the leather to protect from her swings. He moved to the stone bench beside their sparring area,

35

pouring a cup of water from a pitcher and handing it to Raven. "I taught you the move so I *do* win."

She sat, conceding the point to him. Wiping her hands on her hide pants, she took the cup. Practice had chased away her fears, letting it curl deep inside instead of pushing her to the edge like before. Taking a sip of the water, Raven pondered her next words. "Rue…"

His brows creased. He moved to stand in front of her. "Yes, Princess?"

Raven raised a brow.

"Raven," he corrected. He raised his hands in apologies for the formal facade. They held too dark of a secret between them to continue the formalities after all these years.

"Why didn't you tell me?"

He sat beside her, pouring water for himself. "I didn't know about a betrothal. Only a ball. And I still don't have a confirmed list. I…" Ruben watched her face and nodded to himself. "I didn't want to worry you if he didn't come."

Because of the nightmares. They'd just stopped almost two years ago. The guilt hadn't, though.

She sighed, plumes of black hair flying. Damn it.

Ruben laid a gloved hand on hers, which gripped her pommel tightly.

"What Grayson said yesterday," Raven started, licking her lips, "about murder being punished here, do… do you think he suspects something?"

Ruben shifted, leather creaking against the stone bench. "Even if he does, there is no proof." He dipped his head to catch her falling gaze. "It'll be okay. I'll protect you, Raven. You're safe."

With a sad smile, she nodded. Yes, he always protected her, even from herself. But Raven hadn't truly felt safe in years. Worried, guilty, empty. But not safe. She was less frantic, less scared, but there was constant movement within her, constant worry.

The two left their sparring area, down the winding path to the gardens and into the castle's back corridors. Their practice swords remained stashed at the courtyard.

The moment they entered the castle doors, Ruben lost his smile and Raven straightened her shoulders. The whole guard knew of their deep friendship, considering he'd been part of her guard since she was nine and he a green recruit at sixteen, and he had earned his way up the ranks to Captain, but they kept their friendship and professional relationship separate. The guards had to see a strong leader, not a joking man and his best friend.

Raven glanced up at Ruben, his short dark blond hair and hazel eyes, that strong jaw that somehow looked like it could cut the glass windows. Ruben was a constant, steady presence. Always beside her, like a shadow that was a part of her. Yes, he was her best friend. Her only friend—and she didn't need more than that.

Princesses didn't have friends. Their duty was to their kingdom. No friendships, no love, no dreams.

She loved Ecanta, her villagers, and Ruben, and that was enough.

CHAPTER 5

Cindy Arden's hands shook, the bread loaves bobbing on the baking tray. Her fingers gripped the metal, an odd mingling of cold from the tray and heat from the bread radiating. She stared at Flint across the path at the deceased weaponsmith's booth. Standing alone, Flint seemed happier. His brow was smooth, his movements as he adjusted the weapons more sure. Though he tried to hide the relief, his shoulders were straight and unburdened. He was finally free.

They'd rarely talked, but with her booth directly opposite his, she'd seen Barren. She'd recognized those flinches, the distance Flint tried to put between him and Barren.

She recognized the fear.

She stared down at the loaves. Father had told her to put out the fresh bread while he'd started the next batch. To return inside immediately. He never wanted her out in the mornings. She had to observe from the window until the afternoon, until it was time to retrieve the unsold goods and clean the stall.

But Flint... Cindy glanced back at the house. She could be quick. She gripped the tray and weaved around people starting to filter into the market.

Cindy set the tray on the sparse weapons table and brushed her blonde hair back into her loose bun. The curls soft but rebellious never remained twisted in her hair tie.

Flint smiled at her, but his eyes darted to the baker's house over her shoulder.

Just as she knew his pain, he knew hers. Voices carried in a small market.

"I heard," Cindy whispered, keeping her tone politely sad.

He paused, then fingered the tablecloth. Long fingers adjusting the fabric, then stopping. "Yes. It was sudden. I'm—um, I'm selling the last of his wares."

Cindy leaned in slightly over the blades and caught his eye. "Was it —" she lowered her voice further, "*him?*"

Flint held her stare, and his blue eyes grew wet. He let out a shaky breath. "Yes."

Oh, thank goodness. The Red Hood. Cindy had hoped he would help. She hadn't hoped death, just change. She bit her lip. Maybe death was the only way.

Flint stared at the house behind her. "It would be a shame if your father was next."

His tone disagreed.

Cindy tensed, fingers digging into the tray. She wanted change, too, but didn't count on it. "People see, but they don't help."

"The Red Hood does."

She glanced up, his stare catching her. His eyes held the hope that she didn't.

He cleared his throat and returned to a normal volume. "Princess Ravenna visited me this morning."

"She did?" Cindy's heart pounded, and she searched the sparse market quickly. The Princess? She didn't come for another half hour usually.

"At my house."

Cindy breathed a sigh of relief. Not here.

"She offered for me to work with the castle blacksmith," Flint continued, awe in his voice. "And that me and my siblings can move into the castle servants' quarters."

She returned her attention to him, eyes widening at his news. The

39

princess was so kind, always giving food and—a door creaked. Cindy's heart stuttered, muscles tensing. Her gaze froze on Flint's face.

No.

"Go!" Flint warned, his eyes trained on her house.

Cindy sprinted to her booth, moving around people with the tray. She started to set it down on the tabletop but tripped, losing her grip. The loaves cascaded to the ground, tray clanging as she caught herself on the table. No, no, *no.*

She snatched up the tray as heavy footsteps neared.

Father loomed over her, wide face reddened and scrunched in anger.

"Papa, I—"

Pain laced on her right cheek, registering before she'd even seen his hand move. Cindy stumbled, hand holding her stinging face. The baking tray dangled from her fingertips.

The market quieted, eyes turning to her. Her cheeks heated more.

"What did you do?" Her father glared down at the bread lying in the dirt, then turned his angry dark eyes on her. Sweat poured down his wide face, skin rosy from the oven's heat and his ire. "Stupid girl!"

The baker's yell turned the heads of a city guard, but the guard didn't move. The people returned to their wares and purchases. Somewhere in the distance she heard a gate creak.

She shrunk into herself, holding the tray in front of her. "I'm sorry, Papa."

"Sorry?" He gestured to the loaves. "You ruined these! How am I going to sell them now? No one wants dirty bread."

"I didn't mean—"

He tore the tray from her hands and grabbed her by her fallen and disheveled bun. She cried out and stumbled again, knees giving way. He pulled her close to him, gravelly voice whispering, "You're worse than worthless. You cost more than you're worth. But you'll fetch a pretty penny to Ocara traders." Sweat and spittle hit her nose, and she winced. He turned her head, and anger flared in his gaze. "Keep screwing up, and that's where you'll go." He thrust her face to the ground. "Pick them up. Then, get back to the kitchen."

Tears burned behind Cindy's eyes as her father returned inside, but she pushed them back. Her arms burned where the dirt and gravel grated against her skin. She brushed the dirt off with her stained apron.

She didn't know what hurt worse, her cheek or her heart. Would he really sell her to traders? In a few weeks, she'd be eighteen and unmarried, not his responsibility and not worth his time. She swallowed hard. Yes, he would. He didn't hesitate to swing, so why would he hesitate to sell?

She knelt, dirt coating her dress and the golden loaves. Curls fell helplessly around her face, but at least they'd cover the building welt.

Boots and a lightly embroidered dress hem stopped before her, and Cindy edged backward from instinct. She kept her gaze on the bread and tray, not wanting to lift it and her scarlet cheek show.

The woman crouched, and a pale hand reached for a loaf.

Cindy sighed, grateful and ashamed. "Thank you. You didn't need to help."

"I don't mind." The young woman dusted off a loaf. "You didn't deserve that."

Cindy knew that she didn't deserve hate and anger, but sometimes she felt like she did. That she truly was worthless. Her throat tightened. "Sometimes Father… doesn't have patience. We're strained. Well, all the merchants are—" Cindy glanced up, and her words froze.

Black hair, ruby ribbon—no crown, but Cindy knew it was Princess Ravenna Heldt. She saw her from the window every day. The one person she was to avoid.

Father's glare flashed in her mind. And his warning.

Cindy startled, toppling into the dirt. "Oh! Forgive me, Your Highness."

Princess Ravenna reached out to right her. "Are you okay?"

"Yes, Your Highness." Cindy nodded fiercely, feeling her curls bounce. "I've heard of your kindness, the gifts, but didn't expect…" Didn't expect her to help when no one else did. Cindy looked at the princess's now dirty dress hem.

"Don't worry." Ravenna smiled, noticing Cindy's focus, and placed the last loaf on the tray. She paused, staring, then asked, "What's your name?"

"Cindy, Your Highness." Heat flushed her face, and she hoped either dirt or her bangs covered her cheek.

Princess Ravenna's dark brows scrunched slightly, and she continued to stare. "That's pretty, is it short for anything?"

"No, Your Highness."

Why was she staring?

Cindy's heart raced. She was talking to *the* princess. The one person Father wanted her to avoid, to not embarrass him in front of.

"You don't have to call me that." Ravenna brushed off her dress and stood, extending a hand to help Cindy up.

"Sorry." Cindy tried to straighten her tattered apron. "I never thought *I'd* talk to you."

"Why haven't we met before?"

"I'm usually baking now."

Princess Ravenna nodded slowly. "Then, what is your father doing right now?"

Cindy swallowed at the direct question and tone.

"I visit *every day*," Ravenna stated. "And I haven't seen you once over all these years."

The intensity of the princess's gaze made Cindy's resolve fall. "I-I'm not supposed to be out when you're here," she admitted.

Princess Ravenna's eyes narrowed, amber hardening, but not angrily. She held her polite smile. "And why is that?"

Cindy's cheeks heated again, the sting swelling in her bruised one, and she couldn't hold her stare. She placed the ruined loaves on the table. Brushed her hands on her dingy dress. "I don't..."

"Well," Ravenna tapped the table, leaving two coppers. "I hope to see you tomorrow."

Cindy hesitantly looked up. She did?

Princess Ravenna smiled, face softening again. She set her basket on the table, and reached inside the cloth-covered top. She seemed to search inside, hands shifting its contents. After a few moments, she retrieved a carefully wrapped parcel and handed it to Cindy. "I hope your family enjoys this."

The scent of apple wafted in the air, and Cindy recognized the feel of a tart under the cloth. A castle pastry, made from the private orchard's apples? If it weren't rude, she would have said she couldn't accept it. Instead, Cindy smiled. "Yes, of course."

The princess started to turn and paused, her brows dipping in thought. Then, she smiled again and left.

Warmth radiated from the tart in to her fingers, and Cindy felt her chest lighten along with it. Father would be angry if he knew she'd spoke with the Princess, if she saw her again. But... Ravenna had been kind. For once, someone had seen and had helped.

RAVEN RELUCTANTLY TURNED FROM THE BAKER'S STALL. CINDY'S SMILE HAD warmed her heart a little, thawing the freeze that nightmare had left, but her heart now raced for different reasons.

Raven meandered through the market, anger flaring. The urge to do *something*. Her guards had done nothing when the baker had struck Cindy. She knew the baker had purposefully hidden Cindy when she went into the market. Hidden how he treated her, the bruises she'd noticed on the young woman's wrist as well as her cheek.

If she hadn't entered the market when she did... Raven relinquished her clenched fingers.

Cindy had been sweet. Raven had felt compelled to keep talking to her. Something had tugged at the edge of her mind but... what?

She searched the crowd for Ruben. In her rush to get to Cindy, she'd broken away, and they'd gotten caught in the bustling crowd. He stood at the clothier booth a ways back, holding a scarf—probably something for Esme. She needed to return to the castle and plan for tonight. The baker would not hit his daughter again.

"Hello, milady."

Raven tore her stare from Ruben to the person who'd spoken. A young man stood a few paces away, hair almost as black as hers, and confidence layering in his relaxed stance. Looking a year older than her, something mischievous and worn lingered in his eyes. Brown clay dotted the softly tanned boots, barely leaving a print on the ground. He wore the simple, dark olive tunic and burgundy pants of the lower class. But looks could be deceiving.

"Hello," she replied politely. This young man, his face wasn't familiar. A newcomer or a traveler. Uncommon in Ilasia—the capital—with the surrounding forests and lack of trade. Though Ecanta competed with Fovet as second largest Kingdom of Aloria, it was far from second richest.

His skin tan, tunic short-sleeved. She could almost see goosebumps on his arms from the chilled air. Her gaze paused on the toned muscle of his exposed arms. She couldn't help but note the width.

Out of the corner of her eye, she noticed Ruben's gaze from the clothier. She smiled at the stranger to reassure Rue there was no threat.

The young man's dark green eyes roamed her face and down to her basket. His assessing gaze, both sharp and soft, made her curious. "Having a fine day?"

Raven nodded, though this day would improve if he'd move.

"Are you new around here?" he asked, some casual tilt to his words. An accent? If so, it was faint.

"Not particularly. You?" she replied courteously. Though she liked talking with villagers, she needed to return, and he was blocking her path. Her patience had been worn very thin this morning.

The stranger smiled, showcasing a small dimple alongside the right of his mouth. It was oddly disarming. "Would you like someone to walk with? These streets could be dangerous."

Not to her.

She paused, recalling Grayson's glare the day before. Was that still true?

Yes, Ruben had assured her Grayson was in the southern region of the city this morning. She would avoid him as long as she could.

Raven looked this stranger up and down, examining the smile he held too confidently. He expected her to take his hand and stroll with him—all because he smiled. He *was* handsome... She turned. "No, thank you."

Moving around the stranger, Raven casually eyed the walls and the best track to the baker's house upon nightfall. She'd poured her sleeping elixir on the tart to ensure the family would be asleep when she—

Someone tapped Raven's arm, and she reluctantly turned.

The stranger.

He extended his hand again, only this time it held a red ribbon.

Raven's eyes widened, then her hand flew to her hair. The black strands hovered in front of her face, unburdened by the tie. It never managed to stay in place for long, her hair too straight to hold anything beyond a crown.

"You dropped this, milady."

He offered it again, sliding closer, and placed it in her hand. She registered the sound of Rue's armor across the way. Rough callouses rubbed her own as the stranger returned the ribbon. Heat radiated from his touch. Up close, he was tall enough to make her feel short, to raise her chin. No one stood this close, even for a brief second, and his breath touched her face. He smiled, a glint in his green eyes, and his voice deepened, "Have a nice day."

He backed away, still grinning, then turned smoothly to stroll through the people, boots barely marring the dirt path.

In the span of time Ruben had started forward, the stranger had touched the princess and left. Too quick for Rue's protective reaction to register and converge on her. She lifted a hand and waved Ruben's concerned stare away, watching the young man walk her marketplace.

Suspicion filled her. Raven strung her headband in her hair and tied it, her gaze following the stranger. What had been his goal? To just… stroll with her? He'd almost seemed *concerned* for her, asking how she was. His parting words had sounded sincere.

What was this? How was he able to knock her off-kilter in the span of a moment?

He wove through people, pausing beside a noble at the cloth vendor, and Raven's eyes latched onto a flash of his hand.

Did he really?

She watched him lightly bump into another vendor. He steadied the man, then the stranger—thief—sauntered on. *That* was his goal. Had he…? Raven checked her coin purse's weight—same as before. No, he hadn't. But he'd tried to, she was sure.

This annoyance of a man had made her lose track of her plan *and* tried to pickpocket her? The coin for the villagers?

Raven glanced at her guards, who looked from the stranger to the other people around her. *Of course* they didn't notice. The best thieves were never caught. Ruben only assessed people for threats to her, not thievery. And who would be stupid enough to try stealing from the princess?

Granted, this princess dressed like a peasant.

Young, fit, used to hard labor if the tan or callouses said anything… this newcomer didn't need to steal for food or money. She hated *that* thievery.

She turned, keeping the thief in her sight. Ravenna caught Ruben's eye and tipped her head at him before moving to another stall, their signal for a few moments' privacy. Her Head Guard smiled and turned around. He understood, more than any of them, that she was a person beyond her royal duties.

The thief dipped to the side of another merchant with a casual greeting and snaked his hand into the man's bag.

Coming up beside him, Raven shoved his shoulder.

Stumbling into an alley between vendors, the thief caught himself and spun. His eyes lightened upon seeing her face. He strode toward her. "If you wanted me in a dark corner, you only had to ask."

Typical.

"You're lucky I give second chances."

His dark brows crinkled. "Come again?"

Raven faltered her steps and fell toward him. He caught her, hands grabbing her waist and arm. The strength of his steadying grip stole her focus for a heartbeat—she hadn't expected him to actually catch her, or the warmth of his fingers on her side. No one touched her beyond her arms or hands.

She blinked. Raven focused, slipping her hand into his pockets. A woodsy scent engulfed her, like being in the forest.

His hand tightened on her waist, a small sound emanating from his throat. She glanced at his gaze, which locked solidly on her. Her knuckles grazed his thigh, a carelessness she'd never encountered before. His stare dropped to her mouth.

Coins retrieved, she righted herself, brushing off his soft yet firm grip and the warmth it left behind. The unease and coined tension still remailed in her stomach. What was that? She smoothed the folds of her dress.

"Think some more with your head." Raven flashed, then stashed the coppers. "And learn to properly pickpocket. I could see you from across the market."

"You were watching me?" he asked, interest entering his voice. He patted his pockets, brow crinkling, then smiled, lips parted. "Hm. Normally, I'd say it's not needed, but it appears I might require some lessons from you." A twinkle appeared in his dark eyes. "Milady."

He dipped his head, a lock of hair falling forward.

"Take care who you steal from. Others aren't as kind." Ravenna checked between the booths for her guards.

"Oh, come on. You can certainly spare a few coins for a poor peasant."

She returned her stare to him. "And *you* have the authority to assume this?"

He shrugged, that crooked smile back on his face. "I'm just a newcomer to this town. How about you show me around—"

Raven grabbed his extended arm, twisted it behind his back and pushed him face-first into the wall. A low grunt of surprise and pain left him. She leaned in, pressing into his back, to whisper, "How about not."

She released him and moved to return to the marketplace—but his hand clasped her wrist, pulling her back. The grip was firm but not hard, the surprise alone of him touching her enough to move her. She found herself pressed against his chest, his other hand holding her waist. Her eyes widened, inches from his brilliant emerald green. Raven couldn't help thinking they matched the forest—both in color and the vastness within.

Raven didn't think she'd ever been flush against a man—not even killing them. Heat flushed her skin from where his thumb moved small circles on the inside of her wrist to the fingers spread along her side, one touching her hip through her bodice. Even the expansive chest under her palm. She glanced down. Wait, her hand was—her finger touched his collarbone under his shirt. His *shirt?* Raven clawed her fingers into his skin and pushed back.

He gripped her tighter, but let her shift a few inches between them. "Easy, love. I like a few love scratches like the next man," he said, winking at her, "and we can do that if you want. But I have a feeling yours would be more than a scratch."

She felt his hand trace down to her knife, hidden in her skirts. A knowing tap on the metal under the fabric.

"A well-hidden blade is especially one to be aware of."

How had he—She froze. Was that a blade she felt against her thigh? Or…

He grinned, lifting three coppers for her to see in his palm before she felt that hand slip back over her hip and into the purse strapped there. Raven tensed, unsure why she didn't just retrieve her dagger.

She told herself it was because of the damning symbol on its end.

The thief leaned forward, words brushing against her face, her lips, "Just wanted to give you your coin back."

Anger, hot and quick, flared in her, and she pushed against his chest. She stepped back out of his grasp. A soft breeze cooled her flushed skin, making her realize just how warm he'd been. How warm he'd made her by proximity.

Raven glared at the thief. "Touch me again, and I won't call the guards. I'll stab you myself." She smiled ruthlessly. "And as a thief in this starving kingdom, that's a mercy. A starving kingdom is not one to be caught stealing in."

A part of her truly hated that it was a truth.

But it was a truth she couldn't overtly change.

She turned, trying to measure her steps and her emotions as she exited the alley, leaving that frustrating thief behind. As much as her pride raged, she was Princess Ravenna now, not the Red Hood.

He'd stolen the coin presumably when she'd pinned him to the wall —and then given it *back*? Why? Just to touch her?

That felt absurd. She knew, mostly from Mira, that casual—and non-casual—touches were a pastime, a pleasure, but never for her. Not a princess. Not even a passing thought.

It wasn't solely her steadfast objection to temping the idea of love when she always knew she'd be betrothed... No one had been interested. Not a single noble. Now, in a day's time she'd have three princes here vying for her hand. Her *hand*, not her heart, she reminded herself.

With that roguish grin, she wouldn't put it past that thief to want more than her hand.

She shook him—his grip on her waist, his skin under her fingertips, his closeness—from her mind. Raven squeezed between the booths back into the marketplace, clearing her thoughts of that roaming thief. Her guards' gazes combed the light crowd for her. She smiled at them and headed to Ruben. She rejoined him and fell easily into her role as princess, as the Ravenna they all knew. They stopped at the notice board. Nothing of importance again.

A laugh pulled her attention to two young men along the wall separating the market from the forest's edge. The thief stood among them, laughing heartedly. Why was he in her marketplace? Beside him stood a young man with sharp grey eyes, seeming alert even in laughter, shaded by a dark red cap.

"What do you know about that newcomer?" Raven asked Ruben quietly.

He followed her stare. "Not much. He's with a group that just came into town, about four men, I think. If you wish, I could find out more, Your Highness?"

She paused, watching the young man. It would be smart to know more. "Yes, please, Rue."

Ruben's hazel eyes crinkled at her childhood nickname. She used it when he was too *formal*.

Sun shone into her eyes, and she shielded them. The sun had already set into the afternoon. Mother would want her back now to talk about the ball.

She checked her basket's contents. Two apples and a piece of bread. And her light coin purse—normally empty upon returning.

That thief. Because of his distraction she hadn't distributed everything. She'd bring extra tomorrow. Raven had to admit, she could see his smile getting him out of trouble. Probably why he used it so easily.

He was the least of her worries. But she'd keep her eye on him if they encountered again. A thief bold enough to steal that frequently and easily was not one she wanted in her kingdom.

Not while it starved already.

CHAPTER 6

Cloak stashed in her satchel, Raven climbed out her window when the guards below looked the other way and carefully stepped over the ledges to the room three windows away. After prying open the pane she kept unlatched, she maneuvered inside and shut the glass. With the three princes arriving tomorrow, Ruben had increased security—two guards always outside her door and more patrolling the castle corridors and exterior.

Her Red Hood duties would be harder to accomplish. She hoped it wouldn't be this difficult returning to her passage outside, and at least she had another entrance just in case.

Raven slipped into her tunnel, clasped the cloak, and exited into the woods. She knelt to cover the tunnel opening with leaves and dirt, then started her trek down to the walled section. The deep red tree trunks surrounding the market gave her adequate cover from the guards that stayed to the paths and walls.

She skulked up behind the house until she found the door to the baker's home. Hiding in the shadows, she tugged a bundle from her satchel. Picking the lock was easy, and once she stood inside, she knew this night would be one of her favorites.

Raven stopped. Standing in the kitchen of this foreign house, she took in the atmosphere. This could be the last time she settled justice. Her last overt act of ruling. Considering her target, she would savor it.

The first bedroom held a figure with a small scrap of blanket barely covering her form, though the nights had chilled. Cindy shivered in her sleep, blonde hair sprayed on the ground. The welt on her cheek had darkened to a purple.

He won't do that again, Cindy.

The next room held two older young women, probably nineteen, both in beds and covered in thick blankets. And the last: her target. Asleep—as the drugged tart she'd given Cindy assured the whole family would be—the baker snored beside his wife.

Raven brandished a strip of cloth and gagged him, though he didn't stir. Then, she dragged him from bed and onto the floor with a slight *thud* as his heavy body hit the wood. Muscles straining, she pulled his limp body. It seemed the baker ate too many of his own wares. She settled him in the front room and let three drops of her blue elixir fall into his mouth, a shimmer floating over his lips.

The baker startled awake, silent except for the rustle of his clothes against the floor. He stared around his house curiously, until his blood-shot eyes landed on the red hooded figure standing before him.

Soft warmth coated Raven's face. Focus, then glazed disconnect clouded his eyes.

"Red Hood," he mumbled into his gag, brown eyes wide with fear. The baker attempted scooting away, but Raven knelt, and he stilled. "No! No—please, I-I won't do it again."

"But you don't even know what you did," she whispered into his ear. Sitting back on her heels, Raven watched his fear grow. Sweat beaded on his forehead, his red cheeks paling drastically. "I see you know how this goes. You take your punishment, and I leave. You scream for guards, and…well, I stay."

Cowering against the floor, eyes frantically flitting between hers, the baker awaited her sentence.

"Your daughter. You remember what you did to her, right?" Raven lowered his gag.

His brows descended in confusion. "Cresenda and Geraldine?"

"No." She sighed. His third daughter seemed to be an afterthought with everything. "Cindy."

The baker's expression hardened into hatred before Raven's glare sent him whimpering again. She leaned forward, placing her hooded face close to his. A warm mist layered her cheeks and nose as she neared. "You don't care for her. You humiliate her, berate her, and give her less than your other children." Raven raised a gloved hand. "And you beat her."

With a solid *crack*, she landed a punch on his right cheek, exactly where he'd hit Cindy. She relished the impact to her knuckles. Another hard punch, and she felt satisfied that he now knew Cindy's pain.

She raised her hand to strike a third time, for the Red Hood always did more than the target did, to teach a lesson—but the light swish of the back door stilled her fist. Gagging the baker, she rose, silent in her hide boots, and crept to the entrance of the kitchen. The whole family was asleep, so who was this? She'd been careful to cover her tracks, check for guards. She'd even locked the door behind her. Wait… she'd locked it.

A guard wouldn't pick a lock.

Raven dug her Loren knife out of her waistband and waited for the soft footsteps to reach the entryway. The shadow fell into the room, and she leapt. Her blade rested against their throat, her other hand twisting their arm behind their back. Whoever they were, they stood a few inches taller than her, and she had to stretch her arms. She squeezed their arm more for leverage, as Ruben had taught her for taller opponents.

"Well," the figure stated casually. "That's an interesting turn of events."

The slightly joking tone jogged her memory from earlier that morning.

The thief.

Withholding a groan, she pushed the blade further into his skin, not quite drawing blood. Here she could actually threaten him. She knew she shouldn't like that fact. She resisted the urge to push it deeper, remembering his grip on her waist, the way he'd controlled her earlier. "What are you doing here?"

He tilted his head, a lock of hair tickling her nose. She couldn't quite make out his face, but she heard his smile. "Since it seems you picked the lock as well, the same as you."

The baker whimpered, drawing the stranger's gaze. Blood dripped from where Raven had broken skin on his cheek.

"Or not."

She squeezed the handle, debating. She needed him gone, but she didn't want to hurt him. Raven released him, keeping the knife poised. "Leave—if you don't want to be next."

He wouldn't know that wasn't the Red Hood's policy, that she only hurt her targets. But this was the first time someone had broken into the house she was targeting.

Raising a brow, the thief leaned around her and tipped his head to the cowering man. "Hello there, Mr. Baker." Then, he eased around Raven to the hall. "It seems you're busy. So, how about I do what I came here for, and you do your thing?"

"And what is your thing?" She stepped between him and the hall with three sleeping young women.

He wiggled his fingers. Just a thief.

Raven glared.

His smile drooped, and he appraised her outfit. "Given your appearance, I'd say you're the vigilante I've heard about." He leaned forward to whisper, "And given what I felt pressed to my back, you're not the man they think you are." The thief winked, shooting a glance at her breasts— his gaze clouded from the magic, brow furrowing. "If you'll excuse me." He moved for the hall, and Raven blocked him again. He sighed. "I'm getting real tired of this game, Red."

This isn't a game. "Don't steal."

He let out a short laugh and sent a pointed look at the baker. "You're joking, right?"

"No. Leave." Raven adjusted her grip on her knife. He was taking up her time. And she didn't normally talk in front of targets. In and out, that was her rule. No chance for them to attribute anything to her beyond the punishments. She didn't want to tempt the unknown edges of her magic cloak.

"You're one to talk—'Red Hood.'"

"Go, thief," she warned. She might just break a rule with him.

An owl's hoot sounded from outside. Raven looked out the window. There weren't owls in this town. The farthest they reached was Verdan on the boarder.

"The name's Lox, actually." He pointed to the window. "And that's my mate alerting me to the guards. Now how about we stop arguing and get the hell out of here? Shall we?"

Grunting, she circled *Lox* and towered over the baker. "I wasn't done, and we both know it." She punched his nose, leaving a blood trail down his face. "Just so you don't hurt her for this," Raven added, "Cindy didn't contact me. I watched. I saw. I came. And I'll return if you do it again."

When she stepped back, Lox turned to the back door. She grabbed his arm, pausing at the fact her hand couldn't quite grip around it. She blinked, pulling him. "No. This way."

Raven walked down the hall to the window at the far end, leaves and branches obscuring the view of the market. She eased it open and turned to Lox. "We climb this, then down over the wall into the forest."

"Ladies first." He smiled, waving his hand at the tree.

She stared, not sure if he meant to be chivalrous. Not sure she cared.

"Such a gentleman you are, thief." Raven sat on the sill and ducked under the pane, grabbing the trunk to climb.

Even up in the branches, she heard his mumbled, "I told you, Red, it's Lox."

"Locks? Because you pick them?"

He sighed. "No. With an 'x.' *Lox.*"

"Okay, thief."

They scaled the tree, and Raven paused upon a limb, searching for a guard before placing her boot on the wall.

"My scout is over there," Lox said, pointing to the left. His breath rustled the hair under her hood, he was so close, a different kind of warmth flushing her skin.

Tugging her hood lower over her eyes, she held it in place as she jumped on the wall and into the next tree. Her hood's magic only worked if it stayed on her head. Or if someone stayed *outside* its barrier. No one had ever come close to breaching it.

She reassured herself that she'd never been recognized, not by her own townsfolk or nobles, thanks to the enchantment on her cloak. They'd have a sense of familiarity when she wore it, but the second they looked away or blinked, they wouldn't recall her face. Same with her voice.

Then, why did this stranger, this thief, make her worry?

Raven dismissed the thought and descended the tree, hearing Lox above. On the ground, they tiptoed a few trees in, and Lox sent another foreign bird call into the forest. An owl hoot called back. He nodded to himself, gazed around the trees, and stopped on Raven. She had been watching him and sneaking a few glances for the guard.

Lox stepped forward, and she held firm, tilting her chin up.

He doesn't know it's you, she had to remind herself. Though she remembered him from earlier, the magic of her cloak made sure he couldn't. According to him, they hadn't met.

"Do you want to come back to the tavern with me and my mate?"

Normally, she'd do exactly that, though alone—finish with a target and scope out more—from outside. The mystery and fear of the Red Hood kept crime mostly at bay, and she couldn't risk being around people as the Red Hood.

Yet, here she was. It was better to stay away from him. Lox had almost gotten her caught already. And he'd made her take longer. She would've been done with the baker sooner if she hadn't needed to mess with him. "No. I did what I came for."

"Well, I didn't." He shrugged, a slight annoyance in his tone, and looked at the wall like he could scale it again.

Raven moved to catch his gaze. "And don't."

"Or what, Red?" Lox leaned forward, his height making her tilt her head back to hold his stare. "You'll come visit me?"

"Yes."

He smiled, that dimple appearing. "I'll probably be seeing you soon, then."

She took a step, not caring that she'd only been this close to a man if he was a guard or she was punishing him. Close enough that she worried he might see through the enchantment to her real face. He needed to learn she wouldn't tolerate him, that he couldn't smile and get away with everything, make a girl fall for his charms. She didn't fall for charms anymore. "And you won't like it as much as you think you will."

Her heart wouldn't be melted by a smile. She'd been the Red Hood so long that, sometimes, she wondered if it could even be melted at all.

SEATED ON A LOG WITH HIS ARM PROPPED ON HIS KNEE, LOX STIRRED THE FIRE with a stick, sending orange embers flying toward the night sky. He'd foregone the tavern and headed back to camp soon after leaving the baker's house. Their modest setup of campfire and tents rested deep in the forest at the base of the mountain west of the city. He shivered in the cool night wind and knew he would have to buy a long-sleeved tunic tomorrow. "I have to say, men, this town is definitely interesting."

As one of the last kingdoms they hadn't explored, he'd hoped so. For other reasons than a vigilante. But... her hood gave him pause. In the baker's house, he'd passed it off as the darkness, the surprise of finding her beating the man, but outside the house... he'd recognized the cloak for what it was. An enchantment. Concealment magic. Or a muddling spell. No matter how much he'd tried focusing on her face, nothing stuck. Not her eye color, hair, her voice, or a single feature. Did she have freckles?

If it weren't for her form firmly pressed against his back, he wouldn't have known she were even a female. He doubted she ever got that close to anyone, given her surprise at his mention of her gender, let alone body. The enchantment couldn't hide her physical features, only how they were seen. And fuck, he'd been damn tempted to hold her against him like that market girl. She'd been a surprising delight in an entirely different way than this Red Hood woman.

This kingdom was shaping up to be more intriguing than he'd originally imagined.

Lox glanced up at Beast. His comrade's tan skin darkened with ink sprawled in shifting abstract forms, hair turning black and lengthening. Black eyes lightened to a crystal blue, and Beast's cheekbones widened. The curse took hold with the barest of a glance at Beast, turning his friend into a twisted mimic of the man Lox hated. And Lox could never stop the fear that rose with it. The true target of the curse: to show a monster, to strike true fear into those who see Beast. At least over the years, Lox had learned to control his flinch for his friend's sake.

He returned his stare to the fire, pondering. Enchantments were rare finds, indeed, no matter the specific spell. And if that Red Hood hadn't found it but *made* it... maybe he'd finally found something helpful for Beast's curse. A Sandceress was the rarest of all magic, a creator of magic.

Beside him, Scar leaned forward into his view, drawing him out of his thoughts. The bladesman stabbed a scarlet apple with a knife, spinning the handle in his grip to peel it with another blade. Ecanta apples were said to be the sweetest in all of Aloria, and Scar hadn't wasted any time finding the fruit. His grey eyes shifted to Lox, the blade never missing a slither of skin on the apple. "Why's that, boss?"

"You didn't even steal anything," Ramsey chimed in. He leaned back against a tree, resting his boots on a log close to the fire. "Wouldn't call that interesting."

His band had traveled across Aloria many times, and each of his men were searching for something… some unsure what. Lox didn't know, himself. Maybe something to make him feel whole again? Worth something. Every time he found another person to help—his band members before recruiting them, the baker's daughter—he got closer.

Their leader eyed them before staring at the flames. "The woman who caught me sure was."

"Really now?" Rams smiled, the expression tugging the scar running from his temple to the corner of his lips.

"She was already inside."

"Stealing?"

Lox's brows rose toward his comrade. "Beating the baker."

The scarred man leaned forward. "Think she was there for the same reason you were?"

Lox nodded. "Mentioned the girl from the market. She wouldn't let me steal anything. That ass deserved that beating, though."

Thump. A blade protruded from the dirt alongside the fire. Scar had thrown it down, cutting up the apple now. "Deserved worse."

They'd both seen the baker strike his daughter. And if there hadn't been five guards present and they newcomers—always newcomers—the trio would've stepped in. But guards and townsfolk didn't always appreciate their help.

"So… she's not a thief? Then… what?" Rams accepted an apple slice from Scar.

Lox shrugged. "Vigilante. That Red Hood—with the poster in the market."

Considering her target tonight, she wasn't the "assassin" the poster portrayed. And the townsfolk apparently agreed, given its obscured nature. Though if the dead weaponsmith was by her hand, she could still be a murderer, just not a hired one. This criminal didn't make sense. Broke into a house to beat a man but opposed to Lox robbing him? Thievery held above physical assault? Who was this woman, and what were her methods?

He nodded to Rams. "Delve into her reported—and unreported—crimes."

She must be known in Ilasia, especially given she had a wanted poster. Thieves like him were noticed within days of entering a city.

"Is she a threat?" Scar asked, glancing up from his slicing.

Was she? Lox's shoulder was slightly sore from her wrenching it behind his back. And she'd blackened the baker's eye. But she hadn't hurt him, even as she'd held a dagger to his throat.

"No."

Lox rolled his shoulder. Where had she learned to fight like that?

He stared out into the forest, finding a solace that he'd lost for years. None of the other kingdoms had forests quite like this. Not just because of the red trunks known only here, but the thickness of the forests. And he could swear that the moment he entered the tree line, and the deeper he walked, a calmness settled over him. A tingle on his skin.

It reminded him of home.

He shook his head. No. This band was his home.

They were all he needed.

CHAPTER 7

Deep in the forest of Ilasia, surrounded by enchanted vines and branches, Zella tried not to get too close to her tower's empty window frame. It was difficult not to. Stars illuminated the midnight sky, their beauty marred only by the shimmering film left over the bare window by Naja's magic barrier. Zella still treasured the view, limited as it was, of the outside world.

The greatest beauty she'd ever seen was the night sky and its lights. Each one was a mere spot in the deep expanse, but not a single one of them shined alone. Each stood out in the black background. And on rare nights, the full moon illuminated everything below. To shine that bright, it was a wonder to see. She'd read that many people viewed the stars as gods, that fallen stars had created the fae, merfolk, and Vala. Magic fallen to Earth. She wondered what they thought now that magic dwindled?

Some nights, though, clouds coated the sky, or the trees around her tower would blow enough to block her already painfully small view. But tonight, tonight she could see so very much. It made her wonder what else existed outside these magicked walls. What beauty could the whole of Aloria hold.

Tingling, like a sizzle of… something… crept at the base of Zella's neck. She straightened and touched her shoulder.

Naja.

She didn't know how she knew, but whenever she felt that sensation, Naja would enter a mere minute later.

Zella eased away from the window and stepped over her trail of hair across the floor. The motions were routine after the years, the growing length she had to avoid tripping over. With easy and quick steps she tidied her sparse room, though the only mess being the table of books open to varying pages. She checked that the pages were *appropriate* for Naja. There wasn't much beyond a table, a bed on the floor, two book-cases... and the floor-length mirror that Zella tried to forget existed. She knew Naja could see through it if she wanted. Another *precaution.*

Hinges creaked, and a lock turned, though Zella knew no tangible key kept that door enclosed. She faced the doorway and formed a polite smile. She was happy to see Naja, happy, yes. Naja was the only person she had, and she would be grateful for that interaction. Maybe today wouldn't be bad. Maybe.

"Neva," came a gleeful singsong greeting, the name she called Zella. Naja entered, shutting the door with a wave of the hand—never once touching the wood or metal that kept Zella encased like an animal. A smile lifted her slim lips, contrasted with the slender and striking features of the Vala.

Naja brought color to the dank tower. Sandy tan skin flared up Naja's arms, over her chest from her low neckline, even at her ankles as the flowing skirt billowed with each step. Gold snaked in two crisscrossing arcs from her middle fingers over the backs of her hands and wrists. Around and around her arms they curved until they met in a solid ring at her shoulders. The thin and flexible gold moved with her, and Zella could never figure out how.

Black brows curved elegantly over dark eyes that Zella avoided as much as possible. Straight dark hair fell just past her shoulders in smooth waves that Zella wished, *wished,* was the extent of her own hair.

Naja smiled and stopped near the table of books. "Good night, isn't it?"

"Yes, Naja." Zella kept her hands neatly at her sides. Careful not to do anything to set off the Vala. These happy moods were rare. Would it aid her?

"Did you enjoy your dinner?"

An exact copy of whatever Naja ate appeared every morning and night on a plate beside the door. And any scraps or uneaten food disappeared within an hour. Zella took care not to miss one of her three meals by napping. The plate was already empty and clean.

Zella nodded.

The Sandceress held her palm over the thick enchanted book. Purple sparked from her skin, and the leatherbound fell open to the last page Zella had been reading—constellations and spyglasses. Innocent enough. As long as she didn't look back to yesterday's search on Valaran glass that erased enchantments from one's view. And if there were other ways around enchantments.

"I have a question, Naja." Zella hoped her tone sounded mild. That it didn't hold the hope her heart did. "I've noticed there's more guards patrolling."

Naja paused in her inspection of the enchanted book's pages, reading. "That is not a question."

Zella nodded. Sheer persistence held her fingers straight and away from the folds of her dress. "I figure that means the streets are safer right now. And I—" She swallowed as Naja's eyes rose to her own. "I was wondering if we could… go… see the stars?"

Dust puffed from the leatherbound as Naja shut it with a harsh snap. She sashayed around the table corner. A nod to the window behind Zella. "You can see them there."

"But—*but* we could see more of them from the streets." Zella pointed toward the direction she knew the market lay, only from her enchanted book's map. "The market would be the best spot—"

"Neva."

Fear crept in icy tendrils up Zella's spine. Her fingers felt numb and chilled. She forced a calming breath. Naja's tone wasn't angry. Just serious. A warning.

Why a warning? It was a simple request. She didn't have to talk to anyone or see anyone… just the stars. Just a fresh breath of air. That wasn't too much to ask.

Zella sighed, a quiet sound of resignation. "Why am I here?"

Everyone else in the world got to live, why not her?

"You know why, Neva." Naja brushed a sleek strand back from her tawny cheek. "The world is not safe for people like us."

"But you go."

"Ein,"—yes— "but I can protect myself from the likes of which would try to harm me."

Zella took a hesitant step forward. "Then, you could protect me, too—"

"No!" The denial was a roar, culminated by a fierce whip of sandy wind. Grains whirled, scraping Zella's skin—arms, cheeks, neck, hair— while the air both caressed and grated in its force. It swept the room, touching and stirring everything but the Sandceress who commanded it. Naja's sleek hair, fabrics at her waist, and even golden earrings didn't rustle. That eerie calm within the quick and vicious wind froze Zella in place. Not even moving to shield her face. Nothing could shield from Naja's magic.

Damn it, she hadn't wanted this angry Naja. She wanted the caring Naja, the one who brushed her hair, who played dolls with her when she was small, who taught her how to read, and above all, the one who loved her.

The soothing breeze, not the raging storm. But Naja was as unpredictable as the desert sandstorms she commanded.

Zella had hardly seen that side of Naja since she was a child. She always hoped, though.

Deep down, she knew somehow that Naja was not her mother, not any relation, just a captor who sometimes cared. Beyond their vastly differing coloring and complexion, no mother would treat her child this way, not from the books and stories Zella had read. But she still had that sliver of memory of Naja's kindness and craved its return.

Naja stepped forward, her gait like a stalking cat, and the wind dulled to barely a touch of air against Zella's skin. The Sandceress extended a hand to Zella's face but didn't quite touch her. Never a kind touch anymore. "People are cruel, little one. They will strike in the worst way and for barely a reason. Some require none. And you cannot know who those people are until they have already stabbed your heart. You, Neva, are too naive for this world."

"I wouldn't be if not for you keeping—"

"You wouldn't *exist* if not for me," Naja spat. Her hand snapped back to her side. "You know nothing beyond these walls."

"And why is that, Naja?" Ire flamed and sputtered in one second. Zella's eyes widened—she hadn't meant to say that. Not so accusingly.

Why, *why* had she spoken? She opened her mouth to take the words back, but couldn't. Naja's glare had already narrowed. Swallowing hard, Zella backed away, leaning forward and curling into herself. "I-I didn't mean—"

Naja's smooth, sandy fingers curled into fists, and the wind spun again, the whirling lashing as hard as its sand. "Are you not grateful for what I've done for you?" Naja stalked closer, her winds, hot like the desert storms they came from, still not rustling a single aspect of herself. Calm resonated in her tone, but Zella heard the tension, the threat.

Naja's nails dug into Zella's hair, fingers tangled in the thick strands that always grew longer. Pain lacerated through Zella's scalp, and she flinched, shutting her eyes in a far too familiar feeling—the scratches and pinpricks stabbing at her skin and the *burning* magic.

The Sandceress pulled her grip, dragging Zella over and upward until those dark eyes shimmered like her magic mere inches away. Anger and something not quite hatred stared back. Not quite *not*, either.

Naja spread her other palm wide, inches from Zella's face. Purple glinted on the raised and waiting slender fingers.

"I feed you, I give you books to learn, to see the world beyond—I keep you alive."

Alive. Alive did not equal living.

Zella gripped her dress, hating that she still backed away, still cowered after all these years. But she would not bow. She knew that the outside was not always bad. That she should fear the inside and this angry Naja. Not the world.

She swallowed through the pain, trying not to grimace as tears stung behind her eyes from the pulled hairs. "I just want to know the world."

Two fierce tugs, shakes—that would have torn the strands clear out if not for the magic keeping them growing. A cry ripped from Zella's throat against her will. She squeezed her eyes shut—another yank—and peeled them open. Violet eyes glared into her soul.

"Never."

Then, the grip disappeared, and Zella was flung backward without a touch. Three sharp footsteps, a swing of the hinges, and the tower was empty once more except for the cursed girl and her books.

Zella raised shaking fingers to her scalp, wanting to rub away the ache but unable to touch the cursed hair that was always used against her. Tears brimmed, but she would *not* cry.

Her scalp burned with the dark purple bruises she knew would stain her for days. Naja's magic always tainted her skin. Zella didn't move again until her skin only tingled. Careful not to step on her hair, more from revulsion than the usual precaution, she walked to the window and knelt.

Light prickled above, shining amongst the now present clouds. Almost coated, but not yet obscured.

Zella could see how people had believed the Vala as gods and goddesses. But she chose to believe the stars were kinder.

She only wanted to feel the world. Why was that too much? She did not want to settle for this little piece of the world.

This was her true curse.

CHAPTER 8

Raven took the seat opposite her mother at the dark, wooden dining table, nodding to the maid tucking the chair in behind her. Nothing but the scraping of their forks and cups across the tabletop sounded while they ate breakfast across from each other. Silence as usual.

The long table dominated the room, far too long for the royal family —even when they'd been a whole family. At least here, the empty seat was at the head of the table, not between the queen and princess. Here, the loss wasn't as strong as the throne room

Ruben stood beside the head of the table, equal distance from the royal women, ready for whoever needed him. He looked up at the city guard who entered the room. Rue bent his head to listen to the man's report. He caught Raven's gaze just as the doors opened again for several staff members and guards to enter. She sent him a questioning look, and he jerked his head toward the entrance.

"They must've arrived," Vanera commented.

Great.

Staff encircled the queen, informing that the apple courtyard was clear and tents would be arriving soon for the competition. Talk of plans for tent and target placement filled the air.

Raven retrieved her basket from the floor and grabbed the three muffins, small loaf of bread, and cheese from the serving tray—the leftovers.

Ruben came around the table, sword jangling against his armor.

"Found anything on the newcomer?" she asked in a hushed voice. After seeing him last night, she was even more interested than when she'd first asked Ruben. If he'd met the Red Hood, she needed to know more about him.

Rue shook his head. "Not much." He glanced at the city guard exiting the doors. "Just that his band arrived two days ago, and his name is Lox. A Javir is with him, so we should notice them. I don't know why we haven't."

"A Javir?"

Even here, with tanned people roaming the streets, the dark night skin of the rare Javir would flash like stars in the black sky. Especially a town so far northeast. After Valara had burned, the remaining Javir and Vala had spread northwest, forming colonies in Loren for their small numbers near two decades ago. Then again, the broken and starving couldn't provide for the broken and starving. She knew that too well.

"He evaded my scout at the tavern," Rue continued, "and we've asked around, but no one knows anything."

"They're staying at the inn?"

"No."

Raven's brows scrunched. "They don't know anyone in town?"

"Not from what we've gathered."

Which wasn't much. "Then, where?"

Ruben shrugged.

She sighed. If the Royal Guards couldn't get any information, maybe the Red Hood could tonight after her business.

Vanera raised a hand to the staff, pausing their conversation. "What's that, Ravenna?"

She turned to her mother. Shit, she hadn't wanted attention to the thief beyond Ruben. He didn't know Lox stole, and she'd like to not get the man hanged for a simple crime.

"Just looking into a newcomer in town." Bowing to her mother, Ravenna patted her basket. "I shouldn't be too long."

The queen stood, her chair not making a single scrape. She extended a red apple in her slender hand. "You can greet the princes for the competition before doing your… duties." A smile touched her lips. "Treat them nicely, please."

"I always do."

Raven reached the door before her mother's voice called out, "And wear your crown."

THREE WELL-DRESSED ROYALS STOOD AT THE GATES TO THE CASTLE GROUNDS, all with distance between. Each, according to Ruben, had been allowed advisers and guards, but only one it seemed had chosen to. Given the four men surrounding the redheaded Loren prince and the two lapeled men beside him, Grayson Loren had brought both.

Taking a deep breath, Raven headed toward the men. At least they all appeared her age or close. She'd taken time to don her crown but hadn't changed out of her market dress, not when she'd have to visit the market after this. Ruben whispered about their territories while they approached. History and geography were not her strong suits, given she tended to spend more time in the village than the castle, and the other kingdoms only with Ecanta interacted for trade. Names and places of distant kings and kingdoms were of little importance when one's own kingdom starved.

Imports and trade had trended downward since King Elric's death years past. He'd kept strong connections—especially with Ocara—but when the grieving Queen Vanera had been left alone to handle the affairs… the connections with the other kingdoms had starved to almost nothing, same as her people had.

The previously strong bond with Ocara from the kings' friendship had dwindled when Queen Vanera could barely converse with the kingdom where her Eldric had died.

Raven took a breath and assessed the princes. All three young men standing together looked like an absurd group of misfits.

Grayson Loren, from the northwestern region of Loren, with the trademark red hair of his bloodline and elegant attire. The black rose insignia on the lapel of his violet tunic.

Finn Shean, from the southern oceanside kingdom of Ocara, on the western border of Ecanta, looked the part of a seaside prince with his tan skin and sandy blond hair. He didn't have a sneer like Grayson, but Finn eyed the Loren with something mixed between interest and annoyance. The look went up and down, assessing the Loren as much as the Loren assessed her guards.

Raven stared at the Ocara prince warily. She'd never ventured outside of Ecanta, but she couldn't shake the unease that rose every time she considered the ocean kingdom.

Kieran—no last name provided—of the 'southeastern realm and oceanic area.'

"Oceanic area?" Raven interrupted Ruben, puzzled. "As in… the whole damned ocean?"

He shrugged, armor clinking lightly. "My men barely got a name out of him. Ask your mother."

Yes, that would be fruitful.

He lowered his voice. "I heard rumors from the guard of a pirate king manning ocean trade from Loren down to Ocara, but of strife between Ocara accepting him as titled."

"A pirate prince?" She appraised the tall young man. Rings dotted the fingers resting on his crossed arms, muscles evident even from a distance. He was the oldest, probably near twenty, and towered over even Grayson's five advisers. Bracers at his wrists covered ends of black ink slithering from his long ebony sleeves.

Raven watched him, trying to remember the maps of their continent and kingdoms. Nothing remained of the central section of Aloria or the boundaries north of Ecanta. Nothing above the Gilan Pass that ridged diagonally across the Ecanta border. Just cliffs and desert and dead forests. South was just mountains and cliffs, no oceanfront, no towns.

They reached the princes, and Ruben nudged her arm. He departed, leaving her to talk while he met with a guard at the semi-erected weapons tent. She swallowed her pride and greeted them. "Good afternoon. Welcome to our corner of Aloria."

"Definitely a corner," Grayson muttered. The prince was dressed in extravagant violet threads with intricate embroidery and gave her a once-over, sneering at her simple dress.

He wore his crown: a dark gold circlet gemmed with rubies and sapphires. He turned his attention to the high walls around them, examining the courtyard and high windows of the throne room behind her. She ignored his hushed whisper to his men of how it differed from *his* castle. Even without their kingdoms' pasts, he wouldn't be high on her list of prospective kings. But then again, she didn't get to choose—her mother did. Ecanta starved… and she needed to do what was best for all, not for her.

The tall Ocara prince stepped up to Raven. Alone. No guard, no adviser. Turquoise short sleeved tunic ruffling slightly in the breeze, he extended a hand. "Princess Ravenna," he said, clasping her hand and bowing. "I'm Prince Finn Shean. I was wondering when we'd get to meet the favored princess."

An easy smile lifted his sun-kissed face, not easily thrown around like that thief's but genuine and honest. The lack of cockiness surprised her, too. She curtsied.

"It's only been guards since we entered the city," grumbled Grayson.

Raven glanced at Ruben, and she knew from the hint of a grin that he listened. She avoided sending a sharp look at Grayson. Her mother would be proud if she had left the castle to see the visitors. She turned to the last 'prince.'

Like Finn, no guards encircled him, though *he* more than likely didn't require any. Mix-matched eyes met hers, one bright green the other crystal blue. He nodded with a grumbling greeting, "Kieran."

Jet black hair touched his shoulders, clad in the dark leather naval coat, pushed half up his forearms. White sprouted at his chest, a parted tunic under all that leather, and buttons lining the front lapels. Danger oozed from him.

He raised a dark brow at her prolonged stare, and she lifted one back. The crease between his lessened.

Nerves and an undercurrent of sadness hit her when she looked at the Ocara prince, irrational but there, nonetheless. He seemed nice and undeserving of her wariness. He also was the only one conversing—politely. Raven asked, "Did you enjoy your trip?"

Finn raised a hand to ruffle his hair, brows crinkling. "Yes, seeing the forest is—"

"How many guards does one person need?" Grayson Loren observed the five guards spaced around Raven and their group. Three more stood with Ruben paces away.

Ire flared, and she stared Grayson down, heart pounding under her skin. "I apologize if our guards are more than yours, Grayson. We *are* tied as second largest kingdom."

Second to Loren, and tied with Fovet.

Though, standing near the Loren Prince, her market dress felt *less* for once. A beacon of how much they needed this betrothal.

And the Fovet prince had sent a letter declining the betrothal offer entirely.

Grayson's mouth thinned into a hard line. "A kingdom tends to downsize when a royal member is lost." Grayson cocked an auburn brow menacingly, voice cold as a winter breeze, "But you'd know about that, wouldn't you, Ravenna?"

She didn't blink, didn't breathe, didn't move. *Bastard.*

"Why don't I see if we can get started." With a curt smile she gave the smallest curtsy of her life and stalked away, fingers digging into her dress.

When the three princes lied paces behind her, she unclenched her hand and thrust it through her hair. The crown stopped her, almost teetering into her hands. She straightened it, fingers shaking against her scalp. Why'd he have to mention Papa?

Ruben finished conferring with the guards and turned toward her. Though his face was serious with the guard, the moment the man left humor entered Rue's gaze.

"Didn't your mother say to be nice?" Ruben chastised quietly.

"It was a request not an order," she hissed back, moving around him to stand out of Grayson's view.

He bent his head. "No wonder you've never had a boyfriend."

She set him with a pointed stare. He knew why—princesses were betrothed not loved. There was no point in looking if she didn't get to choose.

Why was Grayson even an option? Her mother *knew* the history between the two families. Given, she didn't know the whole story... only Ruben did.

"Will Mother be attending this competition," Raven asked, not bothering to remove her tone.

"The queen regrets to inform you," he started, smiling at her look, "that she has lots of trials and requests and can't make an appearance." She didn't crack a smile, and he cleared his throat. "They'll have the tents and targets prepared by noon. We can show them the grounds and their rooms until then."

"Then let's get moving," she ground out, reluctantly returning to the princes.

Footsteps echoed through the corridors as Raven showed the princes through the castle. The tall tapestries of trees and mountains of the first floor, the statues, the open air courtyard in the center with a white-leaved apple tree and benches for resting. Despite Grayson's demeanor, even he paused to stare at the courtyard. The beauty of the courtyard and relic couldn't be ignored by visitors. Sometimes it still stopped Ravenna in her passings.

It was rumored to be the first apple tree of Ecanta. The bright vermillion trunk matched the shiny skin of the apples hanging from the tall branches. None of the other trees of Ecanta had white leaves, and the wonder of what caused this one alone to differ was a mystery. Some whispered *fae magic*, some worshipped the tree and the rumored faefolk, though no one had seen the fae of Nevrande in at least a decade. Even with fae unseen for years, people of Ecanta still prayed to them like gods.

On the second floor, they neared the throne room where two guards stood post. Ravenna slowed to greet them.

Grayson scoffed. "You'd think with all these guards the grounds would be safer for visitors. Or has nothing changed in the last decade?"

If he didn't shut up, he'd find out.

Kieran and Finn looked from her to Grayson. Raven kept perfectly still, not letting her annoyance show. "If you have any issues with my kingdom, I ask you speak them directly so I can resolve them for you."

"Oh, I have some *issues*." Grayson's copper eyes narrowed into slits. "Starting with your guards following me in town."

Ravenna grasped the handle to the throne room where her mother currently spoke with villagers for inquiries and trials. She recognized the bruised man standing before the silver throne and smiled at the baker's blackened and swollen eye. She tilted her head, a challenge in her tone,

71

"Would you like to see how justice is settled in Ecanta? I'm sure you can bring your qualms to my mother."

Grayson *almost* knocked shoulders with her when he slid through the doorway. And that slightest brush sent her nerves on fire.

Finn, the kind prince, paused at her side. He gestured for her to go first.

The opposite mannered princes threw her for a moment.

"Princess Ravenna?" Finn's light brows scrunched.

"Would you like to enter, Ravenna?" Ruben asked to cover her pause. But he knew she couldn't stand those trials anymore.

She faced forward. "No, thank you, Ruben."

For once, yes, she'd rather be on that throne, with the ghost of her father separating her from her mother, than at Ruben's side. Away from that *menace* of a prince.

But... she hurt too much today.

"I have to visit the village," she stated. "The guards can escort you to your bedchambers. I'll see you at the competition."

The princes filed in and stood along the left wall, the tall windows letting the mid-day sun shine upon them.

Raven turned down the hall. She knew what the trial would hold. For her first year as the Red Hood, she'd watched each interrogation trial, nervousness crawling in her bones. But if she saw one trial, she had to stay for them all day. And she couldn't stomach the other trials.

Queen Vanera would ask the baker why he was targeted. The question she and the guards had pondered for years—how the Red Hood chose targets. But Raven didn't choose based on proximity or status or timing. She chose to punish those who deserved punishing. Not the poor and starving who stole for food, but the killers, the cruel, and the unjust.

The baker would say he didn't know, if he was smart like the others.

Raven had instilled secrecy with her targets. They weren't required to tell their crimes—their punishment was equal enough, they didn't need public embarrassment—but the villagers knew to watch them. They all knew the type of acts she targeted. If her targets didn't tell about her, she wouldn't disclose their wrongdoings. If they behaved, like most did, she wouldn't return.

If they didn't... Well, Barren had found that out.

At her bedchamber, Ruben held the door for her, and she waved away the maid and the other guards.

She sat on the bench at her window.

After a word to his men, Ruben shut the door and sat beside her. He put his arm around her, and she leaned in, resting her head on his shoulder. He whispered, "Ignore that boy. You do your best, Raven. And you are the best princess this kingdom could ask for."

"Thank you, Rue." She sighed. "But I can't say I agree."

Ruben squeezed her lightly. "You are such a caring person."

Raven shut her eyes, remembering the trial that had changed her life two years ago. She'd been lost in a misty cloud of shame and guilt until she'd found a purpose—a way to protect Ecanta.

Orange light streamed through the windows, the sun close to setting, highlighting the haggard man shaking under the pain in his back and the queen's fierce stare.

"You were caught stealing food this morning, what do you plead?" Queen Vanera waited patiently, back as straight as her slender throne.

His voice trembled, "Your Majesty…"

Ravenna had seen this man two other times this week cowering on the floor, both for thievery. The guards saw a repeat thief, not a man who couldn't survive.

A noble had just been accused of not providing enough food for his servants and been let go upon paying a steep fine. What about those starving workers?

What about the thieves too crafty, too fast and healthy to be caught… unlike the beggar kneeling on the floor?

"But—" Ravenna tried to say, heart lodged in her throat.

The queen shot her a stern look. It wasn't her place. Not yet. She was here to learn how to rule. She hated being a princess in this trial where her opinions did not matter. The queen ruled all. Eventually, she would be on that silver throne, decreeing the rulings—and it would be her duty to do it right.

The princess looked upon this man, mercy begging in his eyes, and silently vowed to bring food to the villagers starting that next morning. They would eat, and no one else would be harmed for starving.

But that wasn't enough to right this. Anger twisted with the disgust in her chest.

What about those like the noble? Where money overruled a crime? Not anymore.

She would find those who had evaded their punishments for too long from fear or power or money.

Two guards grabbed the man by his arms and pulled him out of the throne room. Within a minute, the sharp hiss of a whip sounded in the courtyard, rising into the throne room above the cries of the man. Raven cringed, fingers white against the bronze armrest.

This was not justice.

She would be true justice.

CHAPTER 9

Lox measured the weight of the bow in his hands and figured his own arrows would still shoot straight with the worn string. He tried to focus on the weapon and not the raven-haired young woman from the market. He couldn't help his gaze shifting across the courtyard.

When he'd seen the poster about the archery competition in the tavern, he couldn't resist. Seeing her was just a plus.

The guard at her side gave Lox pause. He was the same from the alley. Was he her guard? He didn't remain at her side, but he always returned. He stepped closer than personal guards' protocol warranted. He looked a bit old for her, had to be around twenty-five. They didn't appear to be flirting exactly, just talking. And smiling. That normally meant flirting for Lox, though. Not that it ever managed to come of anything real for him.

Maybe the man was just smitten.

Lox knew he would be.

Not any woman could pickpocket him and then pin him to a wall. Not many people even knew when he'd stolen from anyone. Such was a thief's job. And he was quite a thief.

But she'd been watching him. He smiled.

And her curves under his hands… Damn, he wished he'd had just a few more moments, just another breath that close to her. When she'd grazed his cock while retrieving her coins from his pocket—he'd been about to switch their positions on the wall. He knew she hadn't meant to, but he couldn't resist pulling her close. He'd barely resisted kissing those full lips. Only that dagger, and the intrigue of what woman would carry one, gave him pause.

Lox stored his arrows back in his quiver. He clapped his hand down on Scar's shoulder. "How's it looking?"

The bladesman scouted the growing crowd with his grey gaze, skipping over the neatly dressed young man in a bright blue tunic and the villagers lined opposite the targets to the common villagers. It stuck on the tall dark-haired man with black ink peeking from under his tunic's sleeve. "Not bad. There might be a few people up to our standards."

"Thievery or archery?"

Scar grinned, sheathing a blade in his boot. "Archery. Think they'll let me use something besides arrows? I'll still hit the target."

"Doubtful."

Scar was a master with blades, and Lox wasn't bad himself. But archery—that was his true skill. Being raised in the forests of Nevrande would make even the basic of archers into experts. The fae and magic of those forests were relentless and trickery embodied. Now, he shot for fun and bragging rights. And whatever this reward was. Hopefully, gold. When would this competition even start? They'd been standing there for a while. At least Lox had finally broken down and bought a long-sleeved shirt, so the chilled breeze didn't bother him as much. Though, he kept finding himself rolling it to his elbow, before the cold air would force him lower to it once again.

"Boss."

Lox followed Scar's gaze toward the courtyard entrance. The redheaded prince sauntered in, four men in tow. He stopped near the other prince, his followers apparently not opting into shoot.

"You find anything?" Lox asked.

Scar shook his head. "He just... wanders the city, then visits the tavern. Asks questions about some prince or princess. They're very vague."

Lox rubbed his mouth in frustration. Something that prince had done terrified that young woman. "Keep listening."

Scar nudged his head toward her. "Want me to check into her, too?"

"No. Focus on that prince." Lox watched the raven-haired young woman turn from the guard, smiling, then her lips drooped. She'd spotted the redhead, too. "I want to see what she tells me."

"Seems like a challenge."

Lox laughed, and the young woman's gaze flickered over. He grinned. "I like challenges."

It might be foolish, but there was something about her that drew him in. Tested him.

She raised her chin and headed toward the group of well-dressed men.

Lox couldn't help but smile. She was sharp today, it seemed.

And he was curious if he'd get cut.

BLACK STRANDS FLEW INTO RAVEN'S EYES, A STRONG WIND COOLING HER heated skin. She just wanted that Loren prince gone. She wanted this… darkness to disappear. Raven glanced at Grayson, that red hair too reminiscent of his damned brother. She tried taming her hair but gave up. She'd left her crown again. At least Mother wouldn't see.

Mother couldn't be bothered to leave the castle, leaving Raven to deal with the competition she hadn't known about until yesterday. She'd quickly greeted the princes again and returned to Ruben on the sidelines, watching the crowd of workers and attendees bustle around the courtyard. The event organizer rushed from tent to tent, checking off a list as he moved. Another breeze pushed her hair in front of her eyes and she pushed it back. She sighed and turned to Rue. "When are we starting?"

He observed the weapons station and line of targets. "Should be soon." He gestured to the group of royals paces behind the targets. "Want to stand with them? You *are* the prize."

Raven glared up at him. "No." She crossed her arms. "I'm perfectly fine here."

Rue looked around them at the shaded gap between the weapons and armor. "Yes, here, where practically no one can see you."

She huffed, pointing at the well-dressed men. "They're the show. I'm the *prize* as you say." She glanced up at the stained glass windows above. "Mother hides her way; I have mine."

He watched her for a long moment. "I'll make sure we can start. Are you okay—"

Raven laughed. "We're on castle grounds, Rue, you can take a breath. I'm fine."

Rue nodded and headed toward a group of guards readying the bows and arrows, leaving her alone with her thoughts again.

Why did the prize have to be a dance with her? She didn't want to dance with Grayson. Let alone marry the damned—

"Morning."

Blinking, Raven wiped the annoyance from her face and focused on— oh. The annoyance returned. The thief. Nodding politely, she said, "Hello."

Casual smile already in place, he leaned against a pillar, one hand on the strap of his quiver. Green tipped arrows sticking out over his shoulder, matching his tunic. "Looks like you're having fun."

His doubtful and teasing tone irked her. He was right, but that didn't matter.

She nodded at his long-sleeved tunic. "I see the cold won."

Lox crossed his arms, grinning. "So, you like looking at my arms?"

She rolled her eyes. Though, she did notice they still bulged against the fabric's seams.

"Not even a smile?" Lox leaned forward, trying to catch her eye.

She raised a brow. "What are you doing here?"

"Such a lovely greeting." He grinned, walking a few steps around her and gesturing behind him with his thumb. "You smiled at all the other men you talked to. Why not me?"

Raven followed his gesture to the princes. How long had he been watching her? "Do you think you deserve the same greetings as royalty?"

He grinned.

She faced him fully. "This competition is only for guests. Not criminals."

"It says villagers." The thief nodded to a poster pinned to the pillar. He spread his arms wide. "I'm in the village."

"Technicality."

He shrugged. "We criminals live for those." Lox nodded his head toward Grayson. "Bet I'll give a better show than that idiot."

His tone had darkened, and Raven narrowed her eyes. "Don't think that'd take much."

The thief chuckled, a low, genuine sound. Its warmth startled her. His green eyes wavered over her face. Again, she felt about to fall into their depths.

"Welcome!" The event organizer called from the center of the courtyard, gathering the crowd and contestants' attention. Thank the stars Ruben had hired the man for announcer duties. As princess, it should be her role, but after an emphatic '*no*' from her, Ruben had found a nobleman's head of staff for the task. Ruben stood near the announcer, conversing with another guard.

She faced the men and tried to ignore Lox.

"Thank you all for attending this competition. As you are all probably wondering, we are here to welcome some royal guests to Ilasia." He gestured to the princes and announced their names and territories, reading aloud from a parchment.

"Is there a prize?" Lox asked, stealing her attention.

"No." She smiled. "Technically. Not one you'd be interested in."

"Why is there a competition, then?"

"If you'd listen," she hissed, looking back to Ruben and the announcer.

"Oh, you really don't like me." Lox tilted his head, dark locks falling onto his forehead.

She gritted her teeth. "You're so perceptive."

He laughed, deep and genuine. She found a small smile forming at the sound.

The Head Guard's gaze swept over the crowd while the announcer spoke flickering to Ravenna and back. "Now, what are you competing for? This weekend the queen and princess will host a ball." Cheers and exclamations rose from the crowd. Though, Raven heard some rumbles of discontent, probably those concerned about expenses. The announcer raised a hand and his voice. "There will be a sword fighting competition in two days. The winners are based on skill overall. The prize... a dance with Princess Ravenna."

More cheers erupted, and Raven felt a blush rising to her cheeks, despite being out of their views where she stood.

The announcer started listing contestant names and any existing titles, starting with the princes again.

"Interesting how the only royalty *not* here," Lox said, some harsh tone lining his words, "is the reigning crown."

Raven stifled an eye roll but didn't disagree. "The queen does not like to leave her castle walls." She flickered her gaze from him to the looming building and towers behind them.

"And the prized princess?"

She turned on him, glaring, then caught his curious stare. She glanced down at her market dress. He didn't know... "It might surprise you to know that most women don't like being labeled a *prize*."

He shrugged. "Don't royalty always see themselves as prizes for others to behold?"

"Obviously not Ecanta's." She motioned to the courtyard devoid of Ecanta crowns.

"Or they don't deign their people with enough worthiness to bestow their presence upon them."

She raised her brows, incredulous of his stern opinion. Though, she did share it about *other* kingdoms. "Someone doesn't think highly of royalty."

"I don't like those who ignore their people in favor of lining their own pockets and plates." Lox crossed his arms, momentarily drawing her gaze to the muscles there before his tone captured her attention again. "I've travelled all of Aloria, and the rich always favor themselves over the poor."

"You believe that of a kingdom's royalty whom you haven't even met?" That he knew, anyway. She couldn't resist wanting to know more of this thief's opinion—especially when it oddly aligned with hers to a point. She knew she was the exception not the rule for those in power.

"Royalty is royalty, love." He smiled crookedly at her, and she stiffened at the endearment. "I don't have to meet them to know them. I've seen their people, their kingdom. That's all I need to know."

Their people. The starving people. She couldn't quite argue there. Though, she hated that there was a truth to his words. She tried all she could, but sometimes that was not enough. Not when she didn't have full power to make changes.

"Everyone can participate," the announcer continued, "so this is your chance to sign up," He pointed at the row of unfilled archery stations. As he spoke, more villagers wound their way to the bows.

Lox leaned in, an intensity within his gaze capturing her. "When I win, does it have to be the princess? Or can I dance with you?"

A small laugh escaped her. "Someone's confident."

"That's not a no." Lox grinned. He extended his hand. "I never got to introduce myself before. I'm Lox."

She stared at it, debating.

"Don't want to touch the criminal?" he challenged. Something lied underneath his teasing tone.

She raised a brow, then clasped his hand. "Hello, Lox."

His tan skin was warm, grip encasing hers easily and… comfortably. Not stiff like the princes' had been. Raven let go quickly, but it felt long, and she resisted rubbing her palm on her skirt to erase the feeling of his callused skin.

"No name?" His smile relaxed into something softer, maybe sincere.

A guard stationed outside the tents blew a bugle.

Raven let a small smile rise. "Maybe another time, Lox."

His eyes crinkled, and he pressed his lips together, suppressing a grin. He backed away toward the lineup. "I hope there will be."

The announcer moved to stand between the weapons and supplies tent, Ruben following behind. The crowd hushed. "Archers!" the Head Guard yelled. "Take your positions in front of the targets, weapons down. Viewers—stay at the sides. You have three arrows, three chances."

All three princes grabbed their weapons from the tent and halted at the far starting marks, followed by the villagers—including Flint, Lox, and another stranger. The stranger had short dark brown hair, his deep red tunic accenting the auburn shade, and a clean shaven yet young face. Fierce brows lowered as he readied his grip on the bow. She recalled him from Lox's side in the market. That wasn't a gaze she'd forget.

"Ready."

The archers notched their arrows, staring down range.

"Begin!"

Each man raised their bow, aiming and shooting at varying intervals.

Three of the villagers hit only the outer ring. Flint and Finn managed to touch the inner ring but not quite into the center. Grayson's arrow embedded right on the edge of the center mark, barely qualifying. Raven rolled her eyes before she could stop herself.

The stranger was still aiming, head tilting to the side, as if testing the wind.

Lox hadn't shot yet, still gauging the target, bow at his side.

Raven stared at the empty station next to Flint at the closest end. She glanced at the long windows of the castle, the throne room where she knew mother sat, too far to see.

She headed for the last archery station, appraising the targets and feeling stares follow her movements. Guards, contestants, and onlookers alike. Raven stopped beside Flint. She gestured to his target, pierced by two arrows. "Great shot. Wouldn't expect anything less." Raven opened her palm. "Could I borrow yours?"

His eyes widened, and he relinquished the bow. "Of course."

Armor clanked as familiar footsteps neared along the side of the courtyard. She notched an arrow and tested the pull of the string.

Ruben stopped at her side. "R—"

"You said it was open for everyone." Raven smiled up at him. Chuckles sounded from the contestants and crowd. "Did you not?"

He huffed a sigh, staring her down. Like usual, he lost. Rue waved her on. This wasn't as dangerous a skill to showcase as sword fighting, and he knew it.

She'd win her own damned dance.

Two seconds of aiming, and the arrow flew. The string whipped past her cheek, heat rising on her skin. A moment later, the arrowhead embedded into the center ring. Her following two arrows seated deep, inches away. Close but not quite bullseye.

Better than Grayson, though.

The crowd cheered. She curtsied and returned the bow to Flint. Ruben followed as Raven wound her way back to the side of the courtyard, smiling as the rest of the villagers fired.

A low whistle drew her gaze—Lox.

He winked at her, then let three arrows fly in quick succession, barely looking from her to the target. Each a perfect bullseye. If she weren't annoyed, she'd be thoroughly impressed. Somehow, that infuriated her more.

Lox grinned and bowed in her direction. The crowed clapped

Rue whispered, "Do you want to announce the winner?"

She glared up at him.

"I thought not." He left to speak with the announcer.

Once all the arrows were fired, a guard checked for which contestants qualified while Ruben gathered the crowd's attention. "It appears the winner is clear, but there will be a second attempt with sword fighting." He sent Raven a pointed look. No participating, then.

The thief sauntered over, grinning so wide she wanted to punch him. "Nice shot," he said, as he passed her. He turned, close enough to brush her skirts with his legs as he backed away, holding her gaze. His shoulder grazed hers, a heat touching and lingering as he left. "But I'm getting that dance."

Raven watched him head toward the entrance, the other stranger meeting him.

The announcer named off the continuing competitors, "Grayson Loren, Finn Shean, Flint Oak, Kieran, Lox, and Scar…"

Scar? That was promising for the swordfight.

Two nobles and two merchants had qualified as well. Once the announcer finished all names, he and Ruben nodded to the cheers of the villagers and guests, then Rue headed toward Raven.

He stopped at her side, staring off after Lox. "I don't know how I feel about him possibly winning a dance."

She laughed. "Who do you favor? Kieran?"

Out of Lox or Kieran, the pirate screamed danger.

Rue grumbled, "Probably the Ocara prince."

She watched Finn. "He seems the nicest." Her mind drifted toward the betrothal. The man she'd marry, not just dance with.

Who would she pick?

She forced those thoughts away. "We'll see in two days."

Best not dwell on her wants when the choice was not for her to decide.

. . .

EMERALD GREEN LAYERS OF SILK CASCADED TO THE FLOOR, COVERING Raven's bare feet. Bronze and crimson embroidery raced along the hem, marking trees and apples in a forest of verdant.

The queen had insisted she try on dresses, that they'd talk about the betrothal afterward. She'd much rather sparring practice with Ruben, but her mother had looked so forlorn that Raven had agreed.

Dresses lied on Raven's bed and her window seat, all for her to pick. She couldn't remember the last time she'd worn any of these, and she'd already tried on six. She turned, examining her reflection in the mirror. This was the dress.

She had to admit, though she liked red, green didn't look bad on her. The color made her light brown eyes pop, the red flecks in them standing out. And her hair... the black shined like onyx against the paleness of her skin.

"It's perfect!" Mira clapped, bracelets jingling together, and circled her.

Queen Vanera sat behind her, and Raven had caught sour looks as she'd tried on dress after dress. Now her expression held... something she couldn't decipher.

Did her mother like it? She'd even donned her crown to appear the proper princess for her because gods knew she was a disappointment without it.

Why did she care so much whether she liked how she looked? Whether she looked like a true princess?

Did the why matter?

Did she?

Queen Vanera stared, catching her gaze in the mirror. Raven smiled encouragingly and saw a small tilt to her mother's lips. A smile. Happiness? A nod. She liked it. Raven smiled back.

Definitely the right dress.

"You'll be the hit of the ball—well, of course you will, it's all for your future marriage!" The fortune teller gazed happily at Raven's reflection. "All the princes will be starstruck. I might just have to give you a token to keep their hands off you." She winked at Raven, then at the queen.

Raven looked at the dress folds. After Grayson the day before, she wasn't sure she could handle any attention today. The very thought made her nervous. Partly because she knew she could take a man down

—and that wasn't proper princess behavior. Her mind flitted to Lox, his hands catching her when she'd pretended to fall to pickpocket him. His hand gripping hers. His fingers on her waist. His breath on her face.

She blinked hard. Why had she even—

Mira put her arms around Raven's shoulders, righting her thoughts, and stared into the mirror. "Just imagine, in a few months' time, you could be married. Then, you'll have adorable little ones, and Grandma here will—"

"Stop it!" Vanera jumped to her feet, startling Raven. The queen grabbed the pillow from her chair and threw it at Mira, who stared calmly back, a small glint in her lavender gaze.

Shocked, Raven stepped forward, out of Mira's suddenly tight grasp. "Mother…"

She reached for her, but Vanera huffed and retreated a step. The queen shook her head, some blonde strands falling loose from her braided twist. Her shoulders slumped, and she turned, footsteps clacking quickly down the hall.

Mira patted Raven's arm, then followed the queen, her steps calm and steady.

Raven faced herself in the mirror and couldn't recognize herself for a moment. The day's events had thrown her heart into the past, and her mother's grief had thrown her further. Her amber eyes were wide, skin pale, and something appeared… broken in her expression. Like she was nine and seeing her mother scream and cry when she had to return to the castle alone, a widow—a queen without a king—for the first time of the many to come. King Eldric dead and buried.

Raven grasped the necklace that fell just to her own heart. Even as the Red Hood, she always kept the heart tucked under her tunic. It covered her own scarred one.

Maybe, as the Red Hood, the darkness would fade, and she'd finally have that pure heart.

"Papa," she whispered.

Her legs gave out. Deflated, she sat in the chair her mother had just exited.

And cried.

CHAPTER 10

Bronze metal weighed down Raven's hair, but she lifted her chin to counter the heaviness. This would be the first time she wore her crown into the village since her father's passing. Ten long years of trying to be a good ruler, of finding ways to protect and serve her kingdom. Six years since she'd felt on the right path.

I'll be the person they deserve.

Three Royal Guards accompanied her through the corridor, two in front, one behind, Ruben near her side. Breakfast had been quiet, even with the princes attending.

Noon was close approaching, and she needed to visit her people. To check on Cindy.

Footsteps approached from behind. "Princess Ravenna?"

She turned. Prince Finn stopped a respectful distance away. She nodded to the guard blocking the prince, and he stepped through their boundary. His light blue tunic accented his turquoise eyes, which lent a kindness to his smile. Finn clasped his hands. "May I ask you a question?"

"You may."

Finn's eyebrows dipped. "You wear that dress for them, don't you? Your people, that is."

"I do."

"You love your people."

The weight of her crown felt like it had landed on her shoulders. Her voice came out raspy when she again said, "I do."

"I don't have any simpler clothes, but," Finn said, hands shrugging at his neat shirt and pants, "would it be alright if I accompanied you?" A shy smile lifted his lips.

The princess laughed and nodded. Her guards made room for her companion, and she shared a look with Ruben. Finn was definitely the nicest of the three royals.

A comfortable silence eased over them as they traversed the second floor.

Finn rubbed his thumb over his other hand's fingers, a softness entering his voice. "I expect it will be hard for you to leave Ecanta, then. No matter who your mother chooses."

Ravenna halted, crown almost slipping from her head. She caught it with one hand, straightening it as Ruben's hand met her elbow. She whirled to face Finn. "Leave?"

Her breath barely reached her lungs, feeling trapped somewhere in her throat or her words.

Finn's kind eyes studied her, mouth parting and closing softly. He cleared his throat. "You—you'd be a ruler of two kingdoms, Your Highness, and…" Finn glanced down at his hands and back up. "You can't live in both. You'd have to choose."

Choose?

He was right. Stars above, why hadn't she realized this before? She'd only thought about being queen of Ecanta, not of another kingdom. Of *leaving*.

Choose.

She would always choose her people. But did she have that option? She didn't even get to choose her future husband. Kieran, the pirate prince, was absurdly far and maybe not even on Aloria at all. And if Grayson Loren became her betrothed, she'd never see her home again.

Ruben's gloved fingers gently squeezed her elbow, and she flickered her gaze up to him, then Finn. "Yes. I… I hadn't actually considered that."

Why hadn't Mother talked to her about this? She felt so unprepared.

Not liking their eyes resting so solidly on her, she continued their pace, albeit slower than before.

Finn stared at his clasped hands. "When you become married and queen, you'll move to your betrothed's kingdom. Your mother has ruled Ecanta well for years—which is hard alone. My father has, too. My mother..." Finn caught Raven's gaze and shifted his to the ceiling, a heavy breath escaping him. "Queen Vanera will do well in your absence, too. Your kingdom will do well."

Raven pressed her lips together. Without her. How could she do well without *them*?

"I did want to share my belated condolences," Finn continued softly. "Our fathers were close. I always assumed we would be, too. But I understand his death changed things. I deeply regret it was by the ocean's hands. The ocean can be many things, but sadly, it turned violent that day..." Finn cleared his throat. "I hope you do not fear it because of that incident, though I'd understand. I also love my people, Ravenna," Finn said, warily meeting her eyes. "And I know choosing between people you love is hard, too hard. So... um... well—Ocara rests on the border of Ecanta, you know. And if my kingdom were to become your kingdom, our lands would easily mesh."

Raven stared, the iciness of the startling realization still coursing through her.

Finn smiled nervously. "What I'm trying to say, is that if we become betrothed, I will try to erase that choice for you. We would have not two kingdoms, but one. We could build a castle near Verdan and the border."

"You... you would do that?" Raven watched him for signs of deceit or trickery and found only honesty.

He nodded.

"Why?"

"A choice like that is one we should not have to make."

The earlier smooth cheeriness of the prince's voice had fallen into something more rippling and somber.

She reached for his restless hand—a shuffling sounded behind them, and Raven spun.

Queen Vanera stood at the throne room door, one hand gripping the wood.

"Mother." Raven caught her breath and started toward her, but the queen straightened.

"Apologies," Vanera said, looking at Prince Finn and lastly Ravenna.

"Did you hear what Prince Finn said?" Had it hurt her mother as much to think of her leaving?

Queen Vanera stared at her, eyes distant with a slight shimmer on the navy spheres. "I did."

Hoping for an emotion from the glassy Widow Queen, Ravenna prompted, "That's something to consider."

"Yes. It is."

Ravenna stepped toward her, but her mother disappeared into the throne room, unable to even conjure a smile.

Heart sunken, Raven moved to Ruben's side, and they continued walking. He nudged her shoulder gently, and she smiled, taking comfort in him. She shouldn't be hurt. This… distance was nothing new with her mother. Raven knew their relationship was flawed. They loved each other. But… Well, that was it.

There wasn't supposed to be a 'but.'

Vanera missed her husband. Raven missed her father. They shared a ghost between them, and sometimes love could not overcome all.

A COBBLESTONE PATH LINED BY HIGH WALLS WOUND DOWN FROM THE CASTLE gate. The walls led to another, smaller, gate that opened to the market. Then, rows of houses surrounded outward, walled again. A precaution if Ilasia, being the capital, were invaded. With the castle upon the hill and a miniature forest separating the two walled areas, townsfolk could reach the marketplace and lock the gates. Each region of Ilasia had walls and gates, but those of the market rose highest. As far as Raven knew, it hadn't been needed. But precaution was always safe.

Her guards fanned out, giving her space but keeping a watchful eye, Finn visiting stalls while she talked with the villagers. Raven scanned the crowd, people bustling from booth to booth, merchants calling to other villagers, displaying their goods. She usually searched for targets, but today, she felt she searched for something else. Grayson or Lox? Which did she worry more over? The man from the depths of her past, or the newcomer who threatened the already starving dregs of her kingdom.

Basket and coin purse lighter, Raven meandered to the baker's booth.

When she passed the empty weapons stall, Raven slowed. The other vendors walked a few feet away from it, as if knowing Barren's crime upon his death. She hoped more people learned Barren's lesson.

Cindy stood behind the table, fixing the loaves and pastries. She hesitantly waved and curtsied.

"You're selling these by yourself today?" Raven inspected a loaf. "I thought that was your father's job."

Cindy stiffened. She glanced over her shoulder. "He isn't feeling well today."

"Oh? I hope you don't catch whatever it is." Ravenna withheld a smirk.

"I won't." Cindy twisted her wrinkled apron in her hands, then came around the table. She whispered, "The Red Hood visited."

Raven gasped, as a princess should, making her eyes wide. "Are you sure?"

Cindy nodded and leaned closer. "I saw him."

"What?" Raven halted, fingers pressing into the bread.

Cindy's blue eyes sparkled. "Mom and my sisters were asleep, but I heard—I was worried..." She dipped her head conspiratorially. "There were two of them. The Red Hood had... punished my father, then another man appeared."

Damn, Lox.

"Really," was all Raven could say.

"Mhm." Cindy tugged a piece of her long blonde bangs down over her cheek, over the bruise. "They left together."

Gathering her thoughts, and forming a proper ladylike reaction, Raven asked, "Have you told anyone?"

Cindy shook her head.

Raven withheld a sigh of relief. "Why not?"

She shrugged. "You know how it works."

"I do."

Cindy froze, then reached for Raven's arm but stopped. "Not that I mean *any* disrespect, Your Highness. I know the guards do all they can—"

"I understand, Cindy. Don't worry. And I support your decision." Winking, Raven handed her an apple, who held it softly. Something about Cindy felt… easy and even familiar. Raven didn't feel the strain usually apparent when she tried befriending nobles or other girls her age. Could this actually become a friendship? "On a lighter note, have you heard about the ball my mother is throwing this weekend?"

Cindy's blue eyes widened. "No! Oh, you'll look stunning."

"I bet you will, too"

Cindy's smile drooped, and she tilted her head down. Her delicate fingers picked at a hole in her apron.

Raven ducked to catch her gaze. "Cindy?"

Silent, Cindy pulled more strands over her bruise.

Raven straightened and softly grabbed Cindy's hand. "No. It's okay."

Her throat constricted. Maybe they both needed a friend to ease themselves out of the darkness. But would anyone want to stay after seeing into *her* darkest parts? Hesitant, Raven took a breath and said, "Would you like to come?" Raven licked her dry lips. "It could be more fun with company."

A small smile spreading, Cindy nodded.

Relief rushed through Raven's chest. "Do you have a dress?"

"No."

"We'll figure that out." Raven glanced at the notice board, empty of viewers, and waved goodbye.

She strolled to the board, smiling to herself. Maybe she *could* have someone besides just Ruben.

In the board's center rested a fresh poster for the Red Hood, the reward raised to 600 coppers. Each kill earned another hundred coin, the amount her mother put on a criminal's execution.

A villager approached, pinning a post over the Red Hood's vague sketch of a face. Smile hidden, Raven glanced over and the smile dropped—Flint. The apprentice inspected his note and startled upon seeing her.

"Hello, Flint," she said. "How are your brother and sister?"

"They—they're well, thank you, Your Highness."

"Good."

"About your proposal before…" Redness crept onto his cheeks. Flint cleared his throat, hand on his tunic's collar. "I'd like to accept."

"I'm glad. Visit the castle whenever you want. Win will find you quarters to fit the three of you."

With a nod and thanks, he left. She watched his departure before lifting Flint's post. On the back rested two words written three times in red—once in shaky letters, another with inconsistently sized writing, and lastly in a steady hand—*Thank you.*

Raven smiled, the expression shaky on her lips, and replaced the note. "You're welcome," she whispered.

"This Red Hood," came a venomous voice behind her.

Her teeth clenched, pain spiking up her jaw. She relaxed her mouth and grasped her concealed dagger at her waistband instead. *This is a public place. He can't do anything,* she reminded her racing heart.

Grayson appraised the poster, then lowered his narrowed copper eyes to her. "He kills criminals, right?"

The princess nodded, not trusting her voice.

"If only he'd been around six years ago." He stepped closer, and Raven kept her back straight to prevent retreating. "Then, my brother's death would be avenged."

She swallowed and waited until her words were measured to reply. "The Red Hood only goes after criminals, not accidents."

Grayson's eyes flared, anger like she'd only seen from his brother

The scars under her collarbone prickled, the faded burn of slices pierced her memory and the very real feel of a knife in her grip sent panic through her veins. This knife hadn't always been in *her* hands.

Grayson's boots stepped dangerously close to hers.

She jolted backward. Her back hit the notice board loudly, racking her chest and jostling her crown from atop her head. It hit the dirt next to her feet.

Her fingers clutched the dagger, hoping she wouldn't have to use it on another Loren prince.

Movement in her peripherals stole her attention—but Grayson's voice ripped it back to his face. "I know your guards covered up something. He comes to Ecanta to betroth you, then we're told he's died from a boar attack. I don't think so—I saw his body. The wound was too clean to be a boar's tusk. I'll find out what you're hiding in this damn kingdom, *Princess* Ravenna," he spat her title, nodding to her market dress and crown lying in the dirt. "Then, your kingdom will have something besides starving to worry about."

Her breath stuttered as she tried to calm herself against his accusations. Ruben had been meticulous in staging the body, even King Loren had believed it. She repeated the line Ruben had made her practice for hours after he'd found her drenched in Landon's blood. "His death was a terrible accid—"

Grayson lunged again, nose almost brushing hers, copper eyes wide in rage. "If you say it was an accident, I'll—"

"You'll *what?*" Rage vibrated Ruben's tense voice. His form shadowed Grayson and her, but she couldn't look up to her trusted protector and confidant's face. Couldn't part her gaze from the violent glare perched solely on her.

The prince pulled back, a tendon flaring in his neck, and straightened his tunic. "I was just filing a complaint about the guards."

"Then, file it with me." Ruben moved between them, not bothering with subtlety.

Grayson looked the Head Guard up and down, then slid a slanted look her way behind him. "Guards follow me around the castle and the village. I would like them to stop."

Fire struck in Raven's heart, an anger at her own fear and the disgusting fact that even after she'd served Ecanta for two years as the Red Hood, taken down men twice her size and killed dangerous criminals… she'd been scared by this insolent, arrogant boy.

"They are for your protection and—"

Raven cut Ruben off, voice deadly cold and calm, strained by her own ire, "We don't want another royal fatality of a guest."

It wasn't a threat, but Ruben glanced down at her with an unrecognizable look.

Grayson stared at her for another long second, and her knife-hand shook with her ferocious grip, then he retreated. "Well, I will travel of my own caution."

The prince startled when he turned—the marketplace had almost entirely silenced except for hushed murmurs. Villagers gazed upon their standoff, some crossing their arms when he looked their way. A Javir, standing out in the pale crowd, stood a few paces back, glaring at Grayson. He left into the mass of people.

Grayson Loren clenched his fists and pushed through the crowd toward the castle.

"Raven," Ruben said with a sigh, rotating to inspect her. His hands ran up her arms, warming her from the shock of her roiling emotions. "Are you okay?"

She tore her eyes from Grayson's retreating back, released her white knuckles from her dagger, and bent to retrieve her bronze crown from the dirt. After wiping it with her skirt she held it to her chest, fingers tight enough to draw blood on the points. She shouldn't have worn this today. She was not ready. Raven placed it in her basket, gently covered with the cloth, then looked into her friend's worried eyes. "I want him out of my kingdom. Now."

If Ruben couldn't make it happen, then the Red Hood would.

CHAPTER 11

L ox caught his breath and tried not to stare but couldn't help his gaze from shifting across the market.

He shouldn't approach her. He shouldn't.

Lox usually did things he shouldn't. But this… He shook his head.

The guards were swarming the market, that one who followed her talking to a group feet away. That guard couldn't be hers. The man seemed of higher important than the others, given how they deferred to him, and—despite her obvious wealth—she couldn't be a high noble. No one with enough status to warrant a guard personal behaved like her. Not with how she talked with him, her care with others.

But she had *some* important herself, given she talked with princes at the competition and somehow garnered negative attention from the redheaded prince.

He stared. Both Lox and her stood on the outskirts of the market's growing crowd, separate from everyone. But the dark-haired young woman stood out, while Lox blended in. She scanned the people blankly and looped a red ribbon into her hair, tying it steadily and slowly. For someone who'd just been threatened, she didn't seem shaken. Then again, she seemed the type to hide when she started cracking. Lox knew the feeling.

Daran had barely managed to report to him before Lox ran to the market. And now, he stood there just watching and silently cursing that redhead prince—and Lox used the title with contempt.

"Boss."

Lox didn't look at Scar beside him. He didn't want reason. He knew he shouldn't, he'd already approached her yesterday. But... after seeing her unravel the first time from the redhead royal, he'd wanted to check on her. And her fierceness had utterly surprised him. She'd been like a different person when they'd been between the booths or at the competition. Different with the royal, and different with that guard she talked to now. How many shades did she have?

"Boss," Scar repeated, tapping his shoulder.

Lox looked at the bladesman but ignored the warning in his grey eyes. "What did he do?"

Scar sighed. To his credit, Lox hadn't waited for Daran to say much before taking off. Scar seemed very aware of this fact. "Just that the prince threatened her. Nothing hands-on that he saw."

Lox cracked his knuckles. "Nothing since?"

"No. I've been here since Daran told me and went for you."

She stared at the noticeboard, appearing to read the words posted, but something unfocused touched her gaze.

"She's just been threatened by a prince, so a newcomer approaching her will—"

"Draw more unwanted attention, I know," Lox snapped, harsher than he'd wanted.

She had to be a low noble, he'd bet twenty coppers on it. It was hopeless for him to pursue her. For him to pursue anyone, really. A thief was not a proper fit for wed, and no woman looked at him past a casual night. After this long, it shouldn't hurt—but it did. At least he'd stopped hoping for more.

At the head of the market the gate clattered open, and a well-dressed young man in a naval coat caught Lox's eye. A royal from the competition. But no redhead in sight.

The guard finally stepped away, toward the prince.

Lox stared at the woman. Worry clouded her eyes. Her fingers clasped tightly onto her basket.

He shouldn't. He really, really shouldn't.

"Lox," Scar said, a warning entering his voice.

He flickered his gaze to his bladesman. "What?"

Scar sighed. "You shouldn't—"

"I *know*."

Lox heaved a deep breath and strode forward. He easily weaved through the crowd and stopped close to her side. Her eyes tracked his movement but returned outward without a word or another glance.

Casual smile in place, though his heart beat rapidly, he leaned against the noticeboard. "Afternoon."

She looked to the already falling sun and back into the crowd. "It seems it is."

"Is it a good afternoon?" Lox kept his tone light but peered into her eyes, which held steady forward... then shifted to his. His breath caught, but he forced the calm in his expression.

She examined him, just his face, but he felt like she could see deeper. "Why do you ask?"

Lox grinned, a soft chuckle escaping. Her brows scrunched, and he wondered why. He shrugged and stepped closer. "Friendly conversation, milady."

Her fingers touched the hem of her basket's cloth covering. "Is that all?"

Wind whipped past, ruffling Lox's tunic and her black strands. She brushed them back, and the ribbon fell to her neck. She didn't seem to notice, gaze still trapped on the basket's covering.

"If you want."

She nodded.

The tie floated at her collarbone. He shouldn't.

Lox stepped in front of her, and she blinked up at him, something close to surprise and annoyance in her amber eyes. He thought he heard her breath catch, but it might've been his own. Stars above, her eyes were beautiful—fierce. He grinned and softly said, "But it doesn't have to be."

With a sharp look, she shifted her focus over his shoulder.

He leaned in, and she froze, barely glancing at him, but didn't move back. The lack of movement zeroed in his focus. Just like in the market, when he'd gripped her hand, her waist. She'd hesitated. On some level, she hadn't wanted to move back.

Lox moved his hand toward her neck, and she straightened—along

97

with the guard a few yards away. Lox checked on him, smiled, then looked down at her.

She gazed between his eyes, hers hardening. "What are you doing?"

Only the tip of his finger grazed the pulse at her neck, but he swore it raced. His own beat a staccato. Without breaking her stare, he dangled the ribbon from his fingers. "Your tie doesn't seem to stay in place long."

Her brows descended, and she looked from the tie to him. Sharp as usual.

Oh, he might really get cut.

Unable to resist, Lox whispered, "Going to use your dagger on me, milady?"

She tilted back. "How—" She snapped her mouth shut and looked him up and down, stepping away. She started to speak again, then thought better of it and snatched her ribbon back without touching him. Crumpling it in her fist, she leveled her stare with him.

"Lox—"

He smiled. "So, you do remember my name."

She glared, but something sparked in her eyes.

"I'll leave you to your good afternoon, then, milady." Lox bowed with a flourish and started backing away. He winked. "See you tomorrow."

She didn't agree, but her lips quirked.

He'd gotten a smile. Small, but a smile.

Scar had abandoned the spot across the market, and Lox knew he'd be surfacing at his side shortly. Once out of her sight, Lox turned around a building and crept around the back. Metal jangled against armor, and Lox moved closer to the corner.

Footsteps sidled behind Lox, and he held out a palm. Scar placed a knife in it. Lox raised the blade, watching their reflections around the corner.

The guard spoke, tone exasperated, "I know I told you to be nice but—"

She laughed. "Don't worry, I wasn't." Lox's heart fell a notch, but then interest colored her face. "A name is really all your men have found out about this Lox?"

"Yes," the guard replied with a sigh. "But I'm still looking."

He smiled. She was asking about him.

And it was good to know he still could keep the bands' secrets hidden even with the amount of guards in this kingdom.

"Boss?" Scar whispered, jerking his head backward.

Lox retreated down the alley, returning Scar's blade. Scar sheathed it. "Daran's at the tavern. And the redhead headed that way."

"Then, let's go."

CHAPTER 12

Concealed in the black shadows of the forest, Lox could barely see his most trusted comrade perched in the treetop. Daran usually took spying in the night, his dark coloring and ease at stealth aiding to blend him into the shadows almost seamlessly. He'd lived in the shifting sands of Valara and been a thief for survival long before Lox, giving the skills to remain unnoticed even in the daylight, but especially once the sun had set.

Even with Scar also on scouting, he'd taken root atop houses himself once night fell. Lox whistled low, though Daran surely had already heard him. "What's the word?"

Leaves whispered as Daran lowered himself to another branch. "The villagers don't seem to like him."

A deep, short chuckle left Lox. "Can't imagine why."

"He's spoke to some, asking questions, but they turn away." His comrade smiled. "One even spat on him."

They watched the scoundrel shove the gate open, stomping into the south region. Lox leaned down out of the tree to watch the young man unburdened. A patrolling guard watched as well. The redhead increased his speed past the city guard.

Daran tapped Lox's shoulder and jerked his head to the right, the other side of the gate. Shadows shifted along the wall, and Lox's eyes searched the darkness for the movement again. Another figure, stealthy and silent, treaded atop the stones, dark red cloak around their form. The Red Hood.

She was like a wisp of smoke in the trees. He wondered if that concealment magic on her face also concealed her from view. Or was that just the coloring of the forest's crimson trunks aiding her?

Lox whispered, "It seems he's even caught the resident vigilante's attention."

She disappeared into the crimson trees, and Lox tracked every rustle of the leaves hoping it wasn't merely the wind until he located her lithe shape. The vigilante had wound her way onto a house and crouched, hooded gaze facing the redhead.

Why was she following the prince? Ramsey had investigated her previous targets. Only rumors circulated her targets, no one willing to disclose much information about the mysterious person who punished the people they most wanted punished.

Killed in some cases, like the recent weapons vendor.

Lox wondered what this redhead had done to that young woman from the market. Her face at his appearance had been pure panic. Considering she'd pickpocketed Lox and slammed him into a wall, that prince must've done something deplorable. And Lox would find out *what*.

Lox could kill two birds with one stone and figure out whether the Red Hood had just *happened* upon that enchanted hood. Beast was inside already, and if she was a Sandceress, her reaction to sensing his curse would be obvious.

He checked his daggers, both at his hip and in his boot. "Scar's inside?"

Daran nodded and brought his bow onto his lap.

Good, he might need the bladesman's cool reason.

Lox dropped from the tree and started toward the tavern, ready to knock out the royal redhead's perfect teeth if it came to that.

RAVEN STOOD IN A TREE'S SHADOW, ILLUMINATED ONLY BY THE LIGHTS INSIDE the tavern and the crescent moon above. Rambunctious chatter and voices floated through the cracked windows. Her hood covered her face, but she remained far enough back that no one glancing outside would notice. Standing outside the tavern was part of how she watched, listening to the drunks and easy goers inside for news of potential targets. Tonight, she searched for Grayson Loren.

She'd originally planned to corner Grayson when he entered the tavern, but a guard on duty had ruined those plans. Then, the thief had entered soon after the prince.

Lox's hearty laugh rose over the crowd's mutterings. He'd started at the bar when she'd arrived. Over a half hour, he'd gone from table to table, playing cards, trading small—probably stolen—goods, and now leaned against the fireplace with two men. He charmed and pickpocketed with remarkable ease.

Grayson took drink after drink at the bar, buying some for villagers— the only way they'd talk to him for more than ten seconds. From the red faces that turned away, whatever he said pissed off her villagers. Probably being an arrogant bastard just like his brother.

Nothing she hadn't already learned on either of the men.

But *what* was Grayson saying? He'd already publicly accused her of hiding something about his brother's death... Would he say that to her villagers? She couldn't let one bastard ruin her name and all she—and Ruben—had done to move past that ass of a prince.

Stepping back into the forest, Raven paced, debating her next move. The Red Hood's main rule was don't engage. It maintained the mystery and fear—and aided her secret. The townsfolk and guards believed her a man. The more she talked, the more she gave away. So she'd remained hidden except for punishing her targets. When Lox had broken into the baker's house, he'd made her break her rule

And she had to do it again.

Straightening her shoulders and taking a deep breath, Raven rounded the tavern. She pushed through the door, trying not to make a noticeable entrance. Chin high but hood low, she skirted through the crowd. The magic flowed over her, a light heat cascading over her face, form, anywhere they looked.

Where to sit? Lox wouldn't be in her sights at the bar. The far wall would give a good view of him *and* the door. The Red Hood watched everyone; no one would know her two targets.

She eased around people straight for an empty table near a window. The people she'd pressed past silenced, their gazes reaching her. A few gasps sounded as she moved, each person recognizing her hood. Even if they hadn't seen her, they knew her appearance. Ignoring the hushed awe and fear that her very presence created, Raven reached the table and sat, ensuring her cloak draped over the bench and covered her shape.

The room had almost entirely silenced, and she glanced from villager to villager, each ducking their heads and turning away. Barren's death probably weighed on their minds. But they knew she only killed those deserving. Right?

Within moments of her stillness, the chatter resumed, albeit more hushed. Raven leaned back and settled against the wall. For everyone who looked at her, she held their stare until they turned. The Red Hood didn't cower or embarrass. The Red Hood watched, judged, and punished. And everyone would know that.

Lox stood near the fireplace on the wall to the right of Raven, the bar with Grayson rested along the left. She swept her gaze around, ensuring she didn't land on either too long. Lox laughed and joked with two young men, one she recognized as Scar from the competition—slapping their arms, ruffling their hair—and drank from his glass. Ale or water?

Grayson grabbed another tankard—no doubt ale for him—and approached a man. He stood four people down from her seat, and she angled herself to catch his words over the chatter.

Raven retrieved a long knife from her thigh and sharpened it while she watched, giving her restless hands something to do.

"...young man, Prince Landon Loren," Grayson said, words slightly slurred, to a man with greying hair. "About six years ago, do you remember?"

The man rubbed his brown beard, head tilted in memory. "I was here then," he said, gesturing to the bar they leaned against. "He had a horrible accident. Right cocky fellow, if I remember right—and I do." He didn't notice Grayson's teeth clench behind his raised mug.

"But I heard it wasn't an accident." Grayson leaned closer to the man. "That it was a murder."

"I'd believe it," the man said, taking a swig of his mug. Grayson's eyes lit up, and Raven's heart raced until he continued, "Took different girls home each night from this here place. Probably got done in by one of the ladies—or their men. He pissed off a lot of people."

Before Grayson could control his anger enough for another probing question, the man leaned to his friend. "Can't say I would've wanted him as a king anyhow. Not with our Princess Ravenna."

The prince rolled his eyes and turned, eyes searching for another ear to bend.

Raven dipped her head so the person nearest her table concealed her. She didn't want to be that ear.

Her chest tightened. It was what she feared—Grayson prying into his brother's death, trying to find evidence—*believers*—that she'd covered it up. She needed to silence him before the night ended and he spoke to too many people. Even without proof, rumors could spread.

"...surprised they let another son come here, after that one before," a woman said at the bar. "And the other's disappearance. He's the last son left."

The man she talked to gestured to Grayson down the way. "I heard he was insistent. That group of his talks a lot at the inn."

Raven swallowed hard. *Insistent.* Yes, it appeared he was.

A few tables over came another whisper, "I heard there was someone new with him."

She glanced from under her lowered hood, and the man's gaze flickered from his friend to her figure.

"Where did you hear this?" the other asked, tone doubtful.

"Reggie. He's the most recent—living anyway."

Raven thrust her knife against the sharpener hard, emitting a sharp *zing*. Apparently, the baker hadn't been *too* embarrassed about the Red Hood's visit not to gossip. The two men silenced, glancing her way. She glared, sharpening her blade until they turned around.

Nothing she could do about it now. She just hoped they didn't hear it was Lox.

A shadow fell over Raven, and she changed her grip on the handle. Then, she recognized the face. Lox gave a one fingered salute. Her view of the door and Grayson blocked, Raven moved so she could jump up quickly.

"Finally decide to come inside?" Lox grinned. He jerked a thumb over his shoulder at Grayson. "So, what's that guy done?"

Raven stared, surprised that he'd noticed her interest in Grayson. Lox couldn't have known, he'd entered before her.

Lox laid a hand on the table and leaned in close. "Stolen? Beaten a girl?" His tone darkened, eyes shifting down and brows crunching in a level of disgust that made her wonder if he'd seen her panic over Grayson yesterday. Then, his gaze returned to her. "Or do his interests lie in children?"

She tilted her head sharply. He'd been checking up on her, the Red Hood her.

His comrade appeared, bumping Lox's shoulder—the young man with grey eyes. He quirked a smile and inclined his head in greeting, two slender fingers tapping the brim of his red cap.

Lox straightened to whisper something to him.

The men a table over looked their way again.

"Go away," she ordered. Their proximity would support the towns-folk's new theory of their partnership.

"Whoa there, Red. Just trying to warn you." Lox quirked that dimpled smile.

"About?"

He jerked his head back at the door. "Heard some guards are on their way. And you're known for some hefty crimes."

Damn. She checked out the window.

"Why don't you leave?" Raven asked. "They'll want you, too."

Grinning, he shook his head, black locks flying. "They have nothing on me. But you..." He lifted a crumpled wanted poster with the raised reward.

The door swung open with the soft click of moving armor. The guard tailing Grayson must've seen her enter or came to investigate. Everyone shifted, some calling out greetings, while others shrunk into their chair or coats.

Most surprising, however, were the townsfolk who walked to her table. Some started up conversations with each other while standing around Lox and his friend, others sat directly across from her.

More people joined behind Lox, standing between them and the bar.

Raven glanced around, shocked at the villagers' actions. While those at her table seemed nervous, they made small talk with each other and avoided her gaze.

105

A few minutes passed—what felt like agony for Raven—then the door opened and shut again.

Someone mumbled, "Clear," and the group around her dispersed. They gave her small glances, some even left a copper or two in front of her, and returned to their original positions in the tavern.

They'd all blocked her from the guards.

Coin glinted up at her, her eyes unable to look away from the offered repayment.

Speechless, she placed the coppers in her pocket, knowing it would be rude not to. She would return them, slip them back into their pockets on her next trip into town. Even if she had to search them out, she would.

Only Lox remained, even his friend gone. He sat on the edge of the bench's corner. "The level of respect the townsfolk have for a criminal is astounding."

Raven took a breath, utterly moved by their trust and faith. "I do what the guards won't." She cleared her throat. "Your scouts seem very attentive."

"That's the point of calling them 'scouts.'" Lox patted the table and stood. "Don't rough him up too bad. My men won't have anything left to play with."

Her eyes widened in outrage. How dare he taunt her, make fun of her duty.

He checked on Grayson, then looked at her. "See ya next time, Red."

She stared at her knife, at a loss for what to do. She'd expected to watch the thief, learn his motives. But she'd learned that he protected other criminals. Was it because she was female? He'd noticed; his flirtations the same with her as Ravenna *and* the Red Hood.

The door opened again, and Raven checked the occupant. Grayson's red hair barely rose over the crowd, exiting the tavern. She straightened, about to follow, but the bartender reached her table. He set a shaking drink down, a coaster underneath. He tapped the coaster and napkin once, then departed.

She eyed the coaster and unordered drink.

Reaching into her black satchel, Raven retrieved her bag of elixirs and nonchalantly slipped a few drops into the drink. The liquid remained clear—any tampering, whether with poisons or other elixirs—would have turned a shade depending on the addition.

She took a sip and slid the napkin into her lap with her other hand. The bottom had a handwritten note:

I request your services. Meet me in the market.

This was wrong.

The Red Hood didn't take requests, only hints. The townsfolk knew how to give them, like Flint's siblings had, posting a note under her wanted poster in red ink. She'd scope out the targets and discern whether she'd help.

Who would send a request this way? Only a newcomer wouldn't know—

Lox. Raven eyed him across the tavern. Why wouldn't he just ask her?

Or was it one of the royals? *Grayson?*

Knife gripped tight, Raven left the tavern. Regardless of the sender, she'd check the market—after finding Grayson. Even if it wasn't him, she needed to know who'd dared leaving her a note.

Using the cover of the trees and the staggering trail of footprints leading from the tavern, Raven quickly caught up with Grayson at the gate out of the southern region. She scaled the wall and crouched on top, hidden in shadows, and watched him pass through the creaky metal opening.

The guard in the southern region looked the prince's way, then continued his path. She checked the closest guard in the region leading to the marketplace. This gate connected the southern region to the merchant housing, then the marketplace in the center of that walled region. From the wall, Raven located the guard to the left. She smiled, then crept like Grayson's shadow along the stone enclosure after him.

The prince stumbled, caught himself on a house, then righted himself.

Raven jumped from her perch, holding her dagger and sword close to her side for silence, and leapt from the shadows. Covering his mouth, she swept his feet from under him and pinned him to the ground, the dagger that'd killed his brother at his neck. "Hello, Grayson. I believe you know who I am."

After momentary shock and struggling to focus through the drunken stupor, Grayson's copper eyes narrowed on her hooded face. Warm mist crossed her face, magic engaging. He squirmed underneath her, but she dug a knee into his stomach, causing a grunt. Satisfied he'd stop moving, she moved to pin his thighs to the dirt with her knees. Her elbows bore into his arms, bringing her closer than she'd like to his body and ale-scented breath.

He mumbled something against her gloved palm, but she grinned and whispered, "You've done enough talking tonight."

Grayson's brow lowered.

"I saw what you did to our princess this morning," she said, brushing the blade's edge against his neck softly. Dirt darkened his copper hair, a ruddy color—like her crown this morning. "And the rumors you've been spreading…" she clicked her tongue thrice, "they aren't appreciated."

The prince shook his head, trying to free his mouth, and she squeezed his face hard, earning a grunt of pain from him.

She hissed, "I wasn't done. But since you want to be *impatient.*"

Raven slammed her fist into his jaw. His cheek crashed into the dirt, and he coughed out a moan. She grasped his mouth again. Her anger was slipping away from her, she knew it but couldn't quite lessen her death grip.

This time *she* was the one with the blade, with the reason to silence someone.

Even six years later, staring into those almost exact same copper eyes, she could still feel the metal pressing against her collarbone, digging under the bone and toward her heart. The first slash had burned like white fire. The second had ended quickly because Landon had only carved half of the slow, agonizing slash before she'd knocked the blade away.

Landon, that *arrogant bastard,* had scared her for too long. Ever since he'd waltzed into her castle thinking he'd own the palace, that he'd be the king and she his obeying wife—taunted and shamed and tormented her. Ever since he'd attacked her for speaking and tried to *own* her kingdom. Ever since the life and hatred had drained out of Landon Loren's eyes and onto her conscience. For six years, she'd lived with this guilt, this secret—let it shadow her heart.

And now, this boy came here accusing her of exactly what she'd done, the act Ruben had covered so she could grow past the accident into the princess and ruler she tried to be. A nineteen-year-old boy protecting the shattered innocence of a thirteen-year-old girl who'd lost everything.

The skin around Grayson's mouth faded to white under her unrelenting grasp.

She hadn't meant to kill his brother. Just to escape his hatred, to live.

But sometimes living cost another their life.

Her dagger shook under her tense hold. *No.* She was better than this. She had taught herself to be better.

This blade wouldn't kill its second Loren prince and neither would this princess.

Raven removed the knife from Grayson's throat. Gritting her teeth, she punched him, then whispered into his ear, "Leave this village—leave Ecanta. Or we'll meet again. And your royalty won't save you from me and neither will this kingdom's."

The prince lay stunned from her hit, eyes rolling upward in pain. She stood and retreated into the alley's shadows before he could gather his wits. No doubt he was sober now.

Raven climbed the wall and walked through the forest. Her heart had moved its pounding from her chest up to her throat and temples. She'd almost let her rage and fear get away from her. But she'd stopped.

The market neared, and Raven slowed. That request... was it worth checking? She needed to look for real requests under her wanted poster, but she couldn't chance a trap. Anyway... with the betrothal only four days away the townsfolk should become accustomed to the Red Hood's absence. What would they think of their vigilante stopping the punishments? That she'd abandoned them? Or would they understand she'd served them for two years?

Raven sighed.

Five minutes. She'd watch for five minutes.

She climbed a tree to view the market.

Neither Lox nor anyone else appeared. Maybe they wouldn't approach if she didn't? Too bad. She'd already risked entering the tavern. She wouldn't enter the market.

Raven walked the alleys between marketplace booths, checking the market for movement. After she passed most the stalls, she crossed to the gate to take the long way back to the castle. Steps away, it creaked.

"It's not safe after the killing," a man said. Light metal clanked—armor. A guard.

Shit. The booths' shadows were too far away. She clambered for the wall to escape their notice. In her hurry, her boot slipped on the stone.

"What was that?" another man asked, voice deepening in wary. Two guards, then. Probably the same who'd entered the tavern.

Raven had never feared her own guards before. At least Ruben wasn't here. She'd hate to hurt him.

Raven slowly rose atop the wall until they'd have to strain their eyes to find her in the darkness. She moved her satchel forward and removed the wrap of vials, uncapping the red and stoppering it with her fingertip.

The gate opened with caution, and both men entered, their swords drawn. She needed to knock them out quickly. Though she was the Red Hood, they were still her dutiful guards.

Taking a deep breath to still her nerves and the ache in her heart, Raven jumped from the wall and kicked the second guard's back. He stumbled, and Raven grasped his neck, pulling his head back to drip the elixir into his mouth. He tried to spit, but it took effect, and his body slouched. After lowering him gently, she tracked the other guard who'd walked toward the market's center.

Pale light glinted off his blade as he turned, searching. Hard packed dirt softened her steps, her dark cloak blending her into the night. While he hunted through the center pathway, she ducked under a booth's railing and watched from behind the table. Raven changed her grip on her knife, pommel sticking out the bottom of her palm. She tossed a stone off near the booths on the left. The guard followed the sound, and she leapt, vamping off the table and slamming the handle of her knife against his head.

He dropped, armor clanking in the empty marketplace.

The gate creaked—almost empty.

A figure stepped from the shadows, an indigo cloak covering her form. Her restrained and proper walk stilled Raven's breath. Her mother, Queen Vanera, walked toward her.

Damn it.

Her mother hardly ever visited the market, let alone at night. Raven's heart stuttered—the note. Raven narrowed her shadowed eyes at the queen. An ambush.

Her heart pounded as she surveyed the grounds, ears straining for armor and footsteps. Raven took deep breaths and kept her stance loose. To be revealed as the Red Hood right now, in front of her mother, would be the worst thing imaginable for Raven.

Her mother continued into the marketplace, eyes shifting between the vigilante and the stalls. "I believe you already took care of my guards. And no, this isn't a trap."

The queen moved closer, for once her crown absent, and gazed at Raven. Did that mean she wasn't acting as a queen right now?

Raven straightened and eyed her mother. "Aren't you scared?"

Vanera laughed, a small, cold sound. "No. I have more than just guards on my side. And I have many more than you can harm." She came forward, chin raised high like always but a stilted movement to her steps. "I request your services."

Raven stopped breathing. Who did her mother want punished?

Did her annoyance with Mira finally reach its end?

Raven eyed the unconscious guards. Their faces… they weren't strangers, but unfamiliar. New recruits. Why had her mother chosen them for… Damn. She'd wanted the Red Hood to knock out the guards. No witnesses.

Stay calm. You can always turn this down.

"I don't take requests," Raven said, eliciting a sharp look from her mother.

"You will take this one. Or I'll hire another assassin—and you'll be the first target."

Or not. Raven swallowed, heartbeat pounding in her ears. *Assassin*—she'd never killed for hire. "For what, Your Majesty?"

Vanera tilted her head, as if finding something familiar in Ravenna's words. Maybe her words. Thank the gods, the hood also masked her voice. Her mother's footsteps echoed in the still market until she stopped directly in front of Raven.

"Kill Princess Ravenna."

LOX WATCHED THE REDHEAD STUMBLE PAST HOUSES, MORE LIKELY FROM THE blood running down his nose than the drink in his stomach. The Red

Hood had some good swings, but Lox hadn't gotten his shot yet. Ramsey and Daran trailed the bastard with him, and when their leader nodded, they grabbed him from the darkness and dragged him farther into the trees. They held on to his arms and covered his mouth.

Lox approached and clocked him solidly in the face, effectively breaking the nose Red had injured. "I know you've already gotten a talk tonight, but I want to ensure it sticks."

He turned to the forest and called, "Scar?"

His comrade stepped out of the shadows, two short but deadly knives in each hand. Beast followed, but his black eyes froze on the copper of the prince. Beast tensed, and those cursed depths seemed to fall back in time, the young man turning to a boy for a fraction of a second. Then, a deep hatred flashed, leading way for the iron wall the man always kept between Beast and anyone who hit his curse too hard.

Beast stepped to the side, obscuring his face in the thickest of the night's shadows.

Lox left the prince hanging from his men's hands and stopped close to his cursed comrade. "What's wrong?"

Beast clenched his fists at his sides. Unclenched. Clenched. All the while, his eyes didn't waver from the prince's pain-dazed pair. Reluctant, he gritted out, "He's Loren."

Bloody hell. Lox raked a look over the prince. Despite his anger for the jerk he asked Beast quietly, "Want me to let him go?"

Hardly a breath passed. "No." Darkness covered Beast's grotesque face. "Royals are exempt from nothing. Least of all that family."

"Have any questions for him?"

Pain crossed over those black eyes, a searing hurt that ran too deep to suppress. One shake of his head.

Lox nodded, gently touched Beast's shoulder. "Go back to camp."

No sounds followed Beast's departure, a skill learned from the deadly need to remain unseen and unheard.

Lox turned his glare on the royal bastard. "I don't know what you did, and I don't need to. To threaten a woman no matter your rank— especially *because of* your rank—is something we don't tolerate. And if you earned the wrath of the Red Hood, well…"

Scar grinned a black smile.

"I-I'm a prince, you can't—"

A blade rested upon the redhead's throat before he could register the bladesman had moved. Dark smile widening, Scar leaned in and let his piercing grey eyes shine. "I love teaching royalty their lessons."

CHAPTER 13

"Princess Ravenna?" Raven repeated, her voice low and empty. *What?*

Vanera turned toward the castle, breaking the fierce eye contact she'd been holding.

Raven's heartbeat felt like it'd stopped, but she could feel it in her throat, her head—a pulsing, rushing wave threatening to overtake her thoughts. Thoughts that were stuck on her own name being thrown at her.

When Vanera looked back, the queen's eyes had a glassy sheen, and her voice caught. "Yes."

Cold and hollow, Raven stared at her mother, shock stealing her breath. It took all her strength as both a princess and the Red Hood not to break. *You are not Princess Ravenna right now. You are the Red Hood—act like it.*

She needed to speak. But what could she say? No—what would the Red Hood say, Raven thought frantically. 'No' made her dead either way; her mother would hire another to kill the Red Hood *and* the princess. Play the part—and *evade* the assassination.

"I'm not an assassin," Raven said, trying to make her voice as cold as she felt.

"You are if I pay you. You killed our weaponsmith. You're a murderer, which is only one step from assassin: the hiring."

Raven took a breath. "Is that why you chose me?"

She'd killed a child molester, and now her mother wanted her to kill herself?

Vanera shrugged, her indigo cloak shifting delicately. "You are the criminal righting wrongs in this village."

"And the princess wronged you?" The venom came easily now.

The queen's sad eyes hardened on Raven's hood. Her mother stopped, straightening her shoulders and setting the Red Hood with a cool stare, disgust pulling her mouth down. "Does the murderer finally have a conscience? A line he won't cross?"

Raven watched her mother. "If I'm going to kill a princess, I need a good reason."

"My order is the reason!" The queen shot toward Raven, rage and panic in her wide eyes. Raven almost reached out to comfort her mother, but the *order* froze her hand to her side.

Vanera forced a deep breath and straightened, staring at her tightly grasped hands. "But if you must know *something*... she is a horrible reminder of what I cannot have and what I have lost."

Papa.

"Are you not alone enough in that throne room?" Raven tried to hold her tongue but couldn't squelch the anger that'd been brewing since Grayson. She'd dealt with one threat to her crown, her life, and here she stood, being given—*ordered*—another. One she didn't know how to stop.

Vanera glared with the full wrath of a Widow Queen, reminding Raven she was walking on melting ice. Raven spit out, "Your Majesty."

The Red Hood stared, waiting for an answer.

Vanera sighed, her silver eyes shooting to the stars. "I have not been happy for a... very long time," she paused, "and I'm trying to find a way back."

Pain crested the marble-like composure of the Widow Queen, grief too strong to be contained. Ten years this mourning had built, breaking surface occasionally. Raven had felt it too, but she'd only lost a father—too young to have experienced much time with him—while Vanera had lost the love of her life. The companion she'd vowed to spend her life and reign with, to serve by his side. Now, she served beside an empty throne and crown. With a daughter who didn't even wear hers.

"Don't be mistaken, I do love her," Vanera continued, looking up at Raven. "But not enough."

Raven's nails dug into her palms, that blow piercing her heart. *You're the Red Hood.* "How soon do you want her killed?"

"This upcoming weekend." Her mother paced, smoothing her dress. "She must appear at the ball with the princes to secure a trade deal for Ecanta. So, the next day."

Is that it? The princes? The betrothal? Had seeing Raven with them really caused Vanera that much pain? No... this pain had been growing for a decade. Raven just hadn't known she was part of it.

Four days, how could she get out of this in only four days? Ruben... Raven cleared her throat softly. "How will I get close enough to the princess? She's constantly surrounded by guards."

"So, you've been watching her?" Vanera's tone rose into intrigue.

"I watch everyone. Answer the question."

The queen's mouth twitched, a vein pulsing on her temple. "I'll change her guards, send the newer recruits. You can easily overcome them like tonight and kidnap her."

Her guards were her one thought of safety. Raven stared at the felled men laying in the market. At how easily the queen had orchestrated this to her will.

"Once you have her..."

Raven waited for her mother to say it, to simply say that she wanted her daughter dead. An order from a queen was one thing, a statement from a mother was another.

Vanera didn't continue, just waved her hand and adjusted her cloak again.

Nodding, Raven digested this reaction. Maybe her mother regretted this decision. No—Queen Vanera never made an order she wasn't sure of. She had thought long and hard over this. And decided to kill her daughter.

Raven's stomach riled, and she breathed in the chilled night air before asking, "Is there a certain way you want her disposed of?"

"Make it look like a robbery." Vanera grinned, a sly tone entering her voice. "I heard there's a new thief in town."

Lox. Raven's eyes widened. How did Vanera… Oh no. Raven had ordered Ruben to investigate into him. She'd heard them talking at breakfast. This was *her* fault. Lox couldn't take the fall for this. Not when he'd just helped her. All he'd done was steal and barter. He shouldn't be framed for treason.

"And the body?" Raven asked, forcing herself to stay in this role, this dutiful assassin.

"Burn it. I don't want any reminders. Just ensure there is utter proof that she is dead." The queen paused. "She wears a necklace of a golden heart. Leave it for me."

Under her cloak and tunic, the necklace rested against her skin, with her even as this other deadly self. Raven nodded. Though the queen waved her dismissal, she couldn't move.

"Are you sure?" The question sounded wrong from the Red Hood, her tone too childish if she was honest, so she added in a harsher tone, "Once I leave, this cannot be undone."

She hoped that deep down her mother didn't want to do this. That she'd rescind her order. *Please, Mother.*

Vanera glared, stepping closer than Raven liked, her nearness making her queasy. "You think I make this decision lightly? That I call a criminal to kill my daughter on a whim?" The venom in her voice scared Raven. She'd only heard it toward Mira. "Yes, I'm sure."

Raven dipped her head to the queen and departed, trying to keep her steps even. She faded into the alley behind the stalls and climbed the wall to the east side. Each step shook her resolve, the raw emotions roiling her stomach. The moment her boots hit the dirt in the tree line just touching the marketplace, she ran.

Deep into the forest, past her hidden passage, deeper than usual.

The darkness encased her, cold night air stealing her rushed breaths.

Her legs shook, her whole body quaking. Raven ran until she couldn't see the castle or the lights from the village. Then, she stopped, tilting her head back to gasp in fresh air, not caring when her hood fell back. It had been suffocating her. The whole night had suffocated her.

Raven leaned over, reached up to grasp her hair, and vomited into the grass.

She wiped her mouth and sat at the base of a tree trunk, resting her head against the rough bark.

Gods, what could she do? If she wasn't dead in four days like her mother wanted, she'd have a real assassin on her tail. She couldn't evade that.

Could she tell Ruben? He'd saved her years ago with Landon, so he could protect her now. Her stomach turned at the faces of those new recruits on the ground. She'd orchestrated that easily. Did he even know? Ruben might be Head of the Guard, but her mother was Queen. He had to follow her orders.

Even if she did tell him and he helped her, any of Vanera's orders of the guards would supersede Ruben's. It'd be him against every single guard in Ecanta. If he didn't listen to Vanera, she could demote him or fire him completely to appoint someone who *would* listen. If she didn't hang him for treason.

And any new Head Guard would provide a simple opening for another assassin. Then, what would happen? Ruben would be unemployed, disgraced from a fall in stature like that, and... on the run with the princess? One guard couldn't stop a real assassin.

No, even Ruben couldn't protect her.

Raven sighed, her back rubbing the rough bark. She wouldn't incriminate Ruben. She was on her own.

She could try to overthrow her mother, tell the guards about the treasonous order. Then, Vanera could be thrown from the throne and she'd be the queen. But Raven needed Vanera's guidance as a queen. Vanera could claim Raven lied; she had no proof. Other than being the Red Hood. Could she be tried for her actions as the Red Hood? She *had* killed five people as the Red Hood... but she was the princess, and they'd been criminals. Right? What if they discovered she'd killed Landon? That felt more damning than her acts as the Red Hood.

What if the villagers didn't want a person like her as their ruler? Would they pick her mother over her? Damn it. If so, her mother would have grounds to kill her then.

What was left? Return to the castle and die?

The thought sickened her. Her mother wanted her dead. Her mother had *hired* someone to kill her.

It sounded inconceivable, even in her own thoughts, but she'd been hired to assassinate herself. Raven supposed she should consider herself lucky. If she hadn't become the Red Hood, she wouldn't have known about her mother's plan. This weekend she would've danced with princes, possibly gotten betrothed, thinking she had a future—and died.

It would be morning soon. The night sky had already started to lighten. As much as she dreaded it, she had to return. She had to become ignorant Princess Ravenna again. And face her mother with a straight, innocent face.

She'd always known they had a different relationship, but never that her mother had this much pain inside. What hurt her so much? What had Raven done to cause this? Why was her death the only solution to her mother's undecipherable problem?

Raven buried her head in her hands, gloved fingers burrowing into her black hair. She should've just worn her damned crown.

Did it matter now?

What's done was done. She could never forgive her mother for this choice.

She just had to find a way out of it.

Donning her hood, shaky hands moved to the heart necklace tucked safely beneath her tunic. She removed it, barely able to see the glass in the night.

She'd lost her father. And now, she'd lost her mother.

YET ANOTHER GUARD PASSED THROUGH THE FOREST, MERE STEPS AWAY FROM the hidden trapdoor Raven needed to enter her castle. Damned princes. Damned Queen. Damned whole castle.

The increased patrol made that passage unreachable. She had another entrance behind the castle near Ruben's secret sparing courtyard. Crossing half the castle grounds was risky, and it entered on the opposite wing from her rooms. But Raven had no choice.

She crossed through the courtyard where she'd spent countless hours and days with Ruben. For six years, she'd been training with him. Learned how to fight and defend herself from swords, knives, arrows, even in hand-to-hand combat. In the dim light from the stars and the moon, the courtyard looked so empty and small. Maybe that was just how she felt inside.

There might not be another time she sparred with Ruben here. She hadn't known the last time would be the last. How many other things would be her last in this kingdom, with her people, that she had not known?

Raven shook her head to clear the thoughts. She removed her cloak and stuffed it into the satchel. Creeping through the vine-covered entrance, she placed the bag in the corner of the courtyard pillars, covering it with stones and leaves. The draping vines obscured it completely. Tomorrow, she'd have to retrieve it. Sighing, she stared at her trousers and tunic. Usually, she changed into these clothes in the room with the trapdoor to her tunnel. She was out of options right now.

The trousers could arise questions, but at this moment, she didn't care. Her mother wanted her dead.

Dead.

Tears brimmed again, and she took a deep breath. Not now. She had to get to her room first.

After what felt like an hour or creeping, ducking behind trees and pillars and scaling walls, Ravenna entered the castle at the commoner door near the kitchen and throne room. She forced herself not to look at the throne room. To sneak down the side corridors, the south wing that the workers used, and not think about her mother. The royal bedchambers rested in the east wing, and she knew when she was one turn away because scents of patchouli and cinnamon lingered in the air. Mira always burned incense when she visited.

Raven stopped and breathed in the smells. Light shone through the small crack in the door. The fortune teller also turned away all guards who tried to post outside and rarely liked being shut in. Silence came from inside, only the smells and candlelight to show it was occupied.

She stepped closer, not sure what made her move. Through the narrow opening, Ravenna spied a magenta cloth on a table, a crystal ball that was a touch cloudy, a touch clear. Small containers littered the table-top, their contents a mystery.

Who would want to know their future? Whether it was a certainty or vagueness, the prospect sounded terrifying.

Raven turned away and crept numbly to her room.

Without her title and her people—her kingdom—she didn't think she had a future anymore.

CHAPTER 14

Three knocks rang Ravenna out of the sleepless stupor she'd been in for hours. She blinked hard and rolled out of bed, already dressed in her sparring tunic and pants. She'd turned away the dressing maids earlier, unable to fake a smile for long with them. One deep breath later, she approached her bedchamber door. "You know, you can just come in."

She opened the door to Ruben's towering form and grin. "You know it's not proper." His grin dropped as his gaze stopped on the bags under her eyes and her drooped shoulders.

Ravenna faked a sigh and swept an arm wide to let him enter. "You're married."

"And you're not—yet." He arched a brow. Ruben dipped his head before stepping inside and shutting the door. Mouth open, he paused and appraised her attire. "Why are you wearing that? We haven't sparred since the princes arrived."

Right… They'd stopped because of the increased amount of people in the castle; they didn't want anyone discovering her skills. Or the reason why. She'd been so focused on keeping routine this morning, staying the princess who thought herself betrothed in four days, not dead, that she'd adorned the clothes purely through habit. For a moment, she wondered how her mother would handle the betrothal. Call it off? Or would that raise too much suspicion? Ravenna shook her head. There was too damned much on her mind today for that worry. She had to plan. "I'll change."

Armor clanked softly as he turned for the door. Ravenna stopped him. "Just stand in the corner. I'll go in the other room."

The princess's bedchamber had two separate rooms. One for sleeping and dressing, the other for entertaining guests or relaxing. An open doorway connected the two, and Ravenna slipped into the other, grabbing a light magenta gown, the shade an almost-white pastel. Darker magenta lined the sleeves, bodice, and underskirts that showed in the sides of the dress in slits. Might as well look like a princess if she wouldn't be one for much longer.

Ruben raised a chastising gloved finger. "If anyone—"

"Oh, shut it."

He groaned and gave in, backing until the wall separated them. Grinning, she started stripping off her outfit in favor of the gown.

"I have good news," he called.

That was unlikely.

"Grayson Loren left Ilasia early this morning." Ruben's easy voice brought her back to the night before—before her mother's order. To Grayson. In everything with the queen, she'd entirely forgotten his threat to her reputation. The threat to her life had taken precedence. Ruben continued, "Seems the village let him know he wasn't wanted. And my guards. And a few others based on the injuries my men reported seeing as he left."

The look of fear in those copper eyes last night gave her an odd sense of relief. Always in her nightmares, they held hatred.

She almost couldn't believe he'd been a worry, after her mother's order.

"...broken nose—maybe even shattered—and a nasty cut down his side," Ruben was saying.

Ravenna spun and almost rushed into the other room, had she not been in only a slip of a skirt. She hadn't done that to Grayson. A black eye, and *maybe* a bloody nose. But not broken and not a single slice on his body. She would *never* leave a scar on someone intentionally.

Had the villagers really found him afterwards? Her heart swelled with appreciation for whoever had stood up for her.

"That's a relief," she said, making herself step back and continue dressing.

"Queen Vanera mentioned an idea about changing your guard."

Ravenna froze. Closed her eyes tight. It had already started.

"Maybe introducing newer recruits for training. We're talking it over today."

She forced a *mhm* and breathed deeply.

Ravenna checked her reflection in the mirror. The neckline scooped right under her collarbone, a touch too low for her liking. She much preferred tunics; they covered her chest more and her scars. But as a princess, dresses were a requirement. She swept the heart necklace aside and inspected the fabric's edge and skin around it. Pale skin, but not white skin, showed. It was covered. Her heart still pounded, but she let out a relieved breath. Necklace back in place over the center of her chest, her worries faded. Its heart always covered hers.

"What will you do with all your free time now that you're not following that jerk," Ravenna asked Ruben, as she sauntered up.

He turned with a grin. His eyes examined her necklace, and he straightened the pendant as well. "Escort a beautiful princess through her kingdom."

The beautiful princess rolled her eyes. Coin purse heavy with the extra coppers the villagers had given the Red Hood last night, Raven told Ruben of her plans to visit into the village.

"Do you want all of us to accompany you?" he asked, speaking of her Royal Guard. They always insisted on accompanying her in the busy marketplace. But houses had tight spaces between them, the lack of movement hindering her protection.

Ruben's closeness normally felt like a warm blanket, but today felt like that blanket was fraying to pieces slowly. She shook her head, feeling her traitorous headband slipping looser. "That's not necessary. Just you and me will be fine."

They headed downstairs to the dining room. The walk was blessedly normal, and she could almost believe that last night hadn't happened. Until she saw her mother perched in her chair. Prim and composed as ever, the queen barely turned her head to greet her daughter. Ravenna's breath caught and heart raced in her throat as she rounded the empty chair at the head and took her seat across from her mother. Forcing herself to smile politely, she said good morning and waited for the servants to fill her cup before taking a rough swallow.

Breakfast commenced like usual, the two remaining princes chattering, though Kieran didn't contribute much. Ruben ran reports with Vanera, making plans for his guards to accommodate any changes. No further words between mother and daughter. Ravenna realized that a hollowness settled between them. It was always prominent, but until the Widow Queen's order, Raven hadn't known the depth of the pain. She just finally felt her own side of these emotions her mother kept buried so deep.

Mira sauntered in, her bangles adding a lightness to the room, and sat beside Ravenna. The fortune teller shot her and the queen a dazzling smile, which Vanera ignored, and bumped Ravenna's shoulder playfully. "Gonna be a fun day, hm?"

Confused, Ravenna took another bite of food. She didn't think she'd be having fun for a while.

"In case you haven't heard through the gossip yet," Queen Vanera said, a small smile tilting, "Grayson Loren has bowed out of the betrothal search. He will not be at the competition this afternoon."

Finn and Kieran exchanged looks, and Mira clapped her hands. But Ravenna's focus latched on one word—competition. She'd forgotten all about that damned thing. She didn't have time for this; she had to find a way around her own damned death. Her stomach churned. Standing, she bowed her head to her mother. "Then, I better get a head start on my duties." She quickly gathered her plateful of food and loaded down her basket before stepping back from the table.

Ruben's concerned gaze roamed her face, but it was the queen's focused eyes that worried her. Ravenna forced herself to meet them like usual. With a nod, Vanera dismissed Ruben. "Take extra care, given how Grayson Loren was treated last night by our own villagers."

Ravenna paused and studied her mother. Her tone. Her dipped brows. Why did that concern seem real? How could it even be possible for her mother to love her but also want her dead?

Raven continued out of the dining room, Ruben at her side, ready to plot a way to fulfill her mother's order and flee her beloved kingdom.

How was it possible for Ravenna to want her mother happy, even if that meant her own death?

. . .

SHE FELT EMPTY. WITH EVERY VILLAGER AND BOOTH SHE VISITED, SHE FELT more and more empty. Fake smiles and politeness and pretending she didn't know her mother hated her. It was wearing her down. How was she supposed to do this?

Light glinted in her peripheral, bringing her mind into focus. She shielded her eyes and searched for the source. Mira sat behind a short table not far from the baker's booth, one she must've had a guard bring for her. It was covered in the magenta cloth she'd seen last night in the Rova's bedchamber. Atop lied the crystal ball, which had reflected sunlight into her eyes. Around it rested metal tins filed with what looked like small bones, a deck of cards, and some irregular shaped colored stones. An empty chair sat on the other side of the table. Beckoning someone to occupy its cushion.

Raven neared Mira, eyeing the tabletop. She smiled in greeting.

"Are you okay, my dear?" Mira asked, straightening. Dark eyes roamed the princess's face. The irises swirled, as if they could see her secrets. She raised a tan hand, bangles clinking lightly. "Don't lie. It's the betrothal, isn't it? Sit, sit."

With a sigh, Raven sat and didn't disagree, though her worries were far beyond the betrothal. Yesterday, yes, she worried. Now... she could laugh at the idea.

"Listen." Mira reached over the table, taking Raven's hands in hers. She laid them palm up, tracing her fingers over the lines. "The mean one is gone, though his kingdom *was* the largest." Mira made a face, then continued, "The Ocara boy seems nice, and the ocean is beautiful. You'd love it. Both him and that dark one, oh—he is *handsome*. You'd be in for a treat for sure with him. Love be damned."

Laughter rang from the Rova, joy that Raven just couldn't share. This wasn't what she needed. She didn't care about the betrothal, or even if she ever found love.

Mira seemed to take note. Her voice softened while her gaze locked on Raven. She felt seen. "That's not what troubles you?"

Could Mira see her secrets? *Please, no.* This might've been a bad idea.

Raven took a deep breath. "Do you find that our paths are set in stone? Or can we move them?"

125

Mira drifted a fingertip over the crystal ball, images and light twisting in its wake. "Sometimes fate is fate." She tapped the center of the crystal. It smoothed over into magenta waves. "But we can make a mark on how that fate is shaped. Fate can be a moment, and then we have to decide what happens after that moment has passed. Fate can be an encounter, or an action, but not an end. I have guided many to their own fates and after. You, dear one, will have a grand fate."

Hope swelled in Raven's heart, wetness in her eyes. She glanced at the crystal. "Yes?"

The Rova swept aside the crystal, tin, and deck. "I don't need the cards or bones to see your future. Whatever your outcome, my dear, it will be for the best."

Maybe there was hope... She could tell Ruben about the order. She glanced over to him at the next booth. Gods knew he'd help her. He'd do anything for her. Even finding out she was the Red Hood, he'd help. They could make a plan. They could stand up to the queen. Or he could run with her—

"Ruben!" a voice called from behind.

Raven turned to see Ruben's wife smiling and carrying their newborn girl. Esme's short black curls were pinned back with a simple barrette. One gold earring rested atop her ear's curve. She waved the baby's hand at Ruben, and he headed toward them.

Esme's gaze drifted to her and Mira, and her brows descended. Her expression chilled before she composed herself. She never did like Mira, but Raven couldn't discern why.

The breath left Raven. She couldn't. Stars above, she couldn't. He couldn't take Esme and the baby on the road. Not from a queen's wrath. And she would *not* risk them if Ruben faced off against Vanera.

She was truly in this alone.

THE PRINCESS AND HER HEAD GUARD REENTERED THE CASTLE TO RETURN HER basket and prepare for the competition. Raven walked close to her friend, the sound of his armor clanking with his steps her favorite sound. His steps sounded different than the others' with his larger sword and familiarity of the ten years he'd spent with her. She could pick him out of a group blindfolded.

Raven checked the corridor every few seconds, hoping her mother wouldn't approach. Breakfast had been hard enough, and she didn't want to keep pretending if she didn't have to. She peeked into the throne room where her mother almost always sat, the room King Eldric's ghost haunted the most—probably a comfort to the Widow Queen.

The silver throne sat empty for once, and Raven paused at the double doors. Ruben stepped up behind her as she hesitantly pushed them open.

Opalescent floors greeted her, her slow steps echoing, three empty thrones upon their pedestal instead of that one constant. No king, no queen, and soon no princess.

"Remember the first day we came back?" she asked, knowing he'd understand.

The eerie silence was too alike to that day for him not to know. The kingdom grieving, her mother locked in her bedchamber, and even guards somber. She'd been alone in the silence. None had known how to talk to her, to handle the grief of a child when they struggled with their own. She'd been the only one who'd dared to enter the throne room.

The throne and its room seemed as empty—as deep of a hole in the royal family—today as it did then.

Her Head Guard stepped forward. "I do."

Ruben had just been assigned to her guard a few weeks prior to King Eldric's passing, a green recruit eager to protect the little princess. Only, she was plagued more by inner demons than outer. That day, their friendship blossomed. The day a sixteen-year-old boy had cared for the happiness of a nine-year-old girl. Not a guard and a princess. Just a boy and a girl. Friendship.

Today, she stared at the king's throne, feeling just as empty and alone. Slowly, she walked up to it, Ruben a few steps behind. At its base, Raven raised a shaking hand, fingers pausing above the gold, then stroked the armrest. A tear formed and ran down her cheek. "I miss him."

King Eldric had loved her—Father had loved her.

Ruben came up behind her and laid a hand on her shoulder. "I know. We all do."

She turned to him, checked that the doors were closed, then hugged him. Ruben removed his hand from his sword and wrapped both his hands around her, holding her like she clutched him. Like she was nine all over again, her mother distant—gone—and Raven left staring at an empty throne, not fully understanding what had happened, just that it had. That she was alone.

Soon, Vanera would rotate her guards, and by the ball, Ruben wouldn't be with her on the morning walks or in her guard at all. Ten years later, he was more like a big brother than a guard. She would miss Ruben. Miss his constant comfort and friendship.

Maybe even more than her mother.

CHAPTER 15

"She's got to be a noble," Scar said to Lox, as he tested one of the swords laid out for the competition. Scar twirled it expertly in his right hand. Then, his left. Not a single difference in skill between the two. The bladesman eyed the raven-haired young woman's gown. "Trying to get with a noble now, boss?"

The magenta dress she wore today was not overdone, but elegant compared to the brown dress he usually saw her in. And he'd thought she was beautiful before. Lox kept getting lost in how it hugged her form, the waist and hip he'd touched. The higher curves he hadn't dared try.

Yet.

Lox crossed his arms and shot Scar a side look. "Not trying to get with anyone."

The bladesman nodded and inspected the blade's edge with a thumb. He frowned at the metal. "Never seen you this interested is all."

"They've never been interested in me long."

"And you think she would be?"

The woman greeted the blonde from the market, an easy happiness cresting on both their faces.

"I don't know. There's just..." Lox watched her smile, "something there."

Scar executed a practice swing on a wooden dummy. "Can't win if you don't try."

"I've tried plenty." Loxley picked up a sword. "You can't exactly talk, can you, Scar?"

He'd never seen cheeks redden that fast. Grinning, Lox continued to tease, "Pretty sure, in four years, I've never seen you with anyone."

Of course, Loxley knew the reason, but he wouldn't embarrass his friend by saying he knew about the man Scar loved. And whom who loved Scar back. The hopeless pair hadn't realized the reciprocated feelings. Yet. And Lox wouldn't be the one to key them in. A man had to have *some* sort of pride in love, and he refused to take theirs. One of them would make a move—eventually.

Lox had none anymore, but... after enough pieces were broken from his heart, that was bound to happen. He watched the woman walk with a blonde in a light blue dress that appeared more patches than original fabric. A grey apron covered the skirt, and she held a large basket of bread—the baker's daughter. Whose abusive father brought Lox to meet the Red Hood after he'd seen no retribution for the baker's actions. Lox stared at the pair. It was very interesting that she'd befriended this young woman as well.

The two moved through the crowd of onlookers. The blonde was obviously selling the loaves, but the raven-haired woman would occasionally hand her coppers—and the blonde would give a villager bread still. Was she paying for those who couldn't?

What kind of noble paid for the poor to eat?

The two separated, and Lox started across the courtyard to the raven-haired beauty. Feet away, she caught his approach, and her amber eyes narrowed. He grinned.

"You're as excited as ever," he said, stopping beside her.

She smiled a *polite* smile, but her eyes moved around the guards, the princes. Looking for an escape from him.

Lox's heart plummeted. He swallowed and gestured toward the men. "I see there're less competitors than there should be."

Her brows shifted, and a real lift touched her red lips. He couldn't help but stare at them until she spoke, "Prince Grayson decided his interests lied elsewhere."

Something not-quite contempt underlaid her cordial tone. Showing respect to the prince, he assumed, but she feared the redhead.

"Finally saw he wasn't welcome, huh?" Lox rubbed his right brow with a sore knuckle as he quelled his anger for the royal. "The message had to sink in eventually."

Smirking, she glanced at him before turning toward the guard now looking her way, and Lox knew she was about to leave—then she froze. Her amber gaze snapped to him so fast he forgot what he'd said to make her look at him. What could he say to keep her gaze?

Those eyes latched to the hand at his brow, dropped to the other. The redness of his knuckles, bruises between the notches of his fingers.

Confusion filled her face, full lips parted—and her brows descended in thought. "You…" She stopped.

Her sheer surprise of him standing up for her hit him.

She stepped forward, and Lox's breath halted. "Why—"

A curse and *thud* sounded behind him, and she looked over his shoulder. Her eyes widened, rolled upward, then flickered to him for a fraction of a second. "Excuse me."

For once, he didn't have the impression she actually wanted to leave him.

She stalked across the field, a determination to her steps that amused him. Her destination was the two royals who looked almost about to fight. One, with smooth lapels and pristine boots, rubbed his jaw while the other—who looked more pirate than prince—clenched his fists. That guard separated them, the dark-haired prince trying to get around him to the smaller one.

Lox watched her stop beside the guard, holding her ground with the angry royal. He glared down with a fierceness that made Lox take a step closer—as well as the guard—but her chin remained high. Fire burned in her amber gaze, and the man stepped down. Violence had never entered his body, only his eyes, and Lox sensed he wouldn't have struck her.

He thought he heard something about "save it for the fight."

The dark prince stalked away, and the guard nudged the other royal in the opposite direction. Then, he looked to the woman, who shook her head. Lox smiled. She didn't appreciate their royal egos getting riled.

The thief returned to his comrade sparring at the wooden dummy. Yet, his gaze continued to flit to her.

He hadn't asked around about her like he should, solely because he didn't want to know *how* far out of his league she was. A foolish decision, but Lox was always foolish when it came to his heart.

This raven-haired beauty might catch his eye, but he knew his hopes lied with the Red Hood. *That* woman made his pulse race and his hopes build. Sometimes Red seemed at ease with him and *talked* to him—and he'd gathered she'd never spoken to anyone beyond punishing them, never before appeared in the tavern—but she hid behind that hood. Too well. Lox could see her expressions, but they turned vague in his memory—the magic of the cloak, he supposed.

A noble wouldn't spare him, a thief, a passing glance... but another criminal? A vigilante who hunted the wicked, could she care for a thief like him?

Or was he just another to be thrown away?

RAVENNA STOOD ALONE NEAR THE WEAPONS TENT WITH RUBEN. SHE'D successfully avoided Lox all day, but his damned persistence had found her unaccompanied earlier. She sighed. It would only strengthen her mother's claims later. If Finn hadn't dared to call Kieran 'Pirate Prince' to his face, she didn't know how she would've left the thief. How Finn thought he could take Kieran, she didn't know.

Raven glanced across the field at Lox.

Lox had wounded Grayson. His knuckles hadn't been darkened in the tavern. He'd mentioned threatening Grayson to the Red Hood, but she hadn't believed it. Why would a thief do that? For *her*?

That fact had shocked her into forgetting to stay away from him. And his gaze when she'd noticed, he'd held no qualms with her knowing. No regrets, no secrets. The steadiness of his eyes... she didn't know what to make of it.

Lox was an open book, honest.

So different than her mother, their relationship, her hushed friendship with Ruben—*every damned thing*. Even... even Raven wasn't honest, not about who she was. Not her past and not her present.

Lox had made her smile, almost laugh. And despite the whole damned day and night before, it felt real.

Today, nothing felt real. Not her mother's gaze or words. Because she had to pretend she didn't have only four days left. It took too much effort, especially with Ruben. Her breath caught.

A bugle sounded, and Raven forced a smile as attention rose to her and Ruben. She managed to hold it until Ruben left to announce the match's start, until the villager's faces left their princess, until all focus latched onto Kieran and Finn's fight.

The sword fighting was a tournament of sorts, Ruben had said. Matched up based on their scores with the archery. With Grayson gone, another villager had been placed to fill in. Raven tried to watch, she really did. But this all felt pointless.

Who cared about a competition or a dance or a ball or a betrothal when none of it would matter in a few days? How could *she* care when she had to escape her own assassination?

Apparently, Kieran won—big shock there—and now Flint and another villager were sparring.

After a minute of attempting to pay attention, Ravenna turned her gaze to Ruben. To mourn a loss she would cause. A loss she would *become* for her best friend. Seeing Esme and their baby in the market had crushed any resistance she had left. Ruben couldn't leave the kingdom, and he wouldn't be able to win standing up to Vanera.

She really had to leave.

A shout drew her gaze to the sparring field. Flint stood with the sword brandished at the felled villager. Weaponsmith apprentice, indeed. He looked happier with Barren gone. Stars above, what would people like Flint do without the Red Hood?

Even without her mother's order, she would've had to stop. But this felt… wrong. She hated the Red Hood being used for this… this… unfair deed. Whatever she'd done to hurt her mother, she was sure she didn't deserve death.

Raven sighed. How could she escape this? The queen's road was too popular for a runaway, so she'd need to use the forests. Even if she managed to leave Ecanta… where to then? She'd never been outside the three cities of her kingdom, barely left Ilasia and the marketplace in years. Hadn't visited Verdan, the farthest city resting on Ecanta's boarder, in six years—for good reason.

This felt hopeless. In four days, she'd be blindly walking through the

133

forests, hoping she didn't get lost and find the missing fae of Nevrande. Or be found by them. Maybe she could find some maps in the library at the castle...

Cheers and boos erupted from the crowd around the fight, apparently mixed reactions on the outcome. Raven made herself focus, finding Lox holding Flint at the point of his blade, the boy lying on his back. Lean muscle lined the thief's sword arm, sleeves rolled to expose tanned skin. A large grin spread on Lox's face, and he withdrew the sword, helping Flint up from the ground. He shook Flint's hand and receded to the fray of the courtyard.

His sportsmanship surprised her. Not quite matching the idea she held of him.

Ruben hushed the onlookers. "Due to the double injuries of the fight before, the next will be Kieran and Scar. Winner faces Lox in the final match!"

Rambunctious yells sounded all around as the pirate prince and the mysterious young man named Scar entered the sparring arena.

Both their fights earlier must've been quite the show. At the very least, she could get some entertainment out of this sham of an event.

Raven neared the arena, watching Scar twirl a sword in his left hand, then his right. Damn. She might actually see him beating Kieran, even though Kieran stood a good half a foot taller and definitely had bulkier arms than the lithe bladesman.

Cindy approached her side, smiling before turning to watch the fight. Raven wondered given her father's violent history, if this would be difficult for her. Then, she recalled, she'd faced a violent attack and still relished a good fight. Given, it'd been a one off attack, not what she suspected was weekly, if not daily.

Gods, part of her wished she could visit the baker again.

The two fighters squared off, Kieran having removed his naval coat. He rolled the sleeves of his indigo tunic halfway up his forearm, letting his leather bracers protect his wrists. The silver rings glinted in the afternoon light, apparently not leaving his fingers. Raven wondered if they hurt his hands on the sword grip.

She noticed Cindy's cheeks redden beside her. Raven guessed there were multiple reasons to watch this fight.

"Begin!"

Scar darted forward like a snake, swiping his sword at Kieran's knees. Kieran darted back and to the right, readying to strike, but Scar tossed his sword to his left hand and struck from the other direction. Kieran barely raised his arm to block the hit.

Shit. Whoever he'd fought before this had no chance.

The pirate pushed Scar's sword back and stepped forward to strike while Scar recouped his balance. The bladesman caught himself instantly and ducked, twisting left to avoid the blow.

Scar's blade swept across the front of Kieran's chest. Fabric ripped, and Kieran hissed. Blood dripped off the end of the sword. Crimson colored Kieran's shirt black. He sidestepped, using his free hand to wipe the blood. Under the sliced shirt, ink stained his skin, stretching from below the cut to the flash of his collarbone.

Appreciative hoots came from Raven's left, and she almost laughed.

Beside her, Cindy gasped. Raven noticed her gaze was locked on the pirate's face.

Someone wanted to dance with the pirate prince. Part of her could see why. Toned muscles glinted from every flash of his tunic's folds, from his forearms, his chest, even his thick neck. Something deep within her recognized an attraction to those parts of him, even if she didn't care for the man himself.

Kieran didn't glance away from his opponent. Mix-matched blue and green eyes bored into metal grey. He was fast, but no match to the double handed skill of the bladesman. Kieran lunged, and Scar easily parried, twisting the sword out of Kieran's hand. Before Scar could swing his next strike, Kieran's boot kicked out, knocking into his chest.

Gasps sounded as Scar hit the earth, and Kieran rushed to kneel behind him and grab the man in a headlock. Thick forearms wrapped around Scar's neck, more ink peeking from the edge of his rolled sleeve.

Raven checked on the guards, who watched with vapid interest. Swords weren't required for this competition apparently.

Sweat beaded down Scar's face. He got a foot under himself and pushed against the ground. The force made Kieran tilt and have to adjust his knees to keep balanced and not remove his grip.

Raven found Lox in the crowd. He didn't seem fazed by this development, not worried about his comrade, but he was focused on the prince.

One of Scar's hands clasped the arm at his neck, pulling fiercely. The other elbowed Kieran in the stomach. In the second that Kieran winced, Scar head butted him and ducked to escape.

She blinked, and a sword was leveled with Kieran's neck. Scar panted, but the blade held steady, even his cap still rested on his head.

After a stunned moment, the crowd grew loud, once again with mixed reactions. Ruben came into the arena again, calling the onlookers to quiet. Once Scar lowered the sword, allowing Kieran to stand, Ruben gestured for Lox to enter.

"Our final match!" Ruben called. He left the arena and stopped next to Raven. He mumbled, "What's the point after that?"

She sighed. She'd have to dance with this complete stranger, who now felt more dangerous than Kieran. At least Lox wouldn't garner more attention with her.

Lox spun the sword in his hand, smiling. "You almost got the shit beat out of you, my friend. Sure you're ready for this?"

"Any time."

The two circled each other, soft footsteps in the dirt as they measured their opponent.

"Come on, you know the princess isn't your type," Lox taunted.

Scar raised a brow.

"You don't like royals."

He laughed, the expression lighting his face. "True. But I do like to fight."

Kieran came up beside Raven, shrugging into his coat. A red mark formed on his cheek where Scar had hit him.

"You good," she asked.

He glanced down. "Yeah. You joining this one?"

Ruben answered, "No," before she could even reply.

Metal clashed on the field, the comrades striking and deflecting at rapid speed. Each slash of Scar's was met or countered by Lox's blade. As fast as the bladesman was, the thief was a step ahead. Smooth and quick as the wind, Lox lunged and pivoted with a graceful swiftness.

He sliced high, knocking the red cap off Scar's head.

"Hey, now!" Scar dodged backwards, a laugh sprouting with his shout. He caught his hat in midair and tucked it in his pocket. Black hair danced in the breeze. "Little too close there."

"Like I said," Lox adjusted his grip, "I'm winning."

Raven gaped before she could compose herself. She found Ruben intently admiring the fight as well. The thief moved with remarkable skill; she'd never want to meet him on opposing sides. His speed, his ability to block or deflect each attack, even use Scar's momentum to his advantage. And the blade he wielded wasn't even his own. What would he be like with a well-known sword?

Scar stabbed with his right hand, and Lox side-jumped away. The slash opened the thief's shirt from collar to stomach, but not near enough to scratch the *very* toned body underneath. Lox glanced down at his torn shirt, then shrugged it off.

More hoots came from the women of the crowd. Raven found herself eyeing the rippling muscles of his abdomen, wondering what those would feel like against her own smooth stomach. If the power they hinted at assisted in his fighting here.

If they'd be soft or hard under her fingers.

She blinked and shifted her gaze back to his fighting stance.

The bladesman switched hands and slashed from the left. Lox ducked and rolled across the dirt to hit the back of Scar's leg with the pommel of his sword. He stood while Scar faltered, finding balance.

Lox kneed Scar's other leg, bringing the bladesman to his knees. Scar swung upward and back, but Lox grabbed his wrist tight. The thief's sword rested along the neck of his comrade, his foot on Scar's ankle. Fully pinned and subdued.

The crowd made noise, but the sound was far away for Raven.

Ruben reluctantly announced the winner—Lox.

Everyone watched him bow and help Scar stand. The villagers, the guards, Ruben.

Raven's heart dropped, cold running through her. This was bad. His interest in her was already dangerous, but if he was seen dancing with her at the ball, it would strengthen Vanera's accusations about him murdering her.

Could she leave before the ball? Why couldn't he just leave her alone? Why'd he have to—wait. What if he *left*?

Raven shot her gaze to Lox. His band traveled frequently. So frequently her own guards couldn't even gather information on them. If she got him to leave... she could follow. And if he left a day or two before her "murder," and she ensured Ruben noticed his absence, he couldn't take the fall. Two birds, one stone.

He'd be safe from the queen's wrath and her mistakes.

Only Princess Ravenna would have to die for that.

CHAPTER 16

Less than five minutes of the Red Hood entering the tavern that night, Lox slid casually onto the bench beside her. At least he left a small space between them. "You're back."

Heat roamed her face as he assessed her. Raven retrieved a small meal from her satchel, a purchase earlier at the market. She took a bite and eyed him from under her hood. "Why do you feel the need to approach me?"

"Oh, that hurts, Red." Lox touched his chest. "Considering I've helped you out… two times?—yes, twice—I feel that means I can share a simple meal with you."

He reached for a piece of bread, and she slammed her knife into the table, barely missing his fingers. The tavern's low lighting glinted off the blade and onto a gold crested ring on his finger. Lox pulled his hand back. "Ouch."

Raven gestured around the tavern with her knife point. "Do you see anyone else talking to me? No."

"I thought you and I had something special." Lox scooted closer on the bench, hip and thigh touching hers. His woodsy scent enveloped her nose. Warmth radiated from the solid touch down her leg. She forced herself to ignore it.

"Why? Because I'm a girl?"

His brows rose, and his voice deepened when he replied, "I'd say *woman*. But to answer your assumption, no. It's because, as much as you will never admit it..." Lox smiled, that dimple appearing even in this dark light, "you like me."

Definitely not. But she couldn't afford to antagonize him yet. "The villagers are starting to think we're partners, so I suggest you leave."

He grinned.

"So, thief." She couldn't resist smiling when his dipped. "How long are you in town for?"

Lox leaned in, arm brushing hers. His earthy smell contrasted the beer and musk of the tavern. "How long do you want me in town for?"

Just a few more days. Raven eyed the space between them and shifted away, letting a chill settle in the distance and clear her mind. "I don't. Just curious how long you'll be stealing from my town."

"Your town? Don't you steal, too?" Lox jerked his head at the bar, a purple bruise surrounding the baker's eyes and broken nose. "And worse? What was that guy's name? Barren?"

She stiffened. "I do to some what they do to others."

Lox assessed her face under the hood, the enchantment warming as his gaze travelled over where her eyes would be down to her lips, marring it to his recognition. The heat tingled there as his gaze lingered. He smiled and said quietly, "What will you do to me?"

Her cheeks heated on their own accord, and she found herself staring at his mouth.

"Loxley!" a large man called from across the pub.

Finding her breath when Lox turned, Raven glanced at his friend at the fireplace, who raised a pint for Lox. Everything about her froze—her gaze, her heart, her breath. The man was distinctly Loren but also very not human. She wanted to look away, from the red hair hanging to his shoulders, the arched cheekbones. Bones as angled as a beast's, and skin that appeared leathery and cracked. The pitch-black eyes became Loren copper, deep and fathomless. Fear struck her harder than she could ever remember—and so viciously.

The young man flinched—burgundy brows crumpling, lines creasing on his cracked skin. Something in his expression gave her the impression of confusion, a little shock. His eyes shifted sideways, not quite on her gaze, and the harsh appearance faded to a dull representation of a Loren prince. Black eyes returned, copper hair darkened to auburn, the fear lessened a degree.

When she managed to turn from the undoubtedly enchanted man, the terror subsided instantly. She blinked. What kind of magic was that?

Raven took a steeling breath and turned back to the thief.

Lox was watching her face. He leaned back far enough to wave the cursed man off.

She raised a brow. "Loxley?"

"Yes. But most people call me Lox."

"Lox, sly as a fox." She sipped her water. "Because you're a thief."

He faced her, propping his boot on the bench, and rested his elbow on the table. "As are you, milady."

Raven nodded toward the cursed man without turning her gaze. "Is he part of your band of bandits?"

"It's a band," he said, exasperation filling his voice. "Just a band."

"A group of criminals is a band of bandits."

His forest green gaze hardened. "You really think highly of yourself, don't you, Red? What are you, then, a high-class criminal?"

Good, he was finally serious. Raven leaned forward, grasping the bottom of her hood, and said quietly, "How quickly can your band leave town?"

Loxley sighed, shaking his head. "Red—"

"I'm not threatening," she rushed out.

His dark brows scrunched. "Why do you ask?"

"How quickly?"

"Two days." Lox searched her face. "Why?"

She could plan this in two days. The ball was in three, two not counting tonight. She could still follow his band's trail. "Whatever you call them, I suggest that your band leave this weekend."

"What are you getting at, Red?"

She leaned in farther, ignoring how his closeness unnerved her. "I heard of a plot to frame you for murder."

His brows lifted, but his expression held calm, concentrating. "And whom am I supposed to be murdering?"

"The princess."

Lox sat back against the table, propping his head into his palm. Black locks cascaded over his fingers, almost covering them completely. "Considering I've never met this princess, that's a far stretch."

Yes, you have, Raven almost blurted. Did he not remember pickpocketing her in the market? The competition? She searched her memory. She hadn't worn her crown any of the times he'd seen her.

"Does it have to be the princess—or can I dance with you?" Had that not been a joke? Did he really not know *she* was the princess? Wherever Loxley came from, he'd never seen Princess Ravenna. And if she followed his band, they'd lead her to a place that wouldn't, either.

"No matter," she replied, trying to hide her pause. "You're a newcomer and towns don't trust newcomers."

He glanced around the tavern, catching his friend's look, and shook his head slightly. The cursed man searched as well and slowly walked to the door. Loxley returned to Raven, tone serious, "When is this supposed to happen?"

"This weekend. So, I suggest—"

"Does anyone else know?"

"No—"

"We should tell the guards, then."

"What?" Raven stared, watching him scope the crowd.

Lox whistled, low and quick. Another man at the fireplace looked up —the bladesman. "We have to stop it."

He raised his hand to his comrade, but Raven pulled it down. Loxley's sharp gaze shot to her gloved hand tightly gripping his. She hadn't touched him before—not since the baker's. She forced herself to let go, fighting her panic. He wasn't supposed to do this. He was supposed to be a coward, to run, to flee.

Not want to fight.

"Red?"

Raven blinked. Lox had leaned forward, staring curiously, close enough that she worried about the hood's magic. She grasped its edges and shook her head to clear her panic. *Reason with him.*

"No." She swallowed, throat dry as dirt, his green gaze seeming to penetrate her. *Stay calm.* "The queen will call you out on the accusation, and you'd have to say how you learned of this. I can't stand with you— I'm a wanted criminal. Without proof, she'll dismiss it, and you'll be targeted by the assassin."

Loxley held her gaze and raised his hand again palm out, slowly as if not to startle her. He flickered his eyes to the bladesman, signaling him to stay, then returned to her. "Surely, the queen would protect the princess —and me—for a precaution. She should take these accusations seriously."

You'd think. Raven concentrated on her heartbeat, trying to calm herself so her voice didn't waver. "You're being framed; you should just run. Leave now—make a presence in another town. Then, no one can say you did it."

Please just do it.

If he told someone, her plan was ruined.

She'd have to run tonight. She wasn't prepared for that.

Loxley considered her words, then whispered, "But if we stop the murder, there's nothing for me to be framed for."

Damn you. Her panic burned into anger, and she snapped back, "You don't even know her. Let us in Ilasia deal with it. Just leave."

"Aw, do you care about me, Red?" He dipped his head, that casual lilt back in his voice despite the dark topic.

Raven ground her teeth. "I just wanted to give you a heads up." Standing, she sheathed her knife and stepped over the bench seat. "I'd want the same."

Loxley's hand shot out, grabbing her wrist. His firm grasp held her still. "Hey." He rose a few inches off the bench, gazing into her eyes, examining her face. His voice deepened enough to be called sincere, "Who's supposed to kill her?"

She tried to hold his stare—to be the Red Hood, not the princess who was out of options—but the heaviness of the fate looming over her head was too much. She wrenched her wrist from his grasp and turned to the exit.

"Red!" Lox called, then swore.

Ignoring him, she pushed through the crowd and out into the darkness of the night. With only the stars to guide her way, she headed to the marketplace, staying on the outside edge of the wall behind the stations.

There goes her plan. Why—damn it, *why* couldn't he just act like a normal thief? Run like a coward, not... save the princess? What type of criminal even considered that?

She shook her head, black strands obscuring her vision of the trees. A hand burst from the forest and covered her mouth firmly. The rough skin grated against her shout. Raven elbowed her captor, fighting against the strong arm around her waist constricting hers arms. She wriggled her hand down to her knife.

A gruff, "Be quiet," whispered in her ear. Lox.

Softening her blows, she let him pull her into the shadows. She tore from his grasp, spinning to face him. He motioned her deeper into the trees.

What did he want now? Grudgingly, she followed him until he faced her. She snapped, "What?"

Loxley shifted his eyes between hers. "How did you hear about this plot?"

"I have sources."

He gave her a look of exasperation. "Red."

"Stop calling me that!"

He threw his hands up. "Well, I can't call you 'Hood.'"

She sighed, clenching her fists under her cloak. "Look, just don't call me anything. We shouldn't be speaking. I told you so you could *run*."

As the Red Hood, she'd put him in greater danger than as the princess this afternoon.

Lox stepped in front of her, green eyes shining. The brightest things in the dark forest. His deep voice softened, "How do you know this?"

I shouldn't tell him. But, somehow, this thief had an honest look of caring. He wanted to save her—or, rather, Princess Ravenna—did that mean he'd help her as the Red Hood? She swallowed, a burn creeping up her throat as tears and panic threatened. "I was hired to do it."

He held her stare, nodded lightly, and his posture softened. "And do you want to fulfill this job?"

"No," Raven whispered. Clearing her throat, she looked into the trees. "But if I don't, someone else will."

"And kill you next."

She nodded.

Loxley grabbed her sleeve and gestured deeper into the forest. When the castle and booths weren't in view through the trees, he stopped and asked, "What if we fake it?"

"What," she asked, dumbfounded.

"You heard me. What if we stage the murder but protect the princess? Then, we both leave with her before someone can know."

"Why would you do that?" Wonder pierced her voice. He didn't even realize he knew Princess Ravenna. To him, she was a stranger.

He shifted his shoulders, staring into the forest. "Because it'll get me out of being framed for murdering royalty, you out of the heinous job, and the princess will keep her life. Everyone wins."

Raven could tell he struggled with the answer. *Because it's the right thing to do.* "How could we do it?"

"First," Lox said, pacing, "we'd have to decide when and where. Some place where you can do the deed while I whisk her away."

"Whisk away," Raven asked, tone sharper than intended. She didn't like his phrasing. *She* was the one saving herself. And supposedly killing herself.

"We can't tell her beforehand. She'd panic and probably tell the queen. Or arrest us," he said casually, as if Princess Ravenna was just a dainty, well, princess. "We can explain to her while we're on the run."

"What happens afterward with her?" Raven found herself asking.

He considered this for briefly. "Well, that's up to her, isn't it? She can either live her new secret life, away from responsibility. Or she can return on her own. We'd have to find a way to make her believe, for her sake." He eyed Raven's hooded face. "This town's folk seem to adore you, but not the royalty or guards. Do you think she'd trust you?"

Raven attempted to hold back her tone. "Yeah. I think she would."

She took a deep breath. As much as Raven hated the thought of him kidnapping her, she had to agree he shouldn't talk to Princess Ravenna. "How would we stage it?"

Lox touched his chin, slight stubble dotting the tawny skin. "Does the person want proof?"

"Yes."

He nodded, digesting the information. "Want her body never found or there to display her death? Staging a death is one thing, staging a body is another."

"They want it burned," she said, the simplicity of the words and her mother's order burning her insides.

Both his brows raised. "Well. That's easier."

Raven gripped the sides of her hood, tugging it tighter over her face. How could this possibly work?

Catching her movement, Lox stepped toward her. His face and voice softened, oddly comforting. "Listen, you plan where and when, and I'll plan *how*. Meet me tomorrow night at the riverbank on the north side of town."

"Why not here?"

"Because we're planning the fake murder of a princess, and we can't chance being overheard or repetitive."

Nodding, she pulled her cloak around her body in the cool night air. Raven left Loxley in the forest to plan her death and returned to her castle to be Princess Ravenna once again.

CHAPTER 17

That next morning, Raven walked about the forested castle grounds with her guards, Ruben still at her side.

"Are you ready to go to the market, Princess?" The new recruit in the Guard brought out Ruben's formality—to her annoyance. She wanted Rue, not her Head Guard.

"Soon, Ruben." She ducked under a tree branch, checking the visual of the market or castle towers—none. Close enough to the wall and village that she could hide, but not too far from the castle. If her guards weren't suspicious about this new path today, they wouldn't be the day she'd need it.

She knelt to pick a flower, the guise for traversing off her normal route, and tucked it in her basket.

"You left very early this morning," Ruben observed, watching the new recruit's hesitant steps, the other two usual Royal Guards paces away. He gazed around the trees before stopping on her. "Your mother seemed unhappy."

She'd been unhappy for a long time.

The closer the ball came, the harder Raven found looking her mother in the eye. "I wanted an early start. I intend on having lunch with her, to talk about the ball."

She did not, but she'd find an excuse later.

Brushing off a patch of dirt, Raven sat on a rock to weave the flowers together on a dark blue headband. Her guards moved about, the recruit trying not to let his sword sweep behind his legs and trip him.

Her mother sure could pick them. But that was the point.

With a deep sigh, she leaned back, checking a nearby tree for any holes or rotted parts. Nothing, only a hollow at its base. A perfect hiding spot for her cloak.

After leaving Loxley last night, Raven had planned. Here, she could escape her guards and leave signs of a struggle. Grab her stashed cloak and satchel—then meet with Lox.

Therein lied the dilemma.

She'd planned to *follow* Lox, not plot and escape with him. He would expect both the Red Hood and Princess Ravenna to join him. Only one could show, and she'd debated, decided on the princess. He could leave without the Red Hood, but not without 'saving' the princess. Then, on the road, she could leave his band, don her cloak, and sneak behind them out of Ecanta.

She had to talk to him, maybe convince him that she could keep the princess safe and they could split up. That would be easiest—neither of her identities with his band of bandits. They didn't *need* to travel together. But how to convince him of that?

In theory, it was easy. But she was learning that Lox didn't make things easy.

Please, just let this one thing go as planned.

MOONLIGHT REFLECTED OFF THE STILL LAKE, UNABLE TO REACH RAVEN hiding within the trees. Twenty minutes she'd waited, if she'd calculated the moon's shadow correctly. Loxley hadn't specified a time, and she'd been—for once—too frazzled to get all the information last night. What if he'd brought her here to capture her as proof to inform the queen?

No. The honesty in his gaze and words the night before stilled her worries. His smile and charm might be lies and tricks to evade trouble, but his eyes weren't.

The clock tower rung out once and Loxley appeared, walking to the river. Loxley ran a hand through his thick hair and turned, spotting her striding toward him. He quickly dropped his hand and straightened. "You came."

She nodded. "I also planned."

He sat on a log alongside the river and patted the spot beside him. Raven chose the dirt instead. His charms wouldn't win her over, no matter how hard he tried. More important things were at stake, and his joking manner grated her nerves.

Nevertheless, Lox smiled. "Did you find a spot to take her?"

"Yes. It's in the forest near the castle." Ravenna forced her voice to sound disinterested, formal observation when she said, "Her guards seem to fan out sometimes, so I'll have ample time and space to kidnap her."

His brow rose. "*You'll* have time? I thought I was—"

"No." Annoyed at his objection, she set her tone. "You're going to be accused of her murder, so I should be the one taking the risk. She'll know who I am and that I don't kill innocents."

The thief rolled his eyes. "She's a princess; she'll still scream. Think you can keep her quiet?"

I don't scream. Raven glared. "I can handle it."

With a sigh of disbelief, he stretched out his legs. Shaking his head, Lox stared out at the river. "And what will I do, then? Hm?"

"What were you going to have me do while you 'whisked her away?'" Raven gestured into the air with her gloved hand.

"Build the pyre for her to supposedly burn in, and prepare an outfit or disguise for her."

"That's it?" she snapped and let out a harsh laugh. "Build a fire and find some clothes? That's why you're so hurt about it."

Loxley shot her a look, those forest greens shining darkly. "We can't build the fire beforehand or else chance getting caught. And she can't wear the same clothes while we travel. The smartest thing is to burn her clothes in the fire so they'll believe she's inside. Both parts are equally useful and vital."

"Then, why are you so upset? Hoping to get close to the princess?" His flirtations grew tiresome and frustrating. She didn't have time before, let alone now, for this. Treason was about to be held over his head, and he decided to flirt with both the woman he plotted with *and* to kidnap.

He almost growled his reply, "No." Lox took a deep breath and laced his tan fingers together. "I don't like plans changing."

Frustrated by his audacity, Raven stood and paced the river's edge. "Get used to it. Not a single one of my plans have gone accordingly since I met you."

He followed her to the water. "But—"

"No!" She turned, pointing her finger at him when she'd really rather it be her dagger. "You have changed *everything*. I can change this. This is why we met here—to plan."

All too calmly, Loxley looked from her fingertip to her eyes and replied, "Then, let's plan."

Raven forced herself to lower her hand. "They want her appearance at the ball this weekend, so we should do it the morning after. She takes her walks before noon."

"Okay. I'll start the pyre a mile out of town. By the time the smoke alerts them, we'll be out of Ilasia."

"Good." She nodded, pretending to contemplate his words. How to bring up the issue?

His deep sigh startled her. Lox sat and rested an elbow on his knee, dropping his head into his hand. "I don't get this. I really don't."

She expected a teasing grin, not this. Unsure what to say, she waited.

Moments passed, and he rubbed his brow hard, as if he could soothe the worries that caused its creases. "Everyone in town, all the villagers my band and I have talked to, love the princess—*everyone*. She supposedly takes care of them, feeds them, even visits every day." Lox looked up at her, confusion coating his face, and she lost her breath. "To me, that doesn't sound like a princess someone would want dead, let alone hire to kill."

They loved her. It was all Raven had hoped for—to rule fairly and have her kingdom believe in her. She loved them all so much, even the ones she punished—they learned and became better for it. She didn't want to leave. She wanted to lead and protect them, to be their princess.

But her mother had other plans.

And she could not follow them.

"Red?"

Raven blinked, meeting Lox's eyes. His confusion remained, but his gaze had turned pondering. "Y-yes," she said and swallowed, trying to hide how his words had affected her. "This will probably hurt Ilasia greatly."

Her voice caught in her throat. She hadn't even thought about that yet, only how to survive. If her life weren't on the line, she'd consider herself selfish. *Focus.* "The person who hired me isn't from the village. Their gains are probably political."

"What could they gain? She is unmarried and the only heiress to the throne."

Damn it, she didn't know. What *could* her mother gain from this? No, Lox didn't need that answer, he needed a fake one. "This kingdom is starving. With little money for imports and failing crops, we need money and the princess needs to marry. They are close to a betrothal to rectify this and help the kingdom prosper again. Getting rid of her will provide other kingdoms with power over us."

She had to hold in a sigh. What would her mother do without a betrothal? Would her kingdom truly starve without her hand to give in exchange for gold and food? Would she be killing Ecanta by essentially killing herself?

Lox nodded slowly, absorbing the information. "Possibly the princes in town? Or their entourage."

"Plausible," Raven mumbled.

"Us?" Lox raised a brow, lowering his hand to his knee.

"What?"

"You said 'us' before. You consider yourself one of them?"

"Yes."

The thief watched her unblinkingly, an odd feeling settling over her. Why did his attention unnerve her? "Where I come from, thieves and criminals normally aren't part of who they steal from."

"That must be lonely," she stated, hoping he'd stop staring. When he didn't look away, she asked, "Can we continue the plan to save the princess?"

Lox grinned—he *knew* what his stare did to her nerves and *liked* it— and nodded.

"We have where and when," Raven started, keeping her voice even, "but we need to talk about after."

"After?" Loxley's tone rose, interest piqued.

She crossed her arms slowly, ensuring not to jostle her hood. "Once she is safe and we've left Ilasia."

"Yes?"

His one-word answers and that sly tone irked her nerves. Bracing herself, she continued, "We should go separate ways."

Lox stared.

"It'll be safer for both of us."

He rose from the log and halted about a foot from her. "So... I'll go on my merry way *hoping* I'm not framed for the murder I faked, and you'll go on the run for the fake murder you were hired to commit. Am I hearing you right, Red?"

The cold tone would've shocked her if she weren't used to it from her mother. But it was so out of place coming from the joking Loxley. Raven steeled her expression. "If you get far away quickly enough, you can't be accused, and I—"

"Have you been outside of this kingdom?"

"Yes." She straightened, determined to match his stance.

He cocked his head, a few locks falling into his gaze. "Really? Because I've only heard of your crimes in this area," he motioned to the village beyond the trees. She had no response for that. "So, where will you go? And how will we know that the other doesn't tell of our plan, blame the other?"

"I wouldn't—"

"You wouldn't frame me? Like you're supposed to?" Lox shrugged his broad shoulders. "You didn't plan this? We do this together, and I take the fall?"

What? Did he really think she'd involve him just to *blame* him?

"You..." The thief let out a short laugh and shrugged. "You commit crimes and ignore your illegality, you beat—even kill—but don't steal. I don't know what you will or won't do." Loxley touched his chest, ignoring her silence. "I wouldn't tell. After all, I'm a true thief, and we have honor. But how can you *know*?"

A thief having *honor*?

Raven paused, partially waiting for him to cut her off again, contemplating where this conversation had gone. The problem he proposed didn't bother her. If he claimed the Red Hood's guilt, she'd be fine. She'd never be the Red Hood again. She would be... who would she be? Certainly not Princess Ravenna.

Raven.

She'd be Raven. She just needed to travel far enough that she could remove her magic hood without recognition.

"Tell—I don't care," she countered, her new direction grounding her. "Do you know what I look like? No. No one does." Raven pointed to her hood. "You can blame the Red Hood. I honestly don't care."

Searching her gaze, Lox's eyes fogged before clearing, her hood working its magic. He saw her face, her eyes, but they didn't store in his mind. "No. We can't trust each other—so we go together."

"Lox—"

"Whether you like it or not, Red, we're both criminals. We don't have the luxury of trust."

"I don't need to trust you!" she yelled. She couldn't trust anyone but herself anymore. And she hadn't been able to do that for years. She'd almost killed Grayson in fear a few nights ago. Raven still couldn't trust her darkened heart. She reached for her chest and touched the heart necklace hidden beneath her tunic, then dropped her hand. *I just need to get through this.*

"And what do you suggest happens with the princess, hm? Do you think she goes with you?" Lox shrugged, a sharpness to the movement. "I help you attain her, and you keep her for—whatever you could want?"

She needed to get this back on track. To appease him somehow and separate her two halves. "What if she went with you?"

"And I could be charged with kidnapping," he snapped back.

She balled her fists. Gods damn him. She just wanted to live!

Instead of hitting him, she threw her hands up, knocking her cloak off her shoulders. His gaze drifted to her figure, despite their tense connection. She tried to ignore the darkening of his eyes and the flutter in her stomach.

Raven clenched her fists, refocusing. "Someone already wanted to frame you for murder—and you'll be around here at the time, *faking it.*"

She'd wanted to save him from this, but she'd ended up involving him. The fight went out of her. Raven backed up and rested against a tree. "Lox... you should just go."

"What?" The tension left his brow, and he walked silently toward her.

153

She raised a gloved hand. "We've already planned this. You don't need to be there."

He started to protest, but she shook her head. "Lox, this is my mess. Get out of town. I can figure out the rest on my own."

"Red..."

"Go."

CHAPTER 18

Zella tried to ignore the voice outside her tower. She flipped another yellowed page in the enchanted tomb. *If some Vala glass could see* through *magic, was that canceling —*

"Hello?"

She gripped the table and refocused. That section was the closest anything came to breaking an enchantment. Magic interactions was the most undocumented subject of the Vala culture, Zella was realizing. Magic called to magic—especially magic from the same Sandceress—but magic did not *cancel* other magic. Blocking, muddling, and counter spells existed, but nothing negated or canceled existing magic. And to do even accomplish those tactics, you had to have the exact potion or spell.

This was hopeless.

"I know someone is up there," the voice called. "I saw you."

Zella sighed and walked toward the window, stopping before she could be seen again. She tilted her head enough to peer at the cloaked figure below. The fabric was a deep red, but to Zella, it was a shimmering transparent flow of cloth. Magic flowed across it, though the fibers, shifting the young woman's figure and voice. It swirled in similar patterns to what crawled over the vines, the tower, the empty window. She pondered if the enchantments were reminiscent of each other or if all spells resembled each other. Zella

155

had to wonder if the enchanted empty window pane did the same to her appearance. Or was it just her constant exposure to Vala magic that made her in tune to it, able to recognize? To *see* magic and understand the way it weaved into the core of objects and into the air.

"Fine. Don't answer," the girl huffed, breaking Zella out of her thoughts.

Zella presumed that enchanted cloak was how the vigilante could slip past the vines and trees surrounding her tower. She wished it would stop.

Her heart panged.

The first time the Red Hood stumbled through, Zella had been elated. The girl had given her a nickname—Punzella was too long, she felt—and promised to return.

The second time, all of Zella's hope fizzled. Another enchantment apparently lay on the obscuring vines, a precaution of Naja's surely. Though, there was no way she could've known the torture of possible friendship it inflicted on Zella.

The third time, Zella had cried.

Each time the Red Hood returned, it was her first time.

Zella knelt and put her back to the wooden wall. It was thanks to this young woman that Zella had a secret name for herself, that Zella knew her tower was actually a small cottage suspended on thorny and inter-twined vines.

She also made Zella long for the outside, for friendship, that much more. It made staying in this tower more unbearable. And she didn't think she take much more.

The magic bruises on her scalp still stung from Naja's angry magic a few days prior. Naja had visited another time, and Zella had been sure not to ask for anything again.

"I have to leave."

The Red Hood's words felt like they were torn from her own heart. Zella felt stuck between a sigh of relief and sadness. As much as these random visits were torturous, it was also nice to talk with someone.

"Not just here, but Ecanta." Her voice sounded very sad.

The coolness of the wood seeped into her back. "Why?"

Below, the young woman laughed, but Zella detected no humor. "I don't even know where to start. Someone I love doesn't want me here anymore." After a few moments, she asked. "Why are you here?"

A sigh left Zella. "I just am."

"That's not an answer."

"No. It's not."

Rustling sounded below, and a spark followed by a curse.

Zella stood and turned to the window. The vigilante was shaking her gloved hand. "You didn't touch it, did you?"

She nodded, rubbing her hand. Purple swam across the fingers of leather. Zella knew only she saw it, otherwise the girl wouldn't be touching the glove.

Her suspicions were correct—she'd really wished they weren't. The vines were enchanted with a protection spell as well. Her shoulders slumped, and she had to work to stand upright. How many spells had Naja put around her? *Why?*

Why was freedom constantly denied?

"Well, you'd have to jump," the Red Hood stated.

"What?" Zella whirled toward the empty window, stopping the barest inch before the frame.

The Red Hood stared up at the vines and tower, squinting and focused. "To leave. Climbing is out."

Zella backed away from the window, as if the barrier could feel her thoughts, the proposal to leave. She shook her head violently, sandy strands flying, shifting the mass at her feet. "I-I can't."

She swallowed, trying to tamper down the fearful shake.

Leaving was not something she allowed herself to consider. The enchantment alone burned her skin. The climb—well, jump—down? With her hair? And then pushing through the verdant walls... Zella leaned forward again to peer below.

The grass... She would be able to feel it. To smell it. Stories she read told about the scents of the world. Only the barest smells permeated the enchantments.

No.

Zella repeated the sentiment flooding her brain. "It's impossible."

"My cloak is impossible."

She whirled on the window, grabbing the lantern beside it, and threw it. Glass and metal hit nothing—and shattered into shards and shrapnel, purple tendrils rippling in the empty air. Pain flared in her arms as small pieces sliced her skin, and she felt shards fly into her hair and fall, never, *never* cutting her hair.

The Red Hood's eyes stared wide below.

"It's not the same!" Zella yelled, precariously close to the barrier. Frustration boiled within every fiber of her body. "Don't you see? There are *countless* enchantments, bars to keep me here."

She really, truly, was trapped.

"I..."

"Just go." Zella held back tears, but her voice turned thick. She caught the girl's gaze below. "Be safe."

After another moment's stare, the Red Hood headed for the vines.

Don't cry, not now.

This would be the last time she saw her sort-of friend.

"Thank you," she called out.

The young woman turned, red cloak rustling in the breeze that Zella feared she would never feel. "For what?"

"For showing me that people really care for others." Zella smiled softly. "That the outside isn't as bad as the inside."

The Red Hood waved before pushing through the green wall. Branches and vines wrapped around her, some attaching to the cloak before parting slightly.

Despair started to descend on Zella as she backed away, feet stepping over her hair from instinct. Cold tingled in her skin, and she ignored the slices from the glass. She curled up on the small bed in the corner, far from the window and the door. Pushing down the sadness, she lay on her side to see the stars above the tree tops.

At least one of them got to escape their curse.

SMALL THORNS POKED AT RAVEN'S GLOVES AND CLOAK. THE VINES FELT never ending. Doubts swirled through her mind. Could she really just leave that girl there?

Air brushed her face, and the leaves, branches, and vines finally ended. Raven took a deep breath and faced the wall of greenery, squinting against the light sensation filling her head. The warmth of her cloak intensified, the waves rolling across her face and body heating and shifting. Something seemed to push her toward the vines. Toward the girl and the magic surrounding her.

Raven reached for the vines, stepping forward—and her temples pounded in pain.

She grasped her forehead and turned away to steady her breathing, one step, two—and the pain immediately disappeared. As well as the desire to face, let alone walk toward, what lay behind her.

Teal eyes and impossible branches and vines came to her mind. A meadow full of impossibilities.

That girl—She was why… She was…

Was…

Who?

Ravenna let her hand drop to her side and stared at the forest she knew better than anything else. Her tunnel, she needed to return to her room and wake up the innocent princess without a death toll hanging over her crowned head. Gods, this night had been a whole hell of a wreck.

Not ready for the morning already rising, Ravenna crept through the forest and away from the cluster of trees that no one, save one person, could stare at longer than a moment. And Ravenna, though cloaked in an enchantment, was not that person, though a lost girl on the other side of a different and much darker enchantment needed her to be.

CHAPTER 19

Cindy twisted the cupcakes on the tray. The lily was her favorite of the flowers she'd iced. Her eyes flicked to the passing villagers. Father rarely let her decorate—her hands shook under his gaze—or sell directly. But his bruise was larger and darker than hers to his chagrin. People didn't associate with the Red Hood's targets... so here she stood. And if she didn't sell these today, he'd be angrier.

At least her bruise had started fading, though her pale coloring accented its redness.

Heart racing, she held a breath and waved at a woman. "Fresh baked cupcakes!" Her soft voice barely rose a gaze.

Cindy sighed. She hated her timidity. But every time she showed something more, Father—she squeezed her eyes shut. No, he was doing better after the Red Hood's visit.

"How much?" a deep voice rumbled.

Cindy's eyes snapped open—onto a wide leather-covered chest, flowing white sprouting under the expanse of buttons running down the front of black lapels and naval coat. Her gaze followed the black leather down his large arms to the many-ringed fingers and bracers at his wrist. This young man was dressed for sea. She looked up to his face, realizing her rudeness. Harsh lines made up his cheekbones and jaw, but his mouth was smooth—unlike her father's usual hard line.

She recognized him from the competition the day before—Kieran. The one who'd fought the man named Scar and almost won. She tried to not remember staring at his bare chest when that bladesman had cut him —and his shirt—open. The blood had looked minimal, but she still wondered if he was okay. No wound should be taken lightly.

What held her still now, though, were his mix-matched eyes. The left was a bright green like grass, and the right a crystal blue brighter than the sky. Black brows rose over those entrancing eyes, and Cindy remembered he'd asked a question. "They—" she straightened another cupcake, then folded her hands on the table, "they're six coppers each."

He spilled some coins into his large palm. Coppers, dalions of the northeast, and even rakes from the far west cascaded forward. A man of the sea indeed. After sorting through, he held out the coppers. Didn't drop them on the tabletop like others, but waited for her to take them. Swallowing, Cindy extended her hand, and he kept his palm open and still while her unsteady fingers scooped up the coins.

Grateful not to hold his intense stare, Cindy pocketed the coins and pushed the tray forward.

Kieran didn't move.

She waited.

Nothing.

Cindy lifted her gaze and found him watching her. She tried to cover her start, but his narrowed eyes caught it. Damn her timidity. "You— which one do you…"

"Not sure." He tilted his head. "Which is your favorite?"

She blinked. Looked down at the flowers and back up at him. Pointed to the delicate lily. "This one is the most beautiful."

His mix-matched gaze observed the cupcake, then returned to her. "Have you had one?"

"No."

This man… She didn't talk to people much but this wasn't how sales normally transpired.

He placed six more coppers in her palm, retrieved a rose and a lily. Holding her stare, Kieran leaned forward slightly—making Cindy tense and hold her breath—and set the lily next to her hand.

Cindy glanced from him to the cupcake and back—but he'd already turned away. His dark and solid form cut through the crowd like a knife. Stunned, she looked down at the dessert.

And smiled.

Hesitant, Cindy bit into the cupcake. It was like heaven. Sweet and all hers. She ate half, then stowed the rest gently in her apron pocket. If Papa saw he'd think she'd stolen it, but she would savor the gift.

Gift…

She searched the market. Wished she could thank Kieran, but she stumbled with almost all her words, so it was for the best.

A familiar face flashed in the crowd. Princess Ravenna. She waved at Cindy and headed over.

Cindy combed her hair back uselessly. Something about Ravenna looked… tired. Black locks slipping from the hairband, and darkness rimmed her eyes.

The princess smiled, the expression flickering. There, then not. "These are beautiful!"

"Thank you. I got to ice them." Cindy leaned in and whispered, "It's my favorite part."

"Really?" Ravenna raised a brow, then twisted and called, "Such *delicious* cupcakes!"

Villagers turned, and Cindy tensed. She looked to Raven, but the princess had ducked to the next booth. Footsteps and voices cascaded to the table. Cindy twisted her apron. She'd barely made it through the sailor's sale, how could she do this many?

Breathe. Just breathe.

Cindy nodded to herself and unclenched her fingers.

Townsfolk bought cupcakes for nearly five minutes, and Cindy looked to Raven when she flustered, receiving a wink. She stumbled through prices and accepting the coppers, counting each coin dropped on the tabletop. Until everyone cleared, and only two cupcakes remained.

The princess sauntered up, smiling widely and longer than before. Cindy observed her friend, trying to pinpoint what was off about the princess this morning. Maybe her gaze shifting around the market?

"Thank you, Ravenna," Cindy replied, smoothing her messy bun. She sighed. Papa couldn't be angry now. Well… not ang*rier*.

"You're welcome." The princess smiled. "Raven. Not Ravenna, please."

Cindy smiled and nodded.

Raven dug inside her basket. "I have something for you."

Footsteps approached, and Raven scooted over.

"Can I have another?"

Cindy looked up at the gruff voice. Black leather stood opposite her, tousled ebony hair falling over mix-matched eyes. Kieran. Her eyes widened, and she nodded, grabbing the last lily cupcake.

Again, Kieran held the coppers, not tossing them.

She should say thank you. Just open her mouth and *say it*—

"Kieran?" Raven asked, staring at the young man.

Kieran tipped his head. "Morning, Princess."

"Morning," Raven said casually, not at all phased by the large sailor beside her. Raven was brave like that. Like Cindy wished she could be. But no, she couldn't even thank the young man who'd bought her a cupcake.

She pocketed the coppers, and then Raven presented a headband of blue flowers. "They'll compliment your eyes."

Cindy gasped. Dark blue spiraled from a crystal center. Absolutely beautiful. She wished she could create those in icing. She reached for the headband.

Loud footsteps pounded. *Papa.* Cindy flinched and pulled her hand back. No, not now. Not with Raven here.

Kieran straightened, and Raven's head shot up.

"Cindy," her father yelled, stomping over, eyes still bloodshot from the broken nose. He clasped Cindy's elbow and tugged her back two steps. "Why the hell are you gossiping—"

Metal scraped metal—and Kieran's ringed knuckles rested on the table as he leaned forward to glare at Cindy's father. Rings ground against one another with his movement.

"Do you want your eyes to match?" Kieran growled, one black brow bouncing a threat.

Those rings would leave a *mark*, a scar if intended.

The baker froze, Cindy's wide gaze flying to Kieran. No one ever did this—helped her.

163

Mix-matched eyes never leaving the man, Kieran nodded to Raven and Cindy. "I suggest you *behave* in the presence of women."

Her father's mouth parted in surprise and outrage, but he released Cindy and moved back.

Kieran straightened slowly and turned to Cindy. She flickered her eyes away from his and back. Now she should *really* thank him, but this was so embarrassing. Normally, no one ever saw this. She tugged light strands free from her bun and fiddled with them against her cheek.

Kieran's dark brow softened.

Raven cleared her throat. "Cindy sold the pastries, and I'd like her to accompany me on a walk."

"With you?" the baker repeated, shocked.

She glared with the force of a princess.

His breath hitched. "Your Highness."

Cindy tried to squash the happiness in her chest. Tried.

"Yes. She's coming to my ball."

"She can't go—"

"Yes, she can," Raven stated and stepped toward him. "I've invited her."

Kieran crossed his wide arms.

"Of course, Your Highness." He swallowed hard, then nodded, bowing.

Cindy winced, then squeezed her fingers. Always timid. Always scared of his movements.

Raven circled the table and looped their arms together. The flower headband landed in Cindy's hands, and she cradled it. Then, the princess pulled Cindy into the marketplace, Kieran behind them.

Paces away from her father, Cindy relaxed. Shoulders falling, fingers uncurling from the string.

"See you tomorrow night," Kieran said, tipping his head at Raven, then Cindy, and his mix-matched gaze held hers for a beat before he lifted the cupcake he'd bought and turned.

Cindy sighed, then breathed in courage. Breaking from Raven's grasp, she took three quick steps. "K-Kieran?"

He stopped, rotating to her. Grass and sky stared down at her.

Cindy pressed her lips together and stuck her hand out. "Thank you."

He observed her extended fingers before enclosing them in his large palm. Kieran nodded.

She felt so small with just that handshake. When he let go—quickly— she grasped the headband. With a smile, she returned to Raven.

Cindy stroked a flower petal. A headband, and a cupcake. Two gifts in one day. Maybe things would get better.

THE TWO YOUNG WOMEN STROLLED THROUGH THE MARKETPLACE, RAVEN'S incompetent guards trailing. If Raven wasn't dying in two days, she would've enlisted Cindy as the castle baker, to rid her friend of her father. Cold dread stopped Raven's heart. What would he do to Cindy when the Red Hood left?

A guard bumped into them, and she stumbled forward. The man— boy, really—jumped back, hands shooting to his swinging scabbard. "Oh! Your Highness! I'm sorry—"

Gritting her teeth, she smiled. "It's okay. I'm the one that stopped."

Not a single guard was familiar this morning; one Royal Guard, two recruits, and one inexperienced village guard. And no Ruben. Raven thought it premature, considering she wouldn't 'die' for another two days. Guess her mother was eager.

Raven tensed. As casually as she tried to think about her mother's wish to kill her, she couldn't.

Raven rushed them through the crowd, *away* from the guards. Their presence reminded her that she was alone. In the castle, in the village, and even as the Red Hood.

At breakfast, Ruben had mentioned Lox's band in his report. They were already in Dale. Loxley leaving shouldn't surprise her—she'd told him to—but the quick presence twenty miles away made her feel he'd left in a hurry. Given he'd told her it took two days to leave.

But now she could follow them.

The Red Hood always worked alone, but when Loxley had involved himself, she'd felt... almost not alone. Lox was a pain, and she hated his type of criminal—stealing to steal not to survive—but, honestly, having someone know about the murder and willing to help her, for the responsibility of this impossible task to rest on another's shoulders too, it made her able to breathe again.

But Lox was gone. And so were her breaths.

Raven slowed and glanced at Cindy. She'd helped her, with the cupcakes and the baker. Hopefully, Kieran stepping in made it stick. That pirate prince appearing was curious, but who knew what went on in his mind. Pirates could like sweets.

"Thank you for this, Raven," Cindy said. "It's beautiful."

Regaining her polite smile, she leaned into Cindy. "It'll match you."

A few steps passed silently, then Cindy whispered, "I don't think I should go tomorrow."

Raven stopped. "Why not?"

"I don't think I would be presentable." Cindy pulled on her hair, tugging more forward.

Raven's anger sparked. She caught Cindy's hand and tucked the strands behind her friend's ear. "You are beautiful, Cindy. And this will fade. Whatever remains tomorrow, we can cover with powders." She looked her straight in the eyes. "Either way, I'll be proud to have you by my side."

Cindy smiled, teeth flashing, and managed not to divert her eyes. "You're so kind."

"Ladies," a deep voice said, borrowing their attention. Raven turned to—her most annoying thief. Loxley extended his hand to Cindy, charming smile in place.

Raven glanced at her guards. He shouldn't be there—he'd left—let alone walking up to the princess. *Be calm.* He didn't know she was the princess.

Cindy glanced from him to Raven, then grasped his hand. "H-hello."

"Lox," he said, dipping his head and kissing her knuckles. "And you are?"

"Cindy," she rasped, eyes widening. Raven couldn't tell if it was from Loxley's charm and looks or Cindy's usual shyness.

He turned to Raven, his smile curling. "And you, milady?"

Reluctantly, Raven extended her hand. She needed to leave *now*. This was bad, and he didn't know how bad.

"You've never seen her?" Cindy asked.

Loxley brought her hand to his mouth, and she tried to ignore the softness of his lips and the small race to her heart. He gripped it longer than necessary, warm, rough skin rubbing against hers. His thumb brushed her own calluses—from holding swords and knives—and his brow rose. Any swordsman or archer would recognize them, and he was both.

"We've met before." Raven retracted her hand, setting him with a look. "Without introductions."

"This is Ravenna," Cindy explained. "Princess Ravenna."

"Princess," Lox said, brows lifting. His green eyes sharpened, examining her face, her simple attire. "My apologies, Your Highness. I'm not from here."

If he bowed, she might kick him. She hated bows, it made others appear inferior. His would be a greater annoyance.

"Tell me, Cindy," Lox continued, "what type of ruler is our fair princess?" He winked at Raven. Not amused, she cocked a brow.

Cindy looked between them. "Ravenna is generous and very kind."

"Is she forgiving?"

Cindy paused. "Yes, I suppose."

The too-charming thief's eyes circled the market, landing on her guards far away. "You're missing a guard."

Raven stiffened. He'd noticed Ruben at the competitions. He couldn't know it, but the comment hit her heart. She glanced away before he could see the sadness arise.

"We, um…" Cindy said, trying to fill the gap. Confused, she looked at Raven, who smiled to ease her friend. "We were just talking about the ball tomorrow."

"The ball?" His tone lifted, a sly smile hiding in his appearing dimple.

Don't you dare. Raven wrapped her arm around Cindy's. "Yes, and we really must prepare." The force of her polite smile strained her cheeks. She nodded to Lox. "Maybe we'll see you again."

"Oh, you will."

She moved them down the path and glanced back, hoping he'd been wise for once and left.

Loxley stood where they'd been, staring after her. He grinned crookedly when he caught her gaze.

Damn him.

CHAPTER 20

A black dagger dug into the tree's bark, a breath's mark before Loxley walked past. He halted, readying his own weapon. Red stepped out from the trees, the moonlight catching her hood, and he straightened. "I thought we weren't meeting again for another day? Not that I'm complaining."

She barreled down on him, pushing against his chest with both of her palms. He staggered backwards, her hands pressing him into a tree. "What—"

"You were with the princess—where *everyone* could see! How stupid are you?"

Her words would've wounded his pride had he not caught her tone. Loxley couldn't help but notice her hands were still on his chest, scattering his thoughts. He smiled down at her. "Are you jealous, Red?"

"No!" She took a deep breath, stepping back. She spoke carefully, possibly trying to not throw another dagger at him. "You're about to be framed for her murder. The more you're seen with her, the more believable the lies become."

"I didn't know she was the princess when I walked up to her." Lox shrugged.

Though he'd known Ravenna was out of his league, he couldn't have imagined *that* far. Or *her* a princess. She carried the confidence, but… not the formality or rigidness. The entitlement.

Seeming to capture her anger, Red sighed. "I thought you left."

He smiled. "Did you miss me?"

Did she?

"No!" Red hit his arm. "Why are you still here?"

"Because—" He dodged her next punch and grabbed her wrist, pulling her in close. Her eyes widened. Were they gold? Green? Brown? He could never recall. "You need me to pull this off."

He held her against him, gaze lingering on her lips, wondering if she'd stab him if he kissed her. Probably.

It'd be worth it.

He released his grip, letting her step back. "My band is establishing our presence in Dale, and I'm under the guise of finishing some business. I'll be seen in Dale tomorrow, then return here that night to help you in the morning."

Her gaze narrowed. "Why would you chance this?"

"I told you I would help, Red." Lox searched her face, but the enchantment marred her expression. Mist clouded his mind.

"And what about the princess? Did you figure out a plan for that?"

He grinned. "Now that I know who she is… I think she'll do great with my band. How about we tweak one of your suggestions?" He leaned forward. "She goes with my band, and you and I stay here to ensure everything worked. Then, we meet up with the band on the road."

"You go with your band, I'll catch up."

Her hard gaze made him pause. Why was Red so adamant about *not* coming with him?

"Red. We stick together."

She nodded, gazing into the forest.

Something was wrong.

"But I have to say," Loxley continued, remembering *Princess* Ravenna's calloused hand, "I'm intrigued by her. She's not the typical princess."

Red glared.

"I might just scope out the castle."

Her head jerked toward him. "What do you mean?"

Red's sharpened gaze meant he was onto whatever issue she held. He meandered around her, stepping silently over rocks and twigs. "Well, the ball will be in full swing tomorrow night. I can look around. See the princess."

"No. Don't go near her again." Red raised her finger at him. "You've already put the plan in danger."

"But we need to know where the guards are," he pointed out.

She groaned. "Then, do that from *outside* the castle."

Loxley stepped closer and softened his voice, almost losing its teasing lilt. "You could come with me, Red."

He knew it a foolish offer, but they weren't on the run *yet*. Would she throw him away like everyone else?

"I'd love to see you in a dress," he said, reaching for her hand. He'd love to take her *out* of one, too.

She grabbed his forearm, swinging him around, and pushed him against a tree. The jolt took his breath, and he recalled another grip pressing him into a wall. Red leaned in. "And I'd love to stay out of jail." She squeezed his arm and grabbed her knife, still embedded in the bark, and pulled it free. "Stop thinking about the princess."

Lox turned his head to stare at Red's hooded eyes. That grip had belonged to a very different young woman, though. Her eyes flashed amber. Then, the cloak worked its magic, and he couldn't pinpoint their color. Lox relaxed his arm. "Okay. I'll be good."

After a moment, she released him. "You better. Two days—the lake at noon."

Yes, Red definitely had a secret.

SHE COULDN'T BELIEVE HIM! STOMPING AWAY, RAVEN BARELY TOOK CARE TO quiet her steps and climbed over the wall into the housing area around the marketplace. Even after discovering he'd talked to the person he was about to be accused of murdering, he thought it a good idea to attend the *ball*?

If he—Raven stopped, the hard clomping of metal boots on dirt halting her ranting thoughts. A guard. She glanced around; even covered by the night's darkness she had nowhere to hide. The next wall stood two rows of houses down and—from the loudness of the steps—she didn't have time to scale the one behind her. Raven looked between the houses. No, the guards examined every inch of the village, even alley-ways and shadows. The forest, her only refuge, too far.

A shape appeared beside her and twisted her around. The scent of woods and earth encircled her. "No—Lox, go!" Raven looked for the guard, seeing his armored boot cresting the corner, and pushed against Lox's chest. "We can't be seen together, she—they'll know."

Loxley grasped her cloaked shoulders and pushed until her back hit a house, its shadow barely draping over them.

Her eyes widened and she tried to tear his hands away. "Wha—"

He covered her mouth with his palm, his earthy scent enveloping. "Trust me," Lox whispered in her ear, leaning in so close she nearly felt trapped, his body and heat overwhelming. He pushed her cloak off her shoulders, hands sliding over her shoulders. He kept her hood up, but made the folds tuck behind her, more hidden in the dark. "If we're caught together, we'll escape together. Now play along." Loxley wrapped his arms around her waist, pulling her tightly to him, and lowered his face over hers.

Her breath left her. She could only see him—his eyes, his lips. Only feel him around her. Too stunned and confused to move, Loxley's warmth and closeness froze her thoughts.

The clanking steps neared.

No—they needed to *run*.

"Giggle," Lox whispered against her ear.

A shiver ran down her spine from the heat of his breath. "What?"

"Giggle, moan, something."

She understood the ruse now but still didn't know what to do. She'd never been intimate with anyone. She'd heard Mira's flirtations, seen her rattle some guard's nerves with her dresses and teasing, but for Raven, this was new territory—one she hadn't planned on exploring until a betrothal that now would never happen.

Lox groaned—whether from frustration or the ruse she couldn't tell—and squeezed them against the wooden wall. He brought an arm up to lean on the wall high above her head, his surprisingly muscled forearm blocking her hooded face.

171

Despite the cool night air, his breath warmed her neck, making Raven unsure if she was blushing or if it was his heat. When he pressed even closer, the slight stubble on his jaw brushed her cheek, and she gasped, the sound breathless and surprising her.

Keeping his face tucked into her neck, Lox edged back and mumbled, "Sorry, love."

The guard's armor creaked just feet away but slower now and reached the opening to the small gap between houses they rested within. The gravity of the situation fully dawned on her. If the guard caught her now, the danger would be worse than ever. Discovery as the Red Hood meant her escape foiled, her mother realizing she knew of the plot.

Raven's hands, still resting on Loxley's shoulders and the only thing separating their chests, shook. Fear of being caught or Lox's closeness? Maybe all the above. Her nails dug into his tunic, panic setting her on edge. The last time a man had been this close she'd killed him, but she felt oddly secure with Lox, the young man who didn't treat her like a dainty princess or a deadly vigilante. Who protected her instead of hurting, willing to go down with her and escape the same.

Lox's breath mixed with hers, cheek resting on hers, and she could feel his tension, legs taught against hers. Not soon enough, the guard's footsteps retreated in the opposite direction. Loxley released the tight grip on her waist that she'd forgotten within her fear and looked around, staying close to her. "I think we're clear." Then, he stopped, turning back and placing a hand on her shaking shoulders. He ducked to gaze into her eyes. "Red…"

Magic and warmth swam over her face, marring her expression. Trying to stop the tears prickling, Raven closed her eyes and released her fingers' grip on his tunic, resting them on top. Ever since her mother had ordered her death, Raven had avoided her touch. Ruben was off her guard. She'd felt unloved, unwanted, and truly… *truly* alone for the first time since her father's death.

Lox leaned back. "What's—Red, I wouldn't hurt you."

She couldn't look at him—the only person who somewhat eased this lonely ache even though she hated the idea of him. Who confused her emotions in ways she couldn't understand.

He pulled away completely, and the rush of cold that engulfed her felt far too familiar. Raven opened her eyes and grasped his tunic—and Lox stopped. She instantly let go, lying her hands flat on his chest.

She gaped up at him, not sure what she was doing.

Loxley's forest gaze held hers, pondering, searching. "Red…"

The heat of him flared through his tunic, through her gloves, through his thighs pressing against hers from her tugging him closer. Forget the hood's warm magic, this was *fire*. And Raven didn't know if she wanted it to flare or cool.

Lox edged forward, capturing what he could of her gaze. His breath caught the same time hers did, she felt it under her palms. His hand moved from her waist to her hip. Fingers trailed from her shoulder to the edge of her hood.

"No—"

"I won't," Lox reassured her, lowering his hand to her neck. Her pulse beat against his thumb, heat trailing with his light touch. "If I promise to keep my eyes closed…" he breathed, "can I kiss you?"

The fire inside her grew at his words. The idea of—

She pressed her lips together. "You like the mystery, do you?"

He chuckled, the sound reverberating down her body. "I like *you*. And I don't think you want me to know your secrets." Lox pressed closer, face just on the edge of her hood and whispered, "But I know you want me to kiss you."

"I…" Raven swallowed, skin hot and intensely aware of her heartbeat. Why did she almost feel dizzy? "I've never…"

Lox's eyes widened for a second, but he didn't retreat. His grip softened on her hip, raising to her waist, liquid heat trailing with the movement, through her tunic. "I'd be honored, love."

Any other moment, and she would've rolled her eyes at his words.

"Yes or no, Red." He closed his eyes. His thumb lightly caressed her neck, and something close to a gasp left her. A smile crested his lips, she could almost feel it. "I'll wait. You have to tell me, but I'm perfectly content… right," he squeezed the hand on her waist, "here."

Fire—she was fire. Her gloved fingers gripped his tunic. She shouldn't, her brain warred at her. But why not? What reason was there left not to? She couldn't think of any in this moment.

"Yes," she breathed.

The fraction of space between their mouths disappeared. His lips were soft on hers—at first. Then, she gasped, and the parting of her lips had Lox part his, and his tongue brushed against hers. At that touch, the fire consumed her. Raven pulled on his shirt, one gloved hand raising to his shoulder to bring him closer. His hand spread on her neck, heat flowing with every inch he explored.

Lox's tongue opened her mouth wide, moving with hers furiously. His thumb pushed under her jaw, tilting her more against him at the angle he wanted. Something within her liked him having that inch of control, and she arched into him. His body pushed into hers, until all she could feel or think was Loxley. His chest, his thigh against hers, sliding between her legs—*oh*.

Forget the fire in her before, pure liquid heat pooled at her core, where Lox's leg pressed against her front. Raven's body arched against him, and he groaned, her mouth swallowing the sound as his tongue tangled with hers.

The hand at her waist drifted down her hip, squeezing almost roughly into her skin. Loxley groaned when her tunic shifted and his fingertips touched her bare skin.

She couldn't think, not as his hand traveled up her waist. Raven sighed at the pure heat of his touch, hips arching into him without thought.

Loxley hissed, and his fingers trailed down, cupping and squeezing her ass. Another gasp fell from her as he pressed her into him, and she felt his hard—

He broke away, the barest inch separating their panting breaths. Loxley's hand retreated from her neck to her shoulder, the other shifted up to her waist. "Red…" he breathed, words brushing her lips. "I— bloody hell."

Lox eased his hips backward.

Raven opened her eyes and found his still closed. Just as promised.

Emotion swelled in her chest, something beyond anything else he'd made her feel.

With each breath now that the kiss had ended, reason came back to her. Stars above, that was… more intense than she'd imagined. She still burned but was starting to cool.

Lox leaned back and looked at her. A smile lit his face in the moonlight. He'd stopped, did that mean he didn't… No. He was a breathless as her.

Though he'd barely moved, the chill of the night invaded the space his heat had occupied. It cooled her skin and her mind. Gods, this was Lox—the thief, the criminal who irked her to no end. Why did she *care*— why had she—

Raven sighed, her thoughts racing down different tracks. She blinked hard, still wanting to tug him closer, because the loneliness suddenly felt so much more vast than moments before.

Staring at her hand on his tunic, she wondered what in the world she'd just done. She needed to say something, but she had no words. No explanation she could give.

"Red?" he asked into her silence. His body tensed. Lox removed his leg from between hers but didn't step back further. "Did I—" He cursed under his breath. Lox tilted his head downward until she made eye contact and whispered, tone genuine, "I'm sorry for scaring you—"

"It's not that." Raven swallowed, throat tight.

"Then, what…" Confusion marred his expression.

Everything inside her screamed not to speak, but if she had any hope of leaving Ecanta, she needed him to trust her. Maybe wanted it a little herself, too. "I'm—I'm just…" *Alone.* She gasped in a breath, stilling her voice. "You have your band. I don't."

Loxley's eyes widened, so much that she regretted speaking. She tried to move sideways out from his form but he shifted, placing his hand on her forearm—her cloak was still behind her. "I used to do this alone, too. We all did, that's why we formed our band. You're not alone now."

But I still am.

Even if they executed this plan together, escaped together, she would still leave to be the forgotten, dead princess. To survive in a foreign land, veiled in secrets for the rest of her life.

This moment couldn't repeat. She couldn't… This wouldn't work. Because she'd only be with him for a small time.

Raven took a breath and straightened, hardening herself into the Red Hood. "You can move now."

He smiled, almost in a *there's my girl* way. "Are you sure?"

She glared.

Loxley studied her a moment and finally retreated, heading back to the wall. He placed his hand on the stone to climb, then turned to her. "I'll go with my band. Just keep safe."

And he was gone.

He'd agreed. She might be able to pull this off.

Was that because of their kiss? No… this felt different. Genuine.

Raven crept through the shadows toward the path to the castle, hiding amongst the trees. When she reached her passageway, she paused and glanced out to the village. Did that mean he trusted her?

CHAPTER 21

Double doors loomed over Cindy as she stood next to Ravenna. A real ball. She was about to enter the ballroom with the princess, her friend. She still could hardly believe she was standing there in the castle, in a gown, and her father hadn't stopped her this morning when Raven had approached.

They stood at the entrance to the throne-room-turned-ballroom. From the other side of the double doors, the announcer proclaimed, "Queen Vanera!"

Cindy reached up to pull a lock of hair forward.

"Stop fussing," Raven said, "you look gorgeous." She placed Cindy's hands at her side and tucked her hair back in place. The soft curls fell loose past her shoulders, the flowered ribbon resting atop her head—and the bruise merely a small shadow on her cheek. "It's covered perfectly, I can't even tell."

Her fingers smoothed the dress Raven had picked for her to borrow tonight. The dark sapphire bodice's neckline reached to her neck where a thin collar encircled, leaving her shoulders bare. The sides of the bodice sloped under her arms, the back resting just under her shoulder blades. Her collarbones protruded from the sides of the high bodice, emphasizing her curves with some modesty. Cindy felt exposed, yet tightly covered at the same time. The skirt's slight flare showed her hips. Easy folds flowed to the floor, silver jewels sown in with white thread creating a delicate swirling pattern. She felt like the night sky or what she thought the reflection on a lake might look like.

Both doors swung wide, and Raven stepped through, Cindy easing to the corner behind a butler and a guard.

"Princess Ravenna!"

Raven stepped forward, facing a crowd that filled—*filled*—the room. It was more people than Cindy had imagined. The villagers and nobles alike cheered for their princess, who smiled, curtsied, waved.

The doors parted again, and the girls turned to head behind the crowd. People greeted and smiled at them as they passed, mostly toward Ravenna.

"Mira Glass!"

A moderately tall woman strode onto the raised dais that they'd just left at the door. She waved and winked at the crowd, a jubilant confidence Cindy had never seen on another. This was the Rova she'd seen a glimpse of on rare and unpredictable occasions in the market from afar. A dark purple shimmying dress displayed all her curves and most of her cleavage as she descended the dais. The Rova's dark curls were pinned up and back, some falling gracefully around her fac, with a large amount caressing her bare back.

She turned and walked over to them, making Cindy's heart leap.

Mira Glass hugged Ravenna. Her gaze traveled over Cindy's dress and face. Lavender eyes stopped on Cindy's, and the color startled her.

"Oh," Mira exclaimed. "You look beautiful, dear. You remind me of someone…" She fingered a strand of Cindy's hair, then dropped it. "Have fun tonight!"

Cindy couldn't stop seeing the purple irises, couldn't stop staring after the Rova. "Her eyes," she said breathless, tone hollow. "They were purple."

Raven chucked lightly. "Yes, they were. She's a Rova fortune teller. I believe she said the magic she sees colored them."

Music played around them, an upbeat melody. Cindy nodded blankly, unable to shake the shock of those eyes. They'd seemed to pull her in, to freeze her, to… No. She knew she'd never seen Mira up close, so she couldn't have seen those swirling purple eyes before.

Raven tugged her hand, breaking Cindy's stupor, and brought her onto the dance floor, saying, "Mira probably requested this one. She knows how to start a party."

The two girls danced, swirling across the floor, spinning in circles, Cindy laughing and smiling easily. It warmed her heart and actually made her happy. She truly couldn't remember the last time she'd felt this way. Happy. Carefree. Cindy followed Raven's lead with steps and turns. They almost bumped into a few couples and more than one group of girls.

Three songs and too many feet stepped on later, they broke off from the dancing crowd and rested on the edge of the room, catching their breath.

Cindy brushed some curls from her eyes and sighed. "I honestly didn't think I knew how to dance."

Raven laughed and leaned against the wall.

Looking away from her friend, Cindy realized that most of the crowd was staring their way. Smiles lit their faces, but she still felt nervousness creep in at the stares.

"Ravenna," came a voice from her left.

Beside her, Raven straightened instantly. "Yes, Mother?"

Cindy jolted. The queen was intimidating in her own right, as a queen should be. Her posture, the crown, her voice. It all caused spikes of cold to fill her. Even with her smiles earlier when she'd seen them together and instructed Raven to find a proper dress to fit her, Queen Vanera had still scared her a little.

The queen smiled, a kindness to her eyes. "It seems you're having fun?"

Raven nodded, a stiffness to the action.

Queen Vanera looked from her daughter to Cindy. Her stare remained on Cindy. "Pardon me, but... Cindy... you live in the village?" she asked, brows crinkling.

"Y-yes, Your Majesty." Cindy curtsied, swallowing her unease. It was like the queen was searching for something within her. "I work in the bakery."

Queen Vanera's navy eyes hardened. A new fear struck Cindy at the change. This was the queen, not the mother and kindness she'd shown to Ravenna.

Vanera stepped back, though it didn't seem intentional. She shook her head, whispering something Cindy couldn't quite catch, then her gaze flickered between Raven and Cindy. The queen's mouth opened, then closed. Then, she blinked and the composed surface of Queen Vanera returned.

"Excuse me," the queen said, dipping her head slightly, "I must attend to things."

Cindy blinked in the silence that followed. What was that?

She turned to Raven—who was staring after her mother. A long stare, marred by sadness. Was this how they were? She only saw Raven in the market by herself. Not with her mother. Grief could be a terrible thing to overcome. Cindy placed her hand on Raven's.

Raven jumped, but a polite smile rose instantly when she looked at Cindy.

"It must be hard," Cindy said, "being just the two of you."

The princess's smile faltered. A deeper sadness seemed to enter her expression, just under the surface. Cindy was good at seeing what was just hidden.

A young man in a dark blue suit approached them, cutting off further talk. The handsome prince she'd seen Ravenna with a few days ago in the market. Dark blond locks flowed around his sea-glass eyes. Warmth rose to Cindy's cheeks.

Raven curtsied. He bowed back.

"Hello, Princess Ravenna and..." he paused, eyes on Cindy. He extended his hand.

She hesitantly gave hers.

Polite.

She hoped the bruise had faded enough.

Why was Raven smiling like that? Wait, he was waiting for her name.

"C-Cindy," she answered quickly. She tried to ignore the heat building hotter on her face. Maybe that would block out the mark.

"Ah, Cindy." He bent to kiss her hand smoothly, all the decorum of a royal, and properly released it afterward. "I am Prince Finn of Ocara. And you are from Ecanta?"

Ocara? With the sea-side traders and... *ocean*? Who Father threatened to sell her to?

Cindy blinked. "Yes. I live in the village."

Finn motioned to the wide windows. "You must love it here. The forests are magnificent."

She nodded. She was overly aware of her curls bouncing around. *Stars above, get it together.* "Do you have any forests there?"

"Some." He shook his head. "But they are thin and only at the far borders to yours and Fovet's kingdom. Nothing like this beauty."

He stared only at her as he said the last sentence.

Cindy swallowed and glanced at Raven, who seemed to be biting her cheek to hide a smile, then out to the crowd. *Deep breaths, cool your face down, Cindy. Just—*

A dark figure walked briskly by the edge of the dancefloor. Kieran—dressed in his black naval coat, buttons shining as bright as his silver rings. Underneath he wore an indigo shirt reminiscent of Cindy's own dress. The thought of the similarity felt absurd and also not.

His mix-matched eyes flitted from face to face, the predatory alertness that the guards had. He glanced their way briefly, then flashed back.

Blue and green eyes shifted to her and held. Cindy's heart stilted. Then, his gaze moved to Raven and Finn. Kieran paused.

Cindy lifted her hand and gave a small wave. A hesitant smile.

Tonight was the night for friendship and fun.

Kieran's eyes traveled down her dress and back up her slight frame. He stepped toward their group.

Why did the heat in her cheeks turn to fire? And *spread.*

Black locks fell away from his face, swept back in waves that accented the harshness of his features.

"Good evening," Finn said, stiffly inclining his head toward the other prince. Not as easily polite with Kieran as with everyone else.

Kieran grunted noncommittally.

Finn cleared his throat.

"Ocara…" Cindy said slowly, looking up at Finn. "That's on the ocean, right?"

"It is."

She'd heard it was vast and like an endless lake. "I've never been to the sea."

Raven tilted her head. "Neither have I."

Cindy had almost forgotten her friend stood beside her with these two young men and their apparent discomfort with each other.

181

Finn smiled. "You'd both love it."

She rose her gaze to Kieran, the obvious sailor of the sea. "What's it like?"

His blue-green eyes widened at the question directed at him. He rubbed the ringed knuckles of his right hand thoughtfully with his left. "Each day, it differs. Calm, raging, spirited. But it's always beautiful, *powerful*—and you're at its mercy."

Chills ran down Cindy's spine. She could *almost* picture this chancing body of water. Was it big enough to be all of those things at once in different areas? "That sounds..." she said, awe in her soft voice, "magical."

Kieran raised a dark brow.

Finn shifted his jacket. He gestured to both girls, pulling Cindy out of her thoughts. "Perhaps a visit to Ocara could be arranged sometime?"

Ice chilled Cindy through, slow at first. Ocara was cemented in her mind as a threat from her father. Yes, she might visit, but not free. She looked into the crowd. Father would never let her leave Ilasia, let alone travel out of Ecanta. The only way she'd visit Ocara was if he followed through and sold her to their traders.

Her gaze caught on Raven, who seemed to be frozen in a polite smile. Raven blinked and seemed to thaw. She nodded. "Maybe."

Cindy pressed her lips together and straightened, grip tightening on her dress. "Yes, that—" Cindy smiled, "that would be great."

Another song started, and couples moved to and from the dance floor. The jaunty tone brought a lightness to the group again. Finn turned to the girls, extending a slender hand. "Anyone care for a dance?"

Raven bumped Cindy's shoulder and said, "With an actual partner?"

Her light brows rose. That damned warmth rose to her cheeks again, too. Cindy glanced between them all. Raven smiled broadly. Kieran stared at Finn's hand, then looked at the windows. Finn leaned down for a small bow. Cindy hesitantly placed her hand in his.

"This might not go well," she warned the prince.

Finn laughed lightly as he led her onto the floor. "It will go as well as we want it to. No pressure. Just fun."

Fun.

She turned to him. He touched her waist, and she couldn't stifle the jump.

He smiled softly and eased his hand back. Finn moved them left and right, back and forward, in a light rhythm.

The motions started to calm her nerves, and Cindy smiled.

"How are you enjoying the ball?" he asked.

The lights, the music, the sounds of laughter and chatter. Nothing like her home, nothing like what she felt inside when she was home. No pressure. Just fun.

"It's the best night I've ever had."

Truly, it was.

She couldn't wait to spend more days with Raven, if this was the brightness it brought.

RAVEN WONDERED WHAT WOULD HAPPEN TO CINDY AFTER SHE WAS GONE. How long would it take the baker to realize the Red Hood was gone as well? All she could hope was that her and Kieran's warnings had stuck.

The irate prince watched Cindy and Finn dance silently. He nodded to Raven, then departed, leaving the princess to watch the happy crowd while her heart broke. Alone.

She spared a glance at him as he left. He was definitely a pirate from his description of the ocean. Soon, she'd see the ocean. She'd see so much more than she'd ever thought. Things she'd never thought of seeing before.

None of that brought her solace over this next course.

She always felt so alone. But not more so than now.

Through the crowd of dancers and onlookers, nobles and villagers, Ruben stood with his wife. Esme held their daughter, raising her to Rue's face. He smiled down at her. They swayed to the music lightly, a slow bounce with their infant between them.

A sad smile rose to Raven's lips. She'd never see that child grow up. Never see Rue and Esme grow with their little one. Or if they had more children. Her eyes burned, and she refused to blink.

Leaving was just as hard as if her mother *had* killed her.

Raven forced herself to look at her mother. Queen Vanera sat on her silver throne, observing the festivities. As if she didn't believe it was her daughter's last day alive. She had *chosen* after the ball. *Did she want some sort of good day for me?* Raven sighed. The complexities of her mother confused her.

She recalled her almost *happy* tone when she'd seen Raven bring Cindy to pick out a dress. Then, the reaction again on the dance floor. Was that her mother being excited that she had made a friend, then remembering this was to be her last day?

Her tortured mother had flashed through at that moment.

"Don't be mistaken, I do love her. But not enough."

Why was this so hard? She took a deep, shaky breath.

"Milady," a deep voice said. The young man took her hand before she could compose herself to look over. Something about his grip felt familiar. *No one's* grip should be familiar.

Raven turned and looked up into dark green eyes.

Last night flooded her mind. The wall, the heat, the *kiss*—him everywhere. Warmth coated her cheeks, flushing throughout her body at the memory, and stars above, she hoped he couldn't tell.

What the hell?

Lox smiled. His neatly combed dark locks feathered outward, a tan shirt tucked into trousers. Mischief danced in his eyes. "Would you care to dance?"

She huffed out a disbelieving laugh. No, she would *not*. He was going to get himself killed. Why did Lox never listen?

Though the thought of him pressed against her again—*no*. Raven blinked and forced another polite smile. "Why are you here?"

He shrugged. "You invited the whole village, Your Highness. While I'm here, I'm technically part of the village."

"Technicality," she stated mildly, mimicking their conversation at the competition.

"So?" Lox smiled and raised his hand again. "A dance?"

Her gaze roamed the ball, checking the guards. Found Ruben's hard stare on Lox. She swallowed. This was bad.

"Don't like dancing with a thief, Princess?" Lox asked, hardness to the light words.

Raven looked at him and hated the hurt hiding underneath his charm. "Maybe I just don't like *you*," she quipped with a small smile. "But yes. One dance."

His eyes softened, mischievous spark returning.

If she turned him down, that would bring more attention. This could be a quick dance.

Hard footsteps hit the floor in a steady rhythm. Raven knew it was Ruben without turning around. She should have just danced with him when he'd first asked. Damn it. Too slow.

Ruben's heavy and usually reassuring presence stopped behind her. She withheld a sigh at their circumstances having changed so drastically in just a few days' time and looked up at his tense face.

"Do we have a problem here, Princess Ravenna?" Ruben stared only at Lox when he asked the question.

"No, we do not." Her heart beat in her ears, almost drowning out the lively music.

Ruben turned to her, and she smiled to ease his tension.

"I do believe," Lox said, turning her smile stiff as she stared at him, "my prize for winning the competition is a dance with the princess." He gestured to Ravenna.

Ruben gritted his teeth.

Lox leaned forward. "Or was that only if one of the princes won?"

He was *so* lucky she couldn't use a knife at that moment. Fire rose within her, and she stepped forward carefully to try to dampen her anger. Raven smiled tightly. "I already said I'd dance with you. I just don't like being called a *prize*."

She grasped his hand and turned toward the dance floor, acutely aware of his callused grip on hers. Catching Ruben's focused gaze, she quirked another smile. Hopefully, he believed her ire and tension was due to that and not Lox himself. More attention on Lox might kill him.

Lox matched her pace toward the floor, and she forced her movements to seem relaxed. The princess entering the dancing couples garnered attention, and she needed that to not bring a negative focus. Once through the majority of people and at the center of the marble floor, Lox tugged on her hand and pulled her toward him. A small gasp stuck in her throat when her hand rested on his chest and his touched her waist.

Instant heat flooded her.

Like his hand when she'd grasped it earlier, this touch was also familiar. It and the woodsy smell that engulfed her at his close proximity brought her back to last night—not just the kiss. The warmth, the loyalty he'd shown, the loneliness the moment he'd moved. Everything rose within her, throat tightening with too much at once.

Raven pulled back and glanced up at him. "Don't press your luck, th —Lox."

Damn.

He was confusing her, throwing off the whole night.

"If I didn't, I'd never be here." Lox squeezed her waist, tugging her close again. His warmth felt solid and comforting, despite the fear in her veins. Her nerves swam because this was wrong, treacherous for him. He wasn't protecting her now, he was endangering himself.

The music swirled and rose, dipped. She couldn't remember the last time she'd danced before tonight. Lox was easy on his feet with dancing as well as sneaking, it seemed. He led her around the couples and groups, never letting her stumble or touch anyone else. She found herself having to keep up with his footwork, sliding gently but deftly with the notes and turns. Something lively swept over her, bringing a surge of looseness and excitement.

She glanced up at Lox and found something similar dancing in his eyes. They turned, and she spotted Ruben again on the side of the crowd. His brows were low but not angry. Almost confused. Raven realized she was smiling.

What was wrong with her? How did this thief constantly disrupt her plans and her thoughts? Make her change course without even realizing it sometimes.

Gods, how had one kiss—one breathless kiss—invoked such a war in her?

They slowed as the music fell. The second the last note played, Raven stepped back far enough to knock his hand off and curtsied curtly.

"Thank you." She dipped her head politely. "I—"

A trumpet sounded two quick blasts, drawing the crowd's attention to Queen Vanera standing before her throne.

"Good evening." The queen smiled softly, but it unsettled Ravenna. "As you all know, Ecanta has had its fair share of casualties and fore-sights this season. And, honestly, the last." The crowd mumbled agree-ments. "But I hope to remedy that tonight."

Queen Vanera gestured beside her to a tall and older gentleman with a rose gold crown weaving like thorns into his golden hair. "This is King

Siran of Ocara, and we have come to an agreement. From this night on, my daughter, Princess Ravenna, and his son, Prince Finn..." she looked to Raven, an unreadable expression filling her gaze, "are betrothed."

The crowd erupted into excitement and surprised glee. Their princess was getting married.

But she wasn't.

She was dying.

Ruben had moved to stand at Vanera's left, and his calm face *should've* brought her peace. Her throat clenched. He looked so hopeful.

What is Mother thinking? Why even allow such a promise when she knew her daughter would die the next day?

Raven kept her expression even and glanced at Loxley, still beside her. His eyes had widened. She hadn't known this would happen.

"Excuse me." Raven backed away, knowing she had to go to her mother, to stand in front of everyone, her last duty as Princess.

Just breathe. She took a small breath but couldn't manage more.

She squared her shoulders and watched Finn approach. She would do this last facade as their perfect princess.

She had to. Both for them and for herself.

CHAPTER 22

Loxley watched Princess Ravenna take the blond prince's offered arm. Watched her walk up the steps to the thrones together and face the crowd. He remembered her entering the ballroom. The way that deep green dress shone in the candlelight, the way she looked like the forest embodied. She'd stolen his breath then, and for an entirely different reason, it was tight now as well.

Betrothed?

The word shouldn't hurt him as much as it did. It's not like he didn't know she was far from reach. He still wasn't entirely sure why he'd still come today, not after last night with Red. They'd parted with an uncertainty after the kiss—something had changed in her afterward. He wasn't sure how she felt about him. During the kiss, bloody hell, he'd known for sure what she felt. After? No idea.

Something had tugged him to attend the ball. Now, he was glad he'd come if just to learn of this.

Was this betrothal why there was a hit on the princess? To stop the uniting of kingdoms, for jilted love, or was it to keep the kingdom starving as the queen had alluded to? He stared at the queen, standing to the side of the golden throne, smiling at the princess as she stepped onto the dais. She hugged her daughter, whose face still held that smile but seemed nervous. Upcoming nuptials could do that. That Head Guard who used to always follow her was the happiest of all those glimmering on that small stage.

He should have reminded himself of her title more. Maybe he wouldn't be this hurt if he had.

King, Queen, Prince, Princess, all up there joyful and making a wedding a business transaction for more power. Those happy smiles, those marriages arranged for profit. Surely, not of the people, of the royals. For power. Lox hated it.

The other prince stood along the sidelines, that pirate too tall to blend in with the brightly colored crowd of villagers. Lox couldn't help but think of the redheaded prince who'd threatened Princess Ravenna. He was the only malevolent person he'd isolated against her.

Lox sighed as Ravenna turned to the blond prince. Did it even matter at this point?

The prince took Ravenna's hand, covering it with his own, and looked into her eyes. "I promise to honor you and treat you with kindness, my princess."

His voice was not harsh and arrogant as that redhead. He seemed nicer. A little like how Ravenna appeared with her villagers. Lox couldn't look away from her and her betrothed. The girl who didn't know she'd be gone and never actually married to the young man making vows to her this moment.

Princess Ravenna placed her other hand on top of his. "I promise to honor you and treat you with respect," she took a breath, "my prince."

Another smile. Tighter, if Lox admitted from his practice this week of staring at her from a distance.

Maybe not all that happy about the arrangement.

Loxley forced himself to look away. It did *not* matter. Tomorrow, she'd be with his band and on the run. No more gilded life for the princess. It would be dirt and tents and forests and running. No crowns and thrones and marble floors. He stared at the dais, a different sort of anger brewing the longer he looked at this throne room. The table of food and drinks on the side with guards posted around.

They knew their townsfolk were hungry, thieving for food, and did nothing.

Not caring about others, not their villagers, not their helpers or guards.

He took a deep breath. Except for her. Ravenna gave them food.

Was she the best part of this damned kingdom's structure? And she was being forced out.

The four royals turned to the crowd, waved and smiled.

The bright lights and sounds of laughter as the *betrothed* couple descended the dais was starting to give him a headache. Maybe that was his jaw clenching.

Lox skirted to the edge of the room and headed for the balcony doors. He couldn't stand to be around this happiness right now. He needed air. And to calm himself down.

To be away from this party for the rich and powerful becoming more rich and powerful.

It stole his breath and threw him back too many years in his mind.

Stars be damned, he needed air.

RAVENNA COULDN'T BREATHE—SHE COULD *NEVER* SEEM TO BREATHE anymore—the whole night was overwhelming. The room spun. Why did it spin?

Finn offered his hand for her to descend to the dance floor with him. Raven smiled politely, as was habit. As expected.

Cindy appeared, clapping and hugging her tightly—no, too tightly.

Finn and Cindy talked, their voices buzzing in the background as Raven stared around.

"Of course," Finn said, his soft voice floating into her consciousness, "as long as my betrothed is okay with that?"

He was speaking to her. His betrothed. It took Raven a few seconds to respond to being called someone's betrothed. Five days ago, she would've been perfectly fine with the arrangement. Today, it seemed pointless. "Oh—yes." She smiled politely, no idea what they talked about. Clearing her throat, she motioned to the table of drinks and food. "I'll be right back."

Raven headed for the wall, but at the last second turned. She slipped onto the balcony and rushed to the stone railing. She tried desperately to find air, but only shallow gasps came. Her mother knew this was her last night alive and had treated her kindly, so unusually kindly.

Why was her mother being so nice to her? Pretending she had a future—not just beyond tomorrow, but a whole life with a man to marry and start a family with? Why was she giving her hope?

Why did she want her dead?

Raven almost felt bad for her mother—if she hadn't ordered the kill. *Why am I not good enough?*

"Ravenna?" Ruben asked, worry deepening his voice behind her.

Again, she tried to find any, *any,* air just to smooth her composure but found barely a breath. She forced a smile and faced him. But after ten years, he knew her too well. Her Head Guard and best friend took three large steps and reached out to rub her arms with his gloved hands.

"What's wrong?"

Raven opened her mouth, then shut it when no good lie came.

Worry creased his brow. "Was it that Lox you danced with, the newcomer? If he's upset you—" When she shook her head quickly Ruben took a new track, tone turning earnest. "Is there something going on with him?"

Raven let out a puff of shocked air, hating that something *had* happened with Lox. Just not what he thought. "No. You know I wouldn't risk the betrothal like that—"

"No," Ruben interrupted. He grasped her hand. "But I know love can come out of nowhere."

Love? She was far from any love.

Ruben smiled and pointed to the throne room. "Esme blindsided me. I was hopeless, remember?"

She did. He couldn't take his eyes off Esme the first day he saw her. Raven smiled, despite the burn in the back of her throat and eyes. "I tripped you because you were in *such* a daze. And she laughed so hard."

Her smile faded. She'd never have times like that again. Never see him, joke with him, or see his little one grow up. "Just… give me a few minutes, then dance with me, alright?" She raised her brows.

His descended. "Raven—"

"I don't care," she spat, "about *protocol* or properness or… or rules. One dance. Please, Rue, I want one good night."

Ruben pressed his lips together in debate. His gaze roamed her face before he nodded. He pulled her into a hug that about broke her control.

She squeezed her eyes tight to hold off the tears. "You've grown so strong, Raven."

"I don't feel strong."

He cupped her face and stooped to peer into her eyes. "Are you sure you're alright?"

Raven nodded.

"If something's wrong, you tell me, alright? Anything, and I'll fix it." His thumb stroked her cheek. "I'd die for you, you know that?"

"It is in your job description, but let's steer away from that," she teased, then sobered. She was doing this so he wouldn't be in danger. He'd hurt, but he'd be alive and keep his position. "I'd do the same for you, Rue."

He stiffened. "I'll never let that happen."

Heart breaking for what she would do to him tomorrow, she pulled away without comment. Raven jerked her chin at the door.

Ruben patted her shoulder once, then turned to reenter the ball.

"Ruben." When he looked back, she gave him a sad smile. She tried to strengthen it into something that showed how much he meant to her. "I love you."

He tilted his head slightly, considering her words. "I love you, too, Raven." Heavy footsteps faded into the sounds of the ball, and when the door shut, she stared through the glass at his morphed shape. Tears prickled her eyes.

Another breath hitched because she knew she wouldn't see him the next day. And he'd blame himself so hard after she was gone. Her voice shook as she whispered into the night, "I'm so sorry."

A tear escaped, and she turned to the railing. She laid her elbows on the cold stone, burying her face in her palms.

Why was there no *air* on this damned balcony?

The wind stopped blowing on her, and she looked up—Loxley. Startled, she stepped back, then remembered her tear and tried to erase it without him noticing. Then, she realized the door hadn't opened again— had he been there the whole time? "Did you—" Her gaze flew to the door Ruben had exited barely a minute before.

Lox held her stare a moment. He extended a hand, offering a handkerchief. It stunned her.

He didn't confirm or deny overhearing. But did she want the truth?

Raven let out a deep sigh.

She reminded herself that she was a princess, not a criminal to him. Stars be damned, she'd be relieved not to remember who she was at which moment anymore around Lox. To just be herself—the princess *and* the Red Hood. Raven. Just Raven.

"Come on, that prince probably isn't that bad," Lox joked, quirking a smile.

She took his handkerchief, ignoring his comment and dabbing her eye quickly, because she couldn't tell him the truth any better than Ruben. The vulnerability from last night was hard enough, on multiple fronts, and this would be worse.

Loxley stepped forward, drawing her gaze from the cloth. His eyes watched hers steadily, that honest quality back. Her heartbeat quickened. When he spoke, his tone was gentle, "Are you okay?"

She wanted to laugh. Wanted to cry—to throw her dagger, to scream. "Why do you care?" Her tone wasn't angry, just… there.

She knew he liked the Red Hood, but the princess?

Loxley leaned in, plucked his handkerchief from her hands and stuffed it in his pocket. "I'm a nice guy."

"I thought you were a criminal?"

He grinned. "Ouch." He moved around her and leaned against the stone railing, elbows resting easily behind him. "But to be fair, I did pickpocket you."

"Tried to."

"No—I *did* pickpocket. You just did it first." Lox tipped his head. Moonlight shone, brightening his eyes. "And it seems my apologies are in order."

Raven raised a brow. Him, apologizing?

"You could've arrested me."

"I did the same to you," she replied, resting against the balcony's railing to keep an eye on the entrance. Despite what she'd told Ruben, if he found Lox secluded with her, he'd rip the thief apart. And that was without knowing they'd kissed.

Loxley's brow furrowed, but his smile erased the expression. "Still. My gratitude, Your Highness."

Raven let out a small breath, glad she'd found her air again. Right then, she didn't know what she wanted more—to be Princess Ravenna or not. Out there in the throne room with her mother, and Finn, and the pain she'd cause Ruben, *everyone*, and expectations that she could never live up to—that she wasn't even expected to by her mother—it all suffocated her. But out here with Loxley…

This thief was the only person she could trust. The only person who'd helped her not because she was a princess, or beautiful, or kind… but because of who she was.

In her silence, Lox moved closer, his warmth keeping her from shivering in the cool night air. She usually wore her cloak outside, now her bare shoulders froze. The memory of his hand on her shoulder last night, even with the tunic separating them, made her crave for him to touch her now. Staring up at him, Raven had to fight the building heat in her stomach.

One olive hand rested on the stone beside hers, half of his body leaning over hers. Not quite touching, but *almost*.

"I really like this green on you. You know…" Lox looked her up and down, that fire returning and moving with his slow gaze, "green is my color."

She rolled her eyes and glanced away, trying to focus on anything but his voice. The whispers he'd made on her skin before.

Why was she letting him close? As the Red Hood was one thing, but as Princess Ravenna? It was one kiss, and now she could hardly pay attention when he was near.

Maybe because it was her last night as herself, and she just wanted to not be afraid of someone being *close*. Her mother's nearness repulsed her. Her guards made her feel trapped. Ruben broke her heart. The townsfolk made her feel fake and guilty.

Loxley made her feel strong. And… protected. Not like Ruben and her guards used to, like she should stand back and watch the fight, but like he would be her back up if things went wrong.

"If we're caught together, we'll escape together."

"You look cold." Lox's leg brushed hers through the folds of her skirt, and he whispered in her ear, "I could keep you warm, Princess."

Stars above, she knew he could. He was a flame, and she a match. Once struck, she felt like she'd burn quicker the next time. Raven took a calming breath, tearing her focus away from his thigh on hers.

Beneath the building fire, a twinge of annoyance prickled. He'd just kissed her last night—the Red Hood her. And now he flirted with Princess Ravenna? Had their kiss meant nothing? It hadn't felt like it, but she was inexperienced. He definitely was not. Did she even want it to mean something? "Is that all you think about?"

He chuckled, his breath caressing her skin. Loxley paused inches from her face. His expression went from smoldering to pondering. Then, the focused on her amber eyes, staring deeply. After a long moment, he pulled back. She didn't know what, but he saw something.

Loxley removed his arm from the railing and stepped toward her, making her straighten. "You're beautiful, Princess, but I've got my eye set on another woman. No offense."

"None taken," she replied. Did he mean the Red Hood? Had the kiss —she tore that thought off quickly. Though… he *had* said he liked her…

That paused her thoughts. Would he really choose the Red Hood, someone he considered a criminal, a person whose face he'd never fully seen… over a princess? He'd choose *that* part of her—

"Are you feeling better?"

His question surprised her. A stark difference from his flirtations.

Raven took a deep breath and realized she *was* better. Getting distance from the ball and her mother had righted her. "Yes, I believe so."

Loxley stepped aside and swept his hand to the balcony doors. "Then, you should rejoin your friends."

She let out a small laugh and started toward the door. She paused, hand on the knob, Loxley at her side. She *did* have friends now. For one last night.

CHAPTER 23

Basket in hand and guards at her side, Raven walked through the castle gates. A looser dress concealed her tunic and trousers. Breakfast with a silent Queen Vanera, chipper Mira, and smiling Finn had shaken her resolve. But smiling and waving to Ruben like it wasn't the last time she'd ever see him—that had crushed her. She took a solid breath and blinked to dispel her shattering heart.

They started down the path, and from upon the hill, she could see the bustling marketplace. Raven's chest ached. She couldn't do this, couldn't see all of them—her villagers, her friends, her townsfolk—just to disappear moments later.

"I feel like picking flowers this morning," she said to her guards, voice hollow. Raven turned into the forest. It was best to leave everyone with a memory of her at the ball, not visiting them the morning she died.

Bending to pick flowers every few steps, Raven wound through the trees. The guards glanced away, distracted as all recruits were, and she slipped into the denser trees. Once a good amount of space rested between them, she hurried to the tree hollow and removed her satchel. Within moments she'd latched her cloak, pulling up her hood. Warmth swept over her face, swirling down her figure, the magic a comfort more now than ever.

"Princess?" called one recruit quietly. Still casual, not worried. Rustling sounded. "Princess Ravenna?"

Raven pulled her headband free and placed it on a tree branch. Walking deeper into the forest, she ripped pieces of fabric from her dress, leaving a hurried trail. Their worry would spark soon, then panic when they found her headband. The strips of fabric would solidify their worst fears—the princess was kidnapped.

The guards' armor clanked quickly, searching.

Raven ran in the opposite direction, toward the north edge of the forest. Toward the river.

Almost one mile later, Raven stopped to catch her breath and her thoughts. Lox had agreed to let the Red Hood stay behind and him take the princess, but she hoped he didn't expect for the Red Hood to deliver her. While she stuffed her cloak into her satchel, Raven pondered her plan. Ruffling up her hair and adding a leaf, she took a breath and ran.

Raven looked over her shoulder with a panicked expression and pretended to run with fear, not bothering to silence her steps. The river came into view, and she slowed, staring curiously and confused at the water, and turned to face where she'd come. Backing toward the river she spun around, widening her eyes to feign fear.

Loxley stepped out from behind the trees, and she stopped. With a small smile, he said, "Your Highness."

"You!" She took a step back.

He raised a brow and rushed forward to grab her arms. Firm hands held her in place, and she fought with medium effort. Lox gripped tighter, tensing for a strike. "Going for a stroll?" He looked around into the trees, and his tone deepened. "Alone?"

"No," she spat, pushing against his chest, "I was attacked."

"Really?"

"Yes. By the Red Hood. Now—"

"And where *is* the Red Hood?" Loxley's tone rose, and he stared into her gaze.

"I don't know." *Please don't make this more difficult.*

He investigated the trees again, cocking his ear, then turned back to her. The intensity of his stare stole her breath. "Where?"

Raven shook her head, the leaf dislodging from her hair. "I told you— I don't know. Now will you please help me."

197

"Haven't figured it out yet, Princess?" Loxley chuckled and pulled her toward the river. "I thought you were smarter than this."

Raven wanted to hit him, but she had to play her part. "Figured out what?" she ground out through her teeth.

He simply sat on the log he'd perched on days ago when he'd talked about how he couldn't fathom someone wanting her killed. And he now insulted her. "Sit, Princess."

She ignored his pat on the wood. Why was he taking time to *sit?* The guards would search wider soon—they had to leave! "No. Tell me what's going on!"

When he stared out at the forest, she turned and sprinted. She'd get him to move somehow.

"Hey!" A curse and footfalls followed her, and his speed surprised her. Loxley all but tackled her, grabbing her by the waist. He swung her around with their momentum, making her gasp. Pinning her arms to her sides, Lox squeezed tight and pulled something from his pockets. "Now why did you think that was a good idea?"

He switched his grip to one arm and wrapped a rope around her.

Raven squirmed, but his strength outmatched hers. How was he so strong? "What are you—Stop!"

"If you run, you get tied up." Loxley knotted the rope at her side, where she couldn't reach. Then, he tugged her over to the log and pulled her down onto it.

Did he really just *bind* a princess?

Pent up frustration pounded in her temple. They didn't have much time. She needed to get him to move on with the plan. How could she get him to move?

"Return me to my guards," she ordered.

"It's not safe, Princess."

"What do you mean it isn't safe?"

Loxley sighed, a deep breath that touched her dress. "Look, just believe me. You're safer with me."

Raven narrowed her gaze. "Being *bound*, I'm hesitant to believe you."

His jaw clenched, and he rubbed a hand over his mouth.

"Well?"

Lox's green eyes sharpened on hers. "You really want to know?"

Raven shot him a look.

His nails dug into his hair. "You need to remain calm," he started, raising his hands, earning a glare from her, "but I'm saving you."

"From what?"

"From someone who wants you dead."

What would she have said five days ago? She widened her eyes. "No —no one would—"

"Someone did. They paid for your death."

Shaking her head, she made her voice shake. "But... who?"

Lox shrugged, staring into the forest. "I don't know."

Raven paused, considering her next move. How to remind him of the urgency? "And you're working with the Red Hood?"

"Yes." He nodded sternly. "And we're not leaving without her."

She glazed over the 'her' part. "If someone wants me dead, shouldn't we tell my guards?"

He shook his head. "No. The person will hire another. We're faking your death so you can escape."

"We should run then!"

"Not without my partner. I need to make sure she's safe."

His words—his determined tone—halted hers. *Focus.* "She's a criminal!" The admission burned, but if it would make him *leave*...

"Who just saved your life!" Loxley almost shouted back. He took a breath. "Once I know she's okay, we'll leave."

"And if she's not? What are y—"

Lox turned, a fiery loyalty shining in his narrowed eyes. "Then, I'll help her."

Raven was speechless. Why did he... care? Really and truly *care?* This felt beyond a kiss... this felt—

Bugles sounded.

They both looked toward the castle.

The guards had begun pooling together. They'd found her trail, realized she'd been taken. Loxley didn't have much time. And the Red Hood wasn't coming.

"That's my guard," Raven pressed, desperate now. "They'll catch you and bring me home, you'll see."

No answer.

"The Red Hood probably left without you. After all, you're a criminal."

Loxley sighed and stood but ran his fingers through his hair. His eyes searched the tree line with a fierce determination.

Just give up, please.

He really wouldn't leave. He was… worried. About *her*. Not Princess Ravenna, but her darker half. Damn him. She sighed, and the bindings loosened. Just enough to move.

Fine, he could have the Red Hood. But he couldn't have the princess.

Raven took a deep, silent breath and let it out, pulling in her arms. The rope slipped down to her elbows, and she maneuvered her arms free. Inching over, she put the butt of her knife in her fist and whacked the back of his head. Loxley wavered and dropped. She caught him before he hit the ground. She couldn't risk two bangs to the head—she still had to follow him out of here.

After setting him down, she dashed into the trees and removed her dress for the tunic and trousers underneath. Raven tugged her hood firmly over her head and left her dress deep enough to remain unnoticed. Kneeling, she nudged him awake. "Lox—Loxley!"

His eyes shot open, and he blinked. They cleared on her face, then clouded again from the enchantment. "Red… The princess!" The relief she saw clenched her heart. Lox jolted to upright and looked around. "Where's the princess?"

"She's not here?" Raven asked, feigning confusion. "I sent her in your direction while I tidied up."

"No, she…" He rubbed the back of his head, rustling his dark hair. "I told her what happened, the plan, and she freaked out. Kept wanting to leave. But I…" Green eyes locked on her, and he shook his head. "I guess she knocked me out."

"Wow. Knocked out by a princess."

Loxley didn't return the smirk, but his gaze bored into her.

That fire returned with his stare, but worry undercoated the desire. She adjusted the cloak around her shoulders nervously. "Our princess is smart. She'll realize she needs to hide."

Raven investigated the forest. Now that he knew the Red Hood was safe, she could turn into the princess and—

A trumpet sounded. Closer, maybe sixty yards. Already in the forest.

"Lox, we won't be able to find her quickly." She spoke fast, planning, "The guards are already hunting. We should split up as a precaution."

He still stared, that serious look unnerving her. "I'm not leaving without you, Red."

Her heart raced in her chest, breath catching.

Stars be damned, he'd already made that abundantly clear. "Lox, we'll run, then search for the princess. Whoever finds her starts the pyre, then leaves. We'll meet up in two days. Okay?" She stood.

Loxley held her stare. "Really?" He stepped toward her. "You'd just let her go?"

"Yes." Raven dared a glance over her shoulder, dreading the sparkle of armor in sunlight. "Look, I appreciate you helping me, but we should go our own ways. Go and leave with your band—"

"No. Not after all this." His gaze hardened.

She stiffened. "After what? The kiss?" Raven faked a shrug, hoping he couldn't see the blush on her cheeks.

He shook his head. "Not just that. I can't leave you."

"Why not?" Her teeth ground, but his eyes sent a shiver down her spine. Why didn't he look away?

"You need someone to watch your back."

Was that a threat?

Loxley moved even closer. Her hand went to her knife and paused on the hilt. Raven didn't want to hurt him after he'd been willing to help both her selves. Hell, she didn't want to hurt him for many reasons. But staying meant dying, either as the Red Hood or Princess Ravenna.

Though his gaze rested on hers, she knew he'd noticed her movement. She'd have to be quick. *I'm sorry.*

Lox's hand whipped out, and she stepped forward, brandishing her knife. Instead of striking, his fingers closed around her hood, and too late, she realized her movement brought it down.

His gaze cleared, the magic broken, and remained on hers.

Her knife rested against his tan throat.

Tension sprung in her raised arm. Her blade the only thing touching him, she still felt heat off his body.

"I'll do it."

"I know you will, Princess."

They stood completely still, her blade against his throat, his hand gripping her hood at her neck. Close enough their breaths mixed.

Breathing hard, she stared, his reaction and words confusing her. "You knew?"

"I suspected."

Knife still poised, Raven stepped backward. Lox followed, trapping her against a tree, and raised a hand to rest on the bark beside her head. His muscled forearm inches from her head, she once again felt encompassed by Loxley. He leaned in, her steady knife pinching skin. "What are you going to do now?"

"I should be asking you that," she gasped out. This situation was vastly different from the last time he'd pinned her, but that damned fire still sparked and riled through her body. She hated her awareness of his legs on either side of hers, how she remembered the feel of his mouth on hers. She blinked hard. What would he think of her now? How long had he known?

"You know, when it was just helping a vigilante save the princess, I didn't fully ask myself this, but knowing it's you now..." Lox stared for a long moment. "Who could a princess fear in her ruling kingdom enough to leave?"

Her breath lodged in her throat, pulse beating firmly there as well.

"Who could *you* fear, Red?"

Something in his tone shifted from frustration to actual perplexity. Like he truly wanted and cared about the answer. A small breath fractured out of her. "I can't," she pleaded.

The wind blew past them, rustling her cloak, his hair, and that vulnerable portion of her.

His brows descended. Loxley's tone deepened as he said, "Was this all some trick so you could leave town? Be the vigilante instead of the princess?"

What? Her voice hardened, growing colder with each word, "No. I'm not some frivolous girl wanting freedom or an adventure—"

"You're not escaping your betrothal?"

"I was ready to do my duty!" The anger ran through her faster than she could control. She glared, gritting her teeth to stamp down the yell in her throat. "To marry *anyone* my mother needed me to, to serve my kingdom. I wanted to stay. But—" She broke off, pulling her knife back an inch.

But my mother wanted me dead.

I wanted to stay.

That thought fractured her all over again.

"But you were hired to kill yourself."

Raven swallowed, forcing herself not to look away, and whispered, "Yes."

Lox looked between her eyes and nodded lightly, easing back as well, taking the fire with him. "Good. I don't take liars into my band. We all have to trust each other." He brushed off his hands and turned. "Let's go."

She stepped forward, knife hanging loosely. "You're—you're still going to help me?"

He shrugged. "The princess is already 'dead.' The job is finished. You can't exactly stay. And I suspect you haven't been out of the city, so you can come with my band until you figure out what to do."

The princess in her wanted to thank him, but her pride wouldn't let her. Not with the coldness rolling off him, not with the confusion within her now. Instead, Raven nodded, sheathing her knife and following him toward the river. "Hold on," she said, and retrieved her dress.

Raising a brow, Loxley waved her on and ran through the trees. "The pyre is up ahead a half mile. Think you can run that, Princess?"

"Think you can keep up, thief?" Raven said, pulling up her hood and sprinting ahead of him.

BUGLE CALLS STILL RINGING WITHIN THE FOREST, RAVEN AND LOXLEY SLOWED to a jog in a small clearing. The thief dug in his pouch and procured a match. After striking the fire, he jostled the wood, revealing something slender and white and—Raven stepped back, a gasp on her lips.

Bones.

"What's that?" she asked, jerking a finger at the pile. Her breaths came in angry bursts.

Loxley glanced at the bones, then tossed some more kindling in the bottom of the pyre. "A body my men found."

"Why is it here?" Who was it? How had her villager died?

"It's here because," Loxley stirred the pile, embers flying into the afternoon sky, "a simple fire and dress won't prove anything. There has to be a body."

Raven swallowed. At least he hadn't died *for* her. His resting place would just be upended. Then again... a princess's burial was far better than wherever Lox's men had found this skeleton.

Another horn sounded far away. Raven squeezed her fists, they had to move. There wasn't time for this hesitancy. "The guards will expand their search soon."

"Is that all?"

Lox's tone surprised her. Hard, and so unlike him. He'd always been... soft toward her. Cavalier and flirtatious, especially after the kiss. Not... this. Had her secret changed that much?

His gaze held an icy hint when she met it. "Will your betrothed be looking for us, too?"

That word struck her and latched onto her focus.

"My..." *Finn.* Raven paused, that term still foreign and entirely useless now.

"Yes—prince, crown," his sarcastic tone faded, but that might have been her hearing.

"N-no... I don't think—" She stopped on a breath, as realization hit her.

Her betrothal. The *trade.* What would her mother do without it? Would Finn and his father honor the empty agreement Queen Vanera had knowingly struck and provide free food for a grieving kingdom? Finn had been caring, but Ocara was small, too.

Would Ecanta truly starve without her hand to give?

The fire crackled, and a charring bone tumbled lower in the pile of branches.

Raven stepped back, stumbling over a log.

Lox reached to steady her, but she tucked her arms in and gathered her balance blindly. His voice held less venom, maybe even concern. "Red?"

"We need that betrothal for Ecanta." The quiet words left her numb mouth like a bomb to her soul. Raven turned and glanced into the forest. "I can't do this."

She never should have gone this far. She should have talked to her mother, made a deal to appease her and the kingdom's needs. Let mother kill her, but after—*after*—securing trade, food for her people. That's what she'd do. She'd fix this.

She could still save her starving kingdom.

"What—Red!" Lox jolted around her, trying to grasp her arm, but she yanked it back.

Raven distanced herself from him and examined the forest. Which way was the castle? Which way was home?

The back of her eyes prickled, and she shut them hard.

"Red," came Loxley's soft voice, closer than she realized. She kept her eyes closed against the building tears. "Red, you can't go back."

Her eyes snapped open, and she gasped in an unsteady breath, meeting his gentle gaze. "Yes, I *can*!" Raven ran a hand through her hair, knocking the hood back, and realizing the torn dress was still in her grasp. "I… I can make a deal with—" She broke off, staring at Lox. "I can manage just until the betrothal."

Lox's brows scrunched. He dropped his hands. "Do you think that prince will save you?"

The question threw her off, and she shook her head. "No… I don't," she sighed and rubbed her knuckles against her stinging eyes. "I don't *care* about me!"

Lox held her stare. "Why, then?"

"They—they'll starve."

She'd *known* this, damn it, she had. But she'd thought about losing them, and their loss of the Red Hood, not of the betrothal, the deal. Her own loss had blinded her to it.

"Who?"

"Everyone."

Lox's shoulders sagged.

Confusion and anger burned in Raven. Could she fix this? "Lox, I—"

"Listen, Red." His voice was hard but not harsh. "You need to decide, right now, what you want to do. Because after this, what's done is done. Either you take that dress and run home, say you 'escaped' the Red Hood, or…" Lox sighed and extended his hand, "you run with me."

Right then, she could picture it. Stumbling into the castle, hugging Ruben, telling them the burned body was the Red Hood. Truly killing a portion of herself, just not the one she'd planned. Telling her mother she knew, and begging for the deed being finished after the trades happened. She could see the relief in Ruben's face, her townsfolk. The celebration.

And then her real death months later. Forcing them through all this again. *Rue. Cindy.*

Or...

She could leave with Loxley. She could be free of the duplicity, the politeness, the façade. She could dive into her darker self... and maybe another part she hadn't known existed before.

Raven opened her mouth to speak, but... shut it tight.

She gripped the tattered dress and stared at his hand. Rough and worn and tan—and familiar like her blades and hood.

Why was she more scared to live this new life and future than to die?

She took a deep breath and grabbed his hand.

His fingers clasped hers tight, warm through her glove. Squeezed until she looked into his eyes. Forest green bored into her amber. "You can't come back from this, Red Hood or princess."

Raven focused on his hand, on the steadiness of that grasp and that she wasn't doing this entirely alone. At least not right now. She looked at the pyre, the smoke rising into the afternoon sky and the burning body being stripped of everything that made it recognizable as a person.

She nodded, tearing her eyes from the fleshy bones, and threw her dress over them.

Silence lasted for a solid heartbeat before Lox released her hand and got back to the task of her murder. He observed the pyre, fire steadily growing and lapping at the fabric. "Do you have anything else? A personal belonging—your hair tie?"

She shook her head. "Already used that for the kidnapping." Then, she peered at him. He'd remembered her hair tie?

The mention of the tie sparked an idea. Raven brought her dagger to her hair. A few slices later, and she had a doable amount of black strands. Dropping the inch-long pieces in front of the pyre and on the dress, she ignored Loxley's gaze. No, she most certainly was *not* the princess he'd imagined.

"That's probably good. We should..." Lox trailed off, and the sounds of his boots crunching on leaves came closer. "Red..."

Raven lifted her hand to her chest, the pendant lying under her tunic and cloak. The necklace her father had given her as a child, the one thing she would never part with—even in death. Her guards knew that. Ruben would notice. Gods... Ruben. No. She had to do this to survive. Say goodbye to her life as Princess Ravenna, to her father, her mother, her kingdom. And hello to Raven.

The pendant covered her true heart, and its pain, its scars, well. Now she would be bare to the world.

With a deep breath, she reached up and unclasped the chain, pooling it in her hand. One quick slice of her blade and she let a few drops of blood from her arm drip onto the clear glass. "Here. Give the village and the queen this bloody heart."

Lox took the necklace, glancing between her and the bloodied jewelry.

She didn't take her eyes off the white diamond in the center, the embedded ruby as red as blood inside of the glass heart, now soaked and dripping in her own. A pure heart. That's what her father had said about it, about her. She didn't believe it anymore. Someone with a pure heart would be enough for their mother. Be allowed to live.

Raven touched the empty space under her tunic where the heavy amulet had always rested. Though impossible—the pain far too many years past—she swore the scars ached.

The *shing* of an arrow unsheathing tore her gaze to Lox. He notched his bow and placed the chain around the arrowhead. Then, his soft gaze traveled her face, and that honest tone returned. "Something this beautiful shouldn't be burned."

Taking aim at the tree beside the pyre, the thief let his arrow fly, embedding into the wood. The glass heart dangled from the arrow, alone and fragile. Just like Raven's heart as she turned away from the one thing she never thought she'd lose—her kingdom.

CHAPTER 24

T he sun had set into the trees, sending a dark cast over Raven and Loxley, by the time they reached the outskirts of Dale. When the first building peeked over the treetops, Lox jerked the horse they shared to a stop and dismounted. He traded off the reins to his comrade, Jon, who had been waiting in Ilasia's forests with the pair of steeds.

Loxley offered a helping hand, but Raven ignored it, having grown annoyed with pretending she hadn't been *that* close to him in the damned saddle. She'd tried not to put her arms around him but quickly found that impossible if she wanted to stay on the horse. And the warmth of his body had been hard to ignore. And damn did she want to ignore it given the silence of the ride.

Taking her rejection of his hand in stride, Lox turned to Jon and patted the young man—or rather, the almost boy—on the shoulder. Jon had to be seventeen at most, Raven surmised. His black hair, tossed around his face, accentuated his young age, even though his jawline was hard and strong. He wasn't much younger than her, but an innocence wavered in his easy smile and behind his cool blue eyes.

Jon gave Raven a broad smile like he had upon first seeing her hours earlier, and led the horses forward, bending his tall head under a branch and slipping into the dense trees.

Raven turned a quizzical eye to Loxley. He caught her gaze but headed further into Dale.

When they'd reached Jon back in Ilasia, only a few words had traded between leader and comrade before they'd mounted and raced from the capital's grounds and into the unknown trails of the forests. Merely two sentences from Lox: "There's been a change in plans. My… partner has decided to join us early."

No questions from Jon. Just a simple, "Alright."

Nothing about the changed plans or who she was. Somehow, this irked her.

Lox placed his hand on Raven's back to propel her forward with him, and she lengthened her steps to escape his touch. The heat and emotion it caused confused her, and she was still mad at his coldness. Something felt different between them now.

They wound through the forest, buildings in sight to their left. Raven had been to Dale before, but never in the shadows and alleys like this, only in the daytime with royal duties. This town didn't have walls like Ilasia's market, so sneaking past the buildings required less effort but equal stealth to remain hidden in the alleyways.

Long minutes passed with the soft padding of their boots the only sound, the two silent and smooth as the thieves they were. She sneaked behind him and his invisible trail through the city. Loxley finally stopped behind a tall establishment roaring with loud cheers and rambunctious chatter—a tavern. His hand on Raven's arm halted her too.

"You don't have to grab me, I know to hide," she snapped in a whisper, plucking his hand from her cloak.

"Sorry, Princess, I know you're used to making the orders." Loxley grinned sideways at her, then crept around the corner. "But I know where we're going, so that makes me in charge."

Raven's mouth slackened, but her clenched teeth held it in place. She controlled her steps so she wouldn't stomp after him. "You may know who I am, and you may not like it, but you will *not* make me feel bad about my position."

His swagger didn't miss a beat, and somehow that infuriated her.

She grasped his tunic and whipped him around. Loxley's eyes widened, latching onto hers. "I love my kingdom. I did not order, I protected."

209

"No—you punished. You took lives with your own hands."

"This hood is because I wouldn't sit back and watch crimes be committed. You may see me as lowly because of my crown, but I earned respect from my people. I don't need yours." Raven released his dark shirt, stepping back. "And I don't have a crown anymore."

Lox smiled slowly, looking her up and down. That slow peruse threatened to heat her in a way she did not want to feel toward him right now. "Rightly said, Your Highness. Or rather... Red." Her teeth ground at the nickname. "But I know the way out of your kingdom. So, for now, you follow me."

Raven imagined throwing her dagger at his face as he approached the side of the tavern.

A tree rustled a few paces down from them, and a shadow separated from the tree's trunk. Raven eyed the figure as it solidified into a very tall dark-skinned young man.

Raven tensed, then blushed when she realized this was one of Lox's men. And he'd heard their heated words.

How hadn't she noticed him? Then again, those in Ecanta were unused to Javir, their homeland being in the northwest, while Ecanta rested in the northeast of Aloria over the mountain ridges.

After the city of Valara had burned in its desert a decade past, the surviving Valarans, both Vala and Javir, had relocated to nearby kingdoms, the tribe in Loren. Though, Javir were less common than even Vala after that destruction.

This Javir blended well into the night, a shadow in the darkness, his footsteps near silent despite his size. Dark red tunic and burgundy trousers lent him camouflage to the Ecanta forests, even with the sparse gold rings on his hands.

He gave Raven a once-over look, then neared Loxley.

"Daran." Lox bent his head to him and whispered a few words. Then, the leader gestured into the city. "Check on, Jon."

Then, Daran disappeared into the forest, becoming a whisper in the landscape.

Raven wanted to ask who Daran was and why he'd been there, but if Lox's men didn't ask questions about her, she wouldn't ask about them. They didn't *need* to ask questions of Loxley. And she hated that she did. Hated a few things about them at the moment.

Lox jerked his head to a tall tree. Raven ensured her hood was in place, then scaled the branches, ever aware of people in the nearby alleys and Loxley beside her. Quiet rustling in the night, they carefully climbed the tree, and she tried not to focus on how close he was behind her with each step.

A window opened somewhere to her left, and Raven froze, gripping the branch. Loxley pressed against her back, his steadying hand grasped her waist, his other pulling a branch over them. His hot breath wisped against her cheek, her neck, her ear. She almost lost herself in the pattern of his breathing and the heartbeat racing down low in her core from his proximity. Raven turned her head slightly and thought she heard a low curse from Loxley. Thought his fingers squeezed into her side.

After long seconds, the window slammed shut again, and Raven took a breath to calm her heartbeat and that damned fire she battled around him.

"Just two more over and one up," Lox whispered into her ear, breath hot as his hand that drifted to her hip.

Swallowing her nerves, Raven moved out of his grasp and higher up the branches. The tree didn't quite touch the window he'd indicated, so she sat back against a thick branch. A dark curtain obscured the features within, not even candlelight shone. Lox checked his footing, then stepped toward the pane. He let out a low-pitched whistle, and the window slid open, revealing the angled bones and black eyes of the cursed man from the tavern in Ilasia. But when his gaze met hers, his eyes lightened to a copper, and though his skin remained cracked leather, his hair turned the same red of a Loren.

The man glanced down, breaking the intensity of his curse.

Raven recoiled, and Lox's hand held her shoulder. He whispered quickly, "Whatever you see, it isn't real. Beast won't hurt you."

Beast? That was encouraging.

The cursed man lifted his dark eyebrows, and Lox nodded, then gestured to Raven. With a quick glance at her, Beast leaned farther out the window and stretched his long arm. With their gazes no longer locked, his features retreated from a Loren prince back into the original black depths and strands.

She judged both the distance to the small pane and the hard earth, then pushed off the branch, taking his hand. Boots landing lightly on the windowsill, Raven deftly ducked, and he pulled her inside. Beast's strong grip released the moment Lox touched down on the sill, and he moved to his leader.

Another young man closed the window and curtains, blanketing the outside world. Raven held her hands loosely at her sides, counting her weapons and the men within the room: one on either side of the window, one at the door—whom she recognized as Scar from the competitions—and another sitting on the small bed. Five including Lox. Jon and Daran made seven. One girl with seven men, an excellent situation.

Two lanterns lit the room, dimly highlighting their supplies and bags, and the eyes all turned toward her and Lox. One bed sat along a wall, a simple inn bedchamber. He met their gazes, then said, "Jon and Daran will return shortly, but the plan has been altered slightly."

Slightly? Raven would've gapped had she not found their attention to their leader interesting.

The hood's magic flooded over her face and body, masking her from their recognition. Despite her few trips into the tavern before, the feel of multiple eyes on her still unnerved her. The magic itself had become a comfort, a security. But this much, it almost suffocated.

"We still need to leave at dawn," Lox continued. He pointed to Scar. "Stand watch. Ramsey will trade off in three hours. We all need to get rest, tomorrow's a hard travel. I'll explain later, but for now..."

Lox took a breath, holding their stares. He gestured to Raven, his first acknowledgment of her existence beside him. "She is a secret. No one can know she is here or see her face. Ensure that."

She? He wasn't telling them who *she* was?

Her amazement abounded when every band member nodded, then the bladesman left, barely opening the door in his wake. The others turned to pack supplies or stand before the window.

Lox stepped closer, inspecting her attire. "You need a change of clothes. Get with Jon when he returns."

Then, he sauntered toward the door.

Raven cast a glance about the men, then startled when Lox reached for the doorknob. She darted to him, ignoring the stares. Hissing in his ear, she placed her hand on the door, keeping it shut, "What are you doing?"

He looked at her hand, then to her. "I have to make an appearance. To keep up this alibi."

And leave her with three strangers?

Lox must've caught the anger in her widened eyes because he stepped back from the door. "Don't worry. I trust all my men with my life. And yours."

The last part of his statement took her aback. "I don't need guards, Lox."

"Oh, I imagine you haven't needed them for years." He grinned. "I'll be back—don't miss me too hard, Red."

"Now you call me a name?" she snapped, unable to hold her pent up annoyance. "Not just 'she.'"

Both his brows rose, and he whispered, "If you haven't noticed, we have some members with uncommon names. In this band, what you call yourself is up to you. Princess. Red Hood. The bloody Queen of Daggers, if you want. Whatever you choose, it starts now." Lox turned the knob. "Welcome to the band."

The door opened momentarily to chatter and yells, then shut on the silence within the room.

Raven gripped her gloved hands into fists to prevent herself from storming out and stabbing him. She didn't think his band would appreciate that. Given his demeanor, she would need any goodwill she could gather.

Glancing about the room, she resigned herself to stand. These men don't know her, her training or swordsmanship... or her title—and that was a nice advantage. They could underestimate her, like Lox had.

"Did I hear that right?"

She turned, hand not *quite* touching her dagger, though the young man stood a good few feet away. "What?"

"That you're joining the band?" Dirty blond hair cut hung loosely in front of his radiant blue eyes. A teal compared to the crystal blue of Jon. Freckles dotted across his nose and cheeks. He smiled, an easy lift to his crooked mouth.

Raven slowly moved into the center of the room, not liking her back near the wall. "I'm not sure yet. It wasn't originally part of the deal."

His smile lessened. "Oh. Lox doesn't often offer for someone to join." The man stretched out a hand. "I'm Lance by the way."

Why doesn't he? And why'd he ask me? She eyed his hand but kept hers still. "Raven."

"Raven..." another man said, rising from the bed. A scar curved along his chin and upward along the right point of his smile. Smooth pale skin and soft cheekbones created an otherwise handsome face. His black hair lay almost at his eyelashes, and deep almond-shaped brown eyes that would be entrancing if not casually roaming her body. "Damn, I was hoping we'd finally get a female member."

"You were?"

"Yeah. It'd be a nice change of scenery."

Warm mist traveled across her body, slowing on her breasts. His gaze lingered, apparently. And she'd thought Lox was flirtatious. This one was blatant as hell. Briefly, she wondered if he could even see her figure enough to admire it. "Who are you?"

"Ramsey, madam," he said, extending his hand.

Raven unsheathed her dagger, holding it loosely by the handle. "Bet I can throw faster than you can run. Want to try it out?"

Ramsey's broad grin spread, revealing too-perfect teeth. He must have come from a semi-wealthy family. He probably hadn't starved a day in his life. So, why was he here?

Then again, she was the same. Not all nobility and royalty held perfect lives.

He whistled, low and long. "Noted." Ramsey jerked his scarred chin toward the door. Somehow, the interest he showed in her didn't resonate the same as Lox's had. "Scar can do the same. I'd love to see a contest."

Scar—why did *he* have that nickname if Ramsey had this mark?

Ramsey ducked, trying to peer beneath her hood. "You're safe in here. You don't have to stay under that hood."

Raven readied her dagger. She wasn't ready to lower her hood— anonymity her best defense—not alone and not when she was still so close to her home.

"Hey—you heard Lox," called the bandmember from the window, "no one can see her face. Better to keep it on until we're sure we aren't being followed."

Raven nodded her thanks to Beast. Pitch black eyes locked on Ramsey, who straightened, then they shifted to Raven—not quite meeting hers—and she couldn't help the shiver plunging down her spine.

"Ramsey," Beast continued in his deep voice. "Boss said you're on watch next. You should sleep." His tone lacked the nice sentiment the words otherwise would've implied.

Ramsey moved toward the bed, shuffling the pillow. "Yeah. Sure, Beast. Good call."

Raven adjusted her hood and walked to the wall opposite the bed, distancing herself from them. She'd just left a castle full of people whose closeness suffocated her, and this room of strangers stifled.

Ramsey stopped pulling back the blanket. "Unless you wanted the bed, Raven?"

Startled by the flirtatious criminal's generosity, she blinked. Glad that her hood covered her blank expression, she replied, "No, I'm fine. I'm not going to sleep."

The one at the window—Beast?—shifted his gaze to her, and Lance turned from his post at the door and tried reassuring her, "Milady, you're safe. We always have two men on guard and there's seven of us. No one will get to you."

"That's not the problem."

"Then… what is?"

Too much.

She sighed, a quiet exhale that they didn't hear, but steadied her voice. "This kingdom is broken, and it's my fault."

All three men silently regarded her words, but she didn't bother to check their expressions.

Though she was tired, she couldn't shut her eyes. Or ease her mind.

She'd broken a lot of hearts today—a whole kingdom's worth. Her guard, her village, Cindy. Her own. All except the one that should've truly mattered to her: the queen's.

With a price and a death on her head, Raven didn't think she'd be sleeping for a long time.

CHAPTER 25

H ours later the tavern door opened, emitting the younger
bandmember, Jon. He smiled waywardly at Raven who sat on
the floor, then roused Ramsey, who rolled out of bed, instantly
alert to switch places for watch.

She marveled at the ability and routine this band seemed to have. The
structure.

Lance lay asleep on the floor across the room, but the cursed man at
the window held his position. He looked at Jon, whose feet were whis-
per-silent on the wood, and returned to his watch.

Jon noticed Raven's gaze and neared, crouching before her. "Hi
there." His eyes scanned her shadowed face. "Trouble sleeping?"

She shook her head, checking her hood's placement.

"It's not us, is it? Because I know they look rough but—"

"No, it's… No."

She couldn't explain her troubles. Even to this sweet boy. Considering
the men surrounding them, Jon looked young—and so innocent. His
smile came easier, no scars marring his exposed skin, and… something
about him didn't scream criminal like the others. Why was he with this
band?

Jon nodded and headed to a box beside the bed on the dusty floor. He
removed some pages and a small notebook.

Sometime later, while Raven studied Jon and tried not to study the man at the window, the door opened, three figures in the frame. The bladesman, Scar, slapped one on the shoulder, walked straight to the bed and fell on it. Ramsey entered... back from watch already? The other— oh, she recognized him even stumbling drunk. That low, suggestive tone he'd once had in her ear, whispered to a woman, slightly slurred, "Not tonight, sweetheart."

Loxley slipped his hands down the woman's arm and to her hand, leaning close to her ear, or her neck, Raven couldn't tell.

Part of her screamed to look away. But this was what she'd followed, the emotions she'd indulged—with a man who seemed to indulge with many. This was why he was cold—the kiss meant nothing to him. And it should mean nothing to her.

She didn't bother to hear the rest of his words. After the woman's hands could be seen roaming Lox's shoulders and arms even in this dim lighting, he shut the door with a staggering step back. Gods, she hated that she'd touched him the same just nights before.

The lock clicked, and Lox turned, posture straight, and sauntered calmly and easily into the room. He adjusted the ruffled collar of his tunic but stopped when he saw Raven. She stared, taken aback.

Lox came over, crouching as Jon had. "Guess I shouldn't be surprised you're still awake."

"And I shouldn't be surprised you were flirting. Or drinking. Or pretending."

The corner of his mouth twitched, but Lox rubbed his jaw. "If I didn't know you better, I'd think you were jealous."

"Is that how you make an appearance?" was all she could think to reply.

"Yes, it is actually." Lox jangled the pouch at his side, clanking with coin. "Drink, yell, win rounds of cards—make them notice the drunken, brazen criminal."

She raised a brow, impressed. They'd remember his band's presence the other nights and would assume his as well. "And the woman?"

Stars be damned, why did her tone have to be so sour?

"Paid her to say I stayed in her room." His eyes sparkled in the faint light, the cleverness of his own plan leaking into his expression. Or maybe he caught her tone. "She'll think I didn't want to be embarrassed from my drunkenness, unable to perform—which I assure *you*," Lox winked, "I most certainly can. But she's my alibi for the night."

"And why do you need that?"

"Because we're leaving now."

Raven opened her mouth, but Lox stood and spun to the room. "Jon —are we packed?"

"Yes, sir."

"Guys," Lox said, voice raised slightly. Lance jolted out of sleep, standing a second later. Scar did the same on the bed yet a bit slower, and the cursed man turned to his leader. "We're heading out."

And they were in motion. Checking their weapons—of which Scar had *plenty*—securing their pouches or satchels, talking to Jon while he marked on his pages.

Raven stood, counting her own daggers and hidden weapons. Her satchel still hung over her shoulder, and she knew all its contents by heart, so she headed to Lox in the center of the room.

He looked her over, calculating. "You need new clothes. And have to ditch the hood."

"No," she snapped. Not in the mood for his orders.

"It's too noticeable."

"Lox—no." She stepped closer and said quietly, "It's enchantment prevents anyone from recognizing me."

"Magic or not, *it* is recognizable." He unrolled a wanted poster of a faceless hooded figure. "They know the hood, even if they don't know whose face lies underneath. We can disguise your face but not that."

Grudgingly, Raven unclasped the cloak and removed the soft fabric. The men neared them, apparently finished with their duties. A low whistle came from near the bed, and Raven clenched her teeth.

"Rams," Lox chastised, a harshness she didn't recognize in his voice.

"Sorry, boss."

Lox nodded and handed the cloak to Jon, who stashed it in the box. "You can have it back when we're farther from Ilasia. You have two choices—wear what we give you or pretend you stayed with me last night."

"Does it have to be you?" Her tone was colder than intended. "You couldn't be in two places, and that women seemed happy to serve."

A few coughs covered up laughs and grunts. Some adjusted their gazes away from Lox.

He straightened. "And who would you choose?"

Ramsey raised a hand.

Raven shot him a glare, fingering her dagger.

He shut his mouth with a grin.

"Give me the damned clothes," she ground out.

Lox turned. "Jon."

"Not the best, but it'll do," Jon said. He extended a large, brown tunic, which she put on over her own shirt. The baggy fabric covered her curves, and she left it un-tucked to mask her hips. Scar offered a forest green cap, into which she unceremoniously stuffed her dark hair. Shorter strands fell in front, but it couldn't be helped.

Lox appraised her. "Men?"

Their gazes landed on her, and she resisted the urge to squirm. None of them touched her with quite the same heat Loxley's did.

"Her face is too noticeable," grunted the cursed man. Considering his own face, she wasn't sure it was a compliment.

Raven peered around the room as the men pondered that. Spying a small pile of dirt or dust or something else, she bent and dipped her fingertips in it. Not giving a damn about its questionable origin, she smeared it on her cheek and dotted above her brow, then turned back to the band. "Good?"

The band gave approving grunts, the cursed one staring longer, not quite making eye contact. Lox smiled. "Looks nice, Red."

Gods damn the heat in her cheeks. "Stop calling me that—I don't have my hood."

He chuckled and flicked his gaze to her green hat. "Nope. You're wearing my colors now."

SUN STILL HIDDEN BUT RISING, THE PREDAWN LIGHT GAVE THE TREES BEHIND the tavern an eerie glow. Ramsey led a path through the forest to whatever meeting place Lox had specified. The cursed one—Beast—took the rear, his silent movements contrasting his large build. Raven walked between them, hating that Lox sent the two largest bandmembers with her.

He had ordered they split—Lance, Scar, and Jon descending through the window, then her group. Lox had stood alone in the room afterward, watching them disappear. An uneasy feeling had settled in her stomach seeing him by himself. *He* would be blamed for her 'murder'—he should have the most of his men with him.

And you'll *die if found alive.*

That thought didn't ease her guilt.

Ramsey raised a hand, and Raven stopped, scanning the forest.

Beast circled them, a predatory crouch to his stance—shoulders wide and loose, ready to strike, knees bent. His gaze, dark and dangerous, examined potential attackers. Finally, he straightened with a slight nod to Ramsey.

Raven, not one to blindly trust, unsheathed her dagger and feigned casualness by cleaning her nails.

A snicker—Ramsey eyed her knife. "Don't think we can tell if someone's following us?"

Considering her own *trained* guards—albeit new and handpicked by her murderous mother—hadn't noticed her 'kidnapping,' no, she did not trust these criminals. Not with her life. Raven shrugged. "I've been proven wrong too many times."

"Understandable." Ramsey sauntered closer, and she eyed the few feet between them. "But when the boss gives us an order, we take it seriously. And your safety was a very strict order."

Raven steadied her breathing to calm her heart that leapt at that statement. "Why?"

Ramsey shrugged.

Beast grumbled from the darkness, "We don't ask questions."

Again, *why*? "What has he told you about this?"

"Not much," Ramsey said, eyes returning to the forest. "That a young woman needed out of the city. And that he would be framed for murder." He locked gazes with her. "I assume you're the product of both those problems?"

Ramsey was smarter than she thought.

"It's a little more complicated than that." A lot more. But she was thankful Lox hadn't told her story. Raven sighed. "That didn't disturb you? The framed for murder part?"

220

Beast chuckled, a low slightly scary sound. "Lox being a target of crime is not new."

"When we enter a new city," Ramsey added, shaking his head "they don't want us around long. So, they create excuses and blame us for crimes until we leave."

Just like Vanera. But *every* town? "And you didn't... want to know more?"

"Of course. But we don't need to. Lox never leads us wrong."

Somehow that blind faith sounded... unbelievable. What had Lox said to her? *'We're criminals. We don't have the luxury of trust.'* There had to be another reason. Something linking them all together—blackmail? secrets?—a reason to *follow*. Only her guards did that, and they served the kingdom out of honor. Thieves and criminals didn't have honor.

Raven eyed Ramsey, the talker of the two. "So, you heard someone needed out and... went with it?"

He broke off her stare and leaned against a tree, a sigh in his movement. "We all were that person once. Needed to escape our life, our town, our fate." Ramsey glanced at Beast. "Didn't have a home or a family. Barely able to survive—some not at all. We've all been cast out somehow. You've seen Daran, I presume?" The Javir, the man without a land. She nodded. Ramsey twirled his dagger. "So, yeah... we help when we can. No questions."

Helping those who needed it most. Hadn't that been her goal? Stopping those who hurt others, who stole others' livelihoods. Only she wasn't a 'criminal,' she was 'justice.' But these men did far more than she could. She punished; they protected and provided—a refuge, safety... a home.

She needed all of that. And they'd bring her to a place she could finally have it again... She hoped.

The trio waited as the sun rose, patchy shadows shifting around them. Leaves rustled in the wind, branches whipping. Beast's head shot up and to her left, black eyes searching and latching onto whatever had made the sound. Ramsey twisted his knife in his hand, casually strolling over to Raven and standing between her and the direction Beast looked.

A stick snapped loud in the quiet morning. Then, another, followed by steady crunches of dried leaves. The steps bounded away in a scurry —an animal.

Ramsey sheathed his blade and glanced at her calm expression. "Weren't worried?"

"I've taken down more than a mere animal."

"Really now?" He observed her green cap. "Did you have anything to do with that weapon's merchant?"

Raven narrowed her eyes. "Why?"

"I look into whatever Lox wants me to... and a certain red hooded vigilante was one of them." He shrugged but a hard focus remained in his fixed gaze. "And some would whisper words of the targets, like that baker. But no one seemed willing to talk about the *deceased* victims."

She gripped her knife, uncomfortable about his implied question or his leader's interest. "He'd been... taking advantage of his apprentice. A boy who struggled to feed his siblings."

Beast's expression darkened if that was somehow possible, and Ramsey shifted.

Raven swallowed against the image of the unsure handwriting of a child's plea to help their brother. The three thanks on the paper Flint had nailed to the noticeboard. She'd stashed it in her satchel despite the lack of room. "It was his second chance, and he failed."

Ramsey rubbed his clenched jaw, a wariness in his eyes.

"He'd done it before," she said, somehow hating the idea of this criminal judging her. "Barren *knew* what would happen if he touched another —" She cut herself off, anger staunching her words. "What would *you* say happen to him?"

"I'd say kill him," a voice said from within the trees. Beast didn't so much as turn. Not a threat? Lox stepped out, eyes trained on Raven. "But it isn't my decision—or yours—to make."

Relief that he hadn't gotten captured faded beneath her annoyance at his words.

The bandmembers walked to their leader. Lox held his stare on her, something she couldn't decipher but felt close to her mother's anger in it, then turned to his men. "We're almost there. I came to see what was taking you three so long."

He headed back the way he'd came, not once looking at Raven again.

No flirtation in his tone, no smile. Though it was what she'd wanted for so long before, his seriousness unnerved her.

She'd hate to see him angry. But she had a feeling he already was.

DAMN HER. LOX RECALLED THE WEAPONSMITH WHO'D DIED JUST DAYS AGO, the empty stall a reminder of what breaking the law meant in Ravenna's kingdom. The Red Hood's kingdom. He sighed. Royals. So damned entitled.

Who the hell did this princess think she was?

Loxley eyed her, paces to his right as the four of them walked. Black hair flowed out from under his old cap, and even dirt couldn't lessen the beauty in those amber eyes. His old tunic couldn't hide the curves he knew from touch rested beneath. He could still feel her waist, her hip beneath his fingers if he thought long enough. Her gasps on his tongue—

Damn.

He shook his head. She was a *princess*. A princess who killed her own villagers. Granted, they had committed crimes even he would deem punishable, but... creating laws didn't mean you imposed them personally. But really, what could he expect from someone in power? Power made one ruthless and heartless.

He knew that all too well. He had the scars to remind him if he ever forgot.

He still couldn't quite reconcile the beautiful noble he'd fallen for in the market with the princess—let alone with the vigilante he'd kissed against the wall. It made sense that he'd fallen for both sides of her. The princess and the Red Hood. She was violent and fierce—sharp enough to cut—in both forms. How hadn't he seen it before?

He'd been played like a fool, all the while she'd known him but pretended she didn't when he'd seen her at the competitions. Skilled as they came, she'd brushed it off well. He'd never known—had she not pushed him against that tree the night before the ball... When a woman grabbed you like that, you never forget. And she had done it the same as the market girl when they first met.

The pieces had fallen, but he couldn't believe where they settled.

He'd attended the ball, still not quite believing it. The betrothal had thrown him further into confusion. Wondering if the hire to kill herself was true, or if she had fabricated a way to escape. But... her fear, her openness with him seemed far too genuine. She'd seemed committed as Princess, far too committed to lower herself to being with a thief.

223

Lox was pretty sure he was the only person to see deeply into the Red Hood. Had she bared so much of herself to him?

A grunt came from the side, and Ramsey steadied Raven's arm. Her hand rested against a tree trunk, one leg tangled in its roots.

"You okay?" Rams asked, helping her unwind her boot.

She took her arm back from Ramsey's grip, not unkindly, just... quickly. She'd done it with Lox before, as if touch burned. Were they too *lowly* for a princess to be near?

He recalled his hand on her neck, the pulse beating against his fingertips, her lips on his. She'd let him more than touch her then. He doubted she would now.

"I'm fine, thank—"

"Are these woods too dense for you, sweetheart?" Lox sneered, walking up to separate her from his man. "They're just ahead. Hurry up."

Turning on his heel, he stalked farther east.

"I'm not one of your band."

Lox stopped, glanced over his shoulder. "What?"

Ravenna stood straight, pristine as a princess, confidence pouring from her gaze which was for once unburdened by her hood's shade. He'd wanted to see underneath that cloth, but now he didn't know what to do or feel. Dark brows descended along with her tone. "You don't get to order me around."

His anger flashed, and he spun on her. Jaw pulsing, Lox stepped closer, boots crushing into the dirt carelessly. "No, that's your job, isn't it? Make the rules, order everyone else? Be above the law you create?"

Falling rocks and a thundering crack rocketed through his memory, the shuddering of a city separating from the world. Crumbling to pieces right before his eyes, everything lost to the merciless ocean and man whose greed consumed Lox's home.

Her words were quiet but cracked through his mind. "I didn't create them. My mother did. And I'm not above anything."

"Oh, really?" Venom entered his voice as he took another step. "That's why you're running?"

"Running?" Her brows rose high into his old cap.

"Yes, running—from your home, your people." Lox could curse himself. He wasn't just thinking of her, but himself. Even though he told himself he was doing the right thing, stealing from nobles and royals, he was running. Always running from a responsibility he wished didn't lay on his shoulders.

But he didn't have a home, let alone people. They'd been gone a long time. Nevrande had detached from Aloria, resting to float in the ocean to the whims of a pirate who controlled far more than he should.

His home—gone.

This band… they were his people now.

Ravenna's gaze slid to Beast and Ramsey, but her deadly calm voice didn't waver. "I was forced out. I knew my place, my duty, and I didn't step out of that."

"Except to punish those you deemed should be."

The princess, the vigilante, stepped right up to his face. "Do you know who I punished, Loxley? The killers, the nobles who stole from their villagers, the men who beat their women, their children—the men who *touched* children. All the people whose crimes were overlooked because of power or rank, by my mother. Who could pay a fine and continue on. While beggars stole food to last the damned night!" Her breathing staggered, and she paused to catch her breath. A vein pounded in her neck, beating to her anger, and Lox forced his gaze away. "And they all had a chance, I ensured that. If they committed it again… that was their end."

"An end *you* chose for them," Lox hissed, unrattled by her anger.

She was just like that bastard pirate, forgetting others' lives and choices when making her own. Destroying people in her way.

She sighed, a delicate sound in the cold night air amidst their harsh words and tones. "If you'd seen what they did with their second chance, you wouldn't let them go, either."

A brokenness resounded in her words. Stars be damned, he felt it. She was right, and he couldn't deny it.

He stared, long and hard, trying to measure his thoughts before voicing them.

No. She wasn't like him. Not Hook or himself.

Lox examined Ravenna again, trying to ignore her beauty. Determination radiated from every step she took, even without a crown she was ready to… what? She'd lost a kingdom, *her* kingdom. How could she be so resolved in the face of all this?

Without a home, she was just like him. Only she was better.

He needed to reconcile his anger. She wasn't a normal royal. She was infinitely better than any noble or royal he'd ever seen. He'd wondered before, when he didn't know her a princess, how she paid for food for others. How she cared for them. How the vigilante helped. Why was it so hard for him to combine the two ways she cared for her people? The way she found to help those her station couldn't allow her to?

He released a slow breath, dispersing his anger at himself and Hook. Then, he nodded tensely to her and his men. "Let's go, it'll be dawn soon."

CHAPTER 26

Midday sun beat down on the booth, making the wood too hot for Cindy's elbows. All the pastries and loaves had sold, but she still didn't move. Something was wrong. Raven hadn't visited. And not just Cindy, but the market. Cindy had watched, and a black head and shiny guards hadn't appeared. And yesterday? Cindy couldn't remember. Raven hadn't visited *her*, but had she visited anyone?

She bit her lip. Had no one else noticed? Was she just thinking too much?

Hurried clanking drew her gaze into the crowd. The Head Guard Raven usually had at her side, Ruben she often called him, strode alone. His hard gaze roamed with purpose. Not stopping on faces long. Searching.

Cindy's heart pounded. She stepped around the booth. "Excuse me."

Ruben halted. Lines crossed his forehead. Yes, something was wrong.

"Have you…" Clenching her apron, Cindy forced herself to finish. "Have you seen Ravenna today?"

Dark blue eyes widened. "She hasn't visited you?"

"No."

Ruben's gaze cast out to the people, the houses.

"Have you seen her," she tried again. His non-answer and panicked eyes twisted her stomach tighter than the apron in her fingers.

The Head Guard's mouth hardened, and he finally met her gaze. His held her worry, only deeper. Cindy almost flinched. He sighed. "No."

Then, he turned, leaving her in the dirt path, and the world faded around her. *He*, Raven's best friend and Head Guard, hadn't seen her. She'd seemed fine at the ball, if not slightly flustered after the betrothal announcement. But who wouldn't be?

A passerby jostled Cindy's shoulder, sending her spinning. "Oh! Sorry—"

Deeper in the crowd, a dark head bobbed. Hope lifted until she realized their height. Not Raven. But… she knew him.

"Cindy—*Cindy!*" her father called from behind.

Not now.

Weaving through the people, Cindy bounced around and into villagers, and stopped behind the leather clad young man. She tapped his forearm lightly and said, "Kieran?"

He turned, confusion scrunching his black brows. Sharp features that before had made her wary and nervous, barely fazed through her worry. Even her father's yells didn't tighten her shoulders. "Excuse me, sorry to —" Cindy scanned the crowd hopefully once more. "Have you seen Raven today?"

Mix-matched eyes met hers, then caught onto her fingers still marring her apron, and she shifted them to her bun loosening at the nape of her neck. Kieran shifted his naval coat, and ink briefly escaped at his collarbone. "No."

Fear struck through her core, like lightening spiking. He stayed in the castle. If Raven had been bedridden, he'd have known.

Cindy pressed her lips together, touching them with a soft finger. Where was she?

"Cindy!" came her father's roar. He'd spotted her.

Kieran's gaze traveled from her fingertip to her father.

She winced at the thought of returning. "Thank you." She curtsied, started to turn, then glanced back up at Kieran. "Sorry to bother you."

"It's—" he started, but she'd already been scooped up by the crowd.

Cindy steeled herself for her father's harsh words and hopefully not as harsh grip and returned to the booth.

The afternoon passed with roiling worries and mounting chores. But silence had descended on the market. It seemed worry had traveled. Whispers sounded. Heads tilted together. Shoulders turned.

Something *was* wrong.

Carrying old loaves to the trash, Cindy spotted a lone person in the path. Back to her, he stood before the empty weaponsmith booth. The lanky figure didn't move, just… stared. The wind blew his light brown hair sideways. Cindy rushed forward. "Flint!"

He turned. Distant eyes held her gaze.

Cindy stopped, gripping the tray. "Have you heard…"

His brows crumpled, and he opened his mouth. Clenched it. "She's dead."

The loaves fell, tray clattering.

He came forward slowly, shaking his head, and Cindy stood frozen. A tear left Flint's eye, and she touched his shoulder. Despite everything Barren had put him through, he'd never cried in front of her.

No.

"She… she can't," Cindy's voice thickened.

He dropped his face into his hands and cried while the bruised girl held far too still, afraid the shock would break. Flint took in a ragged breath. "I overheard the guards—they saw a red cloak."

Red… Cindy gasped. Shook her head. "No. *No*. He… he wouldn't…"

Flint wiped his eyes, and she reached for him, hugged him. His shaking shoulders almost broke her.

Cindy tried to breathe, but the air stung and rattled her lungs, and she pulled back from him. She blindly searched the market, not knowing what she hoped to find—something to ease this ache—and glimpsed a figure leaning against the notice board. Rings flashed and clanked as Kieran flexed his knuckles at his sides. He held her curious stare, then looked down, crossing his arms.

What was he doing here?

Flint knelt, and she remembered the loaves.

Cindy crouched to stop him, but her fingers trembled, and she clenched them. She felt fragile, far too fragile to touch. Light hair falling haphazardly, she shook her head and bit her lip hard. "You're sure… the *Red Hood?*"

Flint nodded grimly.

Cindy touched her fading bruise. "I thought he was better than that."

He stared at the weapons booth again, sorrow rooting in his gaze. "We all did."

Silence stretched thin, and he stood, returning to the too-empty castle.

Cindy slowly, too carefully, replaced the loaves on the tray. Fingers shaking, she forced herself steady. For she felt, in that moment, like she was made of glass, that her composure might slip if she moved too much... and she'd shatter.

The Red Hood had protected, saved them both, the entire village. But so had Ravenna. She had fed them all, given Cindy friendship, Flint a home and job. Had loved them.

They had been wrong. The Red Hood hadn't been a savior. He'd been a murderer.

And he'd taken the kindest, the fairest of them all.

CHAPTER 27

The band rode for hours, well into the afternoon. Raven rode silently behind Lox; they'd had enough words between them this morning. She didn't have the energy for another fight. His anger had surprised her. Though she'd wanted him to be serious for so damned long, she hadn't expected that. Loxley didn't appear to do serious or anger well. It a sharp emotion, too hard and icy for the charming man.

She hadn't meant to respond so angrily to the man helping her escape with her life, who continued to aid her when he had no reason to. He could hold her for ransom, knowing her title. She'd bet Vanera would pay good money to have her back—to kill her rightly. Raven sighed. No, she hadn't meant for any of this.

Evening had struck, the sun already dipping into the edge of the forest's canopy when the horses slowed to a trot. Upon their leader's motion, the men dismounted and immediately pulled out things for camp.

With surprising skill, Scar crafted a fire from kindle, the flame burning bright. Four rough but sturdy tents were erected, a hammock strung between two trees. Raven stood by the fire watching, useless, no skill to aid them. Never having seen camp set, let alone attempted herself. Same for a fire. Matches were her starter, not a blade and scraps of twigs and moss. She'd have to watch Scar for tips in the coming nights.

Each man worked, each with their own job but aiding the others. So efficient and… steady. They worked together like her Guard.

When each had finished, they stood at intervals around the fire, Beast and the Javir off on the edges, tilted toward the darkening surroundings.

She halted slightly behind and beside Lox, who gazed into the fire, waiting patiently.

Was this really her life now? These seven men whom she knew almost entirely nothing about and who traveled Aloria on their whims of thievery and crime? She'd chosen this path, but had she really? Die, escape alone, or run with companions… not much choice if she wanted life.

She shivered, missing her cloak like she missed her own men—man. Ruben. Stars, this hurt. Esme would comfort him, her love trying to soothe the loss of his best friend.

Needles prickled the back of her eyes, and Raven turned away from Lox and the joining band. *Not now, don't think of him now.* It wasn't safe.

Crackling filled the cold night air. With one deep, slightly shuddering breath, Raven faced the circle of men and warm flames that didn't touch her frozen heart. To her small relief, they gazed at their leader. Only cursory glances slid her way while Lox stepped forward, the orange light accenting his olive skin.

"Plans changed, and you all reacted well to that—thank you," Lox started, nodding to them all and receiving similar gestures. "I'm sure you're all curious about our newcomer." He rubbed the bridge of his nose, then his fingers disappeared into his dark hair. "And what some of you heard earlier."

Raven shifted, feeling Beast's hard gaze. The bandmembers grunted. Even those who hadn't heard must've noticed Lox's mood earlier. Probably an oddity to see their leader lose his temper.

She would've felt proud if her heart wasn't crushed.

"As you know, we'd planned to stop a murder. The Red Hood vigilante was hired to kill the princess and blame me, and they didn't want to follow through. But if they didn't, someone else would." Loxley stared around, pausing for them to digest whatever new information he'd just given. "So, we decided to fake the death. The princess was supposed to come with us for safety and the Red Hood meet us later. Turns out… they're the same person."

Brows raised in the band. Beast's black eyes stayed trained on her, though not meeting her gaze. Ramsey had the decency to look a *little* sheepish at having flirted with royalty. Though, only a little.

Lox gestured to Raven. "Meet the Red Hood and Princess Ravenna."

The bandmembers took her in under a new light, some dipping their heads, others just considering her. No bows. These criminals didn't see her as a princess, just as who stood before them. Raven didn't know how to feel now.

She stepped forward, closer to the warm fire yet still frozen inside. Her secrets laid before this band of bandits made her fingers shake, but she clenched them. "I'm no longer either of those now, least of all a princess. But I did not run from my crown," she said, voice chilling with a glance at Loxley, "nor did I crave its power. I love my kingdom and people. But I had to leave to survive. Someone too powerful wanted me dead."

Loxley's eyes latched onto hers, but she wouldn't elaborate. *Not* that her own mother had ordered the kill. She would only be with them for days, a week maximum, given Ecanta's size. They didn't need to know her. She was pretty sure whatever connection her and Lox had was broken from her secrets.

The Javir, Daran, caught her eye, flames dancing off his brown irises. His whole kingdom and culture and family had been destroyed—a loss deeper than hers. And here she was… being given shelter and passage by this group of young men who could do much worse things to her.

"I…" Raven paused, unsure but having this urge to… thank them. She tore her eyes from Daran to Lox, then the rest of them. A lump formed in her throat, but she pushed out air. "I know none of you probably expected to be traveling with—a person like me… for many reasons. And none of you asked for this. But I appreciate it." She pressed her lips together to stop more words.

"Not sure how much you'll like being with us," Ramsey said from across the fire, drawing her retreating gaze, "but we'll help in any way we can."

Startled, a soft smile reached her mouth.

Lox cleared his throat, and everyone looked toward him again. "I don't have to impress upon you all the importance of…" he looked to her, brows lowered, then back to them, "Red's secret. She cannot be recognized, Princess *or* Red Hood, which will be tricky. And if she's found with us, that's probably treason, right?"

His eyes shot to her again, and her breath escaped. Treason—they'd both be killed. Her eventually, him almost instantly. Raven managed a nod. "But if that happens, I'll—"

"Be protected by the band."

"What—no. I'd explain and—"

"Red."

Loxley's serious tone, the deep genuine one, stilled her own. Forest eyes pierced into her, stilling the urge to fight. "We won't let that happen. Will we, men?" He turned to the band, raising his voice.

Agreements came from each of them, the strength of their words or grunts or raised fists startling her.

Their support—though mostly of their leader—surprised yet warmed her.

She smiled.

Then, in the quiet of near night, the low, deep, mournful sound of a horn rang out for all of the Kingdom of Ecanta.

Its beat shook Raven to her core, resonating in the breath stuck in her lungs and the frozen beat of her heart. She stilled.

Lox spoke, but it was lost to her as she looked over her shoulder back to her home, to Ilasia and the castle she could not, nor would ever again, see. One more horn rattled her stilled mind.

The silence was deafening, as the announcement of a fallen royal should be.

A horn sounded from ahead, closer. Her three cities would sound a response. The towns' own mourning of their princess.

"Red?"

Loxley's soft voice reached her finally, but she couldn't bring herself to look at him. Her eyes burned, and her breathing again wouldn't reach her lungs.

Warm fingers grazed her own, which unknowingly gripped onto her bare arms. With a jump, she faced him for a second before dropping her gaze and retracting her hand. "Have you scouted the forest here?" she asked, forcing the coldness into her breathless voice.

He assessed her but answered calmly, "Yes, we're close to Terra but not enough for detection."

She nodded slowly, then turned toward the trees.

Beast stood in her immediate path. His gaze did not hold confusion as the others did, but an odd understanding. She avoided his stare for fear of his curse and him resembling a Loren again.

Lox appeared at her side, another bandmember approaching her left. She raised her palm. "I'll be right back."

"Red…"

"I'm not running!" she shouted, more forceful than she'd meant. Why did he have to be so *encompassing*? She needed to think, and she couldn't when he was close. "I… excuse me."

Murmured voices followed her as she rushed around Beast and into the forest but not further than the trees' barrier. Then, it was just the wind and her heartbeat in her ears. She walked, jogged, then sprinted, until the cool air constricted her already tight lungs. Raven halted, panting as she turned in a circle and gripped her head.

The mourning horns had ceased but still rang solidly through her heart. Her whole kingdom knew what she'd done.

She clenched her fingers into her hair and found cloth instead. Bringing it down to her face, she stared dully at the dark green cap. She had nothing but this cap and those men to guide her through her own broken kingdom. Anger and guilt coursed through her, and she tossed it to the ground. Dirt plumbed as it hit the leafy floor. She let out a cry of frustration.

Two short, heavy breaths later, she grasped for her black blade and threw it forward. It sunk into the wood of a tree five yards away.

Everything she loved was over.

Raven pulled out and threw every blade strapped to her. From her other hip—her thigh—her boot—her satchel's band.

Ruben. *Shing.*

Cindy. *Thunk.*

Flint. *Thud.*

Mother. *Crack.*

She'd lost them all, and they'd lost her.

But Mother hadn't lost anything she hadn't wanted to.

After the last blade sliced into the trunk, she stared, panting at the shimmering knives. The hum of vibrating metal soothed into the evening air, and silence reigned. All quiet save her ragged breathing.

Staring at her blades, the anger fading with their hum, she whispered, "What did I do?"

A twig snapped, and an appreciative whistle sounded from behind.

Raven whirled, hands at her empty sheaths. For the first time in years, she was without a weapon. She neared the impaled tree.

Two figures appeared. The bladesman, Scar, and Jon, the easygoing boy. Scar eyed the cluster of blades. "Now how did a princess get an aim *that* good?"

"Practice."

He smiled softly. "On criminals?"

"Scar," Jon chastised. The bladesman grinned at the ground.

Raven pulled her daggers free, sheathing them.

Jon picked up the cap with an apologetic expression. "He's got an odd humor."

"Better than Ramsey's," Scar muttered.

Jon ignored him and handed Raven the cap. He smiled, and the genuine kindness warmed her a little. "Ready?"

With a sigh, she donned the cap and nodded.

Scar lead and Jon walked beside her and cleared his throat. "It'd be an understatement to say today was hard for you."

"Yes, it would."

Ahead, Scar added, "It'll get better."

She raised a dubious brow, and Jon said, "Eventually."

They exited the dense trees into the small clearing of the camp. Raven left them and settled into the grassy dirt beside the fire. Within minutes, Jon had dispersed food from one of his many bags. Beast and the dirty blond—Lance, she recalled—stood on the edges of camp, not taking part in their comrades' merriment and talk. Guard duty?

Lance smiled when Scar neared, a parcel in hand. The smile grew before they even made eye contact, almost a secret to himself, then wider and friendlier when approached. The bladesman handed over some food, their hands never touching. After a few exchanged words, Scar nodded and turned away. Lance's gaze lifted from the gift to the blades-man's back, watching Scar saunter across camp with that small smile again.

Focused on Lance, Raven didn't notice Scar heading toward her. He stopped, and she tensed, sitting straighter in the dirt. She hadn't yet figured him out. He crouched and extended a hand. "Scar. Welcome."

"I remember—from the competition." Her gloved hand clasped his momentarily. "Raven." She eyed Ramsey talking to Lox on the other side of camp.

"Curious, huh?" Scar asked, tearing off a piece of bread. He handed her the piece when she glanced at him again, a light smile tilting his lips. She refused, stomach still unsettled. "Why I have that nickname, not Rams."

"Must be a valid curiosity if you guessed it," she said, hoping she didn't give offense.

"We've been asked it before." Scar bit into the loaf, chewing before saying more. "It's simple—I give the scars."

A cap covered his eyes, blood red over burgundy hair. Pale yet piercing blue eyes shot out from the darkness shadowing them, almost grey like the silver of his blades. Steady and focused, the eyes of an expert swordsman.

She recalled the blood running from Kieran's shirt, the only cut in the fights she'd witnessed. Raven raised a brow.

Scar smiled. "Better reaction than I expected. Most women run when I explain."

"Find yourself some better women. Though, as an opening greeting, it *would* alter your chances with a lady."

The bladesman shrugged, eating more of the food. She glanced at Lance across the way.

"You can have a tent for the night."

"No," she stated without pause. She was already causing them enough trouble. "I'm not taking your tent."

"It's alright. See those three?" He pointed to the three darker ones. "We share them. Only Lox has his own, and he barely uses it."

Indeed, the leader didn't seem close to heading to his slightly larger tent.

"Then, I'd be putting more than just you out of a place to sleep."

Scar's eyes lightened, and he raised a finger to the forest. "Two of us are always on watch, usually another is awake anyway, and Daran only sleeps in his hammock." The bladesman gestured to Beast and Lance, then the Javir in the swaying cloth. "So, when he's off watch, there's an empty tent." Scar sipped from a container, then offered it.

Raven smiled politely and took it—water, she surmised from the clarity and lack of smell. "I'm good here. Don't think I'll be sleeping much."

After the long days of worry and the ride today, her eyes were heavy, but her heart weighed heavier.

"You'll sleep. The forest has a kind of... lull to it at night." He took another bite, and the two listened to the crackling fire. "Have you ever slept outside your castle?"

Raven started to retort but paused on his gentle tone. "When I was younger, I'd travel to the other cities, but I can't remember... no. I'd say I haven't."

"Leaving home can be hard, whether it's a cottage or a castle." Scar nodded. He tilted his head. "Surely, a princess deserves more than the ground."

She shot him an appraising look, his tone neither harsh nor joking. He seemed to honestly mean the comment. Raven shook her head, more strands hopelessly falling. "I'm not a princess anymore, and I don't deserve more than anyone else."

"Not even a killer?" Scar grinned darkly, an eyebrow raised.

A joke, to ease her tension, but her veins ran cold. A sad laugh left her, more sigh than joy. "No."

Not when she was a killer, herself.

Raven stared at the fire until someone called for Scar.

The death knell rang through her mind again, echoing her father's a decade before. The sound of hearts breaking. So many hearts—too many.

Ruben... He'd think he failed—the one time he wasn't with her, she was taken and killed. He'd be distraught. Gods, she missed him already.

Raven didn't want to admit it, but she wondered, truly wondered, if her mother would be happier without her. And part of her hoped that she was. The Widow Queen had lost the most important person in her life, and that loss had never left her.

One of them should be happy at least.

With a sigh, she eased to the side, and her hand brushed a piece of cloth. On it lay the bread she'd refused. Slowly, she lifted it and ate a small piece.

She'd wanted to be tough, to show these men she shouldn't be trifled with, but… her death knell had shocked her soul. It was time to stop pretending. No strong, invincible Red Hood; no dainty and composed princess. Just Raven. Whoever that made her.

JOLTING AWAKE, ZELLA SAT BACK IN HER CHAIR, UNSTICKING PAPER FROM HER cheek. She stared around her room. What had woken her? How late was it? The lantern's candle had burned to almost nothing. She sighed. That was thoughtless. She only had two candles left, and who knew when Naja would come back to replenish the supply.

A prickle washed over her chest, then collarbone. Like a chill or anxiety mixed together. Sadness?

Zella stood and turned toward the window. Long strands trapped her in place. In her pacing last —this?—night, she'd carelessly stopped twinning it and moving it with her. The locks were no longer in one long tail, but part of it lay left, right, spread like a sheet on the floor in some areas. Damn it.

With only the faint light that could stream through the window from the stars and moon, Zella slowly made her way across the room and mess of hair.

She leaned down to see into the sky. Nothing was amiss. No storm, no excess of clouds leading up to one. Usually, she only felt this prickle if Naja was near or a storm was brewing. Sometimes she wondered if it had to do with the pressure of the storm and Naja's sandstorms.

Looking back at the room, she gave up on the source of waking her. Sleep or clean, that was her course at the moment. Probably brushing and cleaning this gold sea of hair was the best, if Naja returned and—a loud and long pulse shot through the air, deep and strong.

Sadness.

Zella spun around—and her bare feet slipped on countless strands. A cry fell from her lips as she hit the hard ground. She tried to catch her fall, but her hands slid more, finding no traction. Only that *endless* hair. Pain pierced her head as more was pulled higher up. Elbows hit floor, and she gave up, sinking into the wood and carpet of hated locks.

Hands, back, and elbows stung, but not as hard as her magic bruised scalp.

Another toll rang through the kingdom, reverberating in the cabin the kingdom didn't know existed, and resonating within the cursed girl on the floor.

Staring at the ceiling, Zella absorbed the deep calling. It was sadness embodied. It was grief, pain, mourning. She did not know its true meaning, what it signified to the kingdom, but she felt what it brought. Her whole self felt like *sadness*.

Starlight glinted off the standing mirror against the wall, shining on Zella's face. She tilted her head, cheek to the cold floor and still cold hair. It reflected her lying there, in a puddle of her own cursed hair. The purple bruises shone and shimmered at the depths of her roots. Markings illuminated in the starlight, mottling her pale skin. Bruises—*shimmering* purple bruises on her arms. The bruises of fingertips and some shaped like splashes, the edges crawling outward in small arms of violet.

Magic trapped her everywhere.

The toll sounded once more from farther off, and the sadness faded within.

Frustration bubbled in her chest, and she pushed herself off the floor, moving the hair aside and toward the mirror. The floor-length fixture that Naja used to spy on her more than Zella ever used to stare at herself. Grasping her enchanted book on the table, Zella threw it. Shards burst from the frame, some still stuck. Many more cascaded down than she needed. But she didn't care.

Cuts appeared and stung on her palm and fingers in too many angles to count as Zella retrieved a large piece. She squeezed it and brought the sharp glass to her neck, lifted her hair in large fistfuls. Slash after slash after harried slash. Breathing raggedly, Zella sliced through the last group of strands and gaped down at the severed ends laying on her lap and feet and stone floor. She dropped the shard and wiped her bloodied palms on her skirt before facing what was left of the mirror and her broken reflection.

Jagged, uneven, and partially red with her own blood, her hair hung from varying lengths of only an inch to cresting her shoulders. It framed her face oddly—most pieces too short to grab.

It was beautiful. And free.

A gleeful smile spread.

Zella fingered the new ends of her hair, loving the fresh cuts. She patted it gently, relishing in the lost weight.

Light purple shimmered over her scalp. In the spots Naja had dug with her nails, then it sparked down her strands until it touched the ends —there it crackled almost angrily.

"No," she whispered desperately.

Zella's knees hit the floor, pain from the glass distant as her gaze stayed trained on her reflection and the purple magic she hated with all her heart.

The pieces of sandy blonde hair on the floor lifted from the stone.

Zella shook her head and bit her lip. She tried to cover her head, but the sparks nipped at her fingers harder than the glass had. "Please..."

But she didn't control this magic, and it or its maker did not take mercy on Zella.

Within a ragged breath, the hair she'd just cut had reached upward and reattached. Smooth strands led from her roots down countless feet on the ground, curling around Zella and the cursed tower. Marking her time there and the time yet to come.

Her hands dropped to her lap, and finally, she let the tears fall. Blood covered her fingers, drops and smears coating her dress. She clasped them into fists and pressed them to her eyes as she cried until the sobs racked her chest.

Why couldn't she have this *one* thing?

Teardrops fell onto her cut and burning palms, down her wrists. With the tears, a cold trickle cascaded. Confused, Zella pulled back—and gasped.

Teal shimmers emanated from her fingertips, like cool water running over her skin. Zella stared, shocked.

This was not Naja's magic.

"People like us," Naja had said before.

The past months or so her fingers had tingled when Zella became emotional or, like before, when Naja neared her door, but she'd never imagined this.

Zella wasn't Vala. And only Vala had ever wielded human magic. Yet the shimmers remained under her nails. Zella wouldn't question this gift; it might be her only escape.

Did she too have magic in her veins?

She looked to the enchanted window.

If this was truly magic, then she could fight Naja's. All she needed... Zella gaped at her enchanted book. She'd already found ways around the spell to block magical learning. She could use it.

She only needed one break on either the window or door enchantment. She wouldn't squander this gift.

What if Naja found out? Would she be able to sense the magic on her?

Zella cupped her face in her tingling hands. She didn't want another angry Naja.

No. I will find a way out.

She had to.

If she hoped to step foot out of this tower, she'd need any minuscule magic she could wield. And if Naja discovered she had magic... Zella knew in her shaking heart that nothing could save her from that raging sandstorm.

Zella stood and picked up the tome. Bringing it to her table, she grabbed some small vials and a bowl. If her blood and tears had caused this to spark, she would collect more. Anything to get free.

She squeezed a few remaining drops of her blood into the glass and raised a vial to the starlight. It sparkled, similar to Naja's shimmering magic.

Practice. That would get her out.

To feel the world.

CHAPTER 28

Deep into the night, Loxley returned from watch, dipping into a tent to rouse Scar. The bladesman stood instantly, hands checking weapons as he followed Lox. The two quietly walked across camp, and Scar smirked at the sleeping person beside the flames before continuing into the trees. Lox stopped, staring at Red… the princess… whoever she was, lying close to the fire. The warmth must have lulled her to sleep. Good, she needed it after everything.

Her borrowed shirt sleeve brushed an ember. He should move her. Lox sighed. But was touching her really a good idea? When he'd first kissed her, he'd worried he wouldn't stop. Now he worried they'd never reach that moment again. Either from his anger or her tendency to throw knives

Lox glanced from the fire to her. As much as he despised royals… she wasn't a typical royal. She'd just lost her entire home and people, whom she apparently loved. She deserved his tent more than he did.

Loxley knelt behind her and slid his hand under her waist to lift her. Raven jolted around, pinning his arm beneath her, hand grasping his arm and pulling him toward her. Dagger poised at his throat.

Her intense amber eyes rested inches from his, he could taste her breath. Lavender filled his nose, a soft opposite to the fire's smoke. He stared at her lips, remembering the taste, the softness.

He grinned at himself. Once again, he'd focused on her instead of the weapon she held.

Lox eased his hand out from under her. Her eyes focused on him, pushing away the sleep from her mind, and she moved backward on the dirt slowly. The caution in her gaze struck him. He whispered, "What made you this way, Princess?"

She recoiled, the caution disappearing into pain—then hardening to solid amber. Raven removed her dagger from his throat and sheathed it hard. "A man who thought charm overshadowed everything."

Settling onto the dirt, Lox leaned closer. That explained her usual annoyance at his flirtations. "That redhead from the competition?"

She shook her head, a scoffing laugh on her red lips. "No, that prince wasn't very charming at all."

"I'd say—" Lox paused, realizing just how both her sides played into that prince. The fear he'd seen at the competition, her being cornered in the marketplace, the Red Hood hunting him down... the beating on the redhead's face before Loxley had thrown his punches. "You protected yourself from him."

"I had to." Raven pulled her legs to herself, arms squeezing them tight. "Even Ruben couldn't do it."

"That guard who always followed you?" The heat from the fire warmed half of his body, and Lox shifted so she could share the warmth.

She nodded, black hair bright from the firelight. "He's my Head Guard—was, I guess," she said, dipping her head as if missing the weight of her crown. He'd only seen her wear it at the ball, and she'd looked magnificent, that bronze in her black hair matching her amber eyes. Raven gave a soft smile. "My best friend. Only friend, really."

"I'd say Beast is close to being your friend."

They both looked toward the tall shadow of a man standing watch a few trees away, the stern expression pulling his brows down and enhancing the monstrous features. He hadn't spoken a single word all night, which wasn't new. Raven turned back to Lox and chuckled, low and even genuine.

Loxley patted her hand, absent of a glove for once, and tried to ignore the heat of her skin. "If you play your cards right, you'll find a place in this band. We all did at some point." He removed his fingers. "That's what we're here for: the people who are lost."

Raven stared out into the pitch-black forest.

She needed him and his band to survive. As a princess—and according to her odd moral code—that must be killing her. He'd given her hell about being royal and distributing justice as the Red Hood, but if she hadn't... she'd be dead right now. This princess had just given up her whole kingdom and a secure future in luxury and power to travel somewhere she didn't know and be someone she didn't know how to be.

"We become our own family," Lox said and rose, offering a hand. "You should take a tent. Your sleeve almost caught fire. I was trying to move you."

She checked the mentioned cloth and backed from the flame.

Stubborn. Lox persisted, "I hardly ever use the tent."

She turned her eyes to the forest. Did she not trust them? He almost laughed, no, he didn't suppose she did. Not only were they a band of 'bandits,' but she'd had guards around her her whole life—his men couldn't possibly measure up to her standards.

Then, why had she kissed him?

That question nagged him more so after learning her title.

"I don't want to put any of you out. You're all risking treason for me, and I don't think—" She stopped, mouth clamping shut.

The thief narrowed his eyes. "What?"

Red shook her head. He doubted she'd speak her mind to him. Yet he wished she would. Bloody hell, he wondered if he'd ruined it all.

"Take the tent—I'm up on guard duty next," he lied.

At that, she looked up at his still offered hand, paused, and took it. "You've been awake this whole time, are you *always* on guard?"

He smirked, a tiny tilt to his mouth and coppered skin. "We protect each other. That's how it is, Princess."

"Don't." The word must've been harsher than she meant, for her brows dipped and she whispered, "Please don't call me that."

Slowly nodding, he led her toward his tent. He motioned to the opening, and the hollowness in her struck him. Unable to hold in the curiosity, he asked, "What were those horns earlier?"

Her back straightened, taut as the tent strings. "Mourning horns. The castle sounds them when a royal passes. The towns sound them in reply of their mourning." A small sigh escaped her.

Lox didn't know what to say, her face seemed so... sad. Red sad was not something he expected to see. Not entirely sure why, he held the tent opening for her. She'd certainly had her share of servants, maids, all the nine gold-encrusted yards, and gods knew he—

"That's twice I've heard those horns," she whispered, stilling his thoughts. Amber eyes melted in the moonlight, capturing him entirely in their honesty. A small, sad smile touched her mouth. "Twice in a decade. Never thought I'd hear my own."

Lox's heart thudded deep in his chest.

His lips parted, but no reply came.

Her eyes widened before guarding themselves once again. Like the night he'd saved her from the guard and she'd released a genuine piece of herself to him, his response had made her retreat. She grabbed the opening from his hand. Before disappearing inside, she paused long enough to say, "Thank you."

And she was gone. Into the tent and herself.

Lox stood there, a thin sheet of canvas separating him from the broken girl who wouldn't let anyone in.

Damn. Damn him. The ball swam into his memory

The queen, regal and beautiful before the three thrones. Queen and Princess.

No king.

He hadn't even thought to consider it then, too caught up in his own hatred for the powerful. All while Raven had lost her father. This princess had suffered, more than he knew. And he'd yelled at her.

Bloody hell.

Lox meandered to the fire. Staring into the dancing flames, he clasped his hands and twisted the bronze ring. How old had he been? Twelve? Little less than a decade ago for him, and he was older than her, probably by a year. Raven must've been young, too young.

It had destroyed him, seeing his home and family destroyed by that greedy monster. And he'd ran—spent the last eight years running far from the cavern of his home's remnants. Tilly had begged him for help, but... what could he have done then? What could he do now?

Hook controlled far too much for him to fight against.

Lox sighed and examined the crest of his father: three gold sand dunes pressed into an auburn expanse. The bronze ring matched Raven's crown, he realized with a soft smile.

If he closed his eyes, he could feel the *heat* of the burning sun, the grains shifting under his feet, but not Valara. Never the sight of those dunes. He'd been merely four when his parents had moved. But he'd bet they were beautiful from what his mother—his *naja*—used to say. Valara had burned far before his adult time. It had only been luck that his parents left a year beforehand. Bad luck that they'd chosen Nevrande.

No one could've expected the fae to be overrun by a simple pirate. A pirate king backed by magic.

He looked across the fire at his tent, the princess inside who'd lost everything but had wanted to do anything for her duty. Yes, they had this loss in common.

But she was so much better than him.

Maybe… maybe that could change.

CHAPTER 29

Threads of dawn cascaded through the canvas opening, rousing Raven to the sounds of movement outside. The previous day and night rushed back to her, and she bolted upright. Lox's tent came into recognition, the bedroll and light blanket draped over her... Had it been there? She couldn't remember. Crying, she remembered that. After that slip-up she'd had with Lox... She hadn't meant for that. Something about the night, the fire, the still calm of the forest, it had all made her feel secure enough to speak.

Gods, why did it have to be to *Lox*? The shock in his eyes, the utter silence of his parted lips, it had made her feel—weak. Broken.

She buried her head in her hands, the green cap falling to the tent floor. She picked it up, inspecting the worn cloth, the green more vibrant inside, not as darkened. Faded, she surmised, an old cap. Whose? Scar had given it to her, but his was red.

"You're wearing my colors now, Red," Lox had said. Was it his?

Sighing, she replaced it atop her hair. Without her cloak, she almost felt naked. For two years, it had covered her, protecting her as much as the Red Hood identity protected her from guilt, but now she was on her own. No cloak, no crown, just her. And this damned cap.

Raven gazed at the opening. Figures moved beyond, smoke ascending to the still dim sky. Scar had said they shared the other three tents, but this was Lox's. Would they think something of her exiting their leader's tent? He was undoubtably flirtatious and charming. She didn't want that impression.

Yes, they'd kissed... but that felt so long ago.

She recalled his face in the firelight last night. Sometimes it didn't feel so far...

Whatever. The opinions of criminals were the least of her worries. She didn't quite give a damn.

After straightening her rumpled, borrowed tunic, Raven emerged into the faint daylight. The band readied themselves packing up the campsite, Lox's tent the only still standing. She adjusted her cap. The men stood near their horses, speaking with Jon at his many bags. Had they left it up for her? They'd could've woken her.

Scar passed, smiling. He touched the tip of his scarlet hat. "Mornin'."

Raven nodded, then stopped short. An apple flew her way, and she barely caught it.

Yet again, the men were busy, and she couldn't help. What the hell could she do? She'd never felt this out of place before. Not physically. She'd always known how she should act, even if contrary to her wants.

These men were strangers, this area foreign even though she'd ruled it. Scar seemed okay, at least—and Jon, the sweet boy. The only person she felt somewhat comfortable around was Lox, and they'd been arguing for two days. Raven sighed.

She looked around the campsite's remains in the dim morning light and spotted Lox sitting on a stump.

The scarred one, Ramsey, walked up to him first. She rotated the apple in her hand, glancing around the campsite for any way to busy herself.

A hand gently retrieved the apple from her fingers, and she glanced up to find Scar. She tensed, hand going to her knife. He smiled, raising a brow. A moment later, he had unsheathed his own blade and was slicing the apple. "Fancy a game?"

"What?"

He nodded toward a tree across the way. "Knife throwing. Whoever's closest to the knot wins. Fun way to start the day."

She watched him finish cutting two slices and then his dagger was embedded in the tree, wobbling from the force in the center of the knot. He handed her one of the slices and popped one in his mouth.

"Do you forget I saw you at the competition?" Raven took the offered food, eyeing the distance to the tree.

Scar shrugged. "That was sword *fighting*. I could be incredibly worse at knife throwing."

"Somehow I doubt that," she mumbled. Readying the dagger strapped to her right thigh, she aimed. Hers landed three inches below his.

"Damn you throw well." He whistled appreciatively, then removed his next red-handled knife. With a grin, he flung the weapon forward, it landing the barest space to the right of hers. Between each throw, he split more of the apple between them, until three daggers each punctured the trunk.

Raven conceded the game to him. "I wouldn't want to meet you on a bad day." She took the last slice from him. "Possibly not even a good day."

The bladesman laughed and went to retrieve their knives. When he returned, handing hers to sheath, he asked, "Tell me—how did a princess learn blades so well?"

He turned to a log by the remains of the campfire. He retrieved a whetstone from his pockets and slid his blades over it.

Raven sat on the ground a foot away, watching his easy smile. He was unexpectedly easygoing for someone who'd taken down Kieran and who she had no doubt could outmatch any of her guards.

What would he think of her if he knew what she'd done? She glanced up to find Loxley staring at her. The intensity in his wondering eyes caught the breath in her throat.

What was he thinking? And why did that look affect her so much?

"Raven?"

She blinked. Scar had dipped his head, gazing into her eyes. Concern laced his brow. The smile gone. She straightened and recalled his question. "My Head Guard. So I could protect myself."

She watched him sharpen his knives, glad not to catch his grey eyes. "Had to've started years ago for you to be this good."

"Six." She nodded at his raised brows. "We practiced every morning. Swords, knives, arrows, until I knew and could defend against anything

—even stronger opponents." Speaking of Ruben made her heart fall, so she turned to the bladesman. "What about you?"

A dark smile shadowed his face. "It's a long story, milady."

She gestured around the campsite. "And I'm so very busy."

One dimple flashed on the right corner of his mouth, lightening the dark expression. "My father's a bladesmith, best in Fovet. Well, the king requested a sword. Balanced perfectly, strongest metal available, and able to take down an opponent in a single slash. That part still depends on the wielder," he added with a smirk. "After my father made the sword, the king imprisoned him—so he couldn't make another.

"He knew father had trained me to fight and that I was his only family, so he took me into his... service as well. Sent me on the quests his men couldn't accomplish, either for danger or secrecy. He used us each as pawns to have the other do his dirty work; my father made the king-dom's weapons, and I..." Scar smiled a deadly, far too dark smile, filled with all the pain those years had served him, "killed the ones no one needed know were dead. Or the other would die."

Silence beaded between them. Raven watched Scar flex his fingers over his blade. "How did you end up with Lox?"

"I hired him."

Her brows rose, and Scar laughed, a soft sound for such a deadly man. "I'd watched him in Fovet. He'd been pickpocketing a few of the king's guards, and his stealth inspired me. He mostly went unnoticed by the right people, but he helped those unseen. I saw a good heart in such a crafty man, and I offered him a deal." Another, lighter smile crested his lips, and he flickered his grey gaze to hers. "Actually, I threatened to skin him and throw him in the dungeons if he didn't help me or if he told anyone of my plan."

"I imagine that went over well," she replied, remembering her threats to Loxley.

"He said he'd already known who I was. I thought he was lying—I was the king's secret, only a rumor—but when he mentioned my father... if Lox knew *that*, he was the man for the job. I wasn't taking any chances. Eventually, I stopped threatening him and he stopped taunting me, and we broke my father out of the castle. Daran and Beast helped, and Lance was already in the band." The bladesman paused, eyes drifting across the camp to the man who'd entered his tent the night before. Raven politely took a bite of her apple, holding back a smile. Then, Scar seemed to notice his slip and quickly rushed out, "So, my father is safe, and I dedicated my skills to something better—protecting instead of harming. My blades are my own now, as is my life."

The two sat, letting those words sink into the air. The words they'd shared just nights ago rang through her mind. *"Surely, a princess deserves more than the ground."*

"I'm not a princess anymore, and I don't deserve more than anyone else."

"Not even a killer?"

She eyed the young man beside her. A killer. Seemed Loxley really did take in the broken, the beaten, and the damned.

This band... their goals aligned more than she'd originally realized weeks ago, and they even seemed to have a deep effect on those in trouble. They stole, yes, but from the rich and cruel—she beat and killed the same type of men. Maybe she fit here more than she'd like to admit. Strong loyalty, and strong ideals.

Stronger morals than her, if she admitted it.

"So, the training," Scar said, pocketing his whetstone. He laid his arms over his knees and leaned forward. "What turned the princess into the Red Hood?"

That was a complex question. Raven took a deep breath. They—at least Ramsey—knew she'd killed Barren, maybe the other three if they'd been looking into the Red Hood. But not... *him.*

Hardness crept into her voice, a long-awaited anger that would not be ebbed, even now, "Take your pick—the starving people being whipped for stealing or the rich going unscathed for worse." Raven shook her head, clasping her hands in her lap. "I started by feeding them so they wouldn't be punished. But... then I learned of more tragedies than starvation in the village. The types of crimes no one reported or who would walk from my mother's trials."

"Let me guess," Scar said, "if they paid, they went free."

"Sadly, yes. Then, I became the Red Hood. To at least help how I could." Raven stared at the dying fire, then found her gaze lifted again to Loxley. Their stares caught—he'd been watching her. Listening? They held gaze for a long moment, then Raven remembered Scar beside her and straightened. The bladesman seemed to be inspecting his knife rather hard with a barely concealed smile. She had to resist the urge to send a pointed look at Lance.

Scar stood, sheathing his knife. "We should be leaving soon, but thanks for story time, Raven." He grinned. "Even though, I beat your ass in knife throwing."

A laugh escaped her before she knew it. The sound surprised her, and she couldn't remember the last time she'd laughed.

Movement returned her attention to the thief and his comrade. Lox, talking with Ramsey, nodded toward her. Ramsey smiled and started across the clearing toward them.

Great. What now?

She stood, pretending to search in her satchel for something. When he stopped in front of her, Raven ignored him. He stood there silent for a while. "Sleep well?"

Eyebrow raised, she finally looked at him. That light scar traveled from right temple to cocked grin. "I've had better."

A spark entered his caramel eyes. "So... Raven," he paused on her name, "what do you think of our band?"

"Not the worst band of bandits I've seen." Raven meant it lightheartedly, given Scar's friendliness both last night and this morning.

"And Lox?"

That was a loaded question. The forest eyes just yards behind Ramsey didn't slip her notice. She shrugged. "Depends on the moment. He's not the usual thief."

And that fact puzzled her amongst others.

Ramsey stepped forward, making her look upward to hold his stare. "That all?"

She squared her shoulders, satchel dropping to her side. Raven leaned in. "What do *you* think of him?"

"He's fair, a good leader." Confusion pulled his brows together.

"Then, I say go for it."

"What?"

Raven shrugged casually, making her voice light, "Ask him out, but I don't think you're his type. You're not curvy enough. But I might be wrong."

She knew she wasn't. Lox had loved her curves.

Ramsey stared, mouth parted.

Raven winked, and a laugh came from behind Ramsey—Scar coughed when Ramsey glared at him. When Ramsey looked back at her, the annoyance disappeared.

Done with him and the useless questions, Raven straightened her satchel.

"Next time you want a bed," Ramsey said, as he backed toward the horses, smirk stretching his handsome yet scarred face, "let me know."

Raven's hand stilled on the leather. Heat poured within her veins, and she narrowed her eyes at the criminal.

He winked, eyes traveling down her tunic. "I'll keep you warm. Better than that guard of yours ever c—"

"Ramsey," Lox growled, anger evident in the word.

Thud.

A breadth from Ramsey's head her dagger hummed, wavering from the strength she'd used to hurtle it across camp into the tree. This time, it was a perfect bullseye in the knot's center.

Silence filled the air, each man stilled.

"Shut. Up." Rage flew through her heart, voice sharp as her favorite dagger.

Finally quiet, Ramsey turned his wide eyes from blade to her.

Lox's laugh shot through the stillness. He came up beside his comrade, patting him once on the shoulder but gaze trained on her. "At least I'm not the only one. You really shouldn't taunt a woman who threw knives with Scar."

"You knew she did that?" Ramsey exclaimed, pointing at the dagger. "At people?"

"Thought only I brought it out in her." His leader shrugged, a grin heavy on his mouth. It faded when he looked at Ramsey. "You deserved that."

Scar winked at Raven from across the burned-out fire. The bladesman grinned and mouthed, "Nice."

Retrieving the knife from the bark, Lox whispered something to Ramsey. The man nodded stiffly before turning away with sulking shoulders. Lox neared Raven and held her gaze. "Rams was out of line. I was close to shutting his mouth myself. That said, if you harm one of my men unjustly, you're gone."

"I wouldn't." She tried to remove the iciness from her tone. "He just needed to shut up."

His seriousness drained after another beat. He handed her the dagger. "You can threaten him, even hurt him, just don't *kill* him, please. We all want to hit Ramsey most days, but when it comes down to it, he's a good man."

She eyed the blond, scar and all. Wondered again how he'd gotten it.

"I don't need talk like that. Especially not about—" Raven pressed her lips together, then let out a short sigh. She couldn't think about Ruben today.

Loxley nodded slowly, taking in her words. He rubbed a knuckle against his eyebrow. "I didn't tell any of them about—" He sighed, glancing down at her. She wished his eyes didn't land on her mouth. "When we…"

Kissed felt like such a small word for what he did to her in that alley.

"Good," she said, not wanting him to voice more. She took a breath, refocusing. "How are we getting out of Ecanta?"

"Daran's the navigator. And Jon does the logistics of when we need supplies, best places to get them and all that." Loxley headed to his horse and patted the beast's neck. "We leave for Terra once camp is packed."

A whistle drew their gazes over to the now-rolled tent. Beast hoisted it onto his shoulder and turned to a horse.

Lox smiled and stroked his horse. "Ready for another ride, Red?"

"Don't call me that."

"What then, milady," he leaned in, that pine woodsy scent enveloping her like the whole forest couldn't, "do I call you?"

She took a deep but silent breath, wishing the ache didn't lessen slightly with his scent. "Raven."

Forest eyes roamed her face, latching onto the cap, and a devilish grin lit the thief's tanned face. He stared at her lips. "Let's ride, Raven."

Yes, this was most definitely his cap. She really was wearing his colors.

Upon reaching the edge of Terra, the band split. Beast and Daran took to the ground, giving Jon their horses. Scar and Ramsey walked the cobblestone path first, and many minutes later, Jon descended on his own horse, two in tow.

Jon had tied the two sets of reins to his pommel and eased all three with a skill she figured he'd learned over much practice. Was he just an errand boy to this band?

Lance and Loxley, with Raven sitting behind him, traversed the forest.

"You don't have to tell them everything," Lox said into the quiet, almost startling her. They'd barely spoken a word since mounting his horse. "We don't lie to each other, but we don't force others to tell their secrets. We all have pasts, but we don't have to spill them."

Raven made herself stay still in the saddle. That was oddly... considerate of him. "What makes you think you don't know all my secrets, Lox?"

He chuckled and tilted his head to eye her over his shoulder. Their faces were so close that she leaned back. "A princess sneaking out of her castle to fight criminals? A princess capable of murder? No," he shook his head once, "you have more secrets."

This time, she *did* shift. "I didn't 'murder.' I killed a killer. Mother would ha—"

Mother.

Her heart squeezed in a vice, cutting off air as well as words.

"Re—Raven," Lox said, skipping over the nickname.

She dipped her head, breaking the spell his eyes tended to put her under. He probably thought her voice choked for another reason. The girl without a father now without a mother. Not because her only parent ordered her assassination while hugging her warmly on her orchestrated last day.

He tugged on the reins and, when she remained silent, looked to his man. Lance stopped his horse a few feet behind.

Raven kept her eyes on the trees while Lox handed over the reins. The two dismounted, and she busied herself while he gave orders. Lance departed with their horse to meet Ramsey and Daran and tie the horses in the forest.

She assumed he didn't want to risk a villager recognizing their deceased princess. Beast and Scar were booking a room at the inn, and Jon would join them once he'd went to the local store. For what, she didn't know.

Once Lance and the horses faded into the yonder trees, they headed in a diagonal direction.

"I hope you learn to trust us," Loxley said, startling her.

Raven stared ahead while they walked. "Trust is difficult to cultivate and even harder to keep strong."

"Especially when someone wants you dead," Lox agreed.

She nodded, fearing her voice. *Someone you loved and trusted.*

"You know who ordered it, don't you?"

Heartbeats pounded in her ears, the rush of her breath dulling the sound of the soft wind.

"I'm not asking who did it." His mouth curved. "You're easier to read without that hood, enchantment or not. I assume your guard didn't know about any of this—otherwise he would've helped with the request."

One small laugh left her. "No. Ruben trained me to protect myself, but he didn't know how I used that knowledge."

"Do you think he would approve?" His question was light, but it weighed on her.

She'd avoided asking herself that at every morning practice and every night she evaded Ruben's guards.

"He'd probably give me a talking to for being so reckless." A smile lifted her mouth at the word she knew he'd use. "Vow to train me harder the next day because we both know he couldn't stop me. And probably insist I let him take over."

Wind blew her hair around her face, each brush soft like her heartbeat.

"He'd understand why." Ruben was the only person who would understand. He wouldn't agree, he'd be angry. But he'd understand.

Lox let her stew in her thoughts, then looked over. "Were you two—"

Raven laughed. "He's married!" She gave Lox a grin to match his look of innocence. "And Esme just had their first child. No—we were best friends, nothing more."

"About Ramsey—"

"It's alright," she cut him off. "He doesn't know, and he's... I've met worse."

Lox raised a brow. "Did the dagger hit its mark, then?"

The canopy thickened above them, obscuring her expression in shadow, thankfully. Raven's heartbeat faltered. The memory of hot blood running down her arms and the cold grip of steel—she swallowed.

She hadn't meant for it, but yes, her dagger had hit its mark. And she'd kept it ever since.

Hollowness filled her soul, a deep cavern taking the place of her heart.

"What if it had?"

Loxley stopped walking and turned to her. He assessed her for a long moment, making her wish she had her hood again. "We've all done something we regret, love. We don't judge for the past."

Why did his gaze give her hope?

Why did she want it?

She nodded, forcing herself to look away. Something stirred in her heart, and she was too scared to identify it.

He continued on the invisible path through the trees, a comfortable silence hanging between them and the branches above their dark heads and hearts.

Daran stepped from the shadows not long after the trees started to thin nearer to town. He and Lox talked easily while she followed close behind. No matter how hard she tried, her steps could not be as silent as the Javir's.

How old was he? At least twenty. Probably close to twenty-six, like Ruben. Had he learned to walk on the shifting golden sands of Valara before it burned? That could be the trick to his never-ending silence.

But what was Loxley's trick? Life as a thief, perhaps.

Like in Dale, the trio snuck through the trees into the back parts of Terra. From there, they wound to the inn without any notice from the Terrans. Daran took to the front entrance and Lox lead her to a beautiful latticework that covered the back. He assisted her up and then they climbed the bricks, stepping from window to window, the ledges their only support. Raven was glad she'd left her gloves in her satchel this morning, otherwise her grip wouldn't be as sturdy.

Two stories up, Lox let out a bird call, and a darkened window opened. An arm reached down, then two hands grasped Raven and pulled her through. Another set of hands steadied her before she touched the floor. Ramsey leaned out to assist Lox while Scar brought her further inside.

"You good?" Scar's focused eyes examined her face.

She nodded.

The window shut behind Lox, and he inspected the three bandmembers. Daran was probably downstairs still, the distraction for their entrance—a Javir or Vala was always so rare that people took notice—and Beast out on watch.

Minutes passed where the men conversed, then Jon entered, a bag on his shoulder. Jon smiled crookedly and crossed the room, Lox reaching her as Jon did, and opened the bag. "Alright, there wasn't much, but this should do for the time being."

He pulled out a maroon tunic, smaller, more her size than whichever bandmember's shirt she currently wore. And dark, almost black trousers. Pockets were sown into the sides, and small slits—no, straps. She'd noticed the same on Scar's pants. For blades.

"You need something besides what you have on," Lox explained.

With another lopsided smile, Jon left. Raven asked, "Where's he going?"

"Supplies. He makes sure we have enough food and everything for the days we won't be near a town."

"Is he your errand boy?"

Lox straightened, seriousness creeping over his face. "What?"

She gestured to the door. "He puts up the horses, buys your supplies —is that all he's good for to you?"

"No." Lox glanced at the others, Lance and Scar talking near the bed, Ramsey at the window on guard. "Jon does that because he's the least recognizable. Ramsey has his scar, Daran is Javir, and Scar has what he likes to call a 'criminal aura' about him that we both carry. You've probably noticed, but Jon doesn't look like a thief or a criminal. I also don't let him partake in our more illegal activities. He does those things so we go unnoticed. Him and Beast."

"Why Beast?" she asked, curiosity of the most mysterious one of the group taking over.

Lox opened his mouth, then paused.

A dark laugh came from the window. "He's a right beast, that one."

The leader shot his man a look. "Ramsey."

He stiffened at his full name and leader's tone. Ramsey dipped his head and walked to the door. Lox grabbed his forearm. "Tell Daran to come up."

Ramsey slipped away with a nod.

Door shut, Lox returned his focus to her. She had an inkling Ramsey had meant Beast's appearance. And another that the reason ran deeper.

"Beast is cursed." Lox shook his head wearily. "By a Sandceress."

Sandceress? Aloria's history was vast, but Raven knew pieces—magic had faded for... years. Since the fall of Valara. Only the Sandcerers and Sages, the Vala and Javir, could wield human magic. Other forms of magic existed, of fae in the fabled Nevrande—which no human had seen or heard tale of for almost ten years—and the rumored mermaids, but finding those creatures was a mix of luck and legend. Up until around five years ago, mermaids had helped sailors and offered magic for those in need, but they'd been gone for so long people wondered if they had even surfaced or existed at all. Any remaining Valarans who'd somehow escaped the destruction of an entire empire lived spread throughout Aloria, but sorcery was sporadic even in those bloodlines... so for one to remain would be true magic.

To be cursed by someone of that lost kingdom, even rarer.

"That's..." Raven started but couldn't find a way to finish.

Lox nodded. "Anyone who sees him will see him a little differently. As far as we can figure, there's a base form, and people's perceptions alter their viewings, but we all see..." he tilted his head in thought, "a monster."

Oh. That's no short order curse.

"Yeah," Lox tugged her farther away from the men, a soft smile appearing when he glanced at Lance and Scar telling stories. "Raven— like I said, we all have our reasons for being here. Beast... Ramsey gave him that name since he didn't like using his own. We use it because he doesn't mind it after everything else he's been called. But he's *not* a monster—he just looks like one. Don't let that scare you."

"The things that scare me aren't monstrous, Lox." A fake smile, a casual touch, *pretending.* No, what she feared was pretty on the surface but dark inside. Beast was the opposite, she supposed.

"If you want to know more about the magic, ask Beast or Daran. He was young, but he lived in the time of human magic more than any of us." He gave her a calculating look, which strayed to the cap. "Your enchanted hood gave me pause at first, but an enchanted item could be a relic of Valara. A person... that's another story. If you had magic, you could help Beast, but you didn't react when he was in the tavern, so..." He shrugged. "Another Valaran out this far would be rare anyway."

Raven raised a brow at his words. Lox caught her look, his eyes widening.

The door opened for Daran, and he observed the two as he shut it.

"Not everyone considers the Javir 'Valarans,'" Raven said, voice soft.

The leader ran an olive hand through his black waves of hair and went to his comrade.

Lox accepted the beaten, the broken, and the cursed. Scarred both physically and emotionally. That's why they all fit so well.

Why Raven felt more understood in this band than in her castle.

CHAPTER 30

Candlelight glinted off Raven's newly sharpened blade, and she checked the edge one last time. Evening had surely struck, and she'd been kept in this room the whole gods damned day. She'd known being on the run wouldn't be a picnic, but being trapped in a room was not on her list of ideas.

The door creaked, stealing her gaze. Beast entered and woke Scar beside the bed. The bladesman stretched and stood. His boot paused mid-step, and he turned to the bed where Lance lay. Softly, gently for such a deadly man, he lifted the rumpled blanket and stretched it over the sleeping figure. Lance didn't even stir.

Scar caught Raven's stare, and a small smile rose to his mouth as redness colored his cheeks. With a nod and dip of his hat, he exited.

Lox had been in the tavern or who the hell knew where for *hours*. Jon was getting supplies, whatever that was, but what could the leader be doing? What had he done in her town? Raven scrubbed her face with calloused hands. *Stole*. She sighed—and help her escape with her life.

Stop thinking the worst of people. These men were more than their appearances. Her eyes traveled across the room to Beast, dark leathery skin shining in the dim candlelight. *No, we are not all what we seem*.

Legs stiff from lack of movement, Raven stood and walked to the door.

"Where are you going?" Daran asked in his deep lilting voice, stepping close to her destination.

"Out." She gripped the handle.

Another deep voice spoke from the blanketed window, "Boss says you stay in here."

Repressing a sigh, she looked at Beast, but he didn't meet her eyes. "He's not my boss, and I'm used to staying in the shadows." She twisted the knob. "If he gets mad, I'll take the blame."

Chatter and clinking glasses filled the air the moment she entered the hall, the sound of people both warming her ears and tearing her heart. Raven tucked more hair under the cap and adjusted the rim over her eyes. The dirt had probably worn off her face by now, so she kept it lowered from view. Terra barely had seen its princess, but Terran people still knew her face even if not as well as Ilasia's villagers. No one looked up to the person descending the stairs in the low lighting's shadows, too busy with their drinks, their talk, their cards, or their women.

"Ravenna was too young."

The words halted her boot on the bottom step. She took a deep breath and forced her feet steadily against the wooden floor and to the back wall where she could see the bar and both the stairs and front door.

"Whole damned family is too young for all this loss," another voice said, gripping her heart further.

Maybe coming downstairs wasn't the best idea... Raven clenched her hand into the new pants Jon had given her. But it was so lonely up there. The camaraderie of the band made her miss Ruben so much that it *hurt*. Her throat tightened, and she eyed the door. Fresh air would help.

The lost princess turned, weaving seamlessly around tables and villagers and various spills, hand reaching the open the door—a laugh froze her fingers. She looked over her shoulder, found Lox in the back corner with Ramsey. The scarred young man held a hand of cards over a large pile of coin, Lox beside him, his hands holding a blushing woman.

Blushing because Lox's hand rested on her hip while she sat on his lap.

Raven stepped back, walking along the wall toward them. The woman was more Ruben's age, she surmised, and wearing a small fine necklace above her bodice. The hefty jewels more than a normal villager could afford. How could a waitress have that?

Lox whispered something into Ramsey's ear and returned to the woman, her face reddening with a few words from him.

"*Red,*" she recalled him whispering against her skin, voice like fire against her bones. What had he said to heat up this woman?

This was why she'd been holed up in that damned room? For them to gamble and flirt?

Another crooked smile from Lox, and the woman looked like she was about to faint. At that moment, he looked like Landon. As if love had nothing to do with affection. As if comments and smiles meant nothing. As if one smile could get him anything he wanted—and it could, from the looks of that woman.

The thief's tan hand slipped down her back and to her waist. Raven was about to look away in annoyance at his blatancy—she'd seen enough of Landon's actions years ago—but then Lox's fingers slipped into the woman's purse while he nuzzled her neck.

Raven glared, anger beating her heart rampant, and tried to separate the dead red-headed arrogant prince from the dark, charming thief before her. But she couldn't.

The fact that she tried, that she—almost desperately—wanted to, confused and irritated her.

Ramsey tugged on Lox's sleeve. Smiling, Lox leaned down to his man, then glanced quickly to her. His smile disappeared like her hope— *hope?*—that he was different. Their eyes locked, his expression unreadable. Raven turned and made herself exit the tavern.

Outside, the late afternoon setting sun lent little in the way of direction and light. Unfamiliar with these streets but just wanting *away,* Raven headed around the inn for the forest. The trees would give her solitude and solace. Footsteps followed mere seconds after she'd reached the trees, and she released a heavy sigh of frustration.

"Red," Lox called. He was right behind her, but thank the gods, he didn't try to stop her.

She whirled around, breath coming fast. He lifted a hand toward her arm.

"No." She raised her hand, gritted her teeth, and gripped her fingers into a fist before lowering it. "Charms will not work on me, thief."

Loxley stopped, face a near shadow. "We're back to that, are we? *Thief?*"

He almost sounded hurt. She could've laughed.

"Raven," he started, "I know that looked incriminating. But I don't like h—"

"Do you think I'm jealous?" She did laugh, a cold sound in the quiet forest. "That I want to be another blushing woman falling for your words and your—" She forced herself to stop. His intoxicating touches, his kisses, his ability to look at her and melt her completely. Raven clenched her fists.

Lox looked confused, examining her face quietly.

Raven stepped forward. "I don't care about you and her, Lox. You can do whatever and *whoever* you want. It's that you use them."

Dark brows rose in shock and outrage. "What?"

"How many times have you taken a woman to bed, just to steal more than a heart?"

Lox let out a gasp of air, mouth open before he clenched it. "I will admit that I flirt," he replied, his words came out strangled, stubbled jaw tight, "but I do *not* bed women to steal. That woman makes her money in secrets and blackmail, and Rams and I were gathering information on any local crime. I wouldn't touch her beyond what you saw." He tilted his head, a dark lock falling forward. "I am not that kind of criminal or man." The anger drained out of his face, brows loosening. That... honesty entered his forest eyes. "I thought you knew that, Red."

Raven had to steel herself against the surprising feeling of guilt. "I know *nothing* about you! Just your name."

Not true, screamed a part of her. She knew he protected others; he would rather face a queen—an assassin—than run to save his name. He would rather get caught with her than abandon her.

Raven backed up a few steps, confusion muddling her emotions. Every time she questioned what type of person—thief—this man was, she questioned herself. And the answer never came clearly for either. She'd let a few whispered words and fiery touches—one damned kiss— muddle her thoughts.

She raised her hands to her chest, reaching for her necklace and grasping nothing. The emptiness shattered her. Her shaky fingers met her hair, absent of a crown or hood, but weighed down by a damned green cap. She removed it, gripping it tightly in both hands.

Loxley's eyes rested on the cap, and his closeness unnerved her.

"Goodnight, Loxley." Raven moved around him, shoving the cap to his chest and releasing it and her anger. She was so damned tired of being confused, of the anger, the guilt. Tired of everything.

A WARM HAND ON RAVEN'S MOUTH WOKE HER. HER HAND TOUCHED HER dagger before the woodsy scent calmed her panic. She sighed. Why did it calm her, damn it? Raven blinked into the dark room, focusing on Loxley kneeling before her.

"No dagger?" he whispered, halfheartedly joking. He jerked his head and rose. Soft leather boots quieted his steps to the window.

She stood, confused, watching him. Did he want to continue the argument? He didn't seem angry. And she didn't want to fight anymore. She followed him to the pane.

Beast stood beside the covered glass.

"Don't tell Daran," Lox whispered to him.

"He'll know anyway."

Lox grinned. "Good point."

He pulled the blanket from the glass and pushed the pane open. With a boot on the sill, he turned and grasped her hand. Her eyes widened, but he stood on the thin sill, head disappearing above and tugged her out. Raven copied his movements, squinting in the darkness to find his form on the roof above and to the right. She followed the tug on her hand, gripping his fingers tight when her foot grew unsteady on a shingle.

"Guess you haven't been on as many rooftops as I thought," he whispered, a hint of apology in the teasing tone. His voice was close, breath on her ear, and another hand touched her elbow to steady her and bring her to the peak of the roof.

Black night surrounded them, only the light of lanterns below and the stars above. The beauty of the night stunned her. Then, Lox shifted, hands dropping from her, and the cold air rushed in, reminding her where she was and why. She took a step backward. His height forced her to look up, those bright eyes shining like the starry backdrop.

"Lox, I don't—"

"You were right," Lox sighed, "you don't know anything about me. I don't know much of you, but I do know some. And you don't have a reason to trust me." He looked down at her. "But you should. After all this, you should know I won't hurt you. I lost my parents and my home when I was twelve."

Raven straightened, staring at his hard face with a new light.

Loxley sighed, gaze sliding to the space beyond her, the muscle in his jaw ticking once. Twice. "We lived in Nevrande."

"Nevrande?" Raven stared, open mouthed.

"Yes. It's real. And the fae. Or was." He scoffed, shaking his head. "The simple answer is it's lost. Ripped from Aloria, my village was broken in the process. My parents, they're dead—I saw—" Lox cut himself off, closing his eyes tight. "And the only home I knew was destroyed. All I know is temporary beyond this band. Nothing else."

Her hand raised to his arm without notice until her bare hand touched his warm skin. He looked at her and moved closer, dark brows crumpling. She shifted her gaze between his deep eyes, hating herself for never wondering why this man—barely older than her—roamed Aloria without family. "I'm sorry. I didn't..."

He nodded, those almost black locks shifting on his forehead. "Yeah... that's the thing about being on opposing sides—we assume the other doesn't have our pain."

Understanding glinted in that emerald gaze, so strong that her throat tightened. They'd lost their parents, their families, in different ways, but the loss was still strong between them. She squeezed his arm lightly and withdrew her hand.

He crouched and sat, easing his legs out. "Or some refuse to notice it."

She knew plenty of people in that category. Raven sat, pulling her legs close to her chest, watching the lights of the town. She stared out at the city, wondering how she could miss so much about people, how she didn't ask questions. Didn't even think to form the questions. Was she so blinded by her own goals?

Lox sighed softly and laid his back against the roof. The movement, the utter relaxation in such an exposed space, drew her eyes to him. He stretched an arm up to rest a hand under his head. She tried not to stare at his muscles and found him watching her when she tore her gaze away. His mouth curved.

Raven traced the buildings with her gaze, wishing again she had her hood to cover not only her face, but her expression from him. The night wind cooled her heated cheeks. She hadn't quite noticed it as much before in Ilasia, not with her hood's covering and the magic's warmth. Here, everything was different. Even the buildings and rooftops had a different pattern, not blocked in by walls. This village she had barely visited but was meant to rule—it was beautiful. And she saw it in mourning.

"Raven." Loxley's deep voice rang through her silence, pulling her to the surface.

She looked over to Lox, simultaneously grounding and trying not to lose herself in his gaze.

"After Ilasia, I didn't think you… I thought you were just using me. To escape," Lox admitted. He shrugged, like he could lift a weight lying on his shoulders. "I felt tricked. And I couldn't reconcile the you I liked with the one who ruled. I've always had trouble with those in power."

He sat up, propped up on his arm. Moonlight cast over his face, and she tilted her head to face him. "When we visit new towns, we use whatever resources we can to get information on those who need help. Often, my *charms* are a valuable asset. Like I said," he reiterated, latching onto her gaze, "I only flirt. I don't bed for that."

"But you have bedded women in these towns you've travelled?"

"Yes."

"For love?" she challenged. Why did she care?

The thief nodded, studying the gold ring on his hand. "What I thought was love. But…" his gaze caught her face before dipping down, "not been loved."

What? The thought dumbfounded her. With all his flirtations and charm and… just how was that possible?

A sheepish smile crested his mouth. "You thought I was the one playing with emotions and throwing hearts around." Lox shook his head, not quite meeting her eyes. "A criminal is not desirable, Red."

Lox finally looked up, eyes widening at her confusion. Raven was stunned into silence, both at his openness about himself and his words. Another lonely person was not what she'd wanted, least of all the always grinning Loxley.

"No one is looking for me to be their husband. I'm not worth anything." That matter-of-fact tone she'd had earlier sounded wrong resting in his voice. Lox shrugged, touching to his chest. "No happy ending for me—I know that."

Raven leaned forward. "Lox…"

Forest eyes moved to her, and her heartbeat sped up at the look held within. "Were you really going to marry that prince?"

"Of course," she stated, surprised by the question. "I was going to marry whoever we needed to support Ecanta."

"So, to hell with love, then?" A not-quite icy tone entered his voice.

"It's not the same." Raven narrowed her eyes. "I'm a Princess, Lox—we don't get to fall in love. We have to marry for power or for necessity. We don't get to choose. And we don't get to love."

Rustling beside her drew Raven out of her thoughts. She focused on the man beside her, as warm as the fire he'd lit within her.

"Red, you're no longer a princess." Loxley leaned in, and Raven forced herself not to look away from his eyes, even as his breath brushed her face. "That means you get to choose now."

Her brow crinkled. *I get to choose?*

"You, Raven, can have anything you want."

A handful of heartbeats passed before she realized… *I get to love?* Raven shifted, uneasy with this topic. She'd never thought love important before. When she realized it could be attained…

When she might actually want it.

Raven shifted to stare up at night sky, unable to hold his stare without her heart racing. She wasn't even sure why. Lox always caused such confusion in her.

"Regarding the flirting before," he continued in her silence. "If it displeases you, love, I'll stop."

She cursed the churning emotion in her chest. "I'm surprised you'd give up a chance to flirt." Raven turned and raised an eyebrow at him. "It seemed to be your favorite pastime."

"Oh, I'd say my favorite pastime is the *outcome* of said flirting," Loxley said, a mischievous grin spreading. "But flirting isn't fun if you don't really want the outcome."

"What do you want?"

"That's a dangerous question, love."

Why did he keep calling her that? She swallowed. "Why's that?"

The wind blew past them, cooling the heat building under her skin and whipping a strand of hair forward.

Loxley leaned in, brushing her hair from her cheek and placing it behind her ear. Warmth followed his knuckle as it trailed down her jawline and up to her chin. "Because after you, Red, I couldn't want anyone else." His stare dropped to her lips. "And I want you in every sense of the word."

"I—" She closed her mouth, words lost somewhere in the shortening distance between them. Had she moved in? Him? She didn't know.

His thumb caressed her bottom lip, igniting fire throughout her body. Something mixed between a whimper and a sigh left her, and that was it. Loxley caught her gaze, and in the next moment, his lips descended on hers, her hands gripping his shirt.

Loxley thrust his hand through her hair, cupping the back of her head to angle her mouth for him to delve his tongue inside. He leaned in, rolling her back onto the shingles and covered her with his torso. She dug her fingers into his neck, down his chest, and found herself wrapping her arms around his back. When his tongue plunged deeper, her nails scraped the muscles of his back through his tunic.

A moan left Loxley, and he eased over her fully, legs twining with hers, propping himself up with the arm still behind her head. All of him touched her—all she could think and feel was Lox. His heat, his woodsy scent, his strength.

Raven arched against him, pulling him closer if that was possible. He hissed—biting her bottom lip lightly. She gasped, surprised and thrilled by the sensation. Loxley chuckled at her reaction. "Like that, do you, love?"

His warm hand drifted down her waist to her hip, and she couldn't form a response. She stared into his forest eyes, panting from their kiss and wanting more. Raven grabbed his head and pulled his mouth back to hers, deepening the kiss herself. Lox moaned and relished her ferocity for just a moment before taking his lips from her mouth to her jaw.

She started to protest until his tongue traced a line down her neck. Days ago, she would have been embarrassed by the sound she made as he kissed—the nip of teeth—the base of her throat, but tonight, she was all consumed by him and every emotion he elicited within her. Heat burned at her core, burned wherever he touched and intensified until she could barely handle it.

Loxley slid his fingertips under the hem of her tunic slowly. Gods, her skin felt too tight, like she would combust and explode any second. He shifted above her, and her breasts rubbed against his chest, the tips burning in a way she didn't know they could. She wanted his touch— everywhere. She wanted to touch *him*.

Raven tugged at his tunic and ran her fingers underneath, relishing the smooth skin of his back. Loxley shuddered, cursing her name into her neck. He leaned back just enough to untuck his shirt from his pants, giving her free access to the muscles of his chest, barely lifting his mouth from her body. Her hands skated up his abdomen greedily, feeling his pounding heart under her fingertips, then around his back again.

He pressed her into the rooftop, hips lining up against hers, and leg spreading hers slightly. She gasped as his muscled thigh rubbed her core and sent an intense wave through her.

"I know, love," he growled against her neck.

Raven's body arched against his in reaction, intensifying the desire pooling low.

"Loxley," she whispered, unsure but overwhelmed with every sensation he sparked. She gripped him, nails clawing into his skin.

He must've heard the desperation in her voice because he lifted his head to gaze into her eyes. His breaths came fast, mingling with her own. He held her stare, watching her expression as he brought his hand from her hip to her waistband. Loxley brushed his fingers down the front seam of her pants directly where the heat coiled and—

A wild gasp left her. She thought she was on fire before now she was the whole damned flame. Her hips jolted upward, pushing into his hand more, eliciting raw pleasure. "Lox—"

"I've got you, Red." He covered her mouth with his, plunging his tongue inside as he rubbed the most sensitive part of her. Heat pooled and swelled within her, building with the friction of his fingers until— she exploded. Waves of ecstasy washed over her, splitting her into starbursts. She gripped him, not caring if she scratched him, if she writhed against his hand and hips—if she never came down.

He carried her through, easing her down as the peak drifted. Lox softened their kiss into a slow tangle of tongues, moving his mouth against hers methodically. He only broke away once her writhing stopped.

Breathing hard, Lox rested his forehead on hers, chest heaving against her own.

Raven blinked up at him, lightheaded. Her face was flushed, and she loved seeing that his was, too.

He grinned, that dimple appearing. Loxley watched her catch her breath.

Something stirred in his eyes, something deep and encompassing. It resonated with some broken piece inside her, and her chest tightened for entirely different reasons than moments before.

"Raven..."

The soft, even sound of metal below the rooftop stole her focus. Her heart fell into overdrive. Armor—steps of armor. Raven pressed her fingers to Lox's shoulder, shushing him, and eased further down on the roof. She could hear him adjusting his shirt before following. Boots hitting the edge, she crouched and peered into the street.

One guard marched across the darkened cobblestone path, steady footsteps beating a rhythm into her heart. A silver crown insignia glinted on his chest—a Royal Guard. How had they reached this far already? The band had ridden hard for the past two days.

She whispered to Lox, "He's from the capital."

He turned back to the man with interest, cursing.

Reaching a noticeboard, the guard placed a single page at its center. After ensuring it would hold, the guard turned down the street and posted more pages on posts and occasional doors.

The two outlaws exchanged a glance before the thief dropped over the rooftop edge. Raven checked the height and found Lox extending his hand toward her. She grasped it and used his lent strength and steadiness to jump down. Through shadows and darkness the two crept to the noticeboard.

What would her reward be now after killing royalty?

The page illuminated in the moonlight—**TREASON: Murder of Princess Ravenna and theft to the crown. Reward: 10,000 coppers.**

A hooded face, dark red splashing against the yellowed paper.

RED HOOD

A silhouette drawing of black hair framing an olive-skinned face stared back at them.

LOX.

What had she done?

CHAPTER 31

L ox appraised the sketch of himself, wondering when the queen
or that Ruben fellow had seen him enough to make a good drawing. They even got his nose right. "Not bad. Ten thousand
coppers is a good reward for treason, right?"

Bloody hell that guard had bad timing. He wanted to return to the
rooftop with Raven and continue what they'd started. To—

Silence rang beside him, and he glanced down at Raven. Wide amber
eyes stayed locked on the poster.

"Raven?"

She blinked. Those entrancing eyes shifted to his—his heart faltered.
Fear, utter fear stared back at him. Exactly like the first competition when
she'd seen that Loren prince. The intensity stole every thought from his
mind beyond protecting her, every thought from the rooftop faded under
her fear. He reached a hand to her shoulder, but she snapped out of
whatever trance she was in. Raven's mouth opened, and her brows shot
to her dark locks, gaze skipping from him to the empty morning street.
She grasped his raised hand and strode toward the trees.

Lox moved a step in surprise, but the grip of her fingers steeled his
boots into the dirt.

She kept moving forward, hand stretched out until forced to stop.
One more tug, and she turned on him, panic flashing in her gaze.

"Raven. What's wrong?"

The fear subsided momentarily for confusion. "What's—we have to leave."

Yes, that they did. But her panic threw him. This level of worry from her was rare. He'd only seen it when she was scared for her own life—that prince, the night she confided the murder. Why now? She wasn't in danger without her signature hood.

"Lox—" she started, voice pleading and strained.

The terror radiating from her made him relent. A sigh on her lips, Raven brought him into the forest and behind the tavern. Each hurried step taken only after searching the area. Eyes locked on her face, Lox followed and tried not to focus on the warmth of her skin. Stars be damned, how did the simple feel of her hand on his ignite this need for her?

Once hidden in the trees, Raven turned and stood inches from him, making him stand straighter at her blatant closeness. Lavender filled his nose when he took in a quick breath. Her gaze traced his face, calculating in their scrutiny. "Do you still have that cap?"

Lox removed the old hat from his back pocket. The soft and supple cloth unfolded in her hands. Seeing it on her head before had added a light feeling to the dark memory shrouding the relic of his father and the childhood he'd never have back.

She smoothed out the creases and stepped closer, raising her arms. Lox inhaled in surprise again—Raven never came near him, not *this* near—and held still as she placed the cap on his head. He always touched her, she never touched *him*.

Her smooth fingers tugged its sides further down, paused, then moved pieces of his hair out from under the front. His scalp tingled at each of her touches.

He could lean down an inch and kiss her. The urge struck him as hard as the heat that flashed wherever she touched his hair and skin, both surprising him with the fierceness. If fear didn't linger in her focused eyes, he would've grabbed her and continued what they'd started on that rooftop right here. The sound of her moans against his tongue—bloody hell. But she looked terrified.

Her fingers finally lowered, and she nodded to herself, gaze dropping to his eyes.

Raven rubbed her fingers together and resumed walking toward the inn. She paused below the tree they'd used earlier and motioned for him to climb first. When he didn't, she pushed him. Her fingers shook against his shoulder.

Lox climbed the damned tree only to calm her. He needed to get her to a place where she felt safe. Scared was not a good color on Red.

At the window, Beast took in Lox's serious stare and had them inside immediately. Dark eyes landed on the hat, and Beast looked between them.

Once Lox's boots hit the floor and the window shut, he shot out orders. "Beast, find Daran and get the horses. Lance—Ramsey's probably still downstairs. Leave as quickly and quietly as you can." That gambler was hard to separate from his cards, but at least he won coin. Lox nodded to Beast, and the cursed man exited into the night.

Instantly, the band jumped into motion—Lance out the door, Jon gathering supplies and dispersing items with Scar.

"Boss," Scar said. The bladesman flickered his gaze to Raven.

Lox neared him, eyes never leaving Raven for long, still alarmed by her panic. The quiet retreat into herself as her fingers checked and rechecked the blades at her waist. Another hand rested at her chest, where that necklace had laid, and rubbed a spot over her heart.

Every ounce of what they'd shared on the rooftop was gone, and Lox was terrified he'd never have it back. Not just the touches, the gasps he rang from her, but the connection. The way she looked at him like she saw him as more.

The bladesman appraised her. "She's got five blades, and I think she's about to throw them."

Lox counted four he could see, but Scar was the master swordsman.

"I know." Lox removed his gaze from her to examine Scar. "Is she okay around you?"

Scar nodded, then straightened. "Not the same as you—"

"No worries." Smiling at his man's worry, Lox raised a hand. "You, Lance, and Jon will take Raven to the horses. I'll—"

A knock at the door silenced him and the two other men. Raven had a dagger removed even before Scar, a feat to beat for sure. Jon rose from the bags he'd packed. Lox raised his palm and crept across the wooden floor toward the entrance.

"It's me," came an ever-familiar lilting voice. Daran.

Lox let the man in, patting his shoulder. "You didn't have to—"

"I did." Bright eyes roamed the dark room, stopping on Raven whose fingers danced over her sheathed blades. "Horses are ready. Two groups?"

The leader nodded, checking on the restless princess. "Go ahead and head to the horses. You'll set off first."

"No." Raven snapped into focus, hands stilling, and rushed across the room to him. Determination set in her gaze, chasing the fear. "You're not going to leave last again. Not with your face plastered out there."

Her words hit his heart. Did she… care? About him? No, it had to be something else.

Daran looked at Raven, then nodded.

"What?" Scar asked, a fierceness directed at his leader.

Lox let out a breath and ignored the swordsman. "I'm not going to get us caught, Red." Her intense eyes remained narrowed, so he added, "I'm not leaving last."

Worry marred that beautiful face in a way that tore his heart. Her tense lips stretched into a grimace.

Scar nudged her shoulder. "Don't worry, Daran won't let him head out alone."

Amber eyes held onto Lox's green, then moved to the cap. Her hand lifted, then dropped to her chest before she could touch him. Raven turned away.

Lox nodded to Scar and Jon. The boy placed a bag at Lox's feet and headed after the others. Scar helped Raven outside, and the small group disappeared.

A long silence filled the air.

"Loxley," Daran said, voice like a shifting breeze. Lox braced himself for his right-hand man's words. "If the guards have reached here, Gilan might not be an option. Verdan is faster—"

"Is he there?"

A sigh. "Yes."

Anger rushed through Lox like his heartbeat pounding in his temples. "Then, Verdan is off limits." He scooped up the bag and stalked to the window. "Beast doesn't need a reminder and neither does she."

. . .

THE MOON STILL SAT HIGH BY THE TIME THE TWO GROUPS MET DEEP IN THE forest. Lox searched out Raven the instant the horses appeared, and her wide eyes caught his. What he'd do to calm that panic roiling within her.

Damn Daran for suggesting Verdan. She didn't need that sadness right now.

After checking headcounts for all seven lost men and the lost princess, Daran took the lead across the black expanse. The Javir had never steered Lox wrong before, but they disagreed now. They'd both watched their families decay, one buried and burned, the other crumpled and drowned. Each lost and roaming Aloria alone. They understood each other better than anyone else, but... their hearts rested in different places. One shifting as the sands, the other rooted as the forests.

Daran, a practical and logical man, never made a move without ensuring it was right. Verdan would be the fastest and safest route, but Lox wouldn't take it if it harmed his bandmembers. Especially not Raven.

Hooves pounded into the dirt and around trees for an hour before the band slowed their pace for the horses' stamina. The moonlight had disappeared, blanketed by clouds. Water splashed against his hand on the pommel, bringing him out of his reminiscence. Rain.

Shit.

Lox halted his horse and looked upwards to the mountains looming over the forest canopy. The Gilan pass would be more treacherous in this weather, the rocks and clay slipping under their boots and horses' hooves.

The band stopped, Daran moving to Lox.

Grudgingly, Lox said, "We'll camp for the rest of the night."

His friend nodded, taking the decision in tow with his leader's earlier anger, and started to dismount. Daran's gaze paused on the hat. "Long time since you've worn that."

"Haven't felt like I should, Daran."

Silver eyes shifted to him. "And do you now?"

Lox sighed, forcing himself not to look at the newest member of the band. "Maybe I'm on my way."

"I'd like to see that," Daran said, dismounting and leaving his oldest friend to his thoughts.

Lox smiled—the two Valarans on even ground once again—then gazed across the lightly sprinkling expanse at Raven.

"Let's get the tents up quick, men," Lox announced to the others. "Everyone inside tonight except watch—only one tonight, no one's getting sick from this."

The drizzle had turned into a light downpour by the time all four tents stood in their circle, supplies and lanterns placed inside each. The number of tents and occupants meant more than two people doubling up, no matter how many times he counted. Stars be damned, he'd normally love any reason to have Raven in his tent, but he didn't know where they stood after the rooftop. After—Lox shook his head.

Last time they'd kissed, she'd been so distant afterward. What would this bring?

How many times had he thought there was something more, but he'd only been an experience, a night, for a woman? Gods, he'd never wanted *more* this much, though.

Raven might break him.

If she wanted, he'd forfeit his tent. Anything to ease what burdened her.

While the men worked, Lox kept glancing at Raven standing to the side. The distant, unsure look on her face.

Black hair whipped around her face with the rapid wind. Hollow amber eyes reflected rain, staring into the stormy night. Silence wasn't unusual for Raven, but this silence was harsh. Not the sad somber of a princess who'd abandoned her kingdom to mourn, but the quiet panic of fear. Where was her mind? She seemed undisturbed by the building gale, though it almost ripped Lox's cap off his head.

How lost was his princess?

"Boss."

Lox blinked and turned to Scar, who held his own red cap tightly. Lox raised his brows in question.

"How d'you want to do the tents?"

"You guys can double up however you want." Lox eyed Lance finalizing a tent's ropes.

"What about you?" Scar motioned to Raven, whose hands had returned to her unruly and rampant hair. "Raven doesn't look well. She probably shouldn't be alone, Lox."

He smiled sadly and shook his head. "She's worried."

"Yeah," the bladesman held his leader's stare, "but I don't think it's about herself." Scar patted Lox's shoulder before heading off to the last tent on the end.

Sheets of rain poured on the lost thief, clouding the distance between him and the lost princess. Lox watched Raven warily and touched his old cap. Unsure, he took a step forward, not ready to let hope back into his heart.

ICE ENCOMPASSED RAVEN, SO ENTIRELY THAT SHE WASN'T SURE IT DIDN'T originate from inside. How had it come to this? On the edge of Ecanta, if she recognized the Gilan mountains correctly. The hearts of all Ecanta broken. On the run from her own damned guards and mother. *Mother.*

Needles pricked at Raven's eyes, harder than the rain. This was all her own damned fault. She'd disappointed her mother, she'd brought Loxley to Vanera's attention, she'd *involved* him in this whole facade. If he died, it was on her hands.

She wouldn't let him die.

Mother would not touch him.

Raven pressed her lips together and gripped her tunic, every comfort she'd ever had gone. No crown, no hood, no necklace, and no Ruben. So gods damned alone.

Warmth touched her shoulder, breaking through the ice. A shiver traveled her spine, and she looked up, focus clearing her gaze—Loxley. Emotion crashed over her, a wave of relief rushing in and guilt pushing it back.

He tried a smile and extended his hand.

She eyed it. She'd done so much wrong, she couldn't touch him. Not after all this.

Lox's smile faded, but he placed his hand on her shoulder again and tugged her along. Numb, both inside and out she realized, Raven followed him. Each step was lead, both from her soaking clothes and the freeze that had settled beneath her skin. Had it really been raining this much?

Her feet halted when she noticed he held the flap open for her. Alone with Loxley. A flush threatened to take over her icy skin, not just from the wicked desire he brought out in her, but because he was a comfort to her. She wasn't sure when it had started, this man becoming the person she turned to. The reason she could breathe.

Stars be damned, she wasn't even sure she should be here anymore. Everything was wrong. He didn't even know how wrong—what she'd done. Landon—her mother's order—the attention she'd drawn to him.

She might break if he got too close. She felt on the edge of a cliff, stuck. Not sure whether to fall into him or run.

"Raven," Lox said, voice soft and tired. She gazed at him, trying to decipher his expression through the downpour. "I just want you out of the rain. There's dry clothes inside."

She nodded and dipped to enter. The quiet and calm inside hit her instantly. As well as the chill in her bones. One lantern rested in the corner, an orange glow illuminating the tent. It was just tall enough for them both to stand, a bedroll in the back and a raised pot in the center. Bootsteps sounded, and she turned as Lox stepped through the opening.

A memory of the sensation he'd elicited from her on the rooftop—had that only been an hour ago?—brewed, not quite enough to dispel the ice in her veins.

He raised his hands, palm out, eyebrows high and honest. Lox pointed to the pot resting, the holes carved in the lid. "I'm going to start a small fire for you."

When she didn't protest, he shut the canvas behind himself. She watched him, wondering why he still cared. He sounded... hesitant, distant. Or was that just her?

She sat on the bedroll beside the pot, wrapping her arms around her drenched body. Gods, she felt so damp and *heavy*. But that could just be her guilt, not the rain. Why was he being so nice? She'd gotten his name plastered throughout Ecanta, all for her murder. He'd *saved* her, he didn't deserve to be charged with this.

"Red..." Lox sighed, taking a seat a foot away. Raven stared at the distance like it was a void she'd never cross again. "You're scaring the hell out of me."

Raven rose a brow half-heartedly.

He placed something in the pot and made a spark within. A small orange flame glittered. Loxley blew into the flame, making the sparks grasp onto kindling. Small heat radiated toward her, but with even her bones frozen, this chill would not ease quickly.

"Seriously, Raven, what's wrong?" Lox's voice was low but filled the quiet tent.

She opened her mouth to snap at him like before, but his gaze stilled her retort. Dark green eyes clouded by worry—*worry*—and… somehow that scared her. He wasn't angry at her, and he had every right to be.

Rubbing her arms to dispel some of the cold, and to give her restlessness something to do, Raven sank into a sigh. "I did this." Her voice cracked, and she swallowed, trying to push down that stupid emotion that rose every time she truly thought of her mother, of being wanted *dead*. "I did all of this."

Raven tried to inhale, but it stuttered, and she gripped herself tighter. Maybe, somehow, she could keep herself together if she didn't let go? Did that give her a chance?

"Hey, no…" Loxley's soft hand brushed back her hair, and she squeezed her eyes shut against the gentleness. Rustling sounded as he leaned closer, his body heat managing to reach through her drenched attire. "What are you talking about?"

"Treason!" Raven gasped, finding a full breath on that horrendous crime of a word. She tried to move his hand away, but her reaching fingers shook, and she dropped them. But not before Loxley's gaze landed on them. Raven pulled back, looking anywhere but his face. "Lox… I didn't want you blamed for this. I thought that if you were out of Ilasia… that… But—I didn't mean for this." She pressed her lips together and squeezed her arms back around herself.

"Raven."

Loxley leaned in again, and she shifted away. She couldn't touch him. No. She was horrible, and Lox was—

"Red." Warm fingers grasped her chin, bringing her gaze to his. She shivered. That honest quality in him shined through his stare. "You didn't do this. Listen, I knew this would probably happen. This isn't the first time I've been blamed for something."

Always the blame of cities, Loxley. He didn't deserve a traitor's death.

Loxley dipped his head, voice deepening, and said, "If you're with me, Raven, you're safe."

Breath halted in her throat. "I haven't felt safe for a very long time."

Neither her hood's invisibility nor her crown's power had made her feel safe. Ruben... he'd been the closest she could remember. But safety didn't include being scared every moment of the day.

His brow furrowed. Of course, to a man who traveled Aloria aimlessly with nothing over his head but a cap, a castle and guards probably seemed safe. "I'm not sure what safe is anymore, Lox."

Clothing rustled amidst the fire's crackling, and Loxley's heat engulfed her icy arms. He wrapped his arm around her, tugging her close against him. A shiver went down her cold spine, and she hoped he didn't notice. She shifted into him.

Loxley laid his cheek against the top of her head. His woodsy scent eradicated every thought of fear from her brain. Her heart pounded in her cold chest. Then, his words touched her heart with hope, "It feels like a warm fire, soft enough to relax but steady enough to keep you alive."

The two hopeful outlaws sat by the small fire for a while, the rain falling from a gale to a trickle. The fire did feel like safety, both its warmth and Loxley's enough to almost lull her to a sleep despite her drenched clothes and bones.

Safety felt like this. And that set her heart on fire.

Oddly content in this thief's—this man's—arms, Raven didn't notice her fingers curling against his scorching skin at his neck. Eager to thaw the frozen fingertips, she pressed them against his warm collarbone and edged them under the brim of his shirt, seeking heat. Loxley's heart beat strong against her fingertips. Bumps rose under her touch, his breath hitched. The pressure on her forehead from his cheek lifted as he tilted his head downward.

He tipped her chin up. The softness to those forest eyes startled her, enough that she didn't move when he leaned forward to whisper, "You are safe."

His hot breath covered her lips with those words, and her heartbeat stuttered. She shivered. In that moment, she was close to believing him.

But something deep and dark within her screamed it wasn't true. And he wouldn't be safe with her there and a price on his head.

Steeling that hopeful part of herself, she whispered, "I could leave." Loxley's fingers fell from her chin. "I could wear my cloak. They'd chase the Red Hood."

As she spoke, he stood, a coldness creeping into his expression with each word. She rose, following him as he moved across the tent, broad shoulders tense. Trying to ease his worry, she rushed out, "It wouldn't take long for them to forget about you."

"And what about you?" he asked, voice harsh. Firelight glinted off his hardened gaze.

"I'd find my way out."

He laughed shortly, a humorless sound. "I meant—" Lox waved his hand in the air. He sighed and rubbed the bridge of his nose. "If you stay with us, then we can at least get you out of Ecanta and settled in a town so you can hide without your cloak. Let me do that for you."

Raven held his stare. He wasn't asking her to *stay*, just not to leave. Was this only temporary, like everything else in his life? Even with her talk of leaving, this hurt. "Is that what you want?"

"I don't think what I want matters here, love." His gaze dropped to her mouth. "I already told you what I want."

He had. But was that just for a night? For passing fun? She'd felt a type of want in his touches and body. She still couldn't believe he'd want *her*. He didn't know all of her yet. Her throat tightened. "Lox, you're better off without me."

"Don't say that." Loxley shook his head, a slow, hollow motion. Those green eyes wavered over her face. "There is not a single way that I'm better off without you. Not one."

Tears brimmed in her eyes, and Raven stepped back, turning away. "Maybe... I'm..."

"What?" he snapped. "Better off out there—alone? You're wanted for enough crimes that they'll kill you without removing your hood."

Raven shrugged. "Then, I'll be gone either way, and you'll be safe."

"Is that what you want, Red? To leave?"

"I—" Raven pressed her lips together and turned away.

He stepped forward, all quiet movements gone, boots crunching against the tent floor. Loxley gripped her arm, making her face him. "Forget the posters, forget the guards—is that what you want?" He dropped his hand but not his stare. Something stirred deep in those green depths, matching what filled her chest. "I want you. In my band. At my side. I want you, Raven, *with me*. If you want that, too, I will do anything to make that happen. But if you want to leave... I'll help with that. Even if it breaks me." He leaned in, and his woodsy scent threatened to still her heart. "What do you want, Red? Stay or leave—choose, love."

Choose.

Princesses don't get to love.

You're not a princess anymore.

He'd asked her this once before, in Ilasia—stay or leave with him. This question was harder, but the answer felt far more important. Before, it was life or death. This was her future.

Fear closed her throat, stole her words.

Lox stared while she stood there, silent. Long heartbeats between them, and then defeat—heartbreak—flashed over him. His shoulders sagged, and his eyes glinted. He nodded and turned.

After everything, the way Loxley's presence chased away the fear she always held, the... whatever they'd shared earlier, the thought of being alone scared her. The quiet as he stepped into the rain threatened to make her explode.

CHAPTER 32

Raven stepped forward—her fingers grasped his hand, halting his duck out the entrance.

She looked down at her desperate grip then up at him, his eyes tracing the same path. Damn. A different kind of fear crept through her chest. "I want to stay," she forced out.

Lox held her stare. Nothing in his expression gave away his thoughts. His gaze remained fixed on hers, steady. He stepped in from the opening, but she didn't release her grip. The closing distance between them felt tangible. "Until?"

Raven shook her head. "Wherever you go, I go, Loxley. I think from the moment I met you, I've been drawn to you. You said I get to choose—what I want…" She took a shuddering breath, swallowing her hesitation. "Who to love. Loxley…"

He stood entirely still; she wasn't even sure he breathed. He blinked, opened his mouth and shut it.

She moved closer, close enough to hear his breath catch when she traced his jawline with her fingertip. "I choose *you*."

Who moved first, she'd never know, and she didn't care. Loxley clutched her to him and kissed her like she was the air he breathed. She twined her fingers through his hair while his dug into her waist. Lox cupped her face, callouses caressing her cheeks and eliciting something thrilling and delirious in her.

Their mouths moved against each other ferociously, just as her hands wound to his shirt and lifted. Lox understood quickly her intent and let go of her only long enough to pull off his tunic, it landing somewhere on the tent floor. Her hands glided over his toned skin and—damn, he was just as muscled as she'd seen at the competition. Gods.

Lox groaned as her fingers roamed up his stomach and to his chest. His hands dug into her waist and then shifted. One gripped her hip, pressing her against him, and she felt another sculpted part of him. The other gripped her ribcage through her wet tunic, thumb spreading forward to land just under her breast, at the base of her sternum. Her heart beat into his fingers, rapid and hard. He squeezed and broke their kiss.

Not again—she wouldn't let him stop again.

The fire under her skin didn't want restraint. It wanted freedom.

"Lox," she whispered into his mouth.

"Mhm?" He bit her parted lip lightly, and she forgot what she was going to say. So, she shifted her shoulder until her breast fit the curve of his palm. Loxley moaned, his fingers instantly clasped around it, thumb moving over the tenderest part. "Bloody hell."

Raven's skin ignited with his swirling thumb and tightening grasp. Her wet tunic was barely a barrier, but she wanted it gone. She started untucking the hem.

His eyes widened. "Raven, are you—"

She tugged her tunic free, and Loxley didn't waste breath finishing his question. He slid his warm hands underneath, starting at her hips and slowly climbing up her sides. His fingers spread wide, encompassing as much skin as possible on their ascent, and he caught her gaze again at the bottom swell of her breasts. He paused the barest moment, in which she leaned forward to ensnare his lips and closing that last inch of distance from his hands.

Loxley shuddered, his hands gliding up her to cup her breasts in both palms. "Oh gods, Red." The heat from his hands scorched as he moved his palms against her nipples, igniting a burn in her lower stomach. He rotated his hands and moved his thumbs back and forth over the sensitive tips.

He drifted his fingertips from one breast to another—then halted on her collarbone. Before she could stop him, Loxley leaned back and lifted her shirt to her neck. He stared at the scars. The unmistakable L. The intentional lines. "Raven—what—" His brows crashed over his eyes, voice darkening, "*Who?*"

"Not now," she begged, lifting his chin. "Tomorrow."

She meant it. She'd find a way to tell him everything, but she needed him now. To fall into the love she'd decided to grasp for herself.

"You asked what I want—I want you. Tonight." She removed her shirt, holding it in her fingertips. "And you said you wanted *me* in… what was it? *Every* sense of the word." Raven grinned, letting it drop. "Show me."

"Fuck, Red," he cursed.

He had her backed onto the bedroll before she could register they'd moved. He laid her down, the tips of his fingers slowly loosening the ties on her waistband. "Then, let's get you out of these wet clothes."

Her sword and dagger clanked with the movement, and they both moved to unbuckle and slide her blades from her pants. Once the pile laid scattered on the ground, Lox slid his hands under her waistband, not breaking eye contact as he pulled her pants down her ass and thighs. Until her legs were bare, and he knelt in front of her, untying his own trousers. Her eyes locked to the bulge at the front.

"Four?" He grinned, gesturing to the weapons. "I would've guessed five."

"There might be another," she said, almost breathless as she watched the skin slowly exposed at his hips.

He freed his cock from his pants—her breath entirely lost—easing down over her naked form. "Where?"

Loxley ran his hand down her stomach and stopped at the apex of her legs. He raised a brow. If she'd had breath, she would've laughed. His deft fingers slid inside, overtaking all thoughts. Loxley moved his thumb over her sensitive nub. His teeth nipped her ear when he whispered, "Not here." He kissed her jaw beneath. "Good because I'm about to be. And trust me, Red—there's no room for more."

From what she saw, she agreed.

Raven shuddered, and he caught her gasp in his mouth.

He grabbed her hips, tugging them against his own as he positioned between her legs. His hands were like a brand on her skin, burning, but it couldn't compare to the flame licking under her skin from his touch. This would be the one time she'd want a scar from a man. To have his touch on her always would be heaven.

Lox bent over her, trailing a tongue over her collarbone and scars. He looked up at her, nibbling at her shoulder. "It's going to hurt, love. But not for long."

She nodded, aware, but if the sensations he'd given her on the rooftop were anything, pain was worth more. And she wanted all of Loxley.

"You continue to amaze me, Raven." He ducked to kiss her neck, eliciting a whimper from her. Her nails marred his shoulders. Thumb still encircling her below, he removed his fingers while the tip of him rested at her core.

Anticipation rode through her, and Loxley eased inside her. Heat—fire—she was entirely filled by him and the piercing pleasure. He continued to graze his tongue up and down the length of her neck, then down to the point of her breast. His lips encased her nipple, tongue encircling and—he sheathed himself inside her.

Pain spiked, but he gripped her hips to still her and rocked in and out slowly, evenly, that thumb still moving. She gasped, nails digging into his scalp and shoulder from the mix of sensations. With each stroke, pleasure overshadowed pain until she had no focus beyond Loxley's forest gaze locked on hers and the feeling of him moving inside her.

Her legs twined with his, and she lifted her hips. Loxley moaned into her breast, eliciting wicked heat across her skin.

He brought his arm up to slide behind her back, holding her still as he quickened his thrusts. She was fire—and she *burned*. Lox's tongue trailed up to her neck, then he captured her lips, that tongue plunging and retreating as he did below. The dual rhythm was going to drive her positively insane. His other hand cupped her breast, squeezing and caressing every ounce of her thoughts into disarray.

Liquid fire flared and lashed deep within her, and Loxley's languid thrusts were stroking the heat into an intensity that couldn't come close to what he'd done on the rooftop. Utterly indecent whimpers feel from her lips, and Lox's breathless groans resounded around the tent.

Lox pulled back, hand trailing down below again, with those intoxicating circles. One strong arm looped behind her knee. He lifted her leg,
placing it over his shoulder, and plunged deeper.

He moaned at the same time she did, the reverberations as he shuddered heightening her gasp. She looked down, and the sight of him fully
inside her brought a new kind of excitement and connection. Loxley
rolled his hips, moving within the deepest part of her. No piece of her
would remain untouched by him. Her fingers clawed into the bedroll as
her hips followed his movements.

She watched his pounding thrusts, each one feeling farther and
deeper, each one stroking the fire she'd become until she came apart—
fractured into nothing and everything at once. Floating in the sensations
of Loxley and love and pure, burning ecstasy. Loxley didn't slow his hips
or his thumb, drawing out every second of her pleasure past the point of
anything she'd imagined.

When she was left breathless and senseless, he grabbed her ankles,
crossing them behind his back, and bent over her. Those muscled arms
pulled her chest to his, eliciting a hiss as sensation spiked over the entire
feeling of his body inseparable from hers. "Hold on to me, love," he
growled against her ear.

Then, he returned to her mouth, devouring her with his. Raven clung
to him, his hips pounding and bringing her to another crest as his own
climbed higher. Their movements became rapid and senseless and then
she was starlight again. The waves crashed over her, and Loxley thrust
hard, pulsing with his own release. He dipped his head, forehead
touching hers as his hips slowed with each pulse.

Rain pelted the tent canvas, the sound strengthening as their breaths
and gasps dulled. They remained locked around each other, past when
their racing hearts calmed. Raven released her ankles, and Loxley leaned
on his elbows to stare down at her. He eased off her, but kept her in his
arms as he lay beside her, not letting any space between them.

His calloused hand cupped her face, and she tilted into the warmth.
"In case it wasn't clear—and I want this undoubtedly clear," Loxley said,
staring into her gaze, making her heart swell, "I choose you tonight,
tomorrow, every damned night, Raven."

Snuggling further into his embrace, she smiled. "You better."

He chuckled and pulled a blanket around them, tucking it over her shoulders. Raven closed her eyes, absorbing his love, his warmth. Steady and soft. She marveled at how she felt more comfortable here with this man, amidst a storm in the wild, than she ever had in her large empty bed in a castle.

CHAPTER 33

Loxley judged the mountain ridges peaking over the forest canopy, trying to keep his mind on today and not falling back to last night.

"Verdan is the best option," Daran said, crossing his arms. He stretched his legs out in front of him and the log. "I know you hate it, but we can't take the Gilan pass."

The previous night's heavy rain had dampened the clay, turning parts to mud and others into potential rockslides. No, Daran was right, the mountain pass was not safe. And he wasn't taking Raven anywhere unsafe. However, Verdan held a certain dangerous visitor—and it was the only way out of Ecanta now.

Behind Daran, whose low voice was still justifying his decision, tent flaps parted. Raven stepped out, squinting at the rays hitting her amber eyes. Eyes that had touched his soul.

Lox wondered if she had slept well, gods knew his heart had been pounding out of his chest while he held her close, mind replaying their conversation. Replaying every kiss, every touch. When cool fingers had dipped beneath his shirt all he'd wanted was to pull her to him and—Loxley clenched his teeth against the race of his heart. She'd felt so soft and—

Stars be damned, he was glad about last night, even though he'd entered the tent wanting only to comfort her, truly, but his heart had other plans when it came to her. Plans that scared him senseless.

But their talk of love and… and when she'd grabbed his hand to stay. Did he dare hope—believe? No woman ever wanted him past a night. Could someone care for him? Could *Raven*?

"I choose you."

She didn't even know everything about him—but, fuck, he wanted her to. He'd told her about Nevrande… partly. Nothing about what'd happened. The responsibility he ran from. His family's origins.

When Lox had woken, he'd watched Raven rest, something he knew she didn't do much recently, and had begrudgingly crept from the tent to plan with Daran. He shouldn't hope.

Now, Raven gazed around the campsite, shared a smile with Jon as he passed her bread, but her eyes kept moving. Until they latched on Loxley, capturing him.

Raven started his way. That damned tunic Jon had given her hugged her waist and chest. He knew exactly how he wanted to take her next time, how he wanted to ring those gasps from her lips. Loxley stood to quell his nerves and sanity.

He turned back to Daran, pretending to listen.

"…the edges of Verdan," his friend was saying.

Loxley nodded, very aware of Raven's steps. "We can scope it out. Get three horses ready, and we'll ride in." With a sound of agreement, Daran dipped his head and tilted toward Raven. A smile rose on his lips. Lox narrowed his eyes at his right-hand man, who had greeted him outside his tent this morning with a knowing glance. "Nothing happened."

"Then, why haven't you been listening to me the past minute?"

Lox sighed, caught.

Daran let out a low laugh and tapped Loxley's chest twice. "Some-thing is happening here." The Javir parted toward the horses with a grin.

Gods, that man knew him better than himself sometimes, to Loxley's great annoyance. He flagged down Ramsey. "Get ready, we're going into Verdan."

"What kind of ready?"

"Scouting."

Ramsey departed mere seconds before Raven stopped beside Loxley.

Her gaze followed the man to his satchel, then to Daran at the horses. "We going somewhere?"

"Not 'we.'" Lox shook his head, steadying his breaths as he looked at her. "You're staying here."

Her mouth parted in surprise. Had his tone been harsh? He'd been trying to stay level with her so near after baring his heart last night. Loxley brushed back stray hairs from his eyes and said, "Just checking things out before moving the whole camp."

Raven appraised him, eyes roaming from his own to his posture and back. She nodded, opening her satchel. "Okay." She removed his cap. He noticed she'd fully stopped wearing her gloves all the time. "If you go near Verdan, though, don't forget this."

He stared at the cap. It had fallen off in the night, and after a year of not wearing it, he'd forgotten it.

Raven lifted her hands, taking a step toward him. Unlike last night, though, panic didn't run through her veins, and when their eyes locked, her raised hands stopped at his chest. Only the cap separated them, her knuckle grazing the skin at his parted tunic.

Lox hoped his quickened breathing wasn't obvious.

Damn, she was beautiful.

Then, she blinked, and her gaze turned to the cap and his hair. Delicately, so delicately for someone he'd seen both frantic and violent, she placed it atop his head.

Her gentle fingers didn't tuck in any hairs this time, and he was thankful because he didn't know if he could stop himself from leaning in just a few more inches—Loxley blinked. Bloody hell, what was wrong with him?

Raven tilted her head to inspect her handiwork.

"How do I look?" He let a smile enter his voice even though he held his breath for her answer.

She grinned. "You still look like a thief. But not a *treasonous* one." The smile flickered, as if realizing her words, and he had her wrist in his fingers before he knew he wanted to touch her. But he always wanted to touch her lately, didn't he?

She froze, and Lox squeezed lightly. He tried to ignore the pulsing of her vein under his fingertips. Was her heart beating as fast as his? Amber eyes leveled with his, steady and strong. "I'll be okay, Raven."

Her cheeks brightened, and he found his knuckle skimming the heated skin. Only after she nodded did Lox turn and join Daran standing at the horses, letting out a long breath.

Daran set his leader with a look. "They both need to know."

Sighing, Lox broke the stare. Beast could probably handle it, that pain so long ago for him. But Raven… That blank look in the storm, the way she'd shaken in his arms even with a fire. Trembles that had nothing to do with cold and everything with fear. He didn't want to make her that way again. But she couldn't go into this blind, and he would *not* lie to her. Now… now he had a plan. He could protect her. Honestly say he could keep her safe. Gods knew she needed to feel safe.

Lox nodded. "Yes, they do."

Adjusting his cap, he remembered her soft touch. Scar was right, she was worried about him.

His heart pounded, the memory of her soft skin against his fingers, her hands touching his hair. Her arching into him last night.

And, damn it, Daran was right, too.

RAVEN STARED AT THE SILVER LIQUID IN THE GLASS VIAL. WHEN MIRA HAD hinted the effect of this particular elixir, Raven had never considered using it. *"For after the fun nights, my dear."*

She tipped back the glass, swallowing a few drops. If every night with Lox was like that, she'd have to find a replacement within a month. At least they'd be in Ocara by then. There must be shops for elixirs and tonics.

She rolled the vials and replaced them in her satchel, glancing up as the sound of horses approaching camp. Lox stilled his horse beside Ramsey's and dismounted. His eyes found her instantly, a smile playing on his lips. He handed the reins to his comrade and stalked across the clearing.

How she didn't notice the way his tunic's sleeves showcased his muscles, she had no clue. Those leather bracers at his wrists emphasizing his olive skin tone. The memory of his hands on her hips threatened to heat her face. Raven bit her lip to stop the creeping thoughts.

Loxley's gaze latched onto that small movement when he reached her.

Desire stirred in his eyes, and her own coiled down low. He rubbed his mouth with a knuckle, a small breath leaving him. "Hey... can we go somewhere to talk?"

She furrowed her brows but agreed. Him asking instead of insisting or just gesturing, wanting them away from the band surprised—worried —her. Lox led her into the darkened canopy of the forest.

Despite her worry, her heart pounded with each step bringing her more alone with Loxley. Her mind raced with his possible reasons. They used to sneak into the forest to talk, back when she was just the Red Hood and he just a thief. But... now they were something different. Gods, one night with the man, and he'd turned her into a blushing damsel.

Did he bring her here to talk about her scars? She'd said tomorrow, and she meant it, but the words felt infinitely harder now. She wanted to be honest with him, not just about Landon but about her mother's order. Lox had spilled a piece of his heart with her, how he'd wanted her to stay with him, how he *chose* her. Could she bare her heart and see how dark or pure it really was? Would this man who accepted her two halves accept her mistakes, too?

Would he still want her with him then?

Lox stopped and faced her, making her halt. Fear choked her breath. He adjusted his cap, dark hair spilling across his forehead and touching his brow. "We go into Verdan tomorrow."

She blinked. "Oh, that..." The unexpected topic threw her. "It's been years since I visited." The thought escaped before she meant it to.

Curiosity tugged his dark brows. "Why?"

Damn it. Jumping right in, weren't they?

Raven stiffened and forced her hand not to clench around her dagger. "There was... an incident." Stars above, how could she even voice this? Loxley's eyes locked on her, open and honest, if not slightly wide. "Ruben wasn't with me."

The words faltered—she pressed her lips together. Permitting her shaking fingers to touch the dagger, Raven took a breath. *Just tell him. He knows you've killed before, it'll be fine.*

Lox's hand stilled hers on the knife handle. "That prince," Lox spit out the word like venom, "the redhead—"

Landon, she almost said.

Did Loxley already know? No, that was impossible.

He gripped the brim of his hat and tugged, then let go. "He's in Verdan. He's been here for a week after leaving Ilasia."

Grayson.

Blood pounded in her ears, waves like the ocean cresting against the shore. Verdan. Of course. Why wouldn't he stop here where his brother died? Raven stepped backward blindly, fingers disappearing into her hair. Panic shot through her, as rough and spiking as when she'd seen Grayson in the damned market. Wild and angry fear coated her, shaking her limbs and her heart.

Despite everything, that *incident* still controlled a vulnerable part of her.

Her eyes prickled with tears. She was almost out, almost *free*. She truly couldn't run from her past, could she?

"He was supposed to leave." Damn it, her voice broke. It was small, but it cracked.

Even if she didn't give a damn about her reputation or her secret—he blocked her escape with the band. Verdan *was* the border for Ecanta. The mountains converged around the town, the buildings and people living at the gap between Gilan mountains. No forests or terrain to skate past the road like everywhere else in Ecanta. The border and end of the queen's road lay on the other side of Verdan. They'd have to pass through town to get to the forested trail.

Even disguised with Lox's cap, she would still have to walk in public. There was no way in hell she could evade Grayson. He'd recognize her. Him or his twenty men.

"Ramsey is watching him. His entire campaign keeps the streets full. Verdan is on guard with him here and holding the boarder to Ecanta."

Her heart thudded, eyes widening—Grayson questions might even find answers in this small town.

These men... they'd hear the rumors and questions as soon as they entered Verdan. No—this couldn't be happening. She'd finally felt like she belonged. Raven squeezed her eyes shut. Damn it!

"Raven." Loxley's solid hands on her arms stopped her backward retreat. A soft grip lowered her hand from her unruly hair. She let him guide her closer. He bent to stare into her eyes. "We won't let him near you. Raven, I can protect you from him."

Protect... Her brows pulled together.

Hardness resided in his voice, sharp as a blade and even stronger. "He's the one who ordered your death, isn't he?"

Why would he think...

Someone too powerful wanted me dead, she'd said to them. He knew she'd been scared of Grayson, and this was a logical explanation.

She stared, shocked and startled. His want to protect her from something like that unnerved her. She shook her head, honest for once with him about a Loren prince. "No, no, he isn't."

Lox paused, confusion deepening in his eyes. Framing Grayson would be so easy—too easy. But she wouldn't frame another man for treason. Something about this band, these men, had altered her heart. Upon trying to right her mistake those years ago, she'd created new ones. And she was determined not to return down that path.

"What did he do?" Loxley asked, words soft. A gentle question with such a harsh and bloody answer.

Broke me.

Her heart faltered. True fear catapulted through her. More than anything, she wanted to be with them—Lox.

Tell him. Just tell him, she begged herself. Here was her opening. That she killed Landon. That he was the one who scarred her heart—the scars Lox had kissed last night. The one who had made her want to be stronger. That her mother hired the Red Hood.

Tell him, her heart screamed.

But how could he want her if he knew her own mother didn't?

Raven opened her mouth.

Her throat trembled, and she shut it.

She was a coward. A damned coward. The tears fell.

Loxley pulled her into an embrace. "It'll be alright." His strong arms wrapped around her, holding her, though her fingers shook between them. She squeezed them into his tunic to still herself. "I have a plan, Raven. We'll get through this."

This man... he was too kind. She didn't deserve any of this, but she couldn't make herself step back. Raven sighed and dropped her forehead onto his shoulder. She would fix this.

These men—*Loxley*—had changed her. For the better, it seemed.

CHAPTER 34

Fear catapulted Raven's feet deeper into the black forest. Only the moon and stars lit her path, but her boots were sure as they pressed into the earth. She tugged her cloak around her shoulders, loving the weight of her hood once again. She'd debated on whether to sneak it from Jon's pack while she'd waited for the men to fall asleep, but she'd rather be seen as the treasonous Red Hood than the dead princess.

She hated sneaking out while Lox was on watch, but she knew she couldn't have lied to him, and if he thought her anywhere except his tent, he'd worry.

Warm mist drifted over her face within the raised the hood, unease roiling as it touched her skin.

Lox may have a plan, but she had her own. She'd scare Grayson Loren into leaving before his words could reach their ears. Then, when they were away from him, out of Ecanta... maybe then she could voice the truth.

Verdan was unfamiliar after these long years, and she barely made it to the tavern unseen—mostly by climbing trees and rooftops. Half an hour later, she perched in a tall tree, watching the prince through the window. His copper hair stood out amongst the dark locks of Verdan's people. The likeness to his brother startled her once again, partially because her mother and her looked so different. But these boys... same hair, same eyes—though these... these didn't hold the same arrogance. Dark red eyes flared in her memory, of hatred and cruelty.

The damned Loren prince, he'd darkened her heart.

In the tavern, Grayson's shoulders drooped as another person turned away from him. His brows tugged downward in a far too familiar expression she'd seen on her mother and in her own reflection for many years. Grief.

Landon—*Landon*—had attacked her, she reminded herself, not Grayson. Grayson Loren's only guilt was badly handled grief. But who was she to talk? Who was Vanera? Grayson could have ordered the Red Hood to kill her, threatened destruction of Ecanta had she not obliged, but he hadn't. He wasn't *really* dangerous to her, just her reputation. Truth was the danger, not lies. And that tore her heart.

Raven leaned her hooded head back against the trunk. What could she do, then? She couldn't hurt this boy for merely grieving. Loxley and the men had gotten into her head—and her heart.

The dead prince was the only thing still hurting her, besides herself and inability to let it go.

The door opened, cascading voices seeping into the quiet night. Boot-steps traveled down the deck into the dirt pathway. The prince made slow, tired steps to the other side of town.

No, she wouldn't hurt him. But maybe she could heal them both. With a heavy heart and conscience, Raven followed the Loren prince, keeping to the shadows. Distantly, a door opened and shut, more yelling from that damned tavern escaping. It punctuated the stillness around them. She'd need to be quiet lest he—or the guards—hear her approach.

Most likely, he'd think she was attacking again. The ale he'd probably drank would slow his reactions. Maybe even make him more pliable to her words. Just what would she say when he looked at her, though?

Steeling her resolve, Raven dropped from the rooftop, boots lightly padding the hard packed earth. She would set one of their broken and damned hearts straight tonight. Grayson turned down an alley into the back rows of houses, probably headed for the inn. Her foggy memory placed it behind the vendors. She had about two turns to stop him before reaching the most strongly populated—and guarded—area.

She paused, listening for armor, and leapt out of the shadows behind Grayson Loren. In one swift move, she clasped her hand over his mouth and the other around his arms, preventing a strike. He jolted under her touch, and she squeezed tighter. Raven whispered, "I just want to talk."

Grayson paused in his struggle, the hood's enchantment masking her voice from his recognition. When he tugged, hands trying to grasp her and failing, she continued, "I know what you're looking for."

That stilled him. The prince contemplated her words, then nodded under her grip. She pushed him farther into the gap between houses, closer to the trees. When she felt secure enough to outrun any guards that may appear, she released him.

Faster than she expected, Grayson spun and unsheathed a knife identical to hers. Dark leather wrapped around the handle, the lightest silver ever crafted in a blade shined to the tip, and at the base, she knew from experience, rested a black rose. The Loren royal symbol.

Grief shined in his red-rimmed eyes. She wondered briefly how he could stand straight after consuming enough alcohol to make the edges as red as his irises. "Well, speak."

She kept her hand loose near her sheathed blade and watched his face for signs of a strike. She didn't want to hurt him, but he very much wanted to hurt her. "You search for answers about your brother." Silence. Dark eyes searching her hooded face, warmth flooding her skin as the magic worked hard. "I know what happened."

"Me too," he spat, eyes flaring. "That bitch of a princess killed him."

"Your brother was arrogant. Cruel and malicious. He attacked her." Raven squeezed her eyes tight for a single moment, trying to staunch the memory that thrust to the surface. With a brother, like the ghost of Landon Loren, standing before her, the similarities between this night and that roared to life. Raven took one careful step forward, her emotions balanced on the edge of a Loren blade. "Landon Loren walked this kingdom as if he owned it."

Grayson clenched his teeth, a flash of white in the near darkness. "He —" A swallow, a pause. He'd lived with Landon, must have known the arrogance was true.

"She spoke back to defend Ecanta and its people. Said she wouldn't be *his* queen as he demanded, but *ours*. And Landon Loren didn't like that." Raven tried to keep her tone even, but fear crept up her throat, choking her in a way too close to that night.

The Loren prince rocked back on his heels, knife lowered to his side. Then, anger flared in those copper depths, and he lunged. Only muscle memory from daily sparring with Ruben readied her reflexes to block his swipe with the knife. His blade was just inches above her arm which had risen to meet his wrist. She unsheathed her own dagger; she'd need something to counter—but Ruben had taught her to use a blade as defense not offense. A shield not a weapon.

She pushed him back toward a wall. Faster than a drunk man should be able to move, he arced his dagger through the air. Her forearm caught his swing a second before contact. How did he have such skill with a blade? His archery performance at the competition had been sad, and at swordsmanship—but no, he'd left that morning before the sword competition. She never saw him fight. Apparently, she wasn't the only royal taught to protect themselves. Grayson's feet dodged her attempt at buckling them. Her eyes widened, his eyes were clear. Not red-rimmed from ale but from tears—grief.

After Landon, she'd been consumed by guilt, and this boy was consumed by grief. In her lifetime, she'd been drowned by both—and grief left you a dark, ravaging hole if you let it. And Grayson had.

He punched her stomach. She curled from the impact, her left arm caving in, and his blade sliced into her shoulder. A searing trail carved into muscle down past her elbow. Hissing, she raised her right hand to block another attack, and her blade slashed toward his chest. She checked it at the last moment, only catching his shirt.

The neck fell open. White shimmered in the moonlight on his collarbone. One straight line down, another cresting to the right, an "L". A scar —right where Landon Loren had wanted it.

Raven gasped and wasn't prepared for Grayson to rush her. Surprise on his side, he pushed her off kilter, and she hit the wall. Her head knocked forward on impact, breath leaving her in a hard burst. Hot, searing blood ran down her arm, *her* blood, she dimly realized. His arm pressed on her neck. She couldn't breathe—couldn't *breathe*. Not again. Her eyes welled with tears, both from the lack of air and from the nightmarish memory trying to resurface.

Grayson's grating voice ground into Raven's senses, bringing her dizzy, breathless mind into focus. "Who killed my brother?" Cold fingers lessened enough for her to speak.

Eyes burning from impending tears, lungs bursting to breathe, Raven rasped out, "I did." Her left arm screamed, but she blocked out the pain to raise her dagger, handle up so he could see.

Her confession startled him. She gasped in air and strengthened her voice. Raven stared at the scar evident in his gaping shirt and asked, "How old were you? When he did that?"

Fear flashed in his copper eyes. Too young, probably.

"I tried…" Grayson whispered on a breath. "But he was too much like our father. And after Cam—" He stopped, tears falling. "He got worse."

"He liked to brand things he called his, didn't he?" she asked, her steady voice surprising her. When Grayson didn't respond, she pressed on, a fierceness and honesty ringing in her tone, "I wouldn't let this kingdom be his."

Pattering sounded somewhere near them. Rain again? Stars above, she needed something to wash this damned night from her mind, both of them.

Grayson Loren snapped out of his trance, grief seeping back into his stare. Fingers trembled against her body. How cruel had that boy been to this one? An anguished sound spilled from his mouth, and Raven's heart clenched.

A blink, and Grayson and his weight disappeared. A thud followed off somewhere, reverberating through the alley. What? She breathed in a sob, a groan, and tried to sit up. Her left elbow dug into the dirt to support her weight, but it faltered, and a cry ripped from her lips.

"Rams!" came a growl.

Two figures moved somewhere to her side, but Raven couldn't do more than lie there and try to breathe through the pain. Stars shifted above, drifting with her dizziness. *Get up,* she commanded herself. She blinked, sighed a moan. Fire seared the length of her arm, blocking out her surroundings.

Soft whispers in her ear broke through the chaos that was her wound. The voice tugged at her heart. Raven blinked hard, recognizing forest green eyes. Lox knelt before her, eyes roaming over her face and body. She managed to dip her burning shoulder under her cloak, the blood soaked arm as deep as the crimson cloth.

"Raven," he breathed, soft hands easing behind her back to bring her to his chest.

She hadn't meant for this to happen. Tears sliced the backs of her eyes and fell. Her good hand gripped his tunic. He was soft and steady, and gods, she needed steady right now. Raven gripped him like he was a rock, and she was the ocean, and she needed so very much to feel still.

Loxley soothed her hair, holding her close, tight enough that it should hurt, but she only felt comfort. "You're safe, you're safe—Raven, I'm here."

Her breathing soothed after a few deep moments, and she edged backward. Lox's pale eyes hardened on the gouge running down her left arm. A sound like a snarl left his mouth, and his head turned toward Grayson behind them.

"He's not dead, is he," she asked, unable to get a full glance. His head leaned in too close to hers.

Warm fingers clasped her waist, bringing her upright as they stood. "Not yet."

"No," Raven gasped, fingers digging into his tunic with the strength to stand.

Confusion pulled his angry brows together. "Red, why were you out alone? And *bloody why* were you with him?" Loxley ground out.

"I wanted to make this better. To... apologize or—I..." She'd tried to fix this. Her lips trembled. Time to bare her darkened soul. "I was betrothed to his brother when I was younger." Raven tugged down the collar of her tunic to expose the scar he'd seen last night. "I wouldn't be his, Lox. I couldn't," she sobbed, hating the weak sound.

"I know." He swallowed hard, jaw clenched. Some thick emotion captured his voice, "That you killed him. I've known since Ilasia. I put it together when I realized you were Red. But..." Dark locks shook in the night. "Not why. Not this. Raven." Loxley's eyes darkened on the scar and softened on her face. He moved a finger to the puckered mark, lightly covering it with his tender touch.

The thief clutched her to his chest, being careful of her wound. His gaze stilled her heart. "I've got you, Raven."

Loxley knew. He'd known this whole time. And he hadn't rejected her, not then, not now. He had a better heart than she thought.

"Boss." Ramsey appeared at their side. "We've got company." His scarred chin jerked to the other end of the alley. Yells sounded, armor clanked—guards.

Loxley wrapped an arm around her waist, Ramsey gripped her hand, and the three ran. Past the houses, down two turns, and into the edge of the forest. With a signal from Loxley, Ramsey sprinted in another direction, and a clattering sounded. A distraction.

Raven was too slow. With the blood loss and the exhaustion from the fight, she'd get them caught. Each jostle, each movement sent flames up her arm. She needed her satchel and elixirs.

They stopped to catch their breaths, Loxley's gaze searching for the best exit. Camp was in the forest on the other side Verdan. They'd wound their way back to the heart of Verdan, but the guards were close.

Raven had done this. She should turn herself in. They'd discover her alive—or kill her first—either way the princess would be found, Lox would be off the hook and free. Her mistakes and failures had brought him here, but they didn't need to kill him.

She reluctantly removed her body from his grasp, ready to run back to the guards. She lowered her hood, ready to unclasp it and throw it on him for protection.

His gaze latched onto her. Flickered between her amber eyes, halting on her lips a breathless moment. Gentle fingers traced her midnight hair before placing his cap upon it. Lox brought his hands to her cheeks and held her still, their hot, rapid breaths mixing in the frozen night air.

Her heart caught in her throat.

Loxley's lips pressed into her forehead, a soft, soothing touch. When he pulled back, a sadness breached the surface of his determined eyes. "Run. Take Jon or Scar and—"

She shook her head. "No, Lox, I'm not—"

Steady fingers caressed her cheek. "They'll get me out. Don't worry, Red." He grinned, that devil smile without the light.

Cold rushed in the distance between them as he let go and stepped back twice. Then, longing flashed on his face, and he grabbed her face, dragging her lips to his. Desperation crashed upon her, in the way his mouth pressed against hers, moved with a different earnestness than before. His kiss strong while she trembled. It ended as suddenly and urgently as he began it.

Before she could open her eyes, he was feet away, out of her grip and running too fast for her to follow.

"No!" Raven reached for him, then clamped a hand over her mouth.

The charming thief turned, a dark emotion broiling in those forest eyes. He sent her one last smile before his figure faded around the corner.

"Lox." The whisper fell from her mouth with the strength of a scream but sadness of her heart.

CHAPTER 35

Never before had Raven hated herself more, wanted to collapse into a heap of guilt. Through sheer force of willpower and the hand on her arm, Raven took each step further into the forest. The warmth seeping through her tunic was meant to comfort, but the fingers, the grip, were not Loxley's.

Ramsey had found her standing frozen, eyes trained on the last spot she'd seen Lox run. Where she'd seen him turn down a street and five guards follow pursuit. Where she'd seen them grab him and shove him into the dirt. They wouldn't be kind to the person they believed killed their princess. Blinded by the pain screaming the length of her arm, and the shock of Loxley's actions, Raven had stumbled from shadow to shadow, all the while her eyes stayed in one direction. As if not losing sight of him meant he'd return.

But Lox hadn't emerged from the shadows, his scarred friend had. Those usually sparking eyes had lost their humor and hardened upon her expression. Traveled to her hand clutching at her elbow to keep her left arm immobile and stanch some bleeding. To the green cap sticking out from her red hood. Ramsey had cursed. "He didn't."

Her words had stuttered, trapped in her throat by the scream still rebounding of Loxley's name. How to tell his trusted men that their leader and friend had traded himself for her? For *her*. A newcomer, a princess without a crown, a girl with a dark heart who failed to amount to anything but a disgrace and a burden. Who had put treason on his head, and he'd taken the blame—for her.

That damned idiot. She wasn't worth this.

"I tried…" Anguish stilled her words. She'd tried, damn it. This was the last thing she'd wanted.

"He did," Ramsey had said on a resigned sigh. Dark blond hair bobbed, and he had taken a long look at her face before grasping her arm and leading her through the maze of a city.

He rushed her as much as her exhausted body could handle, then got her onto a horse, and they rode like hellfire through the forest. He'd questioned her grip on the pommel, but she squeezed all her pain into the saddle. The whole dizzying ride to camp only one thing encompassed Raven's mind—they needed to go back for Lox. Ramsey and her needed the rest of the band

Pushing her horse to its limits, she thundered into camp before Ramsey with a death-grip on the reins. Beast was there and stilling her horse mere moments after she burst through. Thighs throbbing from the pressure she'd used to stay upright, Raven all but fell off the horse. Her knees caved in as her boots crashed to the dirt, sending a sharp bolt through her injury. Fingers digging into the saddle were the only thing keeping her standing.

"Raven!" Scar bolted across the dirt, eyes wide. Others neared, worried. His hands gently took her wrist and pulled her cloak away. He hissed in a breath and eased her tunic's cloth out of the deep wound. Darkness clouded his eyes. "Who did this?"

Raven tugged her wrist free, earning a startled look from the blades-man. "Daran," she whispered. Her eyes searched for the Javir, and she moved sluggishly around Scar to him. Hooves sounded behind as Ramsey arrived. "The guards have Lox. We need t—" A groan tore her words from her throat, and she glanced at her wound in a daze, blood steadily streaming through her fingers. She took a shaky breath and gritted her teeth. "Get back to—Verdan, and… help him."

Cursing, the men burst into action—dismantling tents, throwing packs on horses, dousing the fire. All but Scar, who took a bag from Jon and moved her to the side. Raven wished she could be of help. They needed to *move*.

"I'm…" She gasped, as pain shot up her arm. "I'm sorry."

"Shh," Scar soothed, pulling her to the log beside him and opening the bag. "We're used to moving quickly, just hold on. Let's focus on getting you patched up."

No. No, she'd started this whole damned mess. "I got us caught. I— was about to turn back." Words shot at a random cadence from her clenched teeth and startled breaths. "But… he—"

"He did it first," Scar stated, eyes intent on her wound.

"How do you not hate me?"

Surprise marred his brows. "It takes a lot for me to hate. And this is Lox. He would've done this for any one of us. Especially you."

"They'll get me out," Lox had said. Such faith in them.

"Lox did this to keep you safe, so how about we do that? Hm?" His grey eyes pierced her, calm and sure.

She needed to have this faith. In them. In Loxley to stay alive until they could live up to his trust. That meant her at full strength. Not slowing them down like she'd done Lox. "My satchel. I have elixirs."

The bladesman located the bag. Her shaking fingers lifted the flap and removed the rolled leather pouch. Scar scooped it from her hands and unrolled the securely tied bottles. Raven instructed color vials to use and gave in to his kindness and care. First one to halt the bleeding— careful of the two shades of green liquids—and another to stop infection. Lastly, after far more cursing than she'd ever uttered at court, the elixir to meld the skin together burned her arm from shoulder to elbow.

When finished he glared at the deep wound. She knew it needed more than the elixirs, but she didn't want to make Scar bundle the herbs and wrap her arm.

Two shadows passed over them—Daran motioned for Scar to leave while Ramsey crouched before her. "Beast and Lance went to scout," Ramsey said. "We're almost ready to head out."

Already the pain had dulled, giving her enough focus to think. She nodded. Why was his voice hesitant?

Ramsey's eyes latched onto her wound, blood still drying around the puckered skin. He reached for the cloth-wrapped herbs in her lap. Raven leaned backward, eying his hand, this man who had insulted her repeatedly. A resigned sigh parted his lips. "My mother was a healer. I know these herbs better than you do."

He sorted them and picked out some to both ease pain and quicken healing, making an interesting combination she hadn't considered. Maybe he did know his shit. Ramsey talked as he meshed and bundled them. "The guards at Ecanta's border are distracted with Lox's capture."

When she didn't speak, Daran gestured toward the horses. "Despite Lox's original deal with you, we cannot spare the time to escort you further. You can take a horse, supplies, and money. If you stick to the east with the Gilan Mountains behind, you'll find Merna in ten miles."

"What?" Raven widened her eyes. Were they kicking her out? Her throat tightened. But Scar had said…

"We're hoping Lox isn't with Royal Guards yet," Ramsey said, lightly pressing the herbs to her wound and keeping the cloth tight against the mixture. Winding the bandage around her muscle, his gaze focused on the motion. "If they are, and he's in irons, it's hopeless to try to free him. There'll be too many to stage a breakout."

"So…" Raven shook her head, his tone scared her, "what would the plan be?"

Dark blue eyes lifted to hers. "Follow them to Ilasia."

Dread rushed through her heart. A bronze crown, an empty gold throne, and a cold voice crept into her mind. *Mother.*

A humorless chuckle left him. "Our thoughts, too." His binding reached her elbow, and he tucked in the cloth. "We know it's dangerous for you to return. Someone wants you dead—"

"And the whole damned kingdom wants *him* dead!" Raven exclaimed, standing. Anger at herself and her mother and everything burst through. Did they want her to leave him to the guards' mercy? Because there would be no mercy. Not with Ruben in charge.

She shut her eyes. But how could she return?

"Ravenna," Daran said, his lilting voice breezing over her name, it coming out 'Rah-veen-ah.' His tone calmed her. "We will not make you come with us, nor will we make you leave. We'll gladly take your help. But we'll understand if you don't."

Ramsey stood. "Lox is our responsibility, not yours."

Those words pierced her heart.

"We'll let you think." Daran tipped his head to her, and the men left her by the empty campfire that she'd shared with Lox only hours ago.

Her eyes bored into the place a fire had once burned, and she shivered. *"Soft and steady."* Raven pressed her hand to her lips, remembering his warmth as he'd last kissed her. It had been so quick and yet exactly what he felt like—strong and kind and a little bit reckless. *Lox...*

Cold... the world felt so cold without him near. For the past week, he hadn't been more than a few steps away from her. Even before that, she'd seen him every day since his arrival in Ilasia, whether she'd liked it or not. His warmth had been the only comforting thing in her cold life for a while now.

"I choose you."

He'd become such a constant. Without her even noticing, she needed him. Craved his closeness in a way beyond needing his touch. She needed him beside her. Otherwise the world felt off kilter. Raven and Loxley. Not just Raven.

Raven glanced at Scar near his horse. She didn't have long-standing ties to Lox like these men did. But, gods, she wanted to. To be more than just a person he risked his life for. She didn't know when that feeling had arisen, this love for him, but it had.

This urge to save him went past owing him her life. She wanted him safe.

In her life.

Bugles sounded far off, snapping her eyes to where Verdan rested within the forest. Three consecutive blasts. No. No, no, *no*. Raven blindly stepped past the fire, its residual heat and smoke swirling around her boots and making her shiver. She stopped near the consulting band members who paused to follow the sound.

Scar lightly touched her good arm. "Rave?"

Voice paper thin, she whispered, "They've called off the hunt. He's in the prisoner's carriage." Raven pressed her trembling lips together. "They're taking him back to Ilasia."

The men swore in different colors and shades, and a chaotic eruption of voices started.

"We can attack when they're sleeping and—"

"But the carriage—can we break him out?"

"Not unless we find the right guard with the key."

"—could kidnap one and get the answer—"

"What if he tells?"

"We kill him."

SYLVIA LOCKARD

Jon, always the reasonable one, chastised, "Scar, no we can't do that."

"Well, we can't let him go, now can we?" Scar pointed out, waving a sharpened knife at Jon.

With a growl, Beast silenced them all. Black eyes made their way around the men and stopped on Raven. "Did Lox say anything to you?"

Run. But no, she wouldn't. He'd never run from her, even when she'd told him, begged him to. "That you'd free him."

More curses followed. Jon pulled out a notebook and pencil. "So, kidnapping is out, can we steal the carriage?"

"No." The prisoner's carriage was reinforced with both metal and wood and a lock so thick only the key could unlatch it. And with the amount of guards patrolling Verdan alone, it would be fruitless to guess which held it. These six men, no matter their skill, could not take the whole guard, especially not the Royal Guard who escorted the treasonous prisoners. On the road, it was impossible, the villages too crowded. But... Raven fingered her scar, the spot her necklace had always covered. *Ilasia*—she knew it by heart.

"The castle," Raven said, catching only half the men's attention. Lance nudged Scar mid-exclamation about *bloody castle-trained assholes,* and he sheepishly looked at the former princess. "They'll bring him to Ilasia, into the dungeons. And I can get you in there."

All six men weighed her declaration. Raven locked gazes with Daran, and he watched her a long moment, then nodded.

Lance's brow creased. "Are you sure?"

Raven clenched her fists, her wound protesting angrily. "Yes."

Jon snapped his notebook shut, grinning, and bumped her good shoulder with his. Startled, she gave him a tentative smile. The men turned toward their horses.

"Not the first time I've broken into a castle," Scar said with a black grin, as he helped her mount Loxley's black mare.

She rubbed the horse's mane. "Not mine, either."

Raven just hoped she'd break out. If she had to trade places with him, she would. He wouldn't die for her.

USING THE QUEEN'S ROAD, THE GUARDS' TRAVEL ACCOMPLISHED THE TRIP TO Ilasia in half the time the band had taken leaving. With each city they

312

passed through, the guards surrounding the prisoner's carriage changed, more Royal Guards joining and the city guards trading off. Making them freshly rested while the band rode hard on their tail with barely any sleep. In a day and a half, only half of them had managed two hours' sleep while the other half searched for openings to free Lox.

None came.

Raven had insisted on watching the guard, trying to see how Loxley fared. Three guards on separate occasions had entered the carriage. She doubted it was to bring food. Her heart cried out at the all too vivid ideas rose. She knew how grieving overtook her guards. Knew their anger, their lashing out, their blows. Ten years ago, chaos had descended upon Ilasia as each prisoner barely returned unscathed from the throne room to the streets. Now they had a single person to vent their grief.

Gods, she hoped he made it to the dungeon.

On day two, the carriage and guard of thirty men and women crested the outer reaches of Ilasia. Twilight glinted over the horizon and off the metal as it swayed up the cobblestone path between gates and gates and finally the hill to the castle.

From their perch atop the highest building in the northern district, Raven watched, rapt, as the carriage halted in the courtyard behind the high stone walls. A tall guard stood waiting and stomped around to the opening. Ruben. She'd recognize his gait even in the dark. His face had never been so contorted with anger. She'd seen him stern, yes, but never this furious. Stars above, how could she possibly accomplish this?

The door parted, and another guard thrust Loxley outward. He stumbled to the street. No one bothered to catch him. Arms tied behind him, only his knees broke his fall. A gasp tightened in her throat, and her nails scraped the roof's shingles. Even from here, purple visibly mottled the right side of his face, creeping up his jaw. A red line striped his probably split lip, and standing, Lox favored his left leg.

Raven swallowed hard as they shoved and dragged him through the tall front doors of her once-home. A hand patted her wrist, and she looked up into a pair of grey eyes. "You know this place best," Scar whispered.

"Before they doubled the guard!" she hissed back. She took a calming breath that was more of a hard sigh. "And when there was only one of me. Not seven."

Beast grumbled from his crouch behind them, covered by trees, "We can't keep moving around. They'll notice us eventually."

"Well, we can't go to the tavern," Ramsey shot back, shaking his head in frustration.

Jon whispered softly, "And this rooftop is starting to get uncomfortable."

The men shot him looks, but they all felt the same. Jon shrugged and turned to Raven.

Ideally, the guard would be more relaxed outside the castle, having found the culprit. But Ruben knew Lox had men, but only of four of them. He could definitely pinpoint Daran and Scar. And now he suspected the Red Hood. He could expect a breakout, but would be he too clouded with rage to think properly?

She kept her gaze downward, scanning the houses. The villagers thought she'd killed the princess, so she couldn't seek refuge with anyone. Tying them up wasn't a good option, either. She didn't want to further muddle her hooded name, just save Loxley's ass and run like hell.

A small form stepped out from a house, wiping down a booth. Her light blonde bun drifted to the side in her work. With a triumphant yet small smile, she eased back inside.

"I have an idea," Raven whispered, shutting up Ramsey's bickering.

Jon touched her shoulder. The worry dulled his blue eyes to grey.

She smiled wryly. "It's okay. I have a friend."

She hoped.

CHAPTER 36

Leather pressed onto Cindy's mouth, and she jolted awake, every bruise twinging at the strain. No! He'd come early. She focused on the hooded figure before her, but her father had said three more days before the nobleman returned.

Three days until she was truly, officially, sold off.

At least he'd stopped hitting her. No one wanted a bruised slave.

Then, Cindy's gaze focused on the red hood. The Red Hood. She glared, forehead creasing hard. Anger coursed through her, anger she hadn't felt beyond at her father, shaking her shoulders.

The Red Hood's hand dropped.

"You!"

The vigilante spread his gloved hands wide. "I'm not here to hurt you, Cindy."

Something in the voice called to her memory, but it faded instantly.

"You killed Ravenna!" Cindy threw her legs over the bedside, eyes darted to the hall, fearing she'd woken her father. She lowered but didn't soften her voice. "I thought you were good. We all did."

So many hearts had broken the afternoon Raven had been reported missing. Their faith in a protector had shattered the day her body was discovered.

"I didn't kill her," the Red Hood said quietly, too calmly. "I saved her. Like I saved you."

Cindy wavered, not wanting to fall from this anger into grief again. "What are you talking about? Ravenna's dead," her voice broke.

"Please don't scream," the vigilante whispered. He inhaled unsteadily, then gloved hands lifted the hood.

Silence. A fog Cindy hadn't quite noticed cleared over her mind, and she focused on the black hair, the amber eyes, and the familiar face. *Raven.* She sprang from the bed, arms flying around Raven's middle. The princess stumbled backward from the force. The relief and love warmed Cindy, almost breaking and mending her heart.

She pulled back and her joy faded as she absorbed Raven's tired expression. Absorbed the realization beyond Raven being alive. Cindy glanced toward the window, the castle always in view. Something was wrong. "Wait, so you're... What happened?"

Raven moved from the window. "Someone wanted me—Princess Ravenna—dead. And hired the Red Hood to do it. Lox helped fake my death, and we left Ilasia." She swallowed hard, the sound tightening Cindy's chest. "But he was captured for my murder. And I have to help him."

Cindy stared, head swimming. Ravenna—alive, the Red Hood, and returned to save the man who'd helped her. From treason. A sad whisper fell from her lips, "They're going to kill him."

Raven nodded. "Will you help me, Cindy?"

She glanced to the hallway, fingering the bruise on her jaw. Father wouldn't be happy.

But Raven needed her, and she didn't quite care what he wanted anymore.

She set her mouth set into a line. "What do you need?"

A wicked and proud smile curved Raven's lips. "To house a few criminals, Lox's band." Raven raised her palms to Cindy's widened eyes. "They won't hurt you—and your father won't, either."

After a pause, Cindy nodded. Blonde locks fell in her eye, and she recalled her newly bruised jaw. Damn it! She tugged her hair forward, hoping Raven hadn't already seen.

Cindy checked on Raven at the window, *hoot*-ing into the night, and pretended to straighten her light blue night dress. Father hadn't taken kindly to the Red Hood—Raven, apparently—beating him. And once the vigilante had fled, he took that anger out on her. She tucked her arms behind her back but caught Raven's gaze drifting to her pale skin. Tracing the circular and mottled marks climbing from wrist to shoulder. Cindy drew her blanket around herself.

Knowing her friend beat grown men, Cindy felt infinitely weaker than she already had.

Soon, six men streamed in through her bedroom window. Each with different apology and thankful greetings, oddly polite for criminals. The young man called Beast grunted, dipping his head slightly. The bottomless black eyes bored into her, the wolfish angles took on the likeness of her father. When she flinched, though, he averted his gaze, and she wished she weren't too scared to apologize. The youngest, Jon, smiled and shook her hand. Another man winked, making her cheeks redden in surprise, and Raven growled, "Ramsey," before staring hard at him until he backed to the far side of the room.

The men brought all four of her family members gagged to the living room. Then, Raven tilted their heads and dropped a red liquid into their mouths, making them instantly sleep.

The band settled into the living room, taking up the chairs around the table and near the fireplace. Criminals, indeed, these men—who'd saved Raven from death. Cindy watched them all curiously, and the easy way Raven moved and talked with them. There was a comfortability in her that had been absent in the market and at the ball. She'd truly found her place among these men.

Cindy's throat tightened. Could she be saved? She stared out the window. A nobleman would scour Ecanta for his property. This wasn't the first time she'd considered running, but it'd quickly dissolved under her lack of coin or knowledge of the roads. How helpful were these criminals?

Raven touched her arm, breaking her thoughts. She pulled Cindy aside, whispering, "Thank you for this."

She nodded, hair falling loosely around her face, hopefully covering her jaw and budding tears. "I'll get you all some food."

She slipped into the kitchen and uncovered the cupcakes she'd finished icing two hours ago with woodland creatures. Father wanted them sold tomorrow morning, but she hoped she wouldn't be there. A small smile grew. He'd have to make his own pastries to sell. He'd hate to know she gave them away for free—let alone to criminals.

Cindy carried the tray to the men. Setting it down, she wiped her hands on her dark night dress. "This is all I had ready, but I can bake some—"

Grunts and hollers of approval overran her words. Everyone, including Beast, rose for a cupcake. The tray was half empty before Raven snagged a chipmunk.

"Madam, this is the best thing I've had in far too long," Scar said, patting her shoulder lightly. Right on the cut gouging along her collarbone.

Cindy whimpered—bit the noise off, teeth sinking into her lip—and winced away from his touch. Damn it. She tried a smile to cover the movement, but she knew it was obvious.

She laid a careful hand just under the slice; the last thing her father had done before selling her—by a thrown plate two days ago.

Scar's light eyes flickered to the unconscious baker and back to her. He tipped his head slowly. "Thank you."

She retreated to the kitchen, heart pounding from the pain and his touch. No one touched her, only her father when angry or occasionally someone when paying for food. She wished she were more used to this. To people. Her mind returned to that sailor, Kieran, who'd kept his steady hand out for her to grasp his coins. Then, she remembered his swordfight with the man who'd just thanked her, and her skin flushed.

Raven appeared beside her, and she jumped. "Thank you. Again."

Cindy watched the men. "They're quite nice for a group of criminals."

"Eh, they're not too bad." Raven smiled, gaze softening on the group.

She chuckled. "It's good you found people to help you. People you get along with." Cindy traced her left hand up her arm, over the sore bruises, pausing at her shoulder's gash. Barely a single part of her didn't hurt. Even her knees from the dirt, and her scalp from his nails, his grip.

This from a man who was supposed to love her. What would a nobleman do—her owner?

Cindy swallowed. "Raven... Take me with you."

"What?"

"When you leave—please."

Raven shut her gaping mouth. "What about—" Raven's gaze circled the room, "—your sisters?"

"We've… never been like that. *They're* close, but…" Cindy glanced at her unconscious sisters, who matched each other more than her in so many ways. "We've never truly been sisters."

Family, but not quite.

"They'll be leaving soon," Cindy said, stacking mismatched cups into a tower. "They both have suitors now. They're to be married." Though her smile showed, it dipped.

Cindy almost cringed. She had someone, too, but not a suitor. An owner.

How could her father *do* this?

Raven took some of the cups from her, awkwardly stringing together words. "And Finn? From the ball? You two seemed to have—"

The cups fumbled from Cindy's hands onto the counter, clinking together. She rushed to catch them, then took a deep breath. Their dance had been sweet and fun, his smile enough to warm her cheeks even now. She'd thrown the idea of him away before it had started, especially when he'd been announced as Raven's betrothed. "Oh, um… he and his father stayed for a few days after you… died." She cleared her throat, restacking the cups. "But they returned to Ocara."

Raven's stare held steady. "Are you sure?"

"You don't have to decide now—" Cindy sighed. Fear consumed her, threatening to shake her hands, and her tone turned desperately determined. "I just can't stay here."

She swallowed. Shame over her father *selling* her washed over her, and she knew she'd never be able to tell Raven. Not anyone.

"It probably won't be the best life," Raven said. "On the run, technically becoming a criminal—"

"Yes," Cindy insisted, fire in her voice. She clasped her shoulder, gently fingering her collarbone. Warmth surged, and she tugged the blanket over the reopened and bleeding wound.

Raven's gaze still caught it. She nodded. "I'd be glad to have you, Cindy."

Cindy smiled, relief rushing through her. She couldn't help the sigh, even when Raven tensed. But she didn't care if Raven could tell her father had worsened. Because she would *leave.* She'd be free.

Maybe she'd even get to see the ocean.

They headed out to the men and divvied the cups. Cindy started to pour the water, but Scar took the pitcher. "It's alright, milady. Thank you."

Light brows raised, Cindy smiled and stood to the side. Fingered her skirt, unsure what to do.

"Would you like to sit?" Jon asked, motioning near him and the fire.

She straightened, eyes wide, and walked over to sit. Smoothing her dress, she sighed at the fire's warmth. "Thank you."

His brow crinkled. "We should be thanking you."

"How did *you* meet someone so sweet?" Ramsey asked Raven, devouring another cupcake.

Raven glared. "I know all of my subjects."

His eyebrow rose, and he jerked his head to Cindy. "Yeah, but *her?*"

"She helped me in the market—"

"I beat her father," Raven stated.

Cindy bit her lip and stared at the flames.

Ramsey nearly choked on his cupcake, and Beast had to slap his back. A soft metal-on-metal *shing* came from Scar sharpening a blade.

"He..." Cindy swallowed. "Did better after."

Did.

Beside her, Raven clenched her fists. She knew. But these men didn't need to. Maybe Cindy could have a fresh start where people don't pity her. Where she could speak and not be afraid. Move and not doubt. Be around someone and not flinch.

"Well, he's alive so at least he learned," Lance mumbled with a grin. "Our girl wouldn't have left him breath—"

Raven shot Lance daggers with her eyes, and he glanced to Cindy before tactfully staring at his plate.

Cindy knew the Red Hood's operations. Heard of the deaths. Had always agreed with the punishments, especially with Barren's. Flint was her friend, and she'd hated seeing him with that man. *Raven* committing the actions somehow felt right. The princess taking care of her subjects. Cindy's heart warmed. Her friend truly was brave and selfless.

She clasped her fingers, then looked at Lance. "Without Raven, both as the Red Hood and princess, I would be far worse off."

If Raven hadn't returned, Cindy would've been left alone to a far darker fate than before. Soon, they'd both leave this kingdom. A dead princess, and a beaten girl. No, there was nothing left here for her. Nothing left for either of them.

FOOD CONSUMED, PITCHER EMPTY, AND THE FIRE DWINDLED TO EMBERS, THE band huddled around the table. Raven retrieved a wanted poster and pencil from her satchel, sketching the castle and surrounding forest.

"He'll be kept in the dungeons here," she pointed to the far back. "There are only two entrances to the castle that the guards don't know. One I hope not to use, and then my usual—a passage underground." She drew the trap door outside the walls and a sketch inside the palace. "It opens from the throne room or the royal bedchambers, depending on which turn you take so it won't have many guards. But it's not near the dungeons."

The men studied her drawing. Scar nodded, fingering his blades. "Sounds good. Not near anything heavily guarded, but not *too* far from Lox."

Lance leaned back in his chair, arm brushing Scar's. The bladesman glanced at the hand hear his, then shifted more toward Lance.

The band threw out ideas on how to approach unseen, and everyone shot them down. One after another.

Jon sighed and leaned back on his elbows, gazing up at Raven. "If you can't tell, Lox made most of the plans. He played to our strengths best."

She watched the men. "What'd you do?"

Jon shrugged. "Consulted. Verified the possibility and security of his plans. Lox doesn't want me in the messy areas." He sighed again. "But it looks like I am this time." After another minute of pointless arguing, Jon sat up and placed a hand on the table. "Look, I know we all want to save the boss—"

"Damn right we do," Ramsey exclaimed, raising his hand to slam it on the table.

Raven's dagger shot out and pinned his sleeve to the chair. Their eyes shot to her.

"Hey—keep. It. Down." She sent a pointed look at Cindy sitting mostly upright, her face smushed against the side of Scar's chair. Sound asleep with a bunch of criminals. The blanket slipped down Cindy's shoulders, purple marring the exposed skin. "I don't imagine she gets many good nights."

Scar tilted his head to the young woman, a tender dip to his brows. His gaze hardened when he jerked his head at the baker. "Is she okay?"

Raven stared at Cindy, peaceful in sleep. Though only a year younger, she felt protective of her friend. Fixing the blanket over Cindy's arms, she said, "She will be."

"I want her to come with us," Scar said. "If she wants, I mean."

Ramsey, Jon, and Lance all grunted agreements.

"You just want her with us because she bakes," Raven accused Ramsey. "Just because her father's a baker doesn't mean she'll make—"

"Wait... *he's* the baker?" Scar pointed to the man. "Hey, Dare, isn't this the guy Lox was going to steal from?"

Daran looked to the ceiling in thought, then nodded.

"What?" Raven looked between them.

"Sometimes Lox sees people who...well, like you target. People who need to know they can't get away with things. Only Lox steals instead of beats them."

Raven's eyes widened on the baker's unconscious face. *Lox...*

They had met watching the baker harm Cindy. And again that night for the same goal of punishing him. She'd never pondered why he'd picked the same house as her that night. Never thought past him interrupting her. Their methods differed, sure, but their values aligned.

Did that make her more of a criminal or him less of one?

They weren't all that different... And Lox was in the damned dungeons for her. Her mother. Her murder. Her mistake.

She cleared her throat and leaned into the table. "Okay, enough shit. I propose that I enter the castle, and you all guard the perimeter for when I leave with Lox." Her gloved hand silenced their interruptions. "It'll rouse less suspicions if fewer go in."

Scar grumbled, fiddling with his knives, but Lance nudged him. He sheathed a knife and nodded.

Ramsey spread his hands, pleading. "We can't let you go without backup."

"Lox would kill us," Beast's low voice added.

"That, too," Ramsey agreed, pointing at the cursed man.

"Well, they're about to kill *him*," Raven retorted, more anger than she meant. "And I know how to avoid the guards."

"Ravenna," Daran growled, a deep grumble from the usually quiet man.

She gritted her teeth. This was her mistake damn it. "In case you forgot, I can fight."

Daran rested his hands on his knees, dark muscles tightening. "*You* forget, you're a criminal here. One who murdered the princess." He paused, lowering his voice thoughtfully. "No matter how well you fight, they want you dead, Ravenna. They will not hold back. Can you kill the men who protected you for so long? Who want to avenge your murder?"

Her breath caught. What was she willing to do to save Loxley? Hurt her loyal guards for this criminal—no, he was more than that. He was the man she loved, who'd given her freedom in so many forms. Without Lox, she'd be the one locked in that cell. And *he'd* probably be trying to free her. Hell, she'd already be dead if not for him. Her guards couldn't save her from her mother's wrath, even if they'd known. But they would have tried…

She wouldn't kill them. Only knock them out enough to free Lox. Then, they'd run and never have to see this kingdom again.

"One person," she stated. "One of you can come with me."

Reluctantly, the men agreed.

"Who?"

"Me." Daran leaned forward, silver stony gaze landing on each of the others for protests. Not allowing objections. She hadn't seen him fight, but the determination in his gaze made her fearful for any guard who came in his way. The right-hand man was coming for his leader.

He locked gazes with Raven, and she nodded. "Then, we move at dawn."

CHAPTER 37

Raven tapped her foot on the forest floor lightly, searching for the trapdoor while Daran kept an eye out for guards. The soft give of the dirt hardened. She smiled softly. "Got it," she whispered.

Crouching, she brushed dirt and leaves aside to grab the handle. The Javir appeared beside her, unnervingly quiet like usual but especially in the almost silent night. Again, she wondered if he'd learned his stealth from those sands of Valara. She imagined they would lend an ease to his steps.

Raven lifted the trapdoor just enough to slide inside. Once her boots touched the damp earth underground, she reached up to hold it for him with her good arm. Darkness encompassed the pair when she shut the door. She felt around the dirt wall for the lantern she always left behind. Match and lantern lit, she finally took a deep breath.

They were so close.

Down this tunnel, through the corridors of the castle, and into the dungeon. So close to Lox. What would they find when the got there? Crimson colored her imagination—she forced her eyes open and shook he head to clear it. Whatever they'd done to him, she could use her elixirs to heal him.

"Ravenna?"

She turned to Daran, startled into this moment by his calm voice in the darkness. *Not alone,* she reminded herself. Raven started down the tunnel. "Yes?"

"I know we did not ask this of you, but I want to thank you."

"What?" Raven halted, the lantern almost knocking into her chest. She extended her arm to prevent burning herself. "Why would you thank me? I'm the entire reason this has happened."

Daran shook his head slowly, stopping with her. "Loxley has been in various jails for a few of us, and we've always managed to break him out. This is the first royal dungeon, though," Daran conceded with a pause. "I thank you because you're returning to a kingdom you were forced to leave, where you are both being hunted and supposed to be dead. You are about to face your personal guard in your home."

The breath caught in her throat. His words were all true. Daran's voice turned sad on the word 'home', and again, she remembered the band, and him especially, did not have a home.

"All of these things are impossibly hard," he continued in her silence. "And you're doing them for my friend."

"Of course. He did this for me."

"That does not mean someone would do the same for him." Daran's long breath sounded in the darkness. "Do you care for him?" He raised his hand to halt her reply. "I know you are here to help, that you care for others deeply. But do you care for *him,* the way that he cares for you?"

Raven forced herself to keep walking, despite the question bouncing in her head. The feeling of his lips on hers two nights ago—it felt so much longer—rose, bringing all the emotions of that night with it. The answer to that question felt both complicated and simple. Much like their last harried kiss—desperate and short, strong and soft. A princess fall for a thief? A criminal fall for an honest man?

She took a deep breath and sighed it out.

"I've always felt split." She shrugged, the lantern's light bobbing on the dirt walls with the movement. "Princess or Red Hood. Poised and royal, or violent and criminal. Up there," she gestured to the castle entrance lying ahead in the dark, "I have no control. And I have to pretend that's okay, pretend *I'm* okay. Here and in the village, I have control of myself back. And the only thing I have to pretend is my face, not who I am."

Despite the anxiety and fear of what was to come when she left this tunnel, the atmosphere of it eased her nerves. It was her in between. The passage from the castle to the forest. From the princess to the Red Hood, and back. This was where she felt whole. The forest felt like refuge, like she could be her darker and more dangerous self. The tunnel was the only place she was both halves.

"No matter where I was, I had to only be half of myself." Raven breathed in the earthy smell of the tunnel that came close but not quite to how Loxley smelled of the forest. "Until I met Lox. So, yes, I care for him. I don't think there was ever a way I could not."

Daran smiled. The expression lightened his serious face. "Yes, I don't think he had a choice, either, with you."

Her soft footsteps in the packed dirt were the only sound between them for a minute. If she didn't know Daran walked beside her, she wouldn't have thought it possible a person could be so stealthy. It seemed effortless to him.

"Daran…"

"Yes, Ravenna."

She swallowed. "How did you find your way to the band?"

"I sense the root to your question is how a Javir did?" He raised his hand with a soft smile, once again halting her hurried reply. "It is a reasonable question, Ravenna. Javir usually only join a group of their own, are rarely alone let alone with others not of their tribe, and I know even out here, you are probably aware the remaining tribes are on the other side of the continent."

She nodded.

"I only had my sister in Valara."

Raven held her breath, the name of that magical and broken land amazing her.

Daran watched the dirt as they walked for a moment. "I was there when it fell. We went to the tribe in Loren. She hated it." He laughed, the sound startling her for the words they followed. "She left after a while, and I tried to stop her. I tried to find her afterward… but I'd waited too long to follow. So, I searched Loren for her. Along the way, Lox and I found each other instead. People had questions, stares that were more than curious. Loren hated us for moving into their territory. Towns closer to Valara, or more in its shadow, hated my kind and the Vala for the destruction…the loss of magic, and the existence of it in the first place."

"I would guess that Lox was not like them?"

He looked up and caught her gaze. "No." Daran shook his head. "He kept telling me that my homeland and those from it did not make me anything. That I could be whatever I wanted. A lost Javir in a world that hates him… or a person exploring a world he never thought he'd see." Daran smiled, the expression seeming lighter than the lantern. "I love your forests."

A laugh escaped her. "Really?"

"They are beautiful and expansive. The desert was just one landscape, endless and mostly angry. Trees change color, and the mountains around them are tall and never quite the same shape." Daran's smile faded. "Lox allowed me to have a home again. A family."

Raven smiled. "It seems he does that for a lot of people."

Daran nodded, then slowed.

She turned and stopped. The tunnel had reached its end. Raven hung the lantern on a hook to the left and looked up at the wooden trapdoor above.

"Time to steal ourselves a thief."

NOT EVEN MOONLIGHT REACHED THE CELLS BENEATH ILASIA'S CASTLE, LOX noticed as he stumbled inside his very own small enclosure. Stumbled because the guard shoved his bruised shoulder and his gouged leg took the force of his weight. At least, he mused, this was bigger than that carriage.

Metal clanged, bars slamming shut. Last time he'd been in a damned dungeon, he'd rescued Scar's father. Different castle, same size cells. Loxley shifted his weight, and pain seared through his thigh. Bloody hell. Being the man who'd killed Princess Ravenna had its damned perks, like visits from the guards. They sure *loved* their princess.

Raven would be hard not to love. Lox damn well knew he did.

A gruff voice taunted from the dim hallway, "Filth!"

Spit hit the floor at Lox's feet.

Once the guard left, Loxley leaned his shoulder against the stone wall, his back, his head. Hell, everything hurt. He eased down to the floor with a grunt. Damn, they'd sure cut into his thigh. In one of the visits from guards, a boot heel had caught his leg *just right* and cut into the skin. The second kick had breached. The next visits widened the wound until his leg could match Raven's cloak.

Damn. Lox closed his eyes, bringing up that last image of Red, hood around her shoulders, hair free. About to let the guards catch her. He wouldn't have that. Even now, he'd still trade places.

But hell, he'd wished he'd kissed her longer if that was their last kiss. He'd never said he was smart when it came to love—wore his heart on his sleeve.

Loxley swallowed hard. That strangled cry when she'd realized what he'd done, it had unraveled his tattered heart.

Did she hate him for taking her place? It wouldn't matter—he'd rather him be in this cell than her. She wouldn't have made it unscarred through these past few days. Not that she wasn't strong, but if unhooded, she'd be killed already by whoever had targeted her. And if still hooded, Raven's guards hurting her would kill her inside.

The thief observed the cell bars mildly, curious who would be the one to delve into the dungeon. Or would his men wait until he was moved for trial—executed, rather? Raven should be almost to Ocara by now, depending on who'd went with her. He hoped Scar, their budding friendship an easy guess. Red, daggers, sarcasm. But the bladesman probably would've stayed to free him. Thriving on breaking *him* out of a dungeon for once. Lox grinned.

Jon, good navigator and planner, he'd keep her on track. Inconspicuous was his middle name. Made Lox wonder if the boy was hiding from something. But Jon could keep his secrets—of them, Lox knew Jon had some dark ones. Someone didn't refuse to carry a blade without a reason. Didn't get hidden scars without pain. Didn't look Beast in the eye unflinchingly without being haunted by something far darker and scarier.

No, Jon was entitled to his secrets. He was a good guy who deserved more than this band's criminal reputation. He was the best of them.

Gritting his teeth, Lox moved into a half-sitting half-leaning position and sighed. He just hoped Raven was safe.

. . .

CREAKING METAL HINGES ROUSED LOX FROM HIS MILD SLUMBER, HIS throbbing cheek and thigh not letting him too far under the cloud of unconscious. Slouched as he was against the wall, his back had stiffened and now ached. With a groan, he tried to lift his head toward the door. Not another damned *visit*.

"Lox!"

His heart jolted at that voice—the exact word he'd last heard her say, though far less relieved than she did now.

Wake up.

Red cloak, gloved fingers fiddling shakily with keys—no. This was a dream. An ill-timed and far too damned hopeful dream.

Quick footsteps—the cloudy, *impossible* figure's knees hit the floor, dirt clouding. More jangling of keys.

"Red?" he mumbled, split lip muffling the sound.

No—she should be in Ocara. This couldn't be real… but soft fingers brushed his arm. His eyes cleared with a hard blink. Yes, she was real. Through the enchantment, he discerned her face. Withholding a groan, Lox lowered her hood to gaze fully into her amber eyes. Eyes that had entranced him from the beginning. Light scratches dabbed her forehead and neck, dirt smudged her cheek. Why the bloody hell was she *here?*

Lox sat straighter with a groan, hand glancing her cheek. "Raven!"

She reached for his handcuffs, all the while she searched his face and body, gaze latching onto his jaw and thigh.

"What the hell are you doing here?" He tried waving off the keys, but she unlatched the cuffs.

"Saving you." Raven pushed the metal from his wrists and smiled unsteadily at him. "Not used to being the damsel in distress?"

His crooked smile spread, her gaze dropping to its curve—and his breath caught. "I can see that. But why are *you* here?"

"Because—oh, just let me save your ass." She snaked her arm under his and helped him stand, replacing her hood firmly.

He grasped the bars with a bloodied hand, leaving a smear on the black metal. Lox tried to scope out her injured arm. The cloak covered her well, but a bulge rose in the injured area. Rams would've patched her up nicely.

· · ·

329

"Can you stand?" she asked, worry coating her voice.

"Yeah." He hissed in a breath and eased his grip on her arm, instead clasped her fingers, hating the glove between them. The moment he stood, Loxley grasped her cheek, pulling her in for a kiss. Her gasp gave his tongue entry to explore as he pressed her back against the bars. If he didn't need his other damned hand gripping the metal rung above them to keep upright, he'd be exploring a lot more. She clutched him closer with a need that threatened to drive him crazy and say dungeons and guards be damned, he'd take her there on the floor. He caught her bottom lip between his teeth, eliciting a moaning sigh from Raven that was like fire in his veins.

After a long, senseless moment, Loxley pulled back, leaving them both breathless.

"Loxley," she said, starting to ease away from the bar. He wouldn't let her move. Not yet.

"I'm taking one damned moment to breathe you in, Red, because you are my salvation." Lox placed one soft kiss on her lips, whispering, "Even though you shouldn't be here."

"Wherever you go, I go, remember?"

Fuck, she was going to break him apart. He closed his eyes, against the sentiment, against the emotions stewing at her love. "You're making it very hard for us to leave this room right now."

A small laugh left her, opening his eyes on her amber eyes. "*You're* the one making it hard—"

Lox pressed his hips against hers, shivering at the delicious friction, showing her what she did to him. She gasped, cheeks flushing enough that enchantment couldn't hide it. He whispered in her ear, "Definitely you, Red. *Very* hard."

Her hand went to his hips, his thigh—and his leg faltered. Lox hissed, holding himself up by the bars. Raven wrapped her arm under his and supported his weight as he took a step. "They didn't take kindly to my killing you, apparently."

"No, they didn't," she muttered, stepping around a man on the floor just paces from his cell.

Lox assessed the guard below. Blood trailed down his temple, but his chest rose and fell. His gaze trailed up to Raven's strained face. Her eyes that remained fixed firmly ahead and not on her once-guard. She'd come for him.

She'd come for him.

Fighting.

His outlaw heart started to beat with hope. And he finally wasn't afraid of it. Hope—that this was beyond loyalty. Beyond repaying his saving her. That something deeper propelled her into the dredges of her own damned castle.

At the exit to the dungeons, Loxley held the door open. Raven peeked out, returning with a frown.

Lox's head swam from her enchantment's fuzziness, but he blinked to focus. "What's wrong?"

"Daran—he's supposed to be in the hall. But…" Her black brow furrowed.

Shit. Nothing, *nothing*, made Daran leave his post. Loxley sighed. "You know this is probably a trap, don't you?"

"Probably." She readied her dagger, then handed him one. "He might be in the tunnel. Let's go."

Raven took most of his weight while he hobbled with her down the hallway and the next. He tried not to, but she'd tug him back toward her when he eased away.

Armor clanked ahead, and she stopped them. She cursed. The once-princess looked at the three doors in the hall, and slipped them into the nearest. Months ago, Lox would have hungrily looked around the palace room, tonight he only stared at her. Raven leaned her ear against the door, listening. After a quiet minute, she eased it open, and they left. "Patrol timing can be hard to monitor, *but* the rest of the way should be clear," she explained.

How many times had she sneaked out of her castle with much less danger in her steps?

He'd seen her in both lights of herself, the princess and the Red Hood, but never this in-between. The both. The Raven. She amazed him. She knew these corridors better than any thief could dream to, and she looked terrified because of it.

Each step pounded pain through his leg, making focus hard. Without her pulling him in directions, he would've been lost. At some point, his gaze focused, and they were in a different room, Red kneeling in the center and opening a trap door. Lox blinked hard and neared.

"This leads to the forest," Raven stated and lowered a lantern she'd procured somehow into the tunnel below. "Then, we'll meet Ramsey in the forest."

Lox eased into the trapdoor, readying himself for the jolt as his leg hit the floor. Dust plumed, and pain seared up his thigh upon impact. He crumbled, hands spitting up dirt from the ground. Raven cursed, instantly at his side. Her face waxed and waned in front of him as the pain throbbed through his whole body.

"I was going to help you," she hissed. With her guiding hand, they stood.

"Just excited to get out of the castle."

Raven pushed them forward. "Me too."

As they walked—shuffled in his case—down the dark dirt tunnel, Lox noticed Red's nervousness ease. The closer to the forest, the farther from the castle. He'd think she was more scared of that place than whoever ordered her death. Maybe it was hard to see her family and old life.

The two were most quiet until the end of the path, Lox trying his damnedest to stay upright. He stared up at the exit. "This will go well."

Raven cursed. She pushed her hood off her head and dug into her satchel. "Lean against the wall and hold still."

"Yes, milady."

She shot him a look, but he still saw the smile hiding.

He did as he was told. Raven took out a roll of tied vials, carefully selected a dark green liquid, and unstopped the glass. "This will hurt, but it will also ease the pain for a while afterward."

She pushed the torn portion of his trousers aside, baring the open wound to the damp air. Then, heat struck—followed by a coldness

"What do the rest of those do, love?" He jerked his head at the vials.

Raved paused before rolling them up again. "Some heal, some are for sleep or dulling senses. One might be deadly."

"*Deadly?*"

"Maybe." She patted the wrapped potions. "The labels were a little vague, and I lost it a year ago. One said 'fyre,' but it was spelled with a y.

I poured them onto a plant, and…it wilted the flower. It burned, even melted it." Raven swallowed. "I haven't touched that one since."

Lox didn't think he would, either, but he understood her keeping it. What if the worst happened? But that word…

"Better?" she asked, returning his focus.

He blinked. He was.

Lox pushed off from the wall and waited for Red to open the latch. Stars shone down on them through the hold. It felt like weeks since he'd seen them. He sighed.

They hoisted themselves up into the dawning forest. Cool air hit Lox's skin, and he relaxed a modicum of a degree. Almost out.

Raven closed the trapdoor and pushed leaves and dirt thoroughly over it. She stared for a long moment, then nodded and turned. "Let's go."

Faster than before thanks to the potion, the two criminals crept through the forest.

From behind them, a low horn sounded. Raven cursed. "Run."

Leaves and branches hit them as they raced, dodging trees as they headed for the lower city wall.

"Remember the last time we did this?" Lox asked.

"Shut up!"

He was pretty sure he heard a smile in there somewhere.

"I do believe it ended with a kiss."

"You—"

Lox stopped, realizing Raven was slowing and grasping at her neck.

"Red!"

The hood pulled her backward, the clasp digging into her throat. Red streamed backward, but nothing tangible had caught the fabric. Lox gripped the clasp, trying to stop its pull.

Wind whipped around them, picking up speed by the second. It turned from soft to fast, to… gritty. Instead of leaves moving in the wind, it was almost like sand. The wind heated. Sand in the forest?

They both pulled on the hood, Raven stepping backward to ease the clasp from her throat.

Purple swirled in the darkness around them—and the hood fell, motionless. Raven stumbled with the sudden release of tension.

"What is this…"

Goosebumps rose on Lox's skin despite the heat from the whipping wind, slowly dulling. He knew this warmth, that feeling.

Behind Raven, the air shifted, more violet glimmering in the haze. The shimmer cleared, revealing two women standing amidst the trees.

"*This* is what happens when you don't follow orders," the blonde woman said, voice cold. Black gown, silver perched atop her braid. The queen.

Raven stiffened, hands digging into the handle of her knife.

Lox watched her face war with emotions. Guilt or sadness, he'd understand, but not this. *Fear*. And... anger?

She turned slowly to face her mother.

The queen stood alone except for a Rova woman dressed in indigo, countless bracelets encircling her wrists. Her magenta eyes shined, not a touch of her curly hair moving in the magic. Her eyes curved familiarly, and Lox couldn't look away.

Unease seated in his chest.

She waggled her fingers, and the daggers flew from Raven's and Lox's hands, clattering to the dirt floor at the woman's feet. Her lavender eyes narrowed with excitement. "I'll take those."

Wind whipped around them, impossibly pushing on their backs and legs. Lox and Raven were propelled forward to stop just feet from the women. His leg gave out when it halted him, Raven barely catching him.

The woman smiled.

Not a Rova.

A Sandceress.

Buried deep beneath disguise, Lox recognized the sleek ebony hair and olive skin of a Vala. A soft lilt to her voice, well covered but easily recognizable to another Vala.

Raven gasped, as surprised as him.

"A valiant effort, yes," Queen Vanera purred, "but not enough."

The Sandceress giggled, a wicked sound.

"What do you think, Mira? Should we wait for the guards?" She brandished a small sword.

Damn it.

Raven's grip on his wrist tightened—shook. Loxley pressed his hand against her lower back, and she leaned back into his touch. The thief peered from Sandceress to queen to princess, unsure who would strike first. How to prevent Raven from being stabbed by her own mother. Her guards were one thing, her mother another.

"Let's unmask you before you die. See who's killed my daughter." The queen's fingers grasped the red cloth and threw it back.

Black hair spread around Raven's face. Anger boiled in her eyes.

The sword dipped. Her mother's eyes wavered, mouth parted in momentary shock. A broken whisper escaped, "Ravenna."

Raven grinned coldly. "Hello, Mother."

The ire in her tone drew Lox's gaze despite his wariness of the Sandceress. This wasn't right. No love lost between them, *wrong* given the grief that had swarmed Raven upon leaving and what should be drowning her mother now. *Should.*

Why—oh damn.

Armor clanked, guards advancing for their queen. Vanera steeled her expression into a milder distress and slammed the hood back over Raven's face.

Not a mother's reaction, but a queen whose order hadn't been followed.

'*Someone too powerful wanted me dead.*'

The hollowness when talking about her family.

Damn, Raven. No wonder she hadn't told him.

The Sandceress swirled her hand, and the wind thrust forward, pushing Loxley into Raven's back and sending them stumbling into a tree. With another flick, the daggers flew. Lox reached around Raven in time to grasp one before it hit, the other landing at their feet. He brandished it at the Sandceress, whom Raven could only stare at.

Vanera backed away, dropping the sword on the unconscious guard, and screamed. "The Red Hood! He's returned!"

Five guards broke through the trees and grabbed them—pulled Raven's hands behind her, pushed Loxley against the tree, his already split lip smashing against the bark. Lox eased his head back and spit blood at the guard's boots. The man yanked him backward, causing him to stumble on his bad leg and kneel on the ground.

The queen raised a hand. "Take them to the throne room." Her cold eyes landed on Raven's obscured face. "Where they can pay for their crimes."

CHAPTER 38

Opalescent floors shimmered below Raven's boots. Once, they had been a comfort in her life. A constant she'd walked every day. The most beautiful aspect of the room where justice was served, where her father had sat—her family. Now, it blinded her.

After days in the forest and villages, she wondered how she'd ever withstood the castle in all its shining hollowness. The emptiness in the rooms as well as her mother. An emptiness Raven realized she'd shared, but she'd filled with the village and forest.

Handcuffed and hooded, Raven stood at the center of the throne room beside a mostly upright Loxley, her mother standing before her throne. The king's golden chair rested always empty. Raven's own bronze chair lay barren beside her father's gold. She couldn't keep her eyes off her mother, but she noticed Loxley's gaze drift around the room. No doubt searching for exits, advantages. Raven didn't bother. This was her mother's room, the queen's domain. They wouldn't leave until she ordered it.

Behind them, the doors burst open, steady footsteps sounding in time with armor. Footsteps familiar in a way no else's could be. Raven froze, her heart dropped.

No.

She didn't turn, she didn't need to. She didn't think she could.

Two more guards' steps followed the first. She stared ahead at the king's throne, willing this moment not to come.

But it did.

He stopped directly in front of her and Loxley. Dirty blond hair shined in the dawn light cascading through the stained glass windows, blue eyes narrowed and red-rimmed. He alone had his sword sheathed, but his face held enough rage and pain to gouge her heart anyway—Ruben.

She watched him, trying to breathe, trying to soothe the ache that both swelled at seeing him and fell because he was not seeing *her*. This was her true nightmare, one she'd feared for so long—her guards, her Rue, finding her as the Red Hood.

He stared at them both, chest heaving slightly from the run or the adrenaline of catching them, she wasn't sure. She would have hoped he'd see her, not the Red Hood, but the warmth of magic brushing her face crushed anything that started to build.

"Hello again," Lox said with a sarcastic smile.

The Head Guard turned his focus on Loxley, pure anger radiating from Ruben.

Raven found a small breath with his eyes off her. *Loxley.*

Ruben raised a gloved hand and gestured to the guards. The men came behind them and grabbed their already bound hands. Her heart beat in her throat. One guard pulled Loxley backward a step, and he stumbled to the ground from the weight on his bad leg.

Ruben stepped forward and crouched so he was eye to eye with Loxley. "You'll never escape me, boy."

The guard holding Lox put his boot on Loxley's wound and pressed. Lox clenched his teeth but couldn't stifle the groan entirely.

"No!" Raven tried to move the guard off Lox, but the one holding her pulled her back.

"Red—" Lox started but was cut off by another groan.

"Please," she begged the guard. Why did she even try? There was nothing she could say as the Red Hood that would help her.

Ruben turned to Raven—but not Raven in his eyes, the Red Hood. Her throat seized, and she tried to swallow past the pain. To keep the tears at bay. Ruben stalked to her. The guard holding her arms squeezed harder, but she wasn't moving, she couldn't. Her body felt like it was broken.

The Royal Guard emblem on his breastplate still had her bronze crown encircling the Ecanta crest. He hadn't changed it. Hadn't blackened it in grief or exchanged for silver for her mother. He was still her guard. Oh gods.

"You took her." His voice shook, and because she knew him so well, she heard the grief starting to overshadow the anger. Ruben was not an angry man, but thinking she was dead had channeled that ire stronger.

Raven blinked back tears, felt the heat of magic spread to her neck, as she said, "I—"

"Leave us," Vanera called from the dais.

Silence rang in the throne room. Every guard looked at their queen. She waved a dismissive hand.

Ruben stepped toward Vanera, and Raven clenched her eyes shut. Against his presence, hostile and grieving. Against the voice she'd missed like air. "Your Majesty—"

"Out!" she screamed, perched in hysteria.

Raven dared a glance at Rue... and her heart fractured. He'd never appeared this broken.

Bags under his eyes, rage creased his brow. He shut his mouth tightly, glared at Raven and Loxley. The hood her mother had forced back on to keep her damned secret prevented Rue from any recognition. Only hate and sadness covered his expression. Heavy footsteps retreated, each puncturing her heart. She released a breath when the doors thudded.

Mira waved at the door, a purple sheen spreading over it before fading into the dark wood.

Composed as ever, the queen sighed, a harsh exhale rather than of relief, and descended the steps. She stopped feet from Raven, ignoring Loxley. Her face still composed in its queenly manor. Then, she threw off Raven's hood.

The magic fell, a chill racing over Raven's defiant, exposed face.

Blonde brows clenched above Vanera's hard blue gaze. The only betrayal of her true emotions. No crying. No relief. *Anger*. The menace still alive and breathing, standing before her.

"You." Loxley let out a ragged breath, brows lowering to shadow his eyes. "It was you. You ordered her death."

Raven's chest clenched.

"Well, he sure is a smart one, dear," Mira purred from beside the queen's throne. Her hip rested against the arm, casually leaning on the seat of power. "Not just looks. Good choice."

Mira neared, running a fingernail down his cheek, then she paused, nail digging into his jaw. She leaned in, squeezing his arm when he tried to jerk back, and took a deep breath through her nose. Her lavender eyes hardened to glass, like her crystal ball. "The forest is in your heart, but the sand is in your soul." The Sandceress's voice lowered into something close to a growl. "Where are you from, boy?"

Lox glared, jaw clenching.

Mira slapped the cheek she'd just caressed. "Where?"

He inhaled sharply from the hit, slowly raking his eyes up to hers. "Somewhere long gone."

The Sandceress's lip curled upward, and she backed away.

Raven stared at Mira, confused. Why did Mira care?

Lox looked at Raven, and her heartbeat stuttered at the sympathy in his gaze. She quickly righted her sight to her mother.

Vanera bared her teeth in a wicked form of a grimace. "I have to say, I never saw this coming."

"My secret," Raven hissed, letting her anger roll of her tongue. "Or my still beating heart?"

"This… Red Hood." Vanera waved her hand at the cloak, seemingly unable to touch it. The secret that had helped Raven survive her wrath, her sentence.

"Tell me, your fortune teller didn't foresee this? Oh, wait—she's not a fortune teller. She's a gods damned *Sandceress*!" Metal cuffs clanked as Raven spouted that last accusation at Mira, who was smirking and leaning against the queen's throne. A Sandceress. An impossible force— of both magic and power—standing right before her, who'd been in Raven's life as long as she could remember. An impostor. Were they all impostors? Innocent princess, loving mother, fortune teller, Red Hood, grieving queen, Sandceress.

The queen coolly smiled, barely a lift to her mouth, and turned her back on her daughter, taking a few paces before facing her again. Mira sauntered forward, stopping beside Vanera.

Gritty, hot wind encircled Mira for just a moment, flowing from her hair to her feet. As it moved, her figure and clothes shimmered and rustled, unlike the stillness in the forest before. Her whole self altered. Dark curls straightened, indigo skirt shifted inward to form loose violet pants, connecting to a gold top that hugged her curves but exposed her tan skin. The usually jingling bangles tightened to her arms and snaked into a solid piece of gold that wound and crisscrossed from her middle fingers up and around her arms to wrap solidly into a band below her shoulders.

Mira lifted her arms and smiled. The pose had a flourish that was so characteristic of the jaunty and buoyant and *fun* Mira who Raven had loved that it felt like a shot to her heart.

From Rova fortune teller disguise to a Vala Sandceress.

Her purple eyes, black hair, tan complexion. It all took on a different light.

No wonder Rue's wife hated Mira. Impersonating Esme's culture.

Mira giggled, that light sound she threw so carefree. With a wave of her hand, her appearance reversed, and once again, the Rova in traditional if not over-done garb stood in her place.

The queen sighed, stealing Raven's attention back. Mira shrugged at Vanera's annoyed stare.

"You exceeded my expectations, Ravenna, you really did," Vanera said, looking her up and down. "Distributed justice—or what you *thought* was justice—faked your murder, teamed up with a… criminal," her dark gaze slithered over Lox, who observed their interaction with a calculated gaze, "and survived on your own."

Rage boiled beneath Raven's chest, and she wished for a knife to throw at her mother. "Does that mean I get to live? Meeting your expectations. Or is there another reason you wanted me dead, Mother?"

Vanera stared at Raven for a long minute. This was probably the most honest they'd ever been about their emotions toward each other. Yet Raven couldn't help the small part of her that still cried, *why?*

She swallowed, trying to drown out that weak, childish piece of her. The why didn't matter. She *wished* it didn't matter.

She'd always known there was something wrong and not quite right or loving between them, but never this. She'd lived with this monster so close to her for years. And that Sandceress… the lie of her very existence felt like a looming danger.

Soft steps sounded against the opal floor. Vanera stopped inches from Raven. "I tried to love you. To do the right thing. Despite how sweet and smart and kind you were—it wasn't enough. You weren't enough."

No malice, just a fact.

A strangled gasp lodged in Raven's throat. Her eyes burned with building tears. Though she suspected this, all of it, hearing the truth from her mother's lips grated her heart.

"The betrothal was supposed to fix this. Our kingdom, and my pain. You would leave with a prince and live out a life *away* from me. But somehow, it only made it worse."

Raven recalled Vanera's face in the hallway when the Ocara prince, Finn, had talked about her remaining near Ecanta if they married. *That's something to consider,* she'd said to Vanera. *Yes, it is.*

Vanera had just considered it differently.

"I couldn't take it anymore," Vanera continued. She ran a hand down the side of Raven's head, stroking her black hair like when she was young. "I tried to give you another ending, but it seems this truly is the only solution."

Raven stiffened, tilting toward Lox for his steadiness. *Please, don't make Ruben kill her. Not him,* she prayed to whoever would listen—gods, faeries, *anyone.*

Vanera nodded to Mira. The Sandceress grinned, snapping her fingers. A small bottle appeared in her hand. Dark metal covered the thick cork, crept over the sides of the opening, securing into the bottle in several different points, like an octopus capturing prey.

Black waves roiled within. Though it sat motionless on Mira's palm, the contents moved, folding in on itself, grasping for the glass in search of escape. Not a potion or even a spell—something darker.

"What is that?" Raven asked, voice shaking enough to wound her pride.

The queen's brows tipped downward in... *sadness?* "I've used this once before, and I never thought I'd consider it again. Now, you've given me no choice. It seems you'll suffer this fate as well."

"Fate?"

The black liquid swirled, dense as smoke but thick as syrup.

"Death." Mira tapped the glass. The contents shifted away before pushing against where her finger had touched. "Or very close. This is a curse."

Loxley stiffened beside her, no doubt thinking of Beast's curse.

"It'll render the drinker all but dead," Mira continued. "Your breath, your blood, your heartbeat will stop, all frozen between two moments of time." She grinned, perfect teeth enhancing the sandy tone of her skin. "But you'll be aware. Your lungs will feel the struggle to breathe, like the moment before surfacing from underwater. You will relive the worst parts of your life, and you'll know you're under the magic. It will not be like a slumber. It will be like death. Awake and frozen. While the world continues on without you."

Lead settled in the pit of Raven's stomach, dragging her heart along with it.

Where had this curse come from?

Then, her mother's words registered. Raven's voice hardened, deadly. "Who did you use this on, Mother?"

Please, not Papa.

Vanera's mouth sagged, breaking her ever-present calm exterior. Her eyes lifted to Raven's. "Your mother."

CHAPTER 39

Raven swallowed, all anger wiped away by shock. "What do you —*you're* my mother."

"No." Vanera shook her head, voice unnervingly calm. "I'm not."

Raven shook her head, trying to clear her muddled thoughts. "Wait— you're not—" Emotion seized her throat, her breaths; confusion, anger— relief? Warmth encased her hand. Loxley squeezed once, his touch reassuring her when it shouldn't be possible.

Vanera paced the throne room, grey-blue eyes staring through the stained glass windows at the village below. "Dawn was your mother," Vanera continued, a softness to her voice that Raven hadn't heard toward herself in many years. Then, the queen sighed, and it hardened. "And my best friend."

A harsh laugh expelled from Lox. He glared at the queen, jerking his head at the bottle. "And you gave her *that*?"

"Hush, thief!" Vanera commanded.

He rose his eyebrows at Raven. "So, that's where you get that from."

Mira pointed, and his mouth snapped shut with a resonating *crack*. He glared, and she wiggled her fingers back. "Keep it shut, or I'll do it again."

Raven grasped her rampant thoughts enough to ask, "Did—did she and Papa—?"

"No!" Vanera turned on her so fast Raven almost stumbled backward at the fierceness to the queen's gaze. After a moment's breathing, Vanera composed herself. "No. Eldric was not your father, either." She glanced down at her clasped hands. "He loved you like he was, though."

Something small and broken in Raven fractured more. Was everything in her life a lie? It was one thing for her mother to want her dead—but to not even be her mother? For her scrap of a family to be false. That… did that mean she wasn't truly a princess?

Was that why she couldn't quite fit the crowned mold?

Raven fumed, staring at this woman she hated that she could still recognize. Who still felt a little like family. "Then, why am I here? Why do *you* have me? You cursed her and… what? I was left over?"

Too many emotions flashed over Vanera's face before she could contain them. The beautiful features settled into grief. What had happened to make her this way? What was *her* secret?

Hands still bound, she stepped toward the queen, anger beating a pulse in her chest. "What did she do to you?"

"She had *you*!" Vanera screamed, the shout raising the hairs on Raven's arms. "We were supposed to experience life together. We grew up together. We both found love. We were going to build families together, and—I couldn't." Vanera stopped, voice breaking. "She had *children*—child after child after child… and I just couldn't."

Tears brimmed in the Widow Queen's eyes. The queen who'd lost her husband and apparently her heart with it.

"Eventually, Eldric and I had a girl," Vanera paused, voice thick, "but a few years later, she was taken from me."

"So, you took hers?" Loxley shouted in outrage, breaking the mandated silence. He shot a glare at Mira, daring her to hit him again.

"I didn't know what it would do!" Vanera screamed back. She rounded on Mira. "I didn't understand."

The Sandceress sauntered to the queen, slow and precise steps bringing her inches away. Black brows lay low over her violet eyes. "No, you didn't ask questions," she corrected the queen. Mira held Vanera's gaze, and Raven watched the ire drain out of her once-mother. Watched the power and control of the queen melt under the calm storm of the

Sandceress. "I said it would give you children. And you didn't care enough to ask *how*."

Raven's eyes widened as the queen's and Vala's words replayed in her mind. She swallowed. "Vanera…" She met the queen's gaze. "You said children."

The queen averted her gaze to the windows again. Dread settled in Raven's stomach.

The Sandceress turned to face Raven. She neared, bottle still perched in her palm. Her lavender eyes met Raven's amber as she leaned in, their intensity unnerving her. "Your little friend in the village looks a lot like your mother."

"Cindy," Raven gasped. Her sister? Was that why she felt so connected to her?

Lox leaned on her shoulder, catching her gaze. He whispered, "From the ball?"

Raven nodded, swallowing hard. Poor Cindy.

Mira waved at Vanera. "She gave this to Dawn, who then fell under the curse. And Vanera had children." She spread her hands wide. "Like I said. Two to be exact, since your other sister was off with your father at the time. He fled town quickly with the small remnant of his family."

Other sister, what—

"Then," Mira continued, not giving Raven's thoughts a chance to catchup," Vanera had a choice. What to do with them."

The widow queen glared, silent and fuming, apparently letting the Vala spill her secrets for her.

Raven stared at the bottle, the dark liquid that moved on its own. "Why couldn't you unfreeze Dawn?"

The Sandceress laughed, a sound more maniacal than the joyful one she'd gotten accustomed to. "A curse is different than a spell or a potion, dear one."

Emotion seized her heart at the once-affectionate endearment.

"It doesn't fade or require an antidote like a potion," the Vala explained. Raven felt Loxley tense beside her, focus intent on her words. "It is not a glamor or a layer like enchantments or spells, woven into the fabric of the person or object it is on." Mira clicked her tongue. "A curse *overtakes* the person, it consumes them. Becomes them. Inseparable."

Raven and Loxley shared a glance, both seeming to have the same thought—Beast.

Mira raised the bottle, staring into the glass. "A curse requires conditions to break it."

"Which are?" Loxley asked.

"Tsk, tsk." Mira smiled, waving a finger at him. "That is for Vanera to know, not you. Each curse is specific to the one it is on."

She let the curse go, and it floated in midair beside her, weaving up and down, as she spoke, "Curses are ancient, forbidden magic." The Sandceress leaned in and whispered to Raven, "But there isn't anyone left to forbid it."

With a chuckle, she straightened, stroking Raven's dark hair. "Our dear queen used this particular curse and realized what she'd done. Fate, as I've said before, can be a moment. What comes next is the after. She could only take in one child. You were lucky enough not to resemble the queen's lost daughter. You have your father's hair, but your mother's eyes. Cindy, the opposite. So, off Cindy went, and here you stayed. And I had to play a memory spell on the kingdom to forget, to warp, to recall *you* instead of—"

"Mira!"

The Vala's mouth closed in a wicked smirk, and she faced the queen. "Your Majesty?"

"*Don't* talk about her," Vanera hissed.

"You have me search for months on end with tracking spells, this kingdom and that," Mira stated, turning on the queen, "but you won't have me say her name?"

Raven leaned against Loxley, strength leaving her. So, the daughter was stolen, not dead, it sounded. Pieces were falling into place in her memory, her life. Mira's trips, Vanera's unhappiness increasing when she saw Mira. Because the Vala was empty-handed, no news on the missing child—young woman, if she was Raven's age.

"Gods," she breathed, "what did you do?"

The queen rounded on the vigilante. "A true mother would do anything for her daughter. And I did. Just not with you." Vanera's eyes hardened into navy blue. "I didn't know what this curse would do then. But I do now."

Her hand shot out, grip as hard as steel, and pulled Raven toward Mira and the curse. Raven tugged her tied wrists back.

Lox yelled, his bound hands knocking into Vanera hard enough for her to stumble. With Vanera's grip loosened, Loxley grasped Raven and moved her away, slightly behind him. His leg faltered, the injury flaring. She caught him, using her shoulder under his arm to keep him upright.

Vanera rounded on him, hatred in her glare, then paused. Appraised his bruised face, his arm over Raven's, down to the hand he rested on her bare skin.

"You came back for him. Why?"

Lox's finger ran lightly up and down her wrist, trying to calm the racing heartbeat beneath. It steeled her voice. "Loyalty."

The queen's gaze flickered between their faces and back to his finger rubbing soothingly. Vanera sighed, but her voice rose in intrigue, "Is that all?"

She straightened her shoulders, a coolness spreading throughout her demeanor. That composure that came with orders, with calm logic required of a queen. A chill descended Raven's spine.

"You're not my daughter. Not a princess. You're nothing. Now that you know the truth, *you* can decide. Leave Ecanta and never return, or take the curse."

Raven's eyes narrowed. "What's the catch?"

The corner of the queen's mouth twitched upward. "One of you must drink. If you leave, he drinks. If you drink, he's free."

Bangles jingled as Mira, smirking, lifted the potion and added, "There is no cure or remedy. I suggest you not decide lightly."

"You saved him once," Vanera said. "Will you do it again?"

Raven's heartbeat pounded.

In her chest.

Her throat.

Her head.

"I'll take it!" Lox shouted.

Raven looked to him, her mouth parting in surprise. No hesitation. No debate. Just his love.

"Tsk, tsk," Mira said, shaking her dark curls. "You don't get to decide. She does."

"No!" Lox grasped Raven's head with his bound hands, drawing her attention. The throne room faded, the queen, the Sandceress. Just Loxley stood before her, those deep green eyes that felt like home. "You have a life—I have nothing."

She lifted her hands and touched his cheek, resting her forehead on his. A sad smile crested her lips, and she said the words she'd spoken so long ago. "You have your band. I don't."

In a voice so rough and quiet that the queen or Sandceress couldn't hear, he whispered, "You have me."

"I do," Raven's voice broke, and she squeezed her eyes shut, just breathing. "And I can't do this to you."

"I'd rather be under that curse than know you are." Loxley gripped her face, making her look at him. Why did he always have to be so open when he stared at her? "My life has been nothing but running from place to place. But with you, Raven," his eyes misted, shining emeralds, "I feel like I have a home. I can't wander without you. Not again."

Raven breathed for a moment, hating that she was about to break his heart along with hers. She shook her head, silently begging a question. He held her stare, and his forest eyes carried an answer. He would have her back. Always.

She swallowed and faced the ruler of her kingdom. "I choose me."

CHAPTER 40

Zella stared at the trees beyond the window she had never dare touch before tonight, a makeshift bag of supplies in her hands— filled with a carefully wrapped mirror, the enchanted tome, and other favorite books she had sifted through. Those books, those pieces of her that had been her only friends and refuge. She could only carry so many, but she would find a way to replace the rest she left behind.

Left behind. She really was doing this.

Naja hadn't been back in four days, today starting the fourth. Zella squinted into the night, measuring that dawn was fast approaching. She had to hurry. There was no way to know if Naja would return today or tomorrow.

Numb fingers gripped the half-empty small glass vial until she worried it might shatter. One deep breath. Another.

Zella raised her left palm, coated in the thick red mixture from the vial. Slender fingers trembled and paused a barest space before the window, the tips still singed from previous attempts. She swallowed— and pushed the blackened fingers through to the outside.

Cool wind.

The tiniest hint of a breeze. It *touched* her skin.

She shuddered out a breath. Zella stretched her whole wrist out. Wiggled her fingers. A smile crested, real hope sparking through her.

The air crackled violet and violent, then faded, leaving the sound of its breaking in the air. Red dripped from her magic-stained joints, onto the stone windowsill.

Finally, she would touch the world.

The vial was unstoppered in a moment and fully emptied onto the bottom pane.

Without another pause for thought, fear, guilt—any other emotion that might bar her into this damned tower for another moment—Zella scooped up the bag and bent to tighten the knot she'd tied of her hair around the table leg magically bolted to the ground. Zella stepped onto the windowsill. The stone was an odd mixture of cold and sparking warmth, coated with the thick mixture from her precious vial.

Even if she broke her leg, she'd still be outside. She gripped her hair close to her scalp and jumped.

Air rushed past, stealing her breath as the ground neared and neared and—her hair yanked upward, halting her descent. Zella's grip on the long strands lessened the pain, but the jolt still jarred her scalp. Compared to Naja's grip over the years, though, it was bearable.

The tower on the other hand crashed into her shoulder. She grappled her feet against stone to find placement and felt the faint tickle of grass below on the tips of her toes. Keeping her head high, gaze upward, Zella used one hand to steady her taut hair while the other gripped her bag to her chest and dug inside. Gently, she removed the glass shard, letting the bag fall to the ground. Zella looked up at her hair streaming from the tower. In the breaching morning light, it glinted. She sliced through the cursed strands. One swipe—two—and it crackled as it was severed.

Zella stepped back and watched the locks hang from the tower window.

Two heartbeats later, her scalp prickled. Her smile broke. The hair faded from the tower and reappeared around her shoulders, her frame, her legs. Once again attached and weighing her down.

If this was the price to pay, the curse to bear for separating from that tower, Zella would.

She hefted the hair and wound it around her neck loosely, once around her waist, and thrice around her left arm, ending knotted at her wrist. It was cumbersome, but better than tripping. She grabbed the makeshift bag and walked to the edge of the small circular meadow.

Dense trees and vines secluded the tower from the castle and world. Zella examined the greenery for any weaknesses or gaps. Did Naja squeeze through? Did the vines and branches bend for her? Or did she materialize? Zella never knew. She dared to touch the nearest tree. Rough bark grazed her fingers. No pain.

If the Red Hood had managed a way between the trees, then it was possible.

Deep breaths. She closed her eyes, gripped the bag tight, and ran through the vines.

Harsh branches and greenery dug at her sides, her arms, a mixture of rough and soft. A strand pulled on her wrapped hair, tugging her sideways, but she pursued. This was not going to be what kept her here. She hadn't bled and cried and suffered for *trees* to stop her.

Air brushed her face, and Zella pushed and pushed, and—stepped through. Two more steps, and she halted, breathing heavily. She gaped at the trees, the forest she'd read about in her book, then turned to take one look at the vines. Dense trees packed closely together, wound and wound with vines and tight branches.

She'd done it.

A sob rose to her throat, and she let a fraction escape. Tears prickled her eyes. Zella shook her head, looked away from the green prison, and steadied her breath. That was only the first step. She wouldn't be truly free until she left this damned city.

She observed the trees and still-starry dawn sky hungrily, though she knew what she longed to see most was beyond this. Everything was beyond, and soon, she would be, too. Soft, silky, the grass wiggled between her toes and under the pads of her feet. The blades tickled. She hadn't expected softness. *Later,* she reminded herself.

Zella recalled the map she'd stared at for countless days in the enchanted tomb of Naja's. Left was toward the town. Toward roads. Zella relished each step in the grass, wanting to stretch out her fingers to brush the trees, but reigned in her desire.

Snap—a stick broke under her foot, and she stepped on a piercing rock with the other. "Ow!"

Crouching to rub her bare feet, she looked around for anyone that might have heard her. Thankfully, no one yet. Shoes were definitely needed to make it out safely. Maybe she could find a pair before leaving.

Dawn threatened to break the skyline when Zella made it to the first stone wall. She knew there were two that surrounded the city with walled pathways between the sections. Scaling the wall was no easy task with her hair wrapped around her body and arms, but she grabbed the top and hoisted herself up. Even this early, the marketplace was growing with sound and movement.

Dim light pushed through treetops, adding a small reprieve of the shadows. Zella cautiously walked behind the building before her and toward the center of the market, looking at half-prepared and empty booths, villagers bringing out their wares and waking up to start their daily lives. Nerves crept into her veins.

People.

This in front of her could be what she makes for herself once she gets out of this kingdom. She hoped. Gods, she hoped.

Zella measured the wares at the shops, searching for shoes or clothes. At the end of the market, she found the stall she searched for. Walking toward it, she paused, spotting a sale at the weapons table. The merchant took coin from the shopper and handed over a long knife. Should she have a weapon?

The thought alone scared her.

But she would need coin. Otherwise, she'd get nothing. How, though? Steal? Any attempt didn't bode well for her in adept skills.

Zella watched the beginnings of other sales start with the opened stalls… thinking. She could sell something. *Not my books.* She swallowed. It was all she had.

She gripped the bag.

Glass clinked softly inside.

Not *all* she had.

The vials? Her concoctions? Magic was rare in the world, but especially this queendom, the book had told her. And she felt it, the absence of magic. No prickles on her skin or tugging of her cursed hair. Nothing like the electricity pulsing through her constantly at the tower. Here, the world felt calm in its own way. A way no one else could see.

Stepping back toward the wall around the market, Zella pulled out one of her two remaining prepared vials.

She cautiously went to a woman glancing at the open booths. Zella took a deep breath and approached the woman. "Hello."

The slender woman stopped and appraised Zella in the twilight. "Good morning."

Oh. Should she have said that? "I'm selling a potion to—"

The woman reared back, her nose crinkling in distaste. "I don't mess with that."

"It could protect you." Zella held the vial cradled in her palm outward. "It cancels any magic."

"And there is no magic here, girl."

"But—" she tried.

"You'd have better luck selling me shit," she interrupted, waving at the dark vial. "That, I could use."

The woman left with a grunt.

Fear grasped Zella, turning her stomach and squeezing her throat. This wouldn't work. The woman was right. Who would want a potion that stops magic in a world without magic?

Her neck warmed.

Magic.

Softer than with Naja, but still washing over and under her skin.

Heart racing, Zella forced herself to turn slowly. If it was Naja, she couldn't draw more attention to herself.

She faced the feeling, the sensation now moving to the front of her, almost down her arms. Warmth radiated like a small fire from slightly to her right. She could sense its presence. Two buildings sat before her, probably homes of vendors. The booth in front of this house did not appear touched at all.

Following the trail of magic, Zella walked between the houses, under the shadows cast by both. Near the back of the house, she heard voices and paused. One was rougher, the other sounded slightly younger.

"Beast—what are you? Daran!" A young man sighed, and there was a small shuffle. "I'll get him inside."

"Plan changed."

"Why does the plan *always* change?"

By the time Zella reached the edge of the rising dawn's shadows, she saw a tall young man standing at the back door, a pair of boots disappearing into the home as if they were being dragged. The possible body didn't catch her attention as it should have. What made her stare was the young man himself. Not at his auburn hair, his dark eyes, or his large frame. It was the magic.

Dark magenta spiraled across his skin, mangling the sharp features, entrapping his face and body like chains. The warmth within her flamed. Was that his curse she felt? The chains glowed with a pulse. A pulse that beat in the tips of her fingers opposite the rhythm of her own heart.

Yes, his curse.

She gasped at the strength.

The young man's face lifted sharply, gaze instantly locating her in the shadows. Black eyes faded to purple—short auburn hair darkened to black. She focused, and the curse settled back into chains, only the lavender eyes remaining.

An illusion curse. Interesting.

He stalked forward.

Something within her calmed as the cursed young man neared. She felt less lost, magic reacting to magic.

A few feet before her, he stopped, hulking over her small figure.

Zella held his gaze, and surprisingly, he averted it, his brow furrowing slightly. Their stare broken, his purple-marred skin faded to normal. The curse receding beneath his skin.

"Good morning," she said.

Confusion entered his slightly lowered eyes. "Good morning."

She raised her half-filled vial. "I'm selling my wares. It's a potion."

His black gaze locked on the glass, then roamed over her face—never quite meeting her eyes—and back to her darkened finger on the vial.

"It cancels magic. Temp-temporarily," she finished. The intensity of the magic on him was as loud and deep as her tower, and it was almost dizzying now that she'd started to recognize magic's presence.

"There's no need," he declared. Dark brows crinkled. Harsh features softened. "Why would I want that?"

Magic pulsed across his figure, the purple chains appearing to tug at his skin. She whispered, "You're cursed."

Black eyes froze on her lower face, his expression stuck between anger and… something dangerously close to fear. He rose his gaze to hers. Purple flashed in his eyes. "How do you know?"

She held his stare yet again, wondering why his brow creased. "Magic leaves a trace on everything it touches." Her fingers twisted their grip on the vial, the tips shadowy. The magicked bruises still burned on her scalp. "I should know."

The cursed young man took a fraction of a step forward.

Beside them, the house's door opened. "Okay, so what is the *new* plan? Hello."

The other young man from before—she recognized his voice—stopped beside the cursed one. Black hair fell to the tips of his ears, brushed back by the night's wind. While the cursed young man appeared a few years older, this one looked her age. And he was handsome—really *handsome.*

Dawn light hit his pale blue eyes, and Zella gasped at their beauty. They latched onto her, and the focus, the kindness that softened on her face… her cheeks warmed.

"H-hello." She swallowed whatever this new feeling was and looked back to the cursed man. "I'm selling the potion. Would you like it?"

The second one replied, "No, thank yo—"

"Yes."

The second boy's pale gaze whirled to his cursed friend. He stared, but those cursed purple eyes held Zella's.

The younger's black brows rose in surprise, then a contemplating look crossed his eyes. They swam over her impossibly long hair wrapped around herself, surely spotting her fading bruises, and her bare feet. Finally, he brought them back to her own, and she almost felt more nervous.

"Jon," the cursed man said, "pay her."

The younger one, Jon, nodded and pulled out some coins from a pouch in his pocket. "How much?"

Zella paused. How much was anything worth, let alone a potion? What did she need for shoes, a cloak, and food? Stars above…

"Fifty," the cursed young man stated.

"Fifty it is." Jon handed her coins and easily took the vial from her now shaking hands. One corner of Jon's mouth lifted, a dimple appearing on the side. A small flash of his teeth, then the smile widened. "Thank you."

"Y-you're welcome." Zella let out a small breath, nodded, and backed down the alley toward the market.

She clutched the coins, tears prickling her eyes. At the end of the alley, she looked back at the young men. They were in conversation, appearing casual, but the intensity of the cursed one's gaze on his friend gave away their seriousness.

Maybe the potion would help him. They'd surely helped her.

Now, to get clothes, food, and leave this damned queendom behind.

Zella smiled to herself as she approached the clothier booth. The outside world was truly kinder than the inside.

CHAPTER 41

Darkness swirled inches from Raven's face, trapped, some tendrils almost resembling claws reaching for the glass. Which was impossible. But so was human magic, and a Sandceress extended that very curse.

"Drink."

Raven shook her head, dark locks hitting her dirty cheeks. "I'm not as stupid as you think I am," she snapped at the queen and jerked her head toward Loxley, whose shoulder slumped against her own from exhaustion and pain. "Not until Lox is free."

Vanera sighed. "You can't possibly think he'll save you if we let him go."

"No."

The certainty in her voice shocked the queen, who rose a light blonde brow.

Lox tensed beside her.

"I expect to drink… that and fall under its magic. And stay that way." Raven set her jaw, fingers clenching into Lox's arm. "I made a promise, and I don't intend to break it. So—I don't drink until he's free."

The queen's lips pursed, then she turned to Mira. Bangles jingled as the Sandceress waved at the door, a purple sheen raining down the wood. Whatever magic she'd placed now erased.

357

Her mother—her… queen?—tossed Raven's hood back over her head. For once, the cloak and its magic felt like shame.

"Guards!"

The heavy doors swung open, and two guards followed Ruben inside.

"Take this out of the castle." Vanera didn't even spare Lox a glance as she waved her hand at him. "All charges on him are dropped."

Ruben's dark brows rose in outrage. "Your Majesty—"

A step sounded on the marble floor. "Do you question my orders?"

"No." He swallowed his emotion—anger or shock? "I just wonder what justice will be had for Princess Ravenna."

Old Ravenna would have smiled at Rue having to fight emotions against the queen instead of her. But Raven would never see her true Rue again.

Vanera's mouth set into a grim line, and she shifted her gaze to Raven, hooded. Mira released a low sound like a chuckle, the bottle hidden. "The Red Hood is solely responsible. And will be killed upon the hour."

Raven wished she knew the time. An hour. Or less?

The Head Guard nodded, glaring at Raven's hooded face while he hoisted Lox up and removed his shackles.

Her breath hitched. Once again, she couldn't breathe. Her mother, her death, her unworthiness stole all her breaths.

With a hard swallow of whatever feelings were building inside, Raven took one last look at Lox—and breathed. How could he manage to ease that tightness in her chest by just being there? The bruise on his jaw purpled like Mira's magic against the stubble. Her fists clenched. His eyes caught hers, hidden in shadow. The softness held within stole her heartbeat. "Lox…"

He reached, and she tried to grasp him, to touch him for a moment— but Vanera gripped her shoulder.

Ruben paused, staring, a small look of recognition and confusion sparking on his face. Her voice. He must remember, her most loyal and faithful friend. The boy who'd helped her survive, who had covered her crime, who had… His eyes unfocused. As everyone's always did. Damn her cloak's magic.

She turned her gaze to Lox and gave a small smile.

Ruben pulled Lox toward the entrance and shoved him through. Both thick doors shut with a sound so final Raven thought all her breaths had left with Lox because her chest hitched.

Vanera jerked Raven to her feet, the hood falling uselessly, and pulled her to the window. Mira stood behind them both, a menacing hand on Raven's shoulder. A quiet, eerie whisper sounded in her left ear, and she didn't dare turn, for she knew in the pit of her stomach that it was the curse sitting in Mira's hand. The curse she would drink.

This is my problem not his. My crime.

But what was her crime?

They stood in silence until Ruben exited the castle, until he tugged Lox through the gates, until he released Lox's arm at the cobblestone path.

Vanera sneered, her gaze locked on his back. Did her daughter— her… whatever Raven was to her—choosing to save another's life bring her joy? Or annoyance?

Lox walked past two guards, anxiety spiking under Raven's skin, pulse racing against the metal around her wrists. Not a single guard acted against him as he limped down to the first village gate.

Relief washed over her. How soon would the men find him? She let out a small breath. She didn't need to worry about him anymore.

"See? He's free," Vanera spat, wrenching from the window. "Now take your punishment."

Mira smiled, the whispers growing as she leaned in. "Guess you wouldn't be used to *taking* them."

"I want an explanation," Raven stated, eyes still trained on Lox's limping form.

"What?" Vanera's voice prickled with ice, but Raven was already frozen inside.

"A full explanation."

Why do you want me dead? What did I do to make you this way? If she would be frozen between heartbeats, it really didn't matter how shattered her heart was, did it? She wouldn't get a chance to use it again.

Unless Lox discovered the conditions to break it.

Her throat constricted. No. Best not to think of him. He was safe, finally without her burden.

The queen tore Raven from the window, elegant brows taut. "You can't stall this. He won't save you."

"Like I said," Raven replied, just as icily, "I don't plan for him to."

Light blue eyes at war with the hardness inside them stared back, still and wide.

"I just want to know why, *Mother*." Not a question.

"I already told you—"

Raven shook her head. "No. Why kill me."

After a long pause, Vanera spoke to Mira without breaking their stare, "Ready her coffin."

"Coffin?" Goosebumps rose.

The Sandceress turned, taking the eerie whispers with her, and set the potion in her pouch before working purple shimmers in the air. "It's an encased bed, glass surrounding the resting area. You'll be like the potion." Mira glanced over her shoulder and winked. "Trapped in a bottle. Forever wishing to be free. To breathe. To live."

"Dawn is in another," Vanera whispered, almost to herself as she watched Mira's magic color the air. She glanced at the ceiling, at the point of the castle spire above where Raven knew the ashes and urns of previous royalty lay.

Mira's giggle rang out alongside her bangles. "Like mother like daughter."

PAIN SPIKED UP LOX'S LEG WITH EACH STEP, EVEN THE ONES NOT PRESSING into his right thigh's wound. The jostling sent a fresh wave, but Lox schooled his face to erase any winces. He had to make it far enough they couldn't see him. And he knew those large decorative windows gave a view to about two gates into the village, then the distance was too far for clarity. An advantage. He and Lance could shoot a bullseye farther.

Damn that queen, that bitch. To order her own daughter's death... Despite not being blood, she'd *raised* her. And that Sandceress—

His jaw still stung. He couldn't believe her magic. Its existence and its strength. His parents' stories hadn't told of the like. Neither Sage nor Sandceress. How the hell—No. Now was not the time.

Raven. Focus on her. Only her.

360

Gods, that curse…

The black swirled in his mind. The idea of that inside her—

Damn it.

Lox exaggerated his limp until he closed the second gate, then straightened, walked onto the pathway toward the pub. A guard passed, and Lox leaned against a house to steady himself. The guard looked away, and Lox stepped forward, swinging into the alley and behind the building.

Raven had used her tunnel, meaning his men would be waiting in the forest.

Not five steps beyond the wall and toward the forest, a low whistle brought him to a cluster of trees. A scarred chin leaned out of the shadows. Lox sighed. He'd never been this glad to see Ramsey.

The man embraced him before he was fully into the trees' shadows, patting him on the back. Lox used his friend's strength to ease his leg, then straightened. "Where is everyone?"

Ramsey pulled him along the wall behind houses. "Raven found us a place to hole up." He put Lox's arm around his, not caring that he had to stretch an inch. "Right up here."

Lox was surprised—and grateful—at the house's proximity. The building looked familiar, but he couldn't quite place it. Ramsey took him around back and knocked a pattern on the door. Beast opened it, shadowed from the dark room. Something close to a smile stretched Beast's lips and disappeared as he took in Ramsey supporting Lox. He tugged them both inside, locking the door.

The band gave exclamations of joy and praise as he made his way into a small living room. Then, he recognized the house. He'd been first held at knife point by Raven here. Fond memories.

Four people lay unconscious against the hallway wall, tied and gagged. The baker had another bruise on his face. Which of his men had figured out his actions and delivered the well-deserved blow? If he gambled, he'd bet on his betting man by the way Ramsey's knuckles darkened.

"Raven?" Beast's deep voice asked.

The others silenced, awaiting the answer.

It stuck in his throat. Damn it, he shouldn't have let her offer to take that damned potion, curse—whatever that dark magic was.

Instead he asked, "Daran?"

Lance gestured to a couch, where their friend lay on the cushions, a cloth on his forehead. "They left him unconscious outside the gate. He got hurt bad. Some sort of shifting bruise on his head. Boss, what—"

"A Sandceress."

"What?"

A chorus of exclamations clashed, but he whistled loud and clear. Lox sighed and limped toward a chair. "We don't have time."

At that, they sheathed their weapons, gathering what little supplies they could afford. Jon and Lance tried to assist him in sitting.

He waved away their help. Aid could wait until Raven was breathing and he ensured her heart still beat steadily. "The queen is the one who wanted Raven dead—and she plans to keep to that."

Voices rang out. Ranging from "Her *mother?*" to declarations the likes of which Loxley agreed, in particular Scar's curse, "That conniving *bitch!*"

Though the declarations were deserved, they were unhelpful. "Men!" he yelled, grabbing their attention. "We have to get her out of there. Now."

Lox shook his head, trying to remember what she'd told him while she'd pulled him from the cell. Relief at her appearance had clouded his thoughts momentarily. Stupidly. "Did she say how to get inside?"

Ramsey handed him a wanted poster with a sketch on the back. "Two ways. The tunnel she chose, and another risky one she hoped not to use."

Lox nodded, studying her drawing. He tried not to get caught up in the swirls, the picture that could very well be the last thing she wrote if he didn't *hurry*. "The tunnel sounds like it has a higher chance of being found now—they'll be more alert. My bet would be on the one she hesitated to use. Did she tell anyone what it was?"

They shook their heads, some nodding toward Daran, who lay unconscious on the bed. Lox examined the paper, trying to figure out the placement of the one she'd mentioned. It was on the left side of the castle, opposite the tunnel. Closer to the throne room. She'd told Daran. One person, not a group. Meaning he should take it alone.

Please, Raven, find a way to stall. Even if she didn't believe he'd save her—did she really believe that?—he would damn well do it anyway. Her life would not rest in that castle next to that bitch. Or that Sandceress. If they were too late… he'd carry her damned body out of that castle and find a way to break the curse.

"Listen up."

All five band members turned to him, still readying their weapons.

"I'll enter the castle from one path, and you two," he gestured to Scar and Ramsey, "will use the one she tried earlier, the tunnel—did you see it?"

Scar rubbed the back of his neck. "She didn't want us to follow that closely, but I did anyway."

Lox smiled. Always protective, his caring yet deadly friend. "You'll wait for my signal to come out. I'll find throne room and stop the queen."

He motioned to Jon. "Ready all the horses. When Daran rouses have him help you. If he doesn't, strap him in tight." Lox gazed at Lance. "Position yourself somewhere just outside the castle wall—on it if you can—somewhere you can see the throne room. It has a shit load windows and you'll be able to make us out. Ready your bow."

Each of them nodded and dispersed, readying their gear. Beast held his ground against the wall until Lox met his gaze, deepening the curse's effects on them both. Black faded to blue, rare since Beast hardly matched gazes. But those eyes haunted Lox's dreams too often to affect him on Beast. The cursed man walked over, his hulking form more opposing than his face. "Boss?"

Lox lowered his voice. "You have a choice—come with me and stay back a bit or wait near the entrance. The queen has a Sandceress. I didn't want you too close to her. And we'll need your strength to clear a path."

Beast crossed his arms, considering the options. A Sandceress was his weakness. Being cursed left an impression of the one who worked that dark magic. And Sages, Sandceresses—as far as history showed—didn't like each other's magic.

"I'm with you." His black eyes met Lox's green—lightening to a crystal blue, his features roughening—and the leader nodded. Before Lox could turn away, Beast removed a bottle from his pocket. He held it out to Lox.

Lox didn't touch it. The dark liquid was redder and calmer, but still resembled the curse. It felt… off, like the curse had. "What is that?"

"Supposed to cancel magic." Beast lowered it. "Some girl in the village was trying to sell it early this morning. No idea if it works, but it..."

"Feels like magic," Lox finished for him. He looked up at Beast and reluctantly took the potion. "We'll find out."

Anything that might give him an edge to defeat that Sandceress and help Raven, he would take.

"The guards won't let us go easily and neither will the queen." Lox stood and sighed at the pain in his leg. "Make sure no one stops us."

The front door creaked. Scar sheathed his fifth dagger and headed toward it, a smile softening his face. Lox moved to follow, but a blonde girl rounded the corner, holding the edge of an apron filled with herbs and clean cloth. Cindy smiled hesitantly back at Scar, then stopped as she noticed Lox. Her fingers released the apron, supplies landing in heaps on the floor. She quickly looked between the pile and him, reaching down to retrieve them. Scar touched her wrist and waved her to Lox.

Cindy stopped in front of him, wide eyes taking in his wounds, the tilt to his stance. Her light eyes glistened, and she swallowed. "She's still in there, isn't she?" Lox moved his hand to comfort her, but she raised her chin, eyes narrowing. "The queen has her."

Lox rose a brow. "You knew?"

"Raven said not to trust the queen."

One hollow chuckle escaped him. "That's for damned sure."

Scar nudged him, slipping yet another dagger into his boot. "Boss," he whispered, "She—and we—want her to join."

Lox's eyes narrowed on Cindy's darkened jaw. He nodded. "Welcome. Now let's go rescue ourselves a princess."

FROM THE QUEEN'S THRONE, VANERA WATCHED RAVEN, STILL SHACKLED IN the center of the room. She'd been silent since Mira had started crafting the coffin. Now, Raven declared, "Before you kill your daughter—because to some degree I *am* your daughter—you're going to tell her why."

"'*Why*' what?" Vanera snapped, but her mouth shut into that grim line again. Raven tried not to think it was guilt or regret. Because even if it was, the queen wouldn't rescind her decision. She'd come too far. And Raven would not raise her hopes.

"Why'd you pick me?" She turned her face up to the queen. "Instead of Cindy? Reason says pick the one who wouldn't require a memory charm on the entire kingdom."

The question seemed to throw the queen's emotions off course. She turned her head to stare at the bronze throne across the dais. Quiet stemmed between them, except for Mira's magic swirling in the air, the crackles it sounded every few seconds. A whisper, soft and thoughtful, "I thought it' be easier for me. You looked nothing like my daughter, Cindy did too much."

Vanera gazed at the bronze seat, the crown resting on the cushion. "I thought I could give you a good life. Treat you like I would my daughter. Raise you for Dawn." She stopped, voice catching. One breath. Two. The steel of her cold voice returned, and she said, "I gave Cindy a family. Paid the baker's wife to take her in."

"And did you see what *life* you gave her?" Raven asked, anger shaking her voice. "The brute of a man who abused and beat her for years?"

Vanera's blue eyes widened, rivaling the gems on her crown. It tilted to the side atop her blonde braid as she shook her head. "I... I didn't know."

"No, you didn't. Because after you *cursed* our mother, you dumped Cindy off and never looked back." She stepped toward the queen, shackles rattling against each other like Mira's bangles. "Did I mean that little to you, too?"

The queen jolted upright, standing so fast the crown slipped further. "You meant everything to me!"

Her shout echoed—off the empty thrones, the windows, the opal floors. It rang through Raven's chest. Vanera's breaths came in great heaves, jeweled chest rising and falling quickly. Dark blue eyes stared wide and brimming with... with—Raven had never seen such emotion in the queen.

The former princess stepped back, mouth agape. She pulled it shut and stared at her former mother who could only watch the floor.

Vanera backed until her knees met the throne, and she fell into it. She straightened her crown. "Ravenna, I loved you. *So much*... like my own

365

daughter." Her light gaze rose to Raven. "That was the problem. You started to replace my lost child."

For the first time since she learned of her mother's—the queen's—pain did she finally understand it. If someone had replaced her father—no, King Eldric—Raven would feel the same.

But she wouldn't want them dead.

Raven swallowed down the empathy that clawed to the surface, drowned it with anger and hatred as toxic as that curse. "And, to you, death was the only answer."

"No, Ravenna," Vanera sighed, letting her elegantly braided head fall into her palm. "I pushed through. I knew I couldn't reverse time and save Dawn," she added, throwing a glare at Mira. "And when Eldric died... I felt the distance from you more. I considered telling you the truth, finding you another family. Or bringing you to another kingdom."

"Why didn't you?" Raven's heart pounded. With fear or hate, she didn't know. She was a mess of emotions, hearing the queen's story. She understood, and she didn't. All she could do was listen.

"By the time I couldn't stand it any longer... you were too old." Vanera righted herself, leaning far into the silver seat that she'd always sat tall within. Given orders. Now, she shared her thoughts. "The lie had lived for too long, and I had to live with it. But then I saw you with those princes." Her voice broke, reminding Raven of the morning she'd picked out her dress for the ball. The morning Vanera had broken down.

'Just imagine, in a few months' time, you could be married. And then you'll have utterly adorable little ones, and Grandma here will—'

'Stop it!'

It hadn't been the princes but *Mira*. Mira's images forced into the queen's mind—Mira's taunts.

The Sandceress faced away from them, purple swirling before her as she created Raven's coffin, but Raven knew she listened. Mira always listened. But what did she want?

She brought her focus back to Vanera, tears brimming in the corners of Raven's eyes. "You could have still told me." The queen looked up, lips parted, but Raven continued calmly, "I would have done whatever you needed. You, Ecanta, our people."

Vanera held her stare, and a connection—a real, true connection seemed to bubble—

"Your very existence hurts her, dear," Mira said, stepping beside the queen, whose brows had scrunched in thought. "You *instead* of her daughter."

An olive hand landed on Vanera's shoulder, and the queen paused, then nodded to herself, forehead and expression smoothing into resolve. Blue eyes hardened to ice. "We both made our choices, Ravenna, and it does not do for royalty to go back on our words."

The Sandceress patted the queen and smirked at Raven before returning to the glass enclosure, hands sparking.

Raven moved a few unnoticeable steps away, closer to the window, and her gaze roamed. She couldn't escape this, could she? But she didn't need to now.

She finally knew why their relationship felt *wrong*.

Lox was safe.

They just awaited the coffin.

The queen could have her drink the curse first, but Raven had an inkling Vanera wanted her to squirm. To await her fate, stuck waiting. After all, she'd be stuck between heartbeats, breaths—waiting between seconds. Fitting.

Dark whispers called to her amongst the silence, beckoning her gaze to the bottle resting on the king's throne.

"Where did this... curse come from?"

Mira laughed. Not the high giggle normally accompanying her glee, but a full hearty chuckle worthy of a Sandceress. "You don't really think your thief can figure the conditions, do you?" She shook her head, black curls dancing across her too innocent and beautiful face. "Without that, only one with a pure heart has a hope of breaking it."

Vanera's gaze flashed to the Sandceress, then darted away.

Mira continued, waving at the queen, "Vanera caused the spell to be used, so she'd darkened her heart. And your... thief," her tone deepened in disgust, "Well, that's obvious." She raked her purple eyes over Raven, stepping closer. "But you... you, my dear Ravenna," the Sandceress caressed Raven's hair, making her wince, and tucked a strand behind her ear, "you had potential."

"What?" Vanera snapped, unable to control herself. For all her queenly composure. Raven would've grinned if she wasn't about to die.

Mira turned, cutting the queen with her gaze. "You want her dead, do you not?"

Desperation entered Vanera's eyes as she stepped forward. "But if she broke Dawn's curse—"

"You would still be in pain." Mira stared hard until Vanera shrunk back, shoulders high but not straight. "Dawn would not bring back your daughter, she would only make you feel more miserable. Again."

Vanera opened her mouth and seemed to freeze.

This was the grief Raven had seen for years. For her husband, daughter, and best friend.

"It's too late now." Mira shrugged, returning to the coffin. Violet waves of magic flitted before her, emanating from her raised hands, her skin. "You've surely tarnished that pure heart. Either when you became this... Red Hood, or when you left with that criminal. No matter what—there is no cure for you."

Raven bit her tongue. "I just wonder how it came into your possession."

"You mean a human's possession." Mira smiled, a dark tilt. "How I have magic when the world does not." Mira flicked her hair over her shoulder, lavender eyes alight with magic. "I am the last Vala."

The certainty of the statement was chilling.

"My kind burned a long time ago, and I honed my magic."

So, where... Only mermaids and faeries used magic like this—altering, pausing. And the fae had disappeared from known existence years ago. Raven didn't even know where they lived.

"It's mine."

Raven's eyes widened, a weight settling in her stomach, dragging her down.

The Sandceress grinned, eyes trained on the bottle in question. Raven remembered the way it had clawed at Mira's touch.

The skin of its maker.

CHAPTER 42

"Here."

Raven lifted her gaze from the window to the necklace dangling between her and the queen. The gold glinted purple from Mira's magic just feet away, a red ruby shining in the center of the heart.

"Might as well have him with you. He loved you more than I could." Vanera's eyes held none of the sweetness of the sentiment, only a hard glint of grief. Her dark gaze moved from the pendant to the always empty throne. "But he could balance that love and his grief. What happened—to Dawn—he hated it, but he loved you."

"He knew?" Raven squeaked. If Mira altered memories of the kingdom, she wouldn't put it past the Sandceress to change his as well.

Vanera nodded.

Breath lost, Raven grasped the necklace, the last gift from the man she'd thought was her father. A king who had taken in a lost girl when he'd lost his own. Who had loved her nonetheless, who had been better than both her and the queen.

Vanera calmly walked to Mira, who waved her hands above a glass containment too beautiful to be a coffin. Like the gold winding over the glass of the pendant, a dark brown reminiscent of the trees outside spread over the glass walls and lid.

Raven put the necklace back in its rightful place under her tunic, glaring at the queen. All love for that woman had been lost today. All hope of Vanera's love had followed Loxley out those doors. To make her choose her own death, because really, she couldn't let another—let *Loxley* —die for her... Raven had had enough.

Raven straightened her shoulders, tired as she was, and faced the two wicked women.

The Sandceress lowered her hands, letting the queen inspect the coffin. Purple magic still permeated the air, such a dense, constant plume leaving a light shimmer to the throne room corner.

Raven inspected the room for feasible weapons. The dagger in her boot wouldn't ward off magic. She needed something heavier to knock out Mira, then she could take Vanera.

Her stare locked on the queen, the cold calculated appraisal of the coffin occupying the woman's full attention enough that she missed the hatred brewing in her daughter. Heat spread across Raven's skin the longer she watched the woman who'd pretended to be her mother, who'd cursed her real mother—who had stolen her life. And would end it.

With a clarity she normally felt while watching her targets, Raven knew that if she had the opportunity, she'd punish the queen.

Blood boiling with rage, she forced herself to look away and return to a plan of escape. The gold on the coffin could do, but she'd have to break it off. Maybe an arm from her throne—the king's would be heavier, but... could she do that?

The bottle floating beside Mira's shoulder would make a viable choice. She could break the octopus top, force Vanera to take the damned curse.

Even if she did either, Mira's magic seemed limitless. Even at knife-point, the Vala could just wave her hand to disarm her. Maybe even literally.

Raven sighed. This was pointless. Loxley had *limped* out, so he couldn't possibly be far enough from Ilasia. If she freed herself, she'd have to ensure he'd left the village border before running. But would she really chance Vanera's rage and Mira's ruthlessness not to pursue Loxley?

Too many chances and not enough assurances.

She had sealed her fate. Her or Loxley, and she'd chosen. Raven had to trust Lox to leave.

A deep breath wracked her chest. She'd already escaped her death once, and now she had to face it.

Both queen and Sandceress turned to her, glee lifting Mira's mouth. She came forward, indigo dress sweeping with her saunter, bangles chiming. The potion followed, never dipping in its height. Mira stopped before Raven, smile still in place, and extended her palm to the side. The bottle lowered into her waiting hand.

Vanera stood just behind her cohort and appraised Raven's straight shoulders, her cloak, dirty from the dungeon and blood of guards. Dark blue eyes she'd seen every day now stared with a hollow emotion that, now that Raven pondered it, wasn't that different from every one of those days before. Vanera had always hated her, now she just didn't hide it.

Raven swallowed down her anger. "Any last words for your daughter? Oh, wait," she tilted her head and let out a hard laugh to match her smirk, "you don't have one."

Red splattered her vision at the queen's slap, but her grin stayed—she'd made Vanera lose her coveted queenly composure.

Vanera's usually smooth brow wrinkled from the force of her glare. She jerked a hand at Mira, who moved the curse before Raven. "No, I don't."

Oh, she'd kill that woman.

One day, she would.

Now, she extended her hand.

Mira held the intricate metal top, not quite releasing her grip.

Gently, fearfully, Raven's pale white fingers touched the glass.

Black swirled inside, the bottle ice cold. All the warmth in her fingers faded, chased by the freeze of the curse. Raven reluctantly pulled the vial closer, twisting the octopus's head as the legs relinquished their clutch. Air caught in her chest, but she forced herself to breathe. It would be her last, no need for it to get caught before the potion.

Gods, she hoped Loxley could find a way to break the curse. Tears brimmed in her eyes. She'd truly wanted a lifetime with him.

She swallowed air, relishing the feeling of it sliding down her throat.

The feeling of being alive.

Her heartbeat.

Raven tilted the vial forward, staring at its contents.

A whoosh of air shot past her cheek.

One dark arrow flew into the glass bottle, the *ping* resonating through the room before she could recognize the warmth flowing back into her fingertips as the vial fell.

Not a second later, a dagger embedded itself in Mira's arm, pinning her, bangles and all, to the tall back of the queen's throne. Blood spewed from her olive skin, down the long indigo sleeve. She screamed, more a sound of rage than pain. Lavender eyes flared with anger, bangles trapped around the blade stuck inches into the wood.

Glass shattered, the potion hitting the floor beside Raven's boots. Thick, black bubbles permeated the liquid, rapid and hungry like boiling water, eating through the top layer of marble.

Raven tapped the toe of her boot on the opalescent floor, freeing the knife hidden in the sole. She bent and had it raised to Vanera before Loxley walked in and shot a second arrow at Mira's other now raised wrist, tethering the sleeve and bolting her fully to the throne.

"*That's* where the other one was," Lox said appreciatively from behind her, as he shut the door. Her heart leapt and raced, a shiver descending her spine at the memory of Loxley looking for that dagger.

The Sandceress splayed her fingers, but no purple sparks came. Her magic eyes narrowed on Loxley. "Wretched *gath*! What did you do?" she yelled, her voice distorted in her anger and panic. She yanked fruitlessly at the arrows and dagger. More blood descended from the spot the arrow penetrated her skin. Dark lines spread from the wound, creeping farther and farther.

Fear sparked within Vanera's wavering eyes.

Raven smiled darkly at Vanera and stepped as close as she could stomach to this wretched woman. "I've never killed a woman before. Want to be the first?"

The queen raised her chin, eying the blade and then Raven's steady gaze. "You won't."

"You wanted me *dead*." The handle dug into her palm as hard as its blade dug into Vanera's neck. Like her heartbeat dug into the base of her throat with each beat "I loved you—you were my mother!" Raven screamed, voice shaking and pitched on hysteria. The wideness of Vanera's eyes made Raven clear her throat, harden her voice. "But I'm not your daughter anymore. I'm not a princess. And yes, I'll do it." Raven pushed the dagger into Vanera's slim neck, creasing the skin, blood beading down the knife's edge. She bared her teeth at the queen. "Gladly."

Hurried footsteps approached. Her pounding heart had eradicated them until Lox was a foot away.

"Red."

Her heart stuttered at his voice, and she forced herself not to look away from the queen.

"The guards are coming. I knocked out as many as I could, but hell, you've got a lot." He let out a small, humorless laugh.

"Let me—"

"No." He stepped closer to her side, that woodsy scent engulfing her and almost stealing her gaze.

Blood slipped across the blade, a drop—then another—hitting the opalescent floor.

Just a slice. One slice, and her pain, her anger, her fear would be over. The betrayal and secrets and lies *over*.

"Why are you waiting, hm?" Mira's taunt came from the throne. She'd slouched, letting herself sit upon the silver seat. Her lavender eyes latched onto Raven, glazed like mirrors, like her all-seeing crystal ball. "Guilt? Do you feel bad for being a bad daughter?"

Vanera's eyes widened, flicking between Raven and the woman behind her she couldn't quite see. Her mouth opened, then she winced at the extra slice.

The Sandceress feigned a gasp, her tone all sly. "You don't have the guts, do you, Ravenna?"

Raven increased her grip. Murder wasn't a stranger to her, more like an acquaintance she met only upon necessity. She wasn't scared to kill the queen, and that in itself scared her. When had she become this ruthless, this angry? She used to toe the line, balance between criminal and vigilante. But where was she now? Vanera was a criminal, a villain who had ordered a death, had caused so much misery more than a decade ago from her own selfishness—she deserved this.

Lox leaned in, his breath moving the hair at her shoulder. He slowed his words to emphasize their importance, but he couldn't eradicate the slight panic. "You do it now, and it'll be treason."

Raven held steady, eyes trained on her murderous mother—*queen*.

"What type of vigilante are you?" Mira crooned. "You have your victim, and you won't even strike. You're an unworthy princess *and* protector, aren't you?"

"Shut up!" Vanera shouted, slicing her skin further and spilling more crimson over Raven's blade.

Warm, *hot* blood dribbled past the knife and down Raven's hand.

She shouldn't have liked it.

"Red," Lox all but whispered. His voice brought her back to her senses, grounded her.

She looked at him, deep into his forest eyes. They wavered, brows dipped. He was scared, not of the guards or of her killing the queen, but *for* her.

"If you're really not her daughter," he continued, steadier now upon gaining her attention, "you have no claim. We need to find another way."

Raven glared down the blade at her captive. "I'll see you again." She examined her would-be mother's face once more. "*Vanera*."

Not today, but one day, Raven *would* kill her.

CHAPTER 43

Raven stepped back, knife still poised at Vanera's throat while Loxley checked the hall. "How's it look?" she called.

He shut the doors firmly and sprinted to her side, hand on her left elbow and pointing to the left wall. "The window—run!"

Raven donned her hood and bolted for the beautiful windows. Lox's arrow split the glass, and she jumped through the shattered pieces and metal frame, standing on the stone ledge. Lox joined her, scanning the trees and space below them. He gestured to a tree two window ledges and a story down. "There!"

Within the throne room, a crash sounded, and Raven's heart fluttered into the base of her throat. Gripping onto the window frame, Raven stepped over the empty air to the next ledge as quickly as she dared. Her boot tips gripped the stone, and she hurried to the far edge to give Lox room. Without missing a beat, she crouched to grab the ledge and start descending a story.

Glass shattered—and a large hand grabbed her cloak behind them. The strap dug into her neck, slamming her back against the solid wall. She grappled for the fastener, swinging her knife around to stab the guard, but the grip released suddenly with a scream.

Raven knelt to gasp in air and turned. A dark arrow pierced the guard's hand.

"Lance," Lox said, drawing her gaze. He grinned toward his band member perched on the wall. Lance's bow was raised, another arrow poised.

Raven gripped the stone and swung down to hang above the bottom floor's window. She released her fingers, holding her breath until her feet connected with stone.

Quickly, she shifted to the side and looked up for Lox. He winced as he crouched. Raven waited for him to hang down, then raised her hands. "I've got you," she said, holding on to the boot of his bad leg.

"If we weren't running for our lives," Lox said, then released his fingers and dropped. His leg faltered, but Raven pulled on his tunic, bringing him close. He grinned down at her, and continued, "I'd say something you'd slap me for."

Her grin popped up before she turned to the next ledge. More windows shattered as guards fired more arrows. Lance took out all the weapons that came close. Raven jumped to the window ledge, teetering before catching her balance. These boots weren't meant for this shit. She turned for Loxley, quickly eying the guards above, but he was beside her in an instant.

"Don't worry, Red. I'm not letting you get far away again," he breathed close to her ear, sending a warm shiver down her spine.

Gods, how she'd missed him and the feeling of being alive that he gave her. "Shut up."

Lox winked, then sobered, assessing the tree branches reaching toward them. He let out a *hoot*, then leapt.

Raven sighed at his rash behavior, but she didn't have a better plan, and the guards now spilled through the castle's front entrance. She pushed off, grappling for branches as she crashed into the tree. Leaves whipped at her face, small straggling branches tugging at her hood, her clothes, her hair. A hard grip encased her upper arm and tugged, and her boots found purchase on a thick limb.

Lox's dark green eyes came into focus mere inches from hers.

"Don't say it," she warned, recognizing that grin.

His eyes sparkled. "Got you."

With a small groan that could almost be a chuckle, Raven turned to climb down. Lox's grip strengthened, and she faced him, that spark erased from his gaze.

"I'm serious, Raven." Loxley leaned closer, eyes shifting between hers. His voice deepened, reverberating with its intensity. "I've got your back."

She raised her hand to his cheek, slight stubble rustling against her palm. "I know, Lox. Thank you."

His arm encircled her waist, bringing their bodies together. Her heartbeat raced—

Leaves rustled, and Lox's hand lessened. Lance's face appeared between branches. "Hey, boss—" He glanced at them, then cleared his throat. "Ramsey and Scar are holding off the guards at the gate, but we've got to move. They'll be coming from all sides soon."

A longing smile rose on Lox's mouth before he brought her hand to a branch and made his way to the tree's trunk.

Lance winked and aimed his bow back toward the gate. Indeed, guards streamed out, some with bows, most with swords. The trio descended the tree, not bothering with stealth. Lance hit the ground last, shooting more arrows at the closest guards. Raven checked where some hit—arms, legs, nothing vital—but forced herself to stop looking back. She couldn't let sympathy slow her down. Those weren't her men anymore, these were.

The three of them ran deep into the trees on the cusp of the castle grounds and village. Branches and trunks flew past, the group running fast as they dared, barely dodging trees. Raven only knew where they headed because she'd traveled Ilasia most of her life in light and dark.

The forest was a faster route than through town—houses, villagers, and rows of walls blocking an would-be-easy path—which, with another glance back, she realized was where Ramsey and Scar headed.

"Lox!" she called, catching his attention. She jerked her head toward the men. "Do they know where they're going?"

Lox let out a loud whistle, and the men split, Rams going over a wall, Scar turning left. "Don't worry, they have a hide-out." He slowed, turning around a tree with his hand falling to his knee. His injury must be killing him; they had to stop soon.

She ran closer to him. "What's the plan?"

Lance stopped, firing an arrow behind.

Thud.

Raven tried not to wince.

Lox slowed enough to check on Lance. "Remember where we met to plan before?"

Raven thought back to the night she'd told him to leave and he hadn't, where he'd unhooded her—the lake. She nodded, knowing he hadn't voiced because of the guards.

"Jon is waiting there with horses."

The sound of armor chased them, as loud as the surrounding pound of footsteps and arrows embedding in trees. Once a comfort, now a grating threat at Raven's back. Lox's green tunic and darker complexion lent him camouflage, but Raven's red cloak beckoned. Even with the crimson trunks, this close to the castle they spread father apart, and a bright red while her hood was dark. Quick on her feet, Raven nimbly leapt over roots and swung around trees, ducking when an arrow flew too close.

She would remove the cloak, but her identity staying secret felt even more vital now when she ran for her life. If she were seen alive as Princess Ravenna, the queen could claim treason, paste her face everywhere. But dead, she stole Vanera's power.

But how in the world would they get across the walls and village to the east edge of the forest, to the lake? With this many guards already after them? There were too many, and they could only hide so much in the forest.

Raven caught Lox's attention and neared him to speak softly through her panting breaths. "Have Lance get word to Jon to meet us on the west side."

"There's nothing—"

"There's something. It's hard to find." When he paused, she continued, "Trust me."

Lox nodded. He *hoot*-ed again, and Lance turned to her. She took the bow from his hands and turned to fire into the trees. The leader and his man stopped behind two trees to discuss the change in plan.

Armor clanked, then stuttered, falling behind trunks to avoid her rapid arrows.

While she fired for cover, ducking and leaning out to aim again. A whistle, and Lance was at her side, taking the bow back.

They bolted again—it took a few moments before the guards crashing sounds followed.

Lance's strides shortened, and Lox grabbed her elbow, jerking her right. Lance continued straight, the cacophony of clanking metal following him.

Lox took Raven's hand and lead her in a crouch through the brush until they were distanced from the guards, then they ran. His brow stayed furrowed, and Raven knew it was from his leg. *Almost there.* Then, he could rest. He more than deserved it.

Hell, he'd done all this for her—with all those injuries.

She'd repay him somehow.

"He'll tell Beast, who will find Jon," Lox informed, panting from their sudden stop. "With Jon's inconspicuousness, he might still get there before us."

He gripped his thigh again, knuckles whitening.

She sure hoped so.

Silence greeted them as they crested the last of the trees to the small clearing surrounding the hidden courtyard. Three horses stood by the small stone archway. Beast and Jon paced and instantly spotted them. Relief coated their faces when they saw the pair approach.

Beast started toward Lox, eyes targeting his bad leg. "Jon, do you have any quick fixes for the boss?"

He riffled through a saddlebag. His mouth quirked to the side. "Good but not quick."

"Bring the horses around to the other side," she instructed. Beast followed orders, and Jon took over supporting Loxley.

She gestured them into the courtyard. Though she braced herself, the empty sparring area still pierced her heart. She walked into the center and could almost hear swords clashing, steps hitting stone quickly, and her and Rue's panting breaths—her morning for almost a decade.

Vines crept along the stone walls, up into the surrounding trees and over their heads. Dawn light streamed through the small patches between branches and vines. She took a deep breath and returned to her comrades.

"Sit," Raven said to Lox, gesturing to a low stone bench. "I'll see what he has."

"Hey, Rave!" Beast called from the archway opening farthest from the castle. She rose a brow at his nickname and shout. His monstrous face reddened slightly, and he held up Ramsey's bundle of herbs.

She jogged over, opening her satchel. With a short dig inside, her hand reappeared with her pouch of vials.

Footfalls came from beyond... soft and approaching. From the direction of the castle.

Raven froze. No one should be out here. She raised a finger to her lips, crouching and sharing glances with them. It must be a stray guard. If they were quiet, they could escape out the other side.

Beast's eyes snapped to the forest, narrowing—not one of the band. "On the horses!" he ordered with a whisper, grabbing her arm to propel her onto Lox's horse.

A shout and *thud* drew Raven's gaze back over to Lox. He lay sprawled on the floor, having tripped from his injury. Vines twisted on his foot. Gripping his bloody thigh, he struggled to stand. *No.*

Jon turned on his heel. He sprinted to Lox and knelt, untangling his foot from the vines. Armor sounded through the trees beyond the courtyard. Lox looked behind them, furiously pushing up to right himself, but Jon focused solely on the vines. Finally freeing Lox, Jon helped him up.

A lone guard crashed through the vines into the courtyard.

"Run!" Lox shouted to Raven.

Jon pushed Lox toward the horses at the far end of the courtyard.

He took a fighting stance, and Raven realized he was unarmed— always unarmed—but the guard charged, just feet away, sword raised. Jon had barely squared his stance; he *couldn't* block the strike.

"Jon!" Raven screamed, throwing her dagger. The blade flipped over itself thrice before sinking into the neck of the guard. She froze, arm still extended, staring at the man.

He gurgled and dropped to the grass, now covered in his life blood. Crimson dripped from his neck and onto the stone, the crawling vines.

Still gripping his thigh, Lox stared from Raven to the dead man and to Jon.

Raven's eyes stayed glued to the dead guard. Only one strike, a pierce of a blade, had spanned the moment between his life and death. And *she* had decided its end. A gasp strangled in her throat. She'd really chosen these men over her old protectors. These men who had helped her survive, who had taken her from her poisoned kingdom and gone back for her when she was as sure as dead. They'd chosen her; she'd chosen them.

Over anything.

Jon turned. "Thanks, Raven."

His smile shot through her. She straightened her hood, taking a breath. "You would've done it for me."

Though she'd never seen Jon fight, somehow she knew it was true.

Red splattered the air, and Jon's shoulder flew forward. An arrowhead pierced through his shirt and skin from the back, making him gasp. Eyes widening, he raised a hand to it and fell to the side with a grunt.

She looked past him to the other entryway. Another guard's shape took form through the dense vines and branches covering the far archway, the smooth *shing* of a sword unsheathing rang off the walls.

Beast moved a step, but Raven pressed her hand to his chest. "No. Get ready." She grabbed her vial pouch and ran to Jon. She tossed it to Lox. "Little green bottle—*dark* green. Now!"

The thief caught and unrolled it with shaky fingers.

The guard let out a battle yell, raising the sword high. He stalked toward Jon.

Raven dashed over and snatched up the fallen guard's sword. She slid, skidding to her knees on the leaves and dirt and stone. Right before the guard's sword could come down on Jon, Raven lifted the sword, metal clashing in the courtyard.

Shadows from the covering of branches and vines above covered his angry face. The guard panted, glaring frighteningly at Raven, the person who'd felled his fellow soldier, probably his friend. To him, she had killed his princess and harmed his queen.

With both hands gripping the hilt, she shoved the sword toward the guard, forcing him back a step. She turned her head a fraction and roared, "Jon, run!"

Raven looked back at the guard and froze. Light hit his figure through the leafy canopy above, outlining the strong jaw, the light brown hair and dark eyes.

The sword almost slipped from her fingers.

Ruben.

Not here.

Not where he'd taught her to fight, the very moves she felt her muscles tensing to execute.

He raised his sword for another slash, one experience proved would knock her down. Her arms shifted almost without her thinking, from practiced movements and combinations, from early dawn mornings just like this.

This felt too familiar. Raven strengthened her grip and swung up with both hands, meeting Ruben's strike. Her arms shook from his intensity, but she held firm. His glare rattled her to her core.

This wasn't a practice spar for Ruben—he struck to kill.

He withdrew, shifting his grip on the pommel. Careful steps brought him left, and Raven moved opposite, the pair circling slowly. Her breath stuttered through her parted lips, heart racing through her whole body. Over his shoulder, she saw the band had exited the courtyard.

Ruben lunged while her gaze was averted. Only instincts and muscle memory had her sword raised. She swiped right and moved again to block his return swing. His shoulders dipped, and she stepped left, ducking just in time to dance behind him. As she turned to elbow his side, he spun faster than he ever had in practice and slammed his sword down.

Raven managed to stop the downward strike, her own blade turned longways to hold it above her head. Warmth radiated from her arm as she felt the injury from Grayson reopen. She gasped. One knee hit the stone, pain spiking up her thigh.

Hatred shined in his eyes, darkness shadowing his expression. He bared his teeth and let out a long roar as he pushed and pushed.

With a grunt, Raven's other leg crumpled. She gripped the hilt tighter, gritting her teeth against the pain in her arm. She was too outmatched, Ruben too strong in his hate. He would crush her.

On her knees, the former princess swung her leg and took out the Head Guard's feet.

Leaves flew into the air as he landed hard on the stone floor, a dirt cloud pluming. Ruben's hand shot out, the speed as familiar as their sparing practices, and clamped onto the front of her cloak so tight it stole her breath. His furious strength hauled her down, her boot barely catching herself before she could fall into his raised dagger. The clasp at her neck snapped. One side of the cloak slipped over her shoulder, pulling off her hood.

Raven gasped, black hair flying around her exposed face. *No. Not Ruben.* If anyone should be spared the turmoil of Vanera's horrendous actions, it was him. He deserved better than the queen's wrath and this deadly secret.

His eyes cleared, brows softening from anger into confusion.

Enchantment broken, his hand went limp, freeing her. Armored elbows digging into the dirt, Ruben stilled. His mouth stood agape, as wide as his eyes. A shocked whisper escaped, "Ravenna?"

He rose to his knees, and she stepped back, wary. Reluctantly, she lifted the sword.

Ruben stopped, those too-familiar eyes traveling from the sword quivering in her grip to her pained eyes. Then, he tossed his sword onto the floor. Raven dropped hers, and he rushed forward, her falling into him, best friends who had been grieving each other holding on to a fierce hug.

Raven shook in his arms, arms that had held her when she'd grieved her father as a child, when she'd grieved her innocence after killing Landon. During all the nightmares that had followed both. Tears sprung and fell hard.

"Raven," Ruben whispered into her shoulder. He pulled back. Stared, eyes tracing her face, then her hood. He wiped a stray hair aside with a trembling hand. Ruben's mouth worked for a moment before he managed, "How?"

"I'm so sorry."

"What—"

She shook her head. Raven glanced toward the archway behind him, pulling away to kneel beside him.

Ruben gripped her arm, eyes begging any answer. Something to help him make sense of this.

"The queen ordered my death."

His brow furrowed. "She didn't see it was you under the Red Hood?"

Raven pressed her lips together. "Not the Red Hood, Ruben. *Me.*" She pressed her hand to her chest—where the red heart pendant rested under her tunic. "She ordered the Red Hood to kill me."

Distracted, his eyes followed her hand and landed on the necklace's bulge. She lifted the chain, and his lips parted.

Too little time and too much to explain.

His eyes narrowed, trying to work through her impossible words.

Armor clanked in the distance, heavy footsteps crunching twigs and leaves. Their time was over.

"Red!" Lox called through the opening.

Behind her, beyond the courtyard, hooves neared; the others had mounted.

"Don't trust the queen—Mira's a Sandceress." Raven stepped back. "I'm sorry, Rue."

She wanted to say so much more. *I miss you.* She had wondered if she'd miss him most, and it had been true. Especially now. She had the overwhelming urge to snatch him up and take him with her. This innocent, kind man who had protected her in so many ways from more than the dangers of threats on the crown. But she couldn't. She had to fully— finally—leave this life behind.

She spun and ran through the archway and two steps to the charging horse. Loxley extended his hand and pulled her up when she clasped it, pushing herself up with her boot in the stirrup. Once she settled behind him, Lox gripped the reins.

"Keep her safe." Ruben stepped through the vine-covered archway, his words cutting through the urgency to *move*.

Lox stared down at him. "With my life."

Raven knew he meant it, and that terrified her.

"You're not dying for me," Raven said, stern, a look passing to both men, stopping on Lox. "I just broke into my own castle to save your ass. Don't you dare trade your life for mine again."

"Ditto, love."

Ruben's eyes flew wide at Loxley's endearment, landing on her. Her cheeks reddened.

"No!" she said to Rue, holding up a finger. She swung her gaze to Lox.

Lox quirked a brow. "No? Even after—"

"I won't come back for you next time." She glared at her thief.

Lox twisted in the saddle. He lifted her hood and quickly but gently covered her head, tucking a piece of hair into its dark expanse. "I'll always come back for you, Raven."

Her heart pounded hard at the sincerity in his eyes. "Move the damn horse, Loxley."

"Raven," Ruben called. His gaze was both serious and worried. "Did... did this thief steal your heart?"

She looked from her best friend to Loxley. Lox's gaze held curiosity and a tinge of fear for her answer. "No." Raven gripped his side tight. "I fell for his."

The thief grinned. He looked at the trees, silver shining through, then to Ruben. "Don't die. It'll crush her."

He struck the reins, and they galloped after the others. Raven couldn't stop a glance back at her best friend and former guard. He stood outside their sparring courtyard but hadn't taken a step after her. Rue lifted his hand that'd pulled down her hood and stared at it for a long moment before looking up at her fading face.

"Do we need to worry about him?" Lox asked above the hooves of the horses.

Ruben's eyes didn't waver, his shoulders straightened.

"No."

The pain and understanding solidified in Ruben's gaze struck her heart—mirrored her own feelings. This was the last they'd see of each other, and now they were on different sides.

CHAPTER 44

B ranches and leaves blurred into stripes of color with their speed. Lox's leg seared like a fire had latched onto his muscle, but his mind focused on two things—that guard and Jon.

He hadn't done a damned thing to protect Jon, all because they were busy mending his bloody leg. And now Jon—the boy he'd rescued and vowed never to let get mixed up in this criminal shit—was injured far worse. Damn this leg. Damn him.

If Raven hadn't acted so quickly... His racing heart skipped a beat. Thank the stars for her.

"Beast," Lox called to the horse behind him, "how's Jon?"

Beast had broken off the stem of the arrow and placed Jon on the horse with him behind to keep the boy upright. The third unmanned horse tied to his saddle.

"I'm okay, guys," Jon ground out, his soft voice wavering in pain.

Lox didn't believe him for a second. "Beast?"

"I'm going to say he's lying," he replied, worry in that deep tone. "He's really white and... and there's a lot of blood."

Raven twisted around behind Lox, her hand gripping his waist tight enough to steal his attention momentarily. "That's dried, the elixir stopped the bleeding." She faced front again and whispered in his ear, "But he's still in pain."

Lox tugged on the reins, holding on when the horse surged.

Damn it.

Too much later, they reached their meeting place, Ramsey, Daran, Scar, and Cindy waiting on their horses. Lox barely waited for Raven to dismount. Their horse hadn't even fully halted before both their boots hit the earth.

Beast eased Jon to the side to pull him down. Jon winced, grasping his tunic near his pierced shoulder, and tried to take some of his weight off Beast, though it wasn't needed.

The rest of the band were off their horses and at his side instantly, calling and shouting questions. Cindy stood to the side, concern marring her petite face.

"What happened?"

"Jon—"

"Is he okay?"

Their voices grounded on Lox's ears, solidifying his uselessness. He hadn't stopped this.

Raven stood, spreading her hands wide. "Alright—back UP!" The men froze, even Beast who supported Jon. Lox looked up from where he leaned beside Jon. "We don't have time for this shit. Someone get the bandages from Jon's bag. Who can remove the arrow safely?"

Ramsey removed his gloves. "I can, but you have to be ready with a fresh bandage and herbs."

She nodded, opening her satchel. Lox wondered yet again what secrets she kept hidden inside. She removed the same pouch as earlier, bottles glistening in the twilight, and a bundle of herbs.

Beast lowered Jon to the ground, using his own body to support him. Lox knelt in front of him, somehow managing to withhold a groan at the pain, then relief of pressure on his leg.

"Hey, boss," Jon whispered, a smile flickering on and off his mouth.

"Hey, Jonny."

"Seems I have to be quicker." He let out a small laugh, looking toward Raven as she sorted through the herbs. "But it's a good thing Raven doesn't."

Lox sighed a long breath. "No, she doesn't."

Bandages were handed to her, Scar bending over to appraise Jon's injury. His voice grated like his knives sharpening. "Who the hell did this?"

"A guard shot him while he was helping me," Lox explained.

"I'll kill him," Scar spat.

"I already did that," Raven stated, voice soft and eyes glued on the herbs.

Scar looked at her, and his expression softened. "Rave..."

"Ramsey?" Raven called, her knees digging into the dirt, herbs and elixirs lined up on her thighs.

He appeared beside the four of them, pushing Scar back. "Ready, ma'am."

She eased to the side, elbows brushing Lox's, but he didn't move. He wouldn't leave Jon's side, and her touch grounded him while his world spun. He'd almost lost her—seeing her with that cursed bottle raised to her lips had nearly stopped his own heart—and now he might lose little Jon. The least deserving of them to die. The rest of them were criminals, thieves, killers, bandits, but Jon was the only innocent one of their crimes. And Lox was determined to keep it that way.

Raven eased Jon's tunic open near the arrow, and Jon stiffened. They boy raised a hand, but Lox stopped him. Jon's worried gaze met his, and Loxley nodded. Resigned, Jon let Raven peel back the fabric.

Pale white marred the top of his shoulder, lines whipping out to cross over the crook of the muscle's curve. Behind, Lox knew more criss-crossed the boy's back; he'd spotted them once and never dared ask. Those were marks best not mentioned. Marks of shame.

But neat, precise marks slashed across Jon's chest—not many, but enough that Lox could count on both hands. One raised scar slashed over the left of his chest, wide and dark at one edge. Scars of a fighter.

Scars that didn't belong on a boy who refused to touch a blade.

Raven momentarily appraised the white puckers—and Lox remembered hers hidden beneath her tunic. Jon and her shared at least one secret unknowingly.

Ramsey gently grasped the stem of the arrow, another hand on the back of Jon's shoulder. "Sorry, buddy," he said before pushing on the wooden rod.

Jon's eyes flew wide, and a shout sprouted from lips, but he stifled it.

Teeth clenched, he sagged as Ramsey shoved the arrow through his back and out his shoulder.

Without missing a beat Raven poured drops of a dark blue elixir and a light red on both the front and back wounds. Lox's brows lowered as the wound first foamed indigo bubbles, then shimmered crimson, the dripping blood halting in its tracks.

He eyed the purple bottle warily. Where had she gotten these elixirs?

Raven dabbed a mixture of herbs before Ramsey's steady and bloody hands tightly wrapped the clean cloth around Jon's middle and across his shoulder blade. Something in those herbs or elixirs must have relieved the pain because Jon's arms relaxed, muscles no longer bulging.

"Jon."

He looked up at Lox, relief glazing his eyes. Lox held his voice firm. "Scar is going to teach you about blades starting tomorrow."

Jon stilled, laughed dryly, then winced, hand flying to his bandage.

They stood, giving him room. Jon lifted himself with his good arm, letting Beast help him stand.

Lox eyed the potions bundle as Raven put it away. "Where did you get those?"

"Oh, they were…" She paused, eyes widening. "A-a gift. From *Mira*."

Silence descended on the band around them.

Daran stepped forward. "Is Mira the Sandceress?"

Hearing the name with Daran's true Javir lilt, it was without a doubt Valaran.

Raven appeared to realize the same. "Yes. She… she'd been friends with my—the queen as far as I can remember. She dressed like a Rova, said she was Rova. Acted like a gods damned fortune teller." Raven shoved the potions in her satchel. "She gave me these potions. Said 'an adventurous girl needed adventurous tools.'" She laughed, a sound that fell instantly. "That tricky witch."

Lox watched the pain cross her face. She'd had these two women in her life, and they'd both shown their lies and betrayals.

Hearing her growing hate for that Sandceress, that Vala… it tore a little at the hope within him. Hope that she'd accept that minuscule part of him, too. He didn't have magic, but he knew it was hard for people to separate the hated magic from the Vala race.

"She gave me these potions after she *cursed* my mother with one."

Raven unclasped her cloak and threw it on the ground. "I'm guessing this was her doing, too. Found it in a damned box, probably put there by her."

He reached for her shoulder. "Red—"

"I thought *I* was a lie," she stated, spinning and stepping backward. Away from him. He recognized this panic from before. "Princess, Red Hood, murderer."

Scar stepped forward. "Rave."

"No—" She pointed at him to stop. "I am. But now, my whole *life* is a lie. My mother. My family. Being a princess. I've had magic surrounding me, and I didn't even know. That damned Sandceress tore my family apart, she—"

Raven halted, eyes fixed on Cindy standing to the side.

Lox stepped between them to block Raven's view. She blinked and looked down. "Red. Hey…" He held her cheek, tilted it so she looked at him. The sadness there almost crushed him. "Everything has changed. So much that you knew before. But," he rubbed his thumb over her skin, "we have not. We are all here for you. And we will figure out how to adapt to this with you. This cloak," he pointed to it lying in the dirt, "is yours. Not hers. And until we leave Ecanta, it is your protection."

Scar picked up the cloak and handed it to Raven. "We'll find you something else later. I promise." He winked. "Still red, though."

That tore a small laugh out of her. She nodded and took her cloak.

Lox turned to Beast. "How did you get that potion?"

Black eyes stayed on Lox's cheek. The brows furrowed. "A girl in the market this morning. She was selling it for money to leave town."

"Rova?" Raven asked.

"No," Jon said, stumbling closer. He held his arm close to his chest. "Blonde, blue eyes. *Lots* of blonde hair."

"Barefoot," Beast added. "Looked like she was running from something."

How in the world had someone not Rova or Vala gotten a potion like that?

"That sounds…" Raven trailed off, recognition flaring and then fading in her eyes. "Never mind." She waved a gloved hand at Jon. "You need to sit down or get back on that horse."

Lox smiled at Jon's obedience. Raven ushered Jon over to the horses where Cindy stood, helping him to sit beside one, and examining his wound again. She hesitantly removed the vials from her satchel.

No… there was no way to tell Red now. Maybe once the shock and fear dulled. Maybe.

"Boss," Beast called, stealing Lox's attention. When Beast neared, he lowered his voice. "Girl with the potion, she knew I was cursed."

Lox mulled that over. If she saw something particularly unusual or startling on Beast's face, it wouldn't be a stretch to realize he was cursed. "Maybe part Rova? I've seen some that are lighter, but never blonde." He remembered that Sandceress's outfit and appearance changing. "It could be a disguise if she has magic."

"Rival Vala? Sabotage? Or could be a Rova who figured out the farce. Didn't like being impersonated."

Lox shrugged. "Let's count our blessings. Let me know if you see her again, though."

Ramsey started piling sticks and dead leaves to burn the arrow and Jon's bloody shirt. Lox stared at the rags and broken arrow beside the building fire.

"Once you're done, we're moving." Lox watched his men hustle to build the fire, then turned to Raven and Jon at the horses, trying to ignore the searing pain his leg. Cindy twisted her hands in her apron and Jon tried to stand when he neared. Lox waved him down. "How is it?"

"Right as rain."

"It'll heal," Raven corrected, shooting Jon a look. "But I'll have to check it daily. He might not be able to ride alone for a little while."

Lox nodded. "Cindy, you can ride with him. Wouldn't hurt for Jon to teach you how. We might be criminals, but we're *nice* criminals. Isn't that right?" He winked at Raven.

She elbowed him mildly.

"Raven?"

She raised a brow, and he gestured to the forest. Lox grasped her upper arm and led her away from the group, not bothering to hide his limp anymore. Today had been such a trying and traumatic day for her, he wished he could make it better instead of worse. He wished they could stop running and she could rest after all she'd been through. But they couldn't. They weren't safe yet.

He wouldn't stop until she was safe.

"Jon will be okay for now," Raven said, guessing about what was bothering him.

Damn, this woman.

How did she know his heart so well? How could she care so much about him and his band?

"I was going to ask how *you* were doing. With the rush to escape, I didn't get the chance before." His eyes roamed her face, the worry in her brow, the drag to her mouth. "And I feel the question is needed even more now."

She looked away from his prying gaze.

He stepped closer to lay his hand on her waist, the pain in his leg forgotten. "This is hard, especially with everything that bitch said and did. But you hit a lot harder, Raven."

A smile tugged, but she squeezed her lips together. Her deep amber eyes rose to his, stilling his breath in his throat. Sorrow shook her voice. "I've caused so much pain."

Lox pulled her to his chest, wrapping his arms around her body. The warmth of her hands moving to his back and clenching in his tunic shook him to his soul. She couldn't really believe that about herself, could she? But damn, he knew she did. He thought the same about himself.

Jon. The guard. His own capture. Hell, even that queen. She blamed herself.

"I'm sorry you had to kill one of your guard, but... Thank you," he sighed into her hair. "I cannot thank you enough for saving Jon. That boy... he can't die in this band, Red. I can't let that happen. He is too good for this, for us. You did good."

She let out a short breath, then pulled back, her hands at her sides. But Lox couldn't remove his own. "He'll be fine. If I have to use all my elixirs to ensure it, I will." Her dark brow furrowed. "Maybe I should stick to herbs and pour these out."

Raven stepped away, looking down at the leg he avoided putting pressure on. His hand dropped from her waist, leaving it feeling empty, the ghost of her warmth.

"How about instead of that, you use them on me now?"

"What?" She leaned backward, as if away from the idea.

Lox shrugged. "They helped Jon. You've been using them for years for good. The potions themselves aren't bad. Magic isn't bad. Just the person who wields it *for* bad." He smiled. "Well, maybe that one potion is bad. What color was it?"

"*Light* green." She pulled the pouch out of her satchel. "That's true. It's hard when the only magic I've seen is used for bad. Beast's curse, that cursed potion. Mira."

"But also," Lox dipped his head to catch her eye, "your cloak and these vials."

She nodded and unwrapped the pouch.

After checking on his band members, the fire just growing enough smoke that they could start throwing in the ruined clothes and rags, Lox nodded.

Removing the vials, Raven made Lox lean against a tree while she knelt to inspect his injury. Despite the pain, he couldn't help but imagine her kneeling for an entirely different reason. Desire tightened his skin as she touched his thigh—fuck. She peeled the torn patch of his trousers from the wound, bringing the pain to the surface. Red surrounded the injury, blood and torn skin and muscle. She dribbled the dark green and blue liquids on the gouge. Like Jon's injury, it bubbled, then the skin shined over like glass. The moment she dabbed the herbs on his exposed skin, the pain dimmed by half. Relief almost made him sigh and drop to the ground. He could *stand* without gritting his teeth or wanting to cut off his leg.

Raven's light chuckle made him smile. "Feel better?"

"Immensely," he said, grabbing her wrist and pulling her up against him. She gasped, a hand landing on his chest. Lox ran his hand up her arm and behind her neck, gazing into her wide amber eyes as her breath came in fast bursts against his lips. His other hand squeezed into her hip, pressing hers against his hardened front. Stars be damned, he might just take more time now to—

"Boss!"

The two of them looked up at Scar, who dipped around the trees. Raven tried to move back, but Lox's steady hands kept her against his body. He raised a brow at his comrade, frustration burning in his gaze.

"Oh." Scar cleared his throat, waving his hand in the air loosely before pointing a thumb back at the fire. "We're... done."

"Ready the horses."

"Right. I'll... yup." The deadly swordsman turned on his heel.

Lox flicked his gaze back to Raven, taking in her sweet scent and the beat of her heart against his own. Gods, he loved feeling that still beating, her blood coursing, breath still flowing. Damn, he wanted to take her further into the woods and let it be just them. He sighed, brushing her cheek with his finger. No, he'd make sure she was safe first. But *then*... "You know, I've never interrupted him and Lance."

Raven swallowed, her eyes flickering between his. "How rude," she said, her voice a mere breath.

He grinned, then straightened, easing her when she stumbled. "Let's go, Red."

CHAPTER 45

O pal glistened under Ruben's feet, and he focused hard on its shades not to let his mind shift back to Ravenna and the secrets he now held. The secrets he didn't—couldn't—understand yet.

Queen Vanera sat on her silver throne as straight as the sword before Ruben's kneeling form. Her silence said a lot about her struggle for composure—and even more about the truth behind Ravenna's beating heart and hood.

Words finally boomed from the quaint woman, the command of a crown strengthening them. "I'm disappointed—your men should have recaptured them. At least that *damned*," the queen's voice skipped and returned with conviction, "Red Hood."

Ruben's eyes narrowed, and he took a short breath before gazing upward. "That thief is apparently more skilled than we originally thought."

And with Raven at his side, he better be. Ruben hoped the thief meant his words. By the look he'd given her, even after her teasing, the boy was in love with her. The damned idiot had broken back *into* the castle for her. Ruben didn't know if that scared or reassured him.

"He's still just a thief," Mira spat, a foreign, harsh element to her voice. She stood beside the queen's armrest. A Sandceress, Raven had claimed. The purple of her gaze had always unnerved him, now it made his skin crawl.

He'd have to keep his head around that woman especially.

She looks so much like a Rova, not a Vala. Tonight, he'd ask his wife about the differences between the cultures' appearances.

Clearing his expression, the Head Guard addressed his queen. "You saw the Red Hood yourself?"

"Yes."

"Can you describe him?" Ruben knew this was treacherous questioning but had to feel her out. "Then, we can draw accurate wanted posters to catch him without his hood."

The queen shifted in her throne, leaning slightly toward Mira. "There's an enchantment on the murderer's cloak. It prevents me from remembering his face." Her eyes stared at him a mere moment before shifting through the room. Authority rang through her voice, but he sensed an unease from his questions.

Lies. He'd witnessed the magic break.

This woman was supposed to be the person he served and dedicated his life to until Raven ascended to the crown. But what Raven had told him would shatter his loyalty in a way he couldn't afford to be mistaken about. What reason could the princess have for being with that thief who'd been rumored to be partners with the Red Hood before Raven's "murder," and now had been captured within the castle for said crime?

Ruben *knew* Raven hadn't run away for love, even if that Lox had smiled and tried charming her. Something had forced her out, and it appeared that was the queen.

If Ravenna truly had been the Red Hood for the past two years, that meant she'd put the skills he'd taught her to good use, that she'd killed four men.

Why hadn't she told him? Because he was hunting the Red Hood? No, because the men wouldn't be punished otherwise.

Queen Vanera must have seen Ravenna under the hood. Why would she not revel in Raven's return, even as the Red Hood? Why would she still order the Red Hood's death? She'd wanted Raven dead all along. Had ordered it, *hired* the Red Hood for it.

Everything fit with Raven's words, and none with Vanera's.

"What would you have me do now, Your Majesty?" Ruben asked,

somehow managing to keep the speculation from his voice. Polite and neutral as ever toward his queen's orders.

The Widow Queen eased forward in her throne, hands perched on the armrests, and held his searching gaze. "The Red Hood is to be brought to me unharmed and hooded. He'll use the cloak's magic against anyone who sees his face." Her golden brows rose, and she added, "Have that thief killed on sight. He's too much of a flight risk to keep in chains."

Ruben nodded, though his throat constricted in anger. He rose and sheathed his sword.

That was the damning proof—hooded. So that the queen could finish what she'd wanted without anyone knowing Raven still lived.

The Head Guard bowed and turned to exit the corrupt throne room. His chest clenched. Ravenna had known. She'd gone through hell for however many days, trying to find a way out of her murder and deciding what to do about her fate. She'd concluded giving her mother what she wanted and leaving her beloved kingdom and people her only option. And she'd elicited that thief's help.

At least he'd kept her safe.

Why hadn't she come to *him*, though?

But Ruben knew that answer, too. She wouldn't want him hurt. Accusing the queen of treason would be a feat, and as ruling order, Vanera had power over them until proven guilty. And if Vanera truly wanted Raven dead, she would have executed her as the Red Hood— and him for protecting her as they both knew he would have.

He pushed through the thick wooden doors into the hall toward his guards' barracks. Their words at the ball so long ago echoed in his mind.

"I'd die for you, you know that."

"I'd do the same for you, Rue."

And she had. Gods damn her, she had.

Upon finding his men, Ruben isolated ten of his most trusted guards, those who had been in Raven's daily guard with him for the last three years, and ordered them to head throughout Ecanta. Any and all news of the Red Hood or Lox were to come straight to him, and *no one* could hurt them. Only those ten men could touch or speak to the "criminals" if found.

He may not be able to follow her out of Ecanta, but he'd make damn sure the queen wouldn't get her hands on Raven again.

GOLD GLISTENED OFF THE KING'S THRONE, MATCHING THE GLASS COFFIN beside it, hidden under a cloaking enchantment. Queen Vanera rounded on Mira the moment the Head Guard departed and the doors shined purple to silence those within from the outside. "You did nothing!" she screamed.

Hatred coiled in her stomach, roiling and striking against her heart. Wanting vengeance. Wanting freedom.

Mira remembered when her magic hadn't felt grating and demanding like the sandstorms, but soft and calming like the breeze. Barely, but she remembered. Long before this queen entered her life.

The Vala smoothed her dress, the knife hole at her wrist from that *gath*, that desert boy's dagger. "That fool stopped my magic."

And she would figure out how so the next passing would not go in his favor.

Very few things could cancel out magic.

Vanera glared. "You would've let her kill me."

Mira resisted rolling her eyes. "I would not. I was merely testing her. So, you can truly know who your enemy is."

No, she would not let Vanera die, not yet. But she'd like to see Ravenna try. See if the girl still had a pure heart.

The only thing that could beat her masterpiece, her curse.

Because one who cannot fall before her—and they all did—was a danger to her magic. Only a pure heart could wield the magic she could only imitate. If one could control them… that person would be deadly to not only her, but the whole kingdom.

The Sandceress sighed at the queen, shrugging. "Now you know your daughter. Not the princess we thought, now is she?"

Vanera glared. She hated when Mira called Ravenna her daughter. Hated Mira saying the word at all. But that was the price the queen paid for betraying her. Mira grinned and turned, leaving the Widow Queen to her barren throne room. Finally alone.

She retired to her chambers, lighting an incense with a wave. The burning reminded her of home. Of Valara in flames. Of the screams.

That damned *gath* had ruined her curse, her carefully crafted curse. Mira lifted a tiny vial, barely the size of her smallest finger. With a flick of her hand, a strand of her hair wound a black circle around her neck, the remaining drops of the curse hanging from the center. She touched the glass, and the necklace was safe from anyone else's gaze.

No one would be able to steal this morsel from her. They'd die trying.

She'd had to scrape the drops off the marble floor, the pieces that had clung to the glass for life. At her chest, the liquid warmed, pulsing to her heartbeat.

Once Vanera calmed, Mira would have to travel and gather the ingredients for another. Sandstorm kill her, that'd be a hell of a trek. Maybe her connections could make it faster…

Mira sat before her sphere, the smooth glass holding more power than a human could imagine without their own to channel it. They all thought it was crystal, but it was glass—an item she'd crafted from sands of Valara and her own magic. She tapped it with a fingertip, the clouds swirling.

No, Ravenna was *not* the girl she thought. Ravenna had foiled her long-laid plans. Mira had cared for her, too. Tried to be good to her. Gifted her elixirs, innocent potions she'd had no use for any longer. Not since she'd strengthened her own inner magic. Who knew the gifts would bite her in the ass?

And she never thought that damned cloak would cause her this trouble.

DARKNESS HAD FALLEN HARD BEFORE THE BAND EASED UP ON THEIR HORSES, the crazed, rapid gallops turning into softer gaits. They had ridden through the forest on the outskirts of Ilasia until passing Dale and turned left toward the ocean. Cold air clawed at their clothes, any skin open to the night, burrowing deep into their bones. Deep enough to touch the sorrow of the day that had sank to Raven's marrow.

Wordlessly, the band dismounted when Daran's horse stopped, having signaled they'd left Ecanta. Ramsey gathered wood and kindle for a fire, Lance and Scar setting up tents and sleeping rolls with Cindy trying to help. Beast roamed the perimeter, always on watch with Daran at his side. Raven wanted to ask about his health but knew more important things needed doing first.

Lox helped Jon to sit beside the fire, his wound drastically better after her potions—because that's what they were, *potions*. Magic. No fooling herself anymore. Her world was steeped in hidden magic.

She left camp and searched the base of trees to replenish her herb stash, to delay Jon's and Lox's pain. They would need it for the rides and fights to come. Her own arm burned now that her potion's numbing had worn off, but it was a dull ache compared to two days ago.

"Now that we're safe," Lox's voice on her neck made her jump, facing him. With a grin so wide that the darkness couldn't conceal it, the thief sauntered to her. She raised a hand to hit him for scaring her, and he caught it gently. His thumb stroked the pulse at her wrist.

He glanced at her arm, the bandaged wound, and lowered her hand.

Being free, standing in a forest again with him, it felt unreal—like she was in a dream she never thought she'd reach. Watching him being escorted out of the castle had felt final in a way him being captured hadn't. Unexpectedly, tears welled in her eyes.

"Hey," Lox said, cupping her face. "Raven."

She leaned her cheek into his hand. "I thought I'd never see you again." She swallowed, taking a deep breath. "That curse…"

"You didn't think I'd save you," he stated, sad green eyes meeting hers.

Not a question. She sighed. "Without knowing the conditions, I didn't think there was a way you could. I knew you'd try to find a way to break it."

Loxley's fingers tightened their grip on hers. "There was no way in hell I'd let you drink that bitch's potion." He watched her expression for a moment. "Do you think there's a way—to break it?"

Raven pondered that thought. "Mira mentioned something about a pure heart being the only thing able to undo the curse other than the conditions being met. If we learn more about magic—curses—and whatever a pure heart is… we might be able to."

His brow crinkled. "It's plausible. At least we can figure out how to defend against magic."

She recalled his words on the rooftop days ago. "You know a little about magic, right?" When he remained silent beyond his eyes widening, she continued, "You said you grew up in Nevrande… with the fae."

"Well…" Loxley sighed, running a hand through is hair. His gold ring clashed with his dark strands. "My village was on the edge of Nevrande and beyond the fae border. We avoided the fae because their magic revolved around tricks and time. People claimed it the most dangerous of all types. And I was young when I lived there." He squeezed her hand, then looked down at her, sadness in his gaze. "Raven... I..."

"It's okay. That was a long shot. We'll be in Ocara soon, and there must be information somewhere about at least mermaid magic."

After the Vala, she was certain all magic was real—fae, merfolk, human. No doubt there must be some lore or history on curses in the form of potions.

She looked down at their hands. "Mira said my mother had another daughter, 'child after child after *child.*'" Raven raised her fingers, ticking of two. "Me, Cindy—and then another. She mentioned my father taking the last child. I think they might know more about what happened, if they were there."

"I hate her for all that woman did to you. Hell, Red—your *mother.* I'm so sorry." Loxley's thumb caressed her cheekbone. "It also terrifies me more that you came for me."

She stared at him, incredulous. How could she not?

"I didn't want you die for me. I deserved my fate, Lox!" Raven breathed hard, tears burning at the back of her eyes. No. Not now. "She wanted *me* dead, and she learned about you because I had Ruben look into you after we first met. I came to you to make you leave so I could follow you out of town—and ended up *running away with* you. And—and... you saved me from the guards—another stupid mistake I made. I was meant to be captured. You were never meant to be on her radar, let alone in her grasp. Only me. And you're still wanted for treason."

"Raven." Loxley clutched her hand, entwining his fingers with hers. He wiped away a tear with his thumb. "I chose all of this. When I first saw you in the market... I couldn't help but talk to you. The moment you stole from me, I was captured. When you told me the queen's plans, I chose to save the princess instead of run. I knew you were dangerous in more ways than obvious, but I *kept coming back.* And with that bastard," he spat the word like poison, "I chose to take your place." Lox tugged her closer, their chests pressed together. "I chose you, Raven. Every time, I chose you."

Tears pooled in her eyes, threatening to overflow. "You're the only person who has." She swallowed the thickness of her voice. "And I couldn't be happier."

Lox's fingers touched a lock of her dark hair, relishing the smoothness of it before brushing it back. "Don't leave me again."

Her heart thudded, his breath warming her face. "I don't want to."

Neither of them knew which one pulled harder, but they tangled in each other's arms. Lox's lips crushed hers, his fingers winding into her hair. She grasped his tunic, tugging herself to him, mouth moving with his.

Complete.

This was what it felt like to be complete. Her soul felt like it had been wandering, searching for something to make it whole, and it had finally found it—Loxley. He accepted her as she was, princess, criminal, murderer. All the parts that she'd kept apart to appear like she was supposed to. With Lox, she was loved. Truly loved for the first time in her life.

As Raven.

And she loved him, for the thief, the criminal, the protector that he was.

Lox backed her up to a tree, pressing her there with his body. The bark poked at her through her tunic, but she pulled him closer, wanting all of him.

"Raven," he moaned, dipping his head to kiss her cheek, her jaw, and down to the hollow of her neck as she lifted her head. His tongue, hot and wet, slipped out to glide over her skin, and she gasped. He grinned against the side of her neck, teeth grazing and sending a shiver down her spine.

She gripped the back of his head, angling so he could keep sucking on her skin, and her own fingers plunged beneath the collar of his tunic. He groaned, the vibrations like heaven on her neck. Heat licked at her fingertips, his skin taut and smooth. Raven brought her hand forward and felt his collarbone.

He raised his head for her hand to more easily explore his front, the motion making it dip to his chest, straining the ties of his shirt. His mouth trailed along her jaw, and he pulled back just enough to let her see the desire turning his green eyes into shining emeralds. Lox kissed her again, lips moving hungrily against hers, tongue slipping across them before separating and entering to twine with hers. He kept one hand on her waist, gripping her tunic, but moved to loosen the ties at his collar.

Raven slipped her hand deeper beneath his shirt, his muscles flexing as he breathed. His skin was hot and so soft under her fingers. Ridged where the muscles met and bulged. She wanted more, but couldn't reach. His tongue danced in her mouth, making her lose sense of time and place. All she knew was she wanted *more* of Loxley.

His tongue delved and retreated, running along the bottom of her lip before his teeth bit it. She gasped, and it sounded like a whimper, nails digging into his shoulder.

Lox chuckled. He gripped her hips, lifting her to wrap her legs around him. He pressed her into the trunk again, and—gods, he was hard and right where she wanted him if their clothes weren't still on. She already felt ready to combust.

He raised her tunic with one hand to her collarbone—his hard stomach intoxicating against her—and he bent and— "Lox," she gasped.

His tongue swept along the top curve of her breast, just the tip, soft and deliciously wet. Then, he lowered his mouth, encasing her nipple.

Raven's eyes flew wide open, and she stared up at the canopy of trees, head back and hair tangling against the bark. Her legs went weak at the sensation of his tongue caressing and stroking her nipple, her body sliding down his.

With a sound like a growl, he backed up, removing his shirt in one motion. He laid it on the floor and returned to her. She had hers off before he could try, and a wicked grin spread on his face. "Bloody hell, Raven," he breathed, staring at her openness with him.

Loxley tugged her to the ground, lying her on top of him and capturing her other breast in his mouth. She gripped his hair as he lavished her, his fingers sliding beneath the waistband of her pants, tugging the fabric down over her ass. Raven helped him remove it entirely, throwing blades to the side haphazardly. She started untying his own.

He quickly turned to his pants but hissed at the wound on his thigh.

Raven froze and moved back an inch.

He stopped her. "Don't go anywhere, Red." He tugged the fabric below his hips just above the wound.

Loxley grabbed her hips and pulled her over him, straddling her over his own. The heat of him pressed against her core below, already slick and ready for him again. Her hands landed on his chest, and the absolute fire of his body between her thighs consumed her. The thrill of knowing he was right *there*—she shivered. Lox positioned her directly on his cock and whispered, "Nothing is stopping me being inside you tonight."

Then, he slid her down onto him, and oh gods, he was deeper than before. She thought he'd consumed her then, now she couldn't tell if she'd ever separate. Their moans collided in the night, and Loxley kept one hand on her hip, the other bringing her down to kiss her. He lifted and rolled against her, eliciting another gasp from her mouth.

Raven pushed her elbows into the forest floor around him, trying not to hurt him, causing her lower body to move just right. She moved her hips without thinking—because she couldn't focus on a damned thing beyond the sensation of Loxley inside her.

"Fuck—" He groaned against her lips, then pulled back. "Sorry, love—"

She smiled, shifting against him again and making him repeat the curse with vigor. He'd always cursed under his breath anything worse than 'hell,' and some sort of pride swelled in her to make him say this *loudly*.

Loxley leaned up to claim her neck with his tongue, his teeth catching the delicate skin.

She sat up, wanting that deep overwhelming feeling she'd had when she first mounted him. His hands gripped her hips, thumb sliding forward to circle her clit. Something carnal stirred in her, in the way Loxley stared up at her, the way he thrust into her like he couldn't stop. She dug her nails into his chest, moving wildly against him, getting lost in the clash of their hips, the moans she strung from him, and the waves building from his finger's movements.

Tension coiled, and her skin tightened, building with each filling stroke until she split apart. Loxley clasped her neck and brought her down to kiss him as he continued his thrusts, dragging out every pulse within her. She called his name, clenching him entirely, and he shuddered into her, a deep throbbing wringing another climax from her with the intensity. The forest swallowed their moans as they slowed against each other.

Their breaths came in halting bursts, Loxley gazing up at her. His smile lit up the empty night. Lox's hand traced her lip down to her jaw, then back up to her cheek. "To be honest, for the longest time, I wasn't sure if you liked me or wanted to stab me."

Raven laughed, happy for the first time in too long. "Sometimes it's both."

"Just remember… tonight and every night, love." He smiled, leaned in for another, softer kiss that left her breathless and dizzy.

When Raven and Loxley returned to camp, they were greeted by a roaring fire, most of the band sitting around it at uneven intervals. Seeing their leader, Daran and Ramsey neared, taking their seats.

Scar and Lance shared a log, closer than casual, Cindy on another beside Jon. Beast, apparently deeming the location safe, knelt in the dirt near Jon.

One log was left open for Raven in the center of the circle.

Loxley paced around the fire, wearing a torn expression. He took a few more steps, then stopped and faced them. "There's no lie, it's looking bad, men—and women." He let out a puff of air, locking gazes with each band member in turn. "We've been wanted for things before but never treason. Before, it was false, and we could forge an alibi—"

"It's true this time," Raven said, her voice deadly cold. "Danger to the queen."

Lox's eyes stayed on her for a long moment. Probably remembering how he'd had to talk her down from slicing Vanera's throat. "This act of being captured, then escaping has all but confirmed the queen's accusations against the Red Hood and myself killing the princess. But now, as Raven said, we're probably wanted for threatening the queen herself."

The men grumbled, some shrugging. Ramsey stated, "Her power only stretches in this one kingdom. We can just go elsewhere."

Their leader glanced at Raven, then to her hand that was still stained with Mira's ruthless magic. "We've still got a hard ride to Ocara, and crossing the border doesn't mean safety. We now know the lengths the queen will go, and they are pretty damned far. She has a Sandceress, and they are equally ruthless. Especially this one."

Raven adjusted her seat, fingers itching for her dagger that Lox had kindly returned. Her wrists still ached from Mira's hold, and she could still feel the cold of that curse's bottle if she let the memory creep in. "I don't think there's anything she won't do."

Lox brushed his hair back. "The plan for now is to learn about magic, the different types and how—if possible—to defend against it. And to stay low. Raven and I discovered... some dark secrets of the queen's past."

He paused, seemingly trying to find the words to explain but not reveal Raven's secrets.

This damned secrecy would never end. Raven stood. All eyes turned toward her. "The queen is the one who hired the Red Hood to kill me. And she isn't really my mother. She..." Raven caught Cindy's gaze. Her *sister*. How could she say this to her? She cleared her throat silently. "The queen cursed my mother and took me in. Today, she tried to curse me. We hope we can find a way to break that curse."

Beast leaned forward, intense brows descending in thought.

Sadness, a hint of sympathy, shined in Cindy's eyes. Injured Jon's, too.

Raven took another breath, the damned thing wedging in her throat. "She knows I'm alive, she knows I'm the Red Hood, but she can't reveal that I'm either. She will hunt me down if she can. There is magic, dark magic, on her side. And a kingdom that wants revenge. For their queen," her voice hardened, "and the person they believed was their princess."

Raven tried to look them in the eyes, but the weight of her own words barreled down on her. Her foot stepped backward over the log, the halted breath leaving her.

"You're still my princess," Cindy's soft voice said, surety in her tone. Her chin rose when Raven turned hollow eyes toward her.

Ramsey stood. "Kingdom or not, I'll fight for you."

"I don't care if there's a damned Sandceress," Beast growled his agreement, "I'll fight."

"Rave," Scar said, tipping his hat.

Jon smiled and shrugged. "Don't know if you want me, but I'll give it my best."

Daran nodded.

Lance lifted his cup.

Lox grinned. "You know my answer."

The crackle of the fire burning leaves in the night filled the silence as

Raven took in her new life. Somehow, this criminal group was more solid and trustworthy than her guard had been. A warm fire, a red cloak, and a group of criminals kept her safer than the castle of thrones and guards ever had. Inches separated them here, not whole empty seats.

These people, this band of bandits and runaways, made her richer than she'd ever been as a princess—her outlaw family.

ACKNOWLEDGMENTS

You finished it—the whole book! Woo! And you chose to stay around for this part, where I thank all the people who kept me sane and made this book happen when my brain decided it shouldn't. Part of me is screaming "finally, we're here!" now that this book is in the world for you, reader, to hold. Part of me can't believe it's real.

Raven and Loxley were my solace in a time where I wanted a deep love—when I should've had it. Six years after their first draft and I have a love I literally never dreamed or hoped I would find. A different version of me crafted and dreamed these characters, and to revise and publish it now astounds me.

This book carried me through my divorce and helped me to see the relationship I wanted in my life—and I found it. I found ways to accept the parts of me that I hadn't liked before.

To get real for a moment, this journey with this book has been a very solo one for me until now. I originally wrote this book when I was very alone. This book was written in stolen moments late at night, early mornings, alone in my book room, alone in another room when others were together just a wall away.

The last few chapters of this book were initially written while a family member was in her last weeks of cancer and we were all just waiting. It was the only thing solid I had in a fluid and drifting time.

The outward support from friends, family, readers—hell, even my cover artist, editor, and PA—almost brings me to tears. My first pre-order —first **sale**—was from my critique partner and best friend and I did cry.

I would open a draft of this book once a year for the next five years, making revisions and edits, and putting it away again because it couldn't be my priority—I didn't feel like I could or deserved to make it so.

Heart Of A Forest started as an upper-YA story, and I kept having to drag it back into that age-group (you've met Loxley, it was hard. Pun intended). I dreamed of re-writing the series later and upscaling the age to adult later on. Then, in my last day of development editing—when I was supposed to be just re-reading the edits—I decided to just do it **now**.

Within a week I went through the entire book and let the romance flourish into what it had been trying to be the whole time.

It was glorious. It as freeing.

Through this, I was also able to touch the heart of Raven and Loxley's relationship: accepting all parts of yourself and finding someone who does as well.

To every single person who shows any support or kind words— **thank you**. I know everyone thanks their readers or fans, but it's very true. You all bring me to tears.

There are many people who I can say kept me going over the years, and especially once (and after) I'd decided to self-publish. This is not in any order, and I'm sure there are names I didn't mention. Thank you to everyone who has ever supported me in this venture.

For my cover artist, Amira who did an absolutely stunning work of art. Your idea far exceeded my original picture and I'm so glad I trusted you to create this in your vision. For my editor, Whitney, who cheered my plot twists and my decision to age up to NA. For my cover designer, Cas, who brought so much style into the title and for being willing to alway answer my questions. I truly have the best and kindest team for this book.

Cassidy, I still remember your reaction to finishing the first draft, to "this is what it felt like to be complete."

Raquel, who read the first non-draft, the copy without a middle, you are the best critique partner I could've ever hoped to find. And an even better friend. You are my rock when times are uncertain.

Krissey, I don't know how to find the words for your support and encouragement (and I know you're probably like "well find them, woman."). You continuously guide me through the doubt and will always be my cheerleader and tell me it will be okay. Thank you.

Maegan, you already know more than others how this book healed parts of me, how chasing our dreams have healed us both.

Sierra, for always being my hype even when you hadn't read a word, you just <u>knew</u>.

Courtney, for your constant support and excitement. For your honesty and sass and always building me up the I needed it.

For my B&N crew from Jacksonville. I miss you all and crafting this story while being surrounded by stories with you guys every day. Amber, Alexandra, Jennifer, Amy, Ron, Ms. Sue. I can't separate my time first drafting this book from time working at the store with you all. (Amber, did the acknowledgements make you cry, too?)

Zachariah, for being my Loxley, for the love I'd never hoped existed, for pushing me, for listening to my rants, brainstorms and worries.

I love you all with so much of my heart.

Stories are Sylvia's lifeblood—whether originating from a book, movie, or video game—and she's always been drawn to writing her own. Books have always felt like they held their own kind of magic bound within pages, and that called her away from her Bachelor's degree in Psychology to follow her true passion. *Heart of a Forest* is Sylvia's debut romantasy novel, the first in her *A Pure Heart* series. Despite living in Florida, her favorite season is fall (spooky time!) and she loves staying inside curled up with a good book—while getting side-eyed by her sassy cat. When not writing fantasy adventures with swords and sorcery and morally grey characters, she can be found watching TV with her boyfriend and their four dogs. (She also has two lizards, a menace of a kitten, and a fish that would want an honorable mention, please). She dreams of one day writing full-time and for the rest of her life.

instagram.com/sylvialockardauthor
tiktok.com/@sylvialockardauthor